BRIDE OF THE SHADOW KING

Bride of the Shadow King Series

Bride of the Shadow King
Vow of the Shadow King
Heart of the Shadow King

Bride of the Shadow King

Bride of the Shadow King: Book 1

Sylvia Mercedes

ACE

NEW YORK

ACE
Published by Berkley
An imprint of Penguin Random House LLC
penguinrandomhouse.com

Library of Congress Cataloging-in-Publication Data

Names: Mercedes, Sylvia, author.
Title: Bride of the Shadow King / Sylvia Mercedes.
Description: First edition. | New York: Ace, 2024. |
Series: Bride of the Shadow King; book 1
Identifiers: LCCN 2024021054 | ISBN 9780593952207 (trade paperback)
Subjects: LCGFT: Fantasy fiction. | Romance fiction. | Novels.
Classification: LCC PS3613.E678 B75 2024 | DDC 813/.6—dc23/eng/20240508
LC record available at https://lccn.loc.gov/2024021054

First Ace Edition: November 2024

Bride of the Shadow King was originally self-published, in different form, in 2022.

Printed in the United States of America
1st Printing

Book design by Jenni Surasky

For Stephanie Gail,
woman of valor.

BRIDE OF THE SHADOW KING

1

Faraine

"If you'd managed to snare the crown prince of Cornaith for a husband, we wouldn't be in this situation, now would we?"

I close my eyes, trying to still the shiver running down my spine. My brother's words hit me like slaps. They fall from his lips so casually, one would think he remarked on the weather or the cut of his tunic. But the bitter and unspoken emotion behind the words makes me wince and wish I could somehow sink into the cushions of my carriage seat and vanish.

I draw a long breath before raising my lashes and peering at Theodre seated across from me. He's resplendent in a fur-trimmed travel cloak and a plumed hat that takes up far too much room in this small space. A purely decorative sword is propped by his knees, the jeweled hilt wrought to correspond with his belt. Six fat rings, large enough to fit over his velvet-gloved fingers, flash at every move of his hands. He polishes one of them now, blowing on the faceted stone and rubbing it against his sleeve.

"War is such a fright, you know," he says, as though the thought would never have occurred to me. "Hard for the average man to go about his business, what with having to drop everything and turn out to fight. Crops are left to spoil with only the women to do what needs to be done. And such ugly scarecrows they are! All hollow eyed and bony hipped. It quite turns the stomach to look at them. Out there with their plows and their scythes, and a gaggle of ragged brats trailing behind. It's like they have no pride in king or country."

He looks up at me, his dark eyes flashing in the dimness of the carriage. "Nothing an alliance with Cornaith wouldn't have fixed. Their cavalry would have made our enemies take to their heels! Instead, we've got those gods-damned fae crawling all over the countryside, running raids, burning crops, stealing livestock, all like it's good sport. So the people come crying to Father's gates, wailing and holding up their starving children like there's anything he can do about it. Other than send more of them out to fight."

And it's your fault.

He doesn't say it. He doesn't have to. I feel the accusation underscoring every word, every gesture, every glance. I feel it so profoundly, I begin to believe it.

My fault.

Burned crops. Displaced people. Starving children.

My fault.

I should have done better. I should have *been* better. When Prince Orsan of Cornaith came courting, I should have smiled and flirted and danced and teased. I should not have sat quietly off to one side, keeping to the shadowed edges of the room, striving to find places where the light and the noise and the laughter and the tremendous press of people wouldn't break through all my defenses and leave me gasping with pain. I should have pushed that pain into the farthest recesses of my awareness—it's mostly in my head anyway, isn't it?—and pretended not to feel it. Pretended to be what I ought to be; what I was born to be as the eldest daughter of the King of Gavaria.

But I couldn't.

Even so, Prince Orsan might have taken me. Negotiations were well advanced, all the offers and promises between his kingdom and mine nearing culmination. Perhaps I wasn't the bride he'd always dreamed of. Perhaps every time he looked at me, I felt nothing but disappointment and resignation emanating from his sharp hazel eyes. But he knew the value of a good alliance as well as the next man. He knew the wisdom of uniting Cornaith and Gavaria against the threat of fae invasion. Plus, there was my substantial dowry to consider. Yes, in light of these temptations, he would have gone through with it.

Until he tried to kiss me in the garden.

Oh, gods! I close my eyes again, trying not to remember that terrible moment. We'd been strolling in the moonlight, to all appearances the perfect picture of a courting couple if one were to ignore the careful way I kept a good three feet of distance between us. He was quite handsome in a silver-embroidered tunic, his fair hair swept back from his forehead, a jeweled circlet ringing his brow. I wore a romantic, off-shoulder gown of delicate pink, my hair adorned with pearls. Music trailed after us, played by musicians hidden behind a screen of blooming flowers. I'd turned to the prince, intending to make some remark on their playing.

To my utmost surprise, Orsan had taken two swift steps, caught me by my shoulders, his fingers digging hard into my bare flesh, and pulled me against him. His lips crashed into mine. The abruptness of that contact was too much. Everything he was feeling washed over me in a wave—frustration, determination, fear, anger, embarrassment, inadequacy. All of it. All hitting me in one painful collision of lips and teeth and tongue.

My body surged in reaction. And I vomited. Right down the front of his pretty embroidered tunic.

The party from Cornaith left my father's house the next morning, all negotiations abruptly ended. The day after, Father sent me to the Convent of Nornala. He didn't speak to me, not even to tell me how deeply I'd disappointed him. It was as though he wanted to forget I existed entirely.

That was nearly two years ago. I'd heard nothing from home since then, not even a letter from my sisters. Theodre's arrival shocked me three days ago, when he strode unannounced into my private room, filling the doorway with his big, plumed hat.

"I've come to fetch you home, Faraine," he declared without preamble. "The Shadow King is looking for a bride, and you're needed at once."

I'm still not entirely certain why Father sent for me. Whoever this ominously titled *Shadow King* might be, I'm quite certain I am not the bride he's looking for. But apparently, my younger sister, Ilsevel, declared she would not be bartered off in marriage. She'd thrown an enormous fit and locked herself in the east tower, dropping bits of crockery on the heads of anyone who tried to approach.

"Father seems to think you can talk some sense into the foolish girl," Theodre had said as he looked sneeringly around my small, sparse room at the convent. "No one else can, gods help us. But you've always had a way with Ilsie. Get her to recognize her duty to the crown and all that. Make yourself useful."

Suppressing a sigh, I turn to the carriage window and lift the curtain, peering out at the countryside. We are on a decline, descending the mountain pass. My view extends over miles of lowland beneath a twilit sky. I spy what looks like the remains of a village not far from here: a caved-in hall, smoke still rising from its collapsed roof. Burnt-out cottages, blackened walls. Ruin. Devastation. And what became of those who had once called that village home? Are they dead now, run down and slaughtered? Or do they wander the countryside, homeless, helpless, even as early spring storms batter the land?

The whole world seems to exhale despair.

I sit back, letting the curtain fall. Though it's bitterly cold, I pull the glove off my right hand and slip it under my cloak, feeling for the crystal pendant hanging from a chain around my neck. My fingers close around it, squeezing so that its sharp edges dig into the flesh of my palm. At first, it feels cold and lifeless. Slowly, however, it warms in my grip. I detect the faintest vibrating *thrum* deep inside. Closing my eyes again, I try to synchronize my breathing to that pulse. Pain recedes; the roiling in my gut diminishes. I let out a sigh.

Feeling Theodre's gaze upon me, I open my eyes and look back at him. He raises an eyebrow. "Not a pretty view, eh?"

I shake my head. "I'd not realized just how bad things have gotten." My tongue feels thick and heavy when I speak.

My brother snorts. "You've been hidden away in that convent too long."

Hidden away. Not married and producing babies. Not ensuring the military support of our nearest neighbors. Useless. Disappointment. It's all there. Hanging in the air between us. Unspoken but real.

I drop my chin. Perhaps I'm not being fair to Theodre. After all, I don't know him very well. He's several years my senior and spent most of his childhood away from Beldroth Castle, where my sisters and I were raised. I saw him for state occasions and a precious few family gatherings, nothing more. This journey from the convent is the most time we've spent in each other's company. I doubt we'll seek each other out in the future.

"Ah well," Theodre sighs, twisting yet another of his rings as though it's pinching him. "If Ilsie can snag this Shadow King for her groom, it'll all be made right. From what I understand, he's got quite the impressive army at his beck and call, and no love for our enemies. Never thought I'd see the day when Father bargained with trolls, but hey! Desperate times and all that. Ilsevel's not at all keen on the idea, but Father says you can use your gods-gift and make her see reason. I hope you can, for all our sakes! Though I can't say I blame poor Ilsie when I think about it. I mean . . . *trolls*."

He makes a face at the last word, a wave of disgust flowing out from him. I grip my crystal a little harder, breathing in time to its faint pulse. I've heard tell of trolls, of course: stories from the caravan merchants who stop at the convent for shelter on their way over the Ettrian Mountains. They tell of hideous stone-hide monsters towering seven feet tall and more, with fists like boulders and teeth of shining gemstones. Man-eaters. Bone-crushers. Brutes without brains or conscience.

I struggle to imagine such creatures having a king. I struggle still more to imagine my father bargaining with such a king for Ilsevel's hand. Whatever he may think of me, Father has always loved my sister, with her ready laugh and sharp temper, her recklessness and courage. Of all his children, Ilsevel is the most like him—and many's the time I've heard him sigh that she should have been born a boy.

How bad have things become that he would wed her to a monster?

The carriage lurches to a stop. It's so abrupt, I nearly fall from my seat. My brother curses and flings out both hands to brace against the walls. "What in the seven secret names is going on?" he growls, grabbing his sword and using the hilt to hit the ceiling with three sharp taps. "Oi! Fantar! What's the holdup?"

A muffled shout. Followed by a *thunk* on the roof of the carriage.

My heart begins to race. "Theodre?"

My brother, heedless of me, mutters another curse and flings back the curtain over the window, sticking his head outside. "Fantar! It's gods-spitting cold, man. Don't leave us sitting around all—*argh!*"

A burst of shock ripples out from Theodre. I just have wherewithal enough to reach out with both hands, grab hold of his jeweled belt, and haul him back into the carriage. There's a flash of fire on the other side of the window, the gleam of a sword edge slicing down where his neck had been a moment before.

Theodre falls back in his seat. "Spitting heavens!" he gasps, blood draining from his cheeks. "It's those gods-damned unicorns!"

I don't have the words to question him. All hell has broken loose just outside the carriage door. Men are shouting, horses screaming in terror. Through a crack in the curtain, I see flashes of red heat, flickering flame. And in my head—explosions of terror. Terror not my own. Hitting me with the force of a battering ram.

I sink from my seat onto the floor of the carriage, gripping my crystal pendant. My brother stares down at me. His fear is the worst of the assault. It pounds me with brutal intensity. He blinks once. Then, grabbing hold of his decorative sword with one hand, he fumbles with the door on the other side of the carriage, pushes it open, and falls out. For a moment, I'm overwhelmed with relief as he takes his terror with him.

Another scream bursts in my ears. Theodre? One of our men? I cannot tell, cannot guess. What should I do? Crouch in here like a mouse in a trap, waiting to be found and dragged out by my hair? Surely that must be worse than facing whatever waits outside.

Setting my jaw, I work my way to the half-open carriage door and ease the gap wider. A mistake. Utter mayhem meets my eyes. Riders streak past on creatures shaped like horses with monstrous, flaming horns protruding from their skulls. They're beautiful, terrible, glorious creatures ridden by beings equally beautiful, terrible, and glorious. Long hair streaming, shining faces alight with bloodthirsty joy, they wield swords that flame as bright as their mounts' horns. They wear no armor—in fact, they seem to wear next to nothing at all—their muscled, godlike bodies fully displayed as they circle their prey and cut them down.

I spy the silver helmets of my brother's guards. They fight valiantly from horseback, struggling to defend the carriage. One by one, they're pulled from their steeds. Blood, terror, and death assault my senses. I am frozen in place, paralyzed.

Once again, my gods-gift proves to be a curse.

A rider turns suddenly, violet eyes alight in a face of such heartbreaking beauty, it takes my breath away. He sees me and smiles, flashing sharp canines. Digging his heels into his unicorn's flanks, he urges the beast straight toward me. My vision is full of flames and laughter and the edge of an upraised sword.

Acting on survival impulse, I fall out of the carriage, hit the ground hard, and roll underneath. My skirts drag and catch, but I manage to get myself fully concealed just before cloven hooves skid to a stop at my eye level.

The next moment, a pair of bare feet land on the road. My pursuer drops to his hands and knees, turning his head to smile at me where I'm hiding. "Hullo, pretty thing," he says in a language I do not know, but which somehow communicates perfect meaning as it reaches my ears. "Come out and play?"

He reaches his hand under the carriage, long nails snatching at my face. His savage lust hits me like a knife in the head. I scramble backwards. The horses squeal with fright, and the carriage lurches. I narrowly miss being crushed under a rolling wheel that catches my skirt and cloak, trapping me in place. Choking on a scream, I release the catch of my cloak, then grip my skirt with both hands and wrench free. The fabric rips in a long slash all the way up to my thigh. I stagger back from the carriage, struggling to find my balance.

Movement draws my eye. I look up to see my attacker, sprung to the top of the carriage, looming over me. He holds his sword out to one side for balance, but when he spies me, he raises it high. Tossing back his head, he utters a deep-throated, ululating cry of triumph.

As though by magic, a knife appears in his throat.

His eyes widen. A wave of surprise rolls over me. He drops his sword, and his hand comes up to touch the hilt of that knife. Wondering. As though he cannot fathom how it got there.

The next moment, he falls in a lifeless pile at my feet.

I stare down at the being, so beautiful even in death. The stillness of him is stark, the sudden silence of those powerful emotions that battered me only heartbeats ago. I'm numb, frozen.

Before I can pull a single coherent thought into my head, thundering hooves pound in my ear. I whirl just in time to glimpse a huge dark shape bearing down on me. A figure leans far to the side in a saddle; an arm reaches out. I let out a little bleat of surprise just before the breath is ripped from my lungs and I'm swung up into the air. For a terrible moment, I believe I've been struck.

Then, suddenly—*calm.*

I hardly know how to describe it. Where an instant before, the whole world stormed with horror, my every sense exploding with pain, now there's stillness. Peace. I'm so shocked by it at first, I can't even try to make sense of my surroundings. I can do nothing but close my eyes and lean into that calm, that quiet.

Slowly, my awareness returns. I realize I'm not standing on my own two feet anymore. I'm seated. Seated on the back of a large lurching beast and encircled by a pair of powerful arms. I choke on a gasp and twist in place, trying to get some sense of my captor. A pair of startlingly silver eyes look down at me. It takes me several breaths before I realize the face in which those eyes are set is an unnatural blue. For the moment, his eyes dominate everything.

Staring into them, I recognize immediately the source of that calm.

His lips are moving. He's saying something, but I have no idea what. "I . . . I'm sorry?"

"Are you all right?" he repeats. He speaks my language, but his words are strongly accented with a husky, growling burr unfamiliar to me.

"I hardly know!" I blink, shake my head, and look down at my quivering body. "I think so?"

"Good," he says. Then, "Keep low."

A hand on my back forces me to bend over the neck of the beast on which we ride. A thick, muscular neck with a shock of black mane, which I take at first to belong to a horse. But no, those are scales I see between patches of fur. This is definitely no horse.

I don't have time to question further before a flash of fire draws my gaze to one side. A unicorn rider pounds into our vicinity, his mouth open in wild, murderous laughter. He swings his weapon, but the man at my back pulls on his reins, and his beast sidesteps. Steel and flames whistle past my ear. There's a thick sound of a blade hitting skin. The unicorn lets out a bloodcurdling scream. Both steed and rider go tumbling.

I stare in open-mouthed horror. And yet that quiet, that calm, continues to surround me. The strangest, most unexpected sensation.

An arm wraps around my waist, pulling me back against a solid chest. "Best hold on," the accented voice murmurs close to my ear. I just have time to grab a handful of thick mane before he spurs his beast into motion. It lurches forward, but it doesn't feel like galloping. It's as though the monster has become a streaking shadow. I can still feel the warm solidity of its body beneath me, but I can see no more than an impression of rushing darkness.

We bear down on another flaming unicorn and rider. I turn my face away, closing my eyes even as my rescuer's sword arm moves. Distant screams of rage and death burst in the air but seem to belong in another world while I, here in my own small sphere of existence, am surrounded by peace.

The stranger pulls on his reins. His beast skids to a stop, suddenly solidifying. Its huge hooves clop on the stones beneath us. We're no longer on the road but have ridden straight up the mountainside. No horse could scale such a steep incline. When I look back, the view makes my stomach pitch.

The arm around my waist tightens slightly. "Have no fear, my lady. Knar is as sure-footed as they come. Shall we rejoin the others?"

I seem to have forgotten how to talk. I can do nothing but nod and tighten my grip on the mane. Am I imagining the pulse of a heartbeat at my back? A beat so strong and steady, it works its way into my bones. Like the pulse of my crystal, only much greater, much stronger.

I shake my head and peer down to the road below. The unicorn riders have fled; I can still see a few of them vanishing into the deepening twilight, flaming horns and wicked swords flaring. But far too many broken and crumpled bodies lie around the carriage.

"My brother!" I manage to gasp, finding my voice at last. "Where is my—"

I don't have time to finish before I hear a familiar voice shouting, "Get your hands off me, you filthy rock biters!"

Turning toward that sound, I spy Theodre a short way up the road, surrounded by three tall figures. They are startlingly pale, their skin faintly blue, their hair pure white. Two male, one female, each with their hands up, exchanging uneasy glances. Theodre stands in the midst of them, swinging his decorative sword in erratic arcs. He's lost his hat, and his long, oiled locks gleam in the firelight. He looks rather like a lapdog snarling at a pack of wolves.

"I take it that's the brother in question?" says the voice at my back.

"Yes, indeed." I flush as Theodre spews another stream of invective at our rescuers. Or are they our rescuers? Looking around, I spy more of the strange scaly monsters like the beast I'm currently astride. They're just as frightening as the unicorns, if not more so. And these people, they must be fae. Have I been saved from one set of foes only to be taken captive by another?

"Please," I say, turning to look up at the rider behind me. "My brother is frightened. He doesn't mean what he says."

"Gods blight your nethers with pustule sores!" Theodre shrieks.

The stranger raises an eyebrow. "He sounds fairly impassioned."

His mouth quirks in a half smile. "But here, he's had a fright. Not all men are built for battle. Shall we see if we can ease his fears?"

So saying, he rides his monster up to the little circle. Theodre spies him coming, his face paling at the sight of the awful steed. His knees knock, and I fear he will faint then and there.

"It's all right, Theodre," I call out. "You're safe now."

My brother's gaze snaps to my face, his fear momentarily displaced by surprise. "Faraine! What in the seven gods' names are you doing up there?" His voice is accusing, as though I've betrayed him somehow.

I press my lips into a line, then start to slip from the saddle. The stranger immediately moves to assist me, setting me lightly on my feet. I wobble, a little unsteady, but manage to make my way between the tall figures to my brother's side. His churning fear lashes at me like a whip. I wince but extend a hand to him even so. "You're safe, brother," I say again. "These are our rescuers. I don't sense any threat from them."

"They're fae," Theodre spits, his lip twisting with disgust. "They're always a threat."

"Perhaps." I glance around at the crumpled bodies surrounding us, both human and otherwise. "But not to us. At least, not this time."

Theodre struggles to master himself. After a moment's hesitation, he takes my offered hand. I bite back a cry as that contact of our skin sends his emotions jolting up my arm. Bracing myself, I try to send something back through that connection, some small measure of the calm I just experienced so unexpectedly. Theodre shivers and starts to pull back, but when I squeeze his fingers a little tighter, he stops trying to resist. After a moment, he seems to gather strength. Lifting his chin, he turns and addresses the stranger still mounted on the beast's back. "This road belongs to

King Larongar of Gavaria. I demand to know who you are that you would dare ride it."

Cringing with embarrassment, I glance up. The stranger tilts his head to one side, looking contemplatively down at my brother. That half smile is still present at the corner of his mouth. "I am the man who has just saved you from becoming unicorn fodder."

Theodre draws himself up, chest swelling, nostrils flaring. "I will have an answer from you! In the name of the King!"

One of the pale figures standing close at hand takes a step forward, touching a hand to the sheathed sword at her belt. "I'll warn you, sir, to show proper respect," she growls ominously.

"Peace, Hael," the stranger on the monster says. He swings down from his mount and approaches us. A flaming sword lies close at hand, its red gleam shining against his blue-tinted skin and making the planes of his face stand out at sharp angles. "I'm sure the little human means no harm."

"*Little human?*" My brother sounds as though he's about to burst. I try to squeeze his hand again, but he shakes me off. "Do you know who I am? I am Theodre, Prince of the House of Cyhorn, heir to the throne of Gavaria!"

"Indeed?" The stranger looks down at Theodre, his brows rising ever so slightly. "And I am Vor, King of Mythanar, Lord Protector of the Under Realm."

I stare up into those shining silver eyes. My heart seems to catch in my throat. I realize suddenly who our rescuer is: the Shadow King.

2

Vor

Stepping lightly from shadow to firelight to shadow again, I make my way through the fallen, both the dead and the wounded. I saw young Yok topple from his morleth in the midst of the attack, and I'm determined to find him. He's much too inexperienced for a mission like this. He only just completed his *va*-trek earlier this cycle, leaving behind childhood and becoming a man. Though brave and determined, he is untested. But he was so keen to join this mission, bursting with need to prove his mettle. When he begged to accompany me into the human world, I hadn't the heart to say no.

I didn't reckon on encountering Licornyn Riders.

I find the boy in a crumpled heap within a meter of one of the riders. At least he seems to have fared better than his foe, who lies spread-eagled, his sword still gripped in one hand, his glassy eyes staring into the vault of purpling sky, his spirit fled to his god.

I sidestep around the corpse and crouch beside my fallen warrior. He clutches his arm. Blood gushes thick and blue between his fingers. "What's this, Yok?" I say, gently prying his hand away from the wound. "What have I told you about flinging yourself bodily onto the blades of our enemies?"

"You're against it, sire," Yok speaks through gritted teeth. "Dead against it."

"That's right. Next time, maybe you'll listen to your sovereign." I inspect the gash by the flickering light of a flaming sword dropped close at hand. It's deep. Down to the bone. And there's something about the color of the flesh I don't like. "But you didn't come by this blow from a sword, did you?"

Yok shakes his head. His skin has gone a ghastly gray, his eyes hollow in their sockets. "I'm afraid not, sire."

He doesn't want to say it, not out loud. But we both know the truth. This wound could only have been made by a licorne horn. Which means poison.

I sit back on my heels, looking round at the carnage. By the grace of the Deeper Dark, my people have escaped relatively unscathed. Aside from Yok, only two others suffered superficial wounds. The humans have not fared so well. By the time we came upon the scene, the armed escort had already been cut down, leaving only the blustering Prince Theodre and his fair companion. The only reason they're still alive, I suspect, is because the Licornyn Riders intended to make them hostages.

As though drawn by some invisible force, my gaze shifts to the carriage where the prince paces back and forth, wringing his jeweled hands. But it's not he who draws my eye. His sister stands close by, observing her brother. Her face is quiet and still, a stark contrast to the prince's manic mannerisms.

His sister.

One of the three princesses of Gavaria.

Interesting. Very interesting.

With a quick shake of my head, I search among my own people for my captain. She crouches over the body of a smoldering licorne, attempting to cut the still-flaming horn from its forehead with her big stone knife. "Hael!" I call.

She turns, sees me, and quickly rises and hastens to my side. As she comes down the slope, her gaze shifts to the fallen young warrior beside me. "Yok! You devil-gnawed little cave fish! I promised Mar I wouldn't let anything happen to you. Are you determined to make a liar out of me?"

Yok tries to smile. The result is ghastly. "Sorry, sis," he manages, his voice painfully weak. "I mean, it's not as though I *wanted* to have my arm torn off."

"Torn off?" Hael drops in a crouch, her gaze running over her little brother. Upon seeing his limb still attached to his body, she smacks him upside the head. "Ow," he protests.

"Have done with mauling my soldiers, Hael." I show her the wound. "I'm afraid it's more serious than I first thought. A licorne got him."

"*Morar-juk!*" Hael spits.

"Language, sis." Yok shakes his head weakly. "You know Mar doesn't like it when you swear like that."

"Yeah, well, Mar doesn't like it when her baby boy gets himself ripped up by licornes either." My captain turns to me, her face set in a scowl that doesn't mask the anxiety simmering in her eyes. "We have to get him home."

"No!" Yok yelps.

She rounds on him. "What, you think we're going to take you along with us just so you can die a slow, agonizing death while Vor dances with the human princesses? Think again, little brother!"

"I'm not going to endanger the mission." Yok sets his jaw stubbornly and tries to sit up. Blood immediately drains from his face. He groans.

"Down, boy." I plant a firm hand on his chest. He resists only a moment before sinking back to the ground. "Believe it or not, you aren't vital to the success of this little venture."

"Are you sure?" Yok murmurs. Sweat beads his brow, and his eyelids droop heavily. "Don't you need my winning smile to sweeten up the human maidens?"

"They'll have to make do with mine." I turn to Hael, meeting her gaze. "He needs the *uggrha* healer. Before it's too late."

"I'll take him," she answers at once.

But I shake my head. "I can't let you. I don't know what to expect upon our arrival at Beldroth Castle. Larongar has been profuse in his promises of friendship, but humans are born liars. I don't want to venture into the human king's house without my captain at my side."

She bites her lip as though she's actively biting back protests. Swallowing hard, she gives a short nod. "I'll send Wrag and Toz with him then. They both sustained minor injuries but are capable of providing escort. It'll reduce our party rather more than I like, though."

"It can't be helped." I look down at Yok again, pat him gently on the shoulder. "I'll send Umog Zu to prepare your wound and speak a blessing over you for safe travel. Then it's back to Mythanar for you, my friend. Be sure to give your mother my best."

Yok's lip twists in a bitter snarl, but he can't even open his eyes. The poison is already spreading fast. I pray he'll make it back to the healer before it reaches his heart.

Leaving the boy to the ministrations of his sister, I go to fetch the priestess as promised. Zu is busy applying a poultice to a gash on Toz's forehead, but at a word from me, she tells Toz to hold the poultice in place himself and hurries off to see to Yok.

"Are you well, Toz?" I ask, pausing a moment. "Your pretty face broken beyond repair?"

He chuckles, flashing sharpened teeth. "I'll use this pretty face to smash in the nose of the next elf who takes a stab at me!" Unlike most of our companions, his hide is made up in large part of crusty stone, his features craggy and rough as a slab of basalt. His head is as good a weapon as the club he likes to carry. Still, the Licornyn Rider somehow managed to deliver that cut to his forehead. Which can only mean they're carrying *virmaer* blades, spelled with magic powerful enough to pierce even trolde hides. Not a comforting thought.

And here I thought this little jaunt into the human world would be simple.

Slapping Toz's shoulder, I turn from him and seek out the two humans by the carriage. Prince Theodre is still pacing. I can just hear his haranguing voice running up and down the scales as he gesticulates wildly, the rings on his fingers flashing in the firelight. All the while, his sister stands quietly by, hands folded. Every so often, she offers a low answer, but I'm too far away to discern any words.

There's something strange about that girl. Something . . . I cannot quite put my finger on. Her gown is torn, her hair pulled down from her neat cap and veil, her face smudged with dirt. Yet she carries herself with such dignity, I would have guessed at her royal lineage without being told.

But that's not why I struggle to tear my gaze away from her. There's something else. Something more. It's as though, when I look at her, I can almost, *almost* hear a single note of sweet, sweet song. And as that note hums around her, it creates a radiant aura.

I blink, turn away, and look again. The impression, whatever it was, is gone. Nothing is there but a small, delicate, human woman in a ragged, mud-stained gown.

"Enjoying the view?"

Sul stands at my elbow. My brother's arms are folded across his polished breastplate, which still gleams, unmarred by battle. Not a hair on his head is out of place, and his face is as cool and easy as though he's just come from the dinner table, having enjoyed a hearty feast and fine wines.

He catches my eye, grins, and waggles his eyebrows. "You know, I've never been a fancier of human women. But I'll admit, that particular specimen is striking. I notice you wasted no time in scooping her up for a little ride. How did she feel in the saddle, eh?"

I give him a look. "Get your mind out of the *vruhag*. I did what I had to do to keep the poor girl from harm. Nothing more."

"Oh, certainly!" Sul's grin widens. "No one doubts your honorable nature, most noble of kings and best of brothers. But while I'm sure your sterling virtue would prevent you from noticing, that's rather a large rip in the demure maiden's gown. When she was astride your steed, there was more than a little shapely leg on fine display. You, naturally, would have averted your gaze from such a sight, but the rest of us got an eyeful when you rode down the mountainside."

Warmth pools in my gut. I had not been unaware of the amount of skin my passenger inadvertently showed during our brief ride together. I'd made a point to wrap a fold of my own cloak around her for modesty, but there was nothing I could do when she slipped from my saddle. The gown hangs in such a way now that one would not guess at the slit. I doubt the girl has any idea exactly how much she revealed in the heat of battle.

As though reading my mind, my brother prods me in the shoulder. "Now you've had a look into the human king's larder, are you ready to make your selection? Or do you plan to taste a few more of his sweets before deciding which one to bite?"

I glare at him. "Keep your tongue behind your teeth where it belongs, or I'll remove it and give you a proper lashing."

"Steady, brother!" Sul laughs outright. "At the risk of losing my tongue, I feel I should point out that the humans' carriage is going nowhere anytime soon. The traces were cut, and the horses escaped. I'm afraid your pretty little human will need to beg a ride wherever she's going." He places a hand on his heart. "I'm happy to volunteer a spot on my saddle. No need to thank me for my sacrifice."

I don't grace this with an answer and leave my brother chuckling behind my back. The prince and his sister are certainly in a vulnerable state. With neither horses nor escort, they are entirely helpless out here on the mountain slope in the deepening night.

My people have been hard at work, already dragging away the bodies of fallen Licornyn Riders as well as humans. Troldefolk do not believe in leaving the dead untended, especially our dead enemies. Souls unclaimed by the gods may latch on to their killers, haunting them unto death. Our priestess will perform sending prayers over the bodies of the slain before we continue on our way. Their weapons, however, we leave where they fall. It's bad luck to claim the blade of a dead foe for fear it may seek vengeance. Thus, the burning blade of a Licornyn Rider lies near the carriage, smoldering into low embers and casting a red glare on the scene of Prince Theodre and his sister.

"This is your fault," I hear Theodre muttering furiously. He waves his arms in a grand but futile gesture. "You realize, I hope? If you'd married Orsan like you were meant to, Father never would have sent you to that gods-forsaken convent. There'd have been no need for me to come out all this way to fetch you home again. Gods above, it makes me sick to think of it! I hope you're prepared to explain to Father exactly why good men died tonight."

I step a few paces closer. Theodre continues his rant, unaware of my presence. But his sister—the princess—turns and looks directly at me. At least, she seems to. I'm fairly certain she cannot see me in the dark. Her brow puckers with faint uncertainty, but her gaze never wavers.

For the first time I notice: her eyes are two different colors—one blue, one gold.

"Are you listening to me?" Theodre demands, whirling suddenly on his sister. He takes three aggressive steps toward her, his fists clenched and threatening.

"Brother!" She shoots him a warning glance and nods significantly my way.

Theodre stops abruptly, his mouth open. He turns, blinking against the glare from the burning sword. In another step, I fully enter the circle of light. Blood drains from the human prince's face, leaving him ashen. He swallows hard. By human standards, he might be considered handsome. It's difficult for me to judge, but his figure seems broad and sturdy enough, and he's dressed impeccably after human fashion. If his jaw is a little weak, it's nothing a neatly shaped beard cannot disguise. But there's a smallness to him that is difficult to define. As though his spirit has atrophied, rendering him faintly contemptible.

His sister, however . . . I find myself searching in vain for that strange aura I'd sensed earlier, that indefinable music I'd felt, not heard. Perhaps I imagined it. Nonetheless, I'm oddly reluctant to look away. By the standards of my people, she's hardly what one would consider pretty, being far too small and fine boned and delicate. Her hair is the color of warm *jiru* nectar, her mouth wide and pink beneath a long narrow nose. Her brows are dark, as are the thick lashes framing her unusual bicolored eyes. I wonder if she's considered beautiful among her kind.

I wonder if I might learn to think her beautiful, given time.

A pink stain creeps up her cheeks. She drops her gaze, sinking into a respectful curtsy. I've been looking at her far too long without speaking. Hastily, I offer a short bow. "Princess."

"Good King," she answers, casting me the briefest of glances before her lashes fall once more.

"Don't talk to the troll folk, Faraine," her brother growls. My hackles rise at the word *troll*, but I force my expression to remain calm when the prince turns to me. He takes a half step to place himself a little in front of the young woman. "You'll have to excuse my sister's manners, Shadow King. She's been out of society for some years now and easily forgets herself."

Swallowing back any comment on whose manners I find lacking, I force a cool smile and address myself to the girl. "It would appear the gods have smiled upon me this evening, for I have the pleasure of offering you and your brother aid twice over."

She glances uncertainly at Theodre before answering in that soft voice of hers, "You and your people have already done us great service at the risk of your own lives, good King. We are in your debt."

"Aaaaah, that is to say, not *exactly* in your *debt*," her brother jumps in. "Rather, I should think we'd call it *even*, what with you making use of King Larongar's road on your way to enjoy his hospitality. It's only right you should render aid to your host's kin, wouldn't you agree?"

"Theodre!" the girl hisses.

"What?" the prince snaps back. "They're fae! Don't you know anything? Never let yourself become indebted to the fae!"

"Quite right, my friend," I say smoothly, more to assuage the guilty expression his sister shoots me than from any desire to pacify the prince. "I would not dream of collecting on such a debt in any case. Rather, I beg you would do me the honor of allowing me to assist you further. I cannot help noticing you are now without guard or means of transportation. It would be my great pleasure to escort you to your father's home, as I am even now on my way there to pay my respects."

Theodre looks at his sister. She raises her eyebrows. Her expression is difficult for me to read, but she seems to be communicating silently to her brother. He purses his lips, glancing at the carriage, at the cut traces, then around at the night-darkened mountain. "Very well," he says at last, turning back to me. "We'll stay here tonight. In the morning your people can find our horses, and we'll continue together."

I suppress a snort. "My people prefer to travel at night. We will go on and hope to reach Beldroth before dawn."

The human prince stares at me. "How exactly do you expect us to travel without our horses?"

"Simple. You'll ride with us."

Theodre slowly turns, peering out beyond the ringing firelight to the ominous forms of our morleth steeds standing in the deeper shadows. They toss their heads, stomp their hooves, and lash their sinuous barbed tails irritably. One of them snorts, emitting a red spark. Smoke trails from its nostrils.

The human prince's eyes goggle. "Surely you jest!"

"You'll find them quite comfortable. Far better than lurching along in that box on wheels."

But the prince shakes his head and goes on shaking it, as though some mechanism in his neck has broken. "I will *not* be hauled around on the back of one of those monsters!"

"Theodre," his sister says softly, "be reasonable. We cannot stay out here all night, alone. The fae might return, and we have no weapons, no guards."

"I don't care!" Theodre braces himself, looking from the princess to me to the shadowy morleth. "I'd rather be trampled to death by unicorns than ride on one of those devils!"

"Very well." The princess draws her shoulders back, her eyes narrowing. "I'll go then." She turns to me, completely ignoring her brother's spluttering protest of "Faraine! I absolutely forbid it!" Tilting her head slightly to one side, she says, "I am ready to ride whenever you are, King Vor."

I meet and hold her gaze. There's courage in her eyes, unexpected and defiant. She may not be a warrior; that doesn't mean she's weak.

I extend my hand. She hesitates. Her lips press into a thin, contemplative line. Then, taking a quick step, she places her fingers lightly on my arm instead. She doesn't meet my gaze. I feel the warmth of her touch through the sleeve and find myself wishing she'd accepted my hand. Perhaps it would go against standards of etiquette in human society. We're going to have to take care not to inadvertently offend one another.

"Faraine!" Theodre growls. I ignore him and lead his sister away from the carriage to where my own morleth waits. He champs at his bit and flares his wide nostrils. The air of this world disagrees with him, and he's losing large clumps of fur from his withers and flanks, revealing ugly scales underneath. Even I, used to morleth as I am, cannot help a little shudder at the sight of him. Compared to the blunt-toothed, long-nosed creatures humans use to pull their carriages, Knar must appear positively demonic.

But the princess approaches, her footsteps steady, the hand on my arm betraying only the slightest tremble. I find myself straining for another hint of the melodic song I'd heard surrounding her. I can almost, *almost* feel it, tantalizingly just out of range of perception.

"Have no fear, princess," I say, hoping to put her at ease. "I've had Knar since he was a foal, born from a burst of sulfur and smoke in the land beneath the Fiery River."

"Really?" She shoots me a quick glance. "He looks quite vicious."

"Oh, he absolutely is. He would devour me in a couple of mouthfuls if he thought he could get away with it. But that's the great virtue of morleth—you never doubt where you stand with them. They don't pretend to be your friend, but if you treat them with respect, you can find ways to coexist to mutual benefit."

She considers this. "Sounds rather like life at court."

My mouth quirks. "Certainly not. Morleth are far better mannered than any courtiers I know."

At this, Knar tosses back his head and lets out a honking bray that elicits a little scream from the girl. Then she presses a hand to her heart and laughs outright. It's a bright, warm sound here on this cold mountainside. I have a strange feeling I could spend a great deal of time and effort contriving to hear that laugh again.

She looks up at the saddle high above her. "I'll need a little help," she says.

"Certainly, Princess."

A gasp escapes her lips as I catch her around her slender waist and lift her off her feet. She weighs so little, it's but the work of a moment to set her lightly in the saddle. As I do so, however, the split in her gown opens again. She looks down, sees her own bare leg, and fumbles with the folds of fabric, trying to cover herself.

I turn my gaze pointedly away and mount behind her. Once settled in the saddle, I remove my cloak and drape it across her shoulders. She grabs the edges and gratefully wraps them around her for modesty. "Thank you," she murmurs.

A lump forms in my throat. I swallow it back and answer, "Of course." Once again, I'm almost certain I detect a whisper of song. But it's gone again before I can lay hold of it.

I turn Knar's ugly head around, facing the carriage where Theodre still stands, gawping at his sister. "You have a choice, my friend," I call out to him. "You may ride with us to Beldroth tonight or wait for dawn and hope someone comes along to help you chase down your horses. It's up to you."

The prince looks as though he's about to choke on the expletives rising in his gullet. Instead, he manages a single, curt nod. Taking this as acquiescence, I turn in my saddle and call out, "Hael!"

"Yes, my king?"

"Find someone to give Prince Theodre a lift."

My captain growls but salutes. Trusting her to accomplish the task, I urge Knar into motion, guiding him to where two of my men are helping young Yok into his saddle. Wrag and Toz, already mounted, hover close by, their faces wreathed in concern. Toz still has the poultice pressed to his forehead, and Wrag's arm is in a sling. But they're both in better shape than Yok, who looks ready to faint. Will he be able to make the ride back to Mythanar?

"Watch over the boy," I say, addressing the other two. "Bring him home safely."

Wrag nods solemnly. Toz grins, flashing sharp teeth. "Best of luck, Your Majesty. May you find success at the end of your mission."

"From where I'm sitting, success seems to be well in hand!" my brother's voice declares. I turn to find Sul mounted on his morleth, flashing me a suggestive grin. Wrag and Toz both laugh, and I'm suddenly grateful the girl riding in front of me doesn't understand a word of troldish.

With a sharp pull on the reins, I angle my morleth down the descending road. "Hold on, Princess," I murmur close to the girl's ear. I watch her fingers twine in handfuls of Knar's dark mane. Then I urge my steed onward, into the night.

3

Faraine

If someone had told me mere hours ago that I would, before the night's end, find myself riding on the back of a great, spined, nightmarish brute, wrapped in the arms of a magnificent, blue-skinned warrior king, I'm sure I would have laughed out loud. I'm not a romantic. I never have been. I've spent the better part of my life avoiding such powerful and problematic emotions. Yet somehow, I find myself suddenly playing the role of a heroine straight out of a ballad!

After the first interval of riding, the initial shock begins to wear off, and I'm better able to comprehend that which takes place around me. The trolls are talking in their rough, rock-grinding language. The man riding at the king's right hand is particularly chatty. I study him with covert glances, trying to get a clearer impression of him. He looks a lot like the king, with a similarly shaped brow and strong jaw. He's taller and paler, however, and his skin is only faintly blue.

Once, he looks my way and catches my eye. Just for an instant.

But in that instant, I get such a jolt of suspicion, it turns my stomach. I look away quickly and avoid his gaze going forward.

The rider to the king's left is the one he called Hael. I can't get a clear sense from her, for she has my brother riding behind her, and his anxiety is so potent, it dominates everything around him. Still, if I push through Theodre's storm, I can just catch a sense of something strong emitting from her. *Worry*, if I'm not mistaken.

"Are you comfortable, Princess?" The king's voice startles me. He's been quiet for some time.

I shiver a little at the sensation of his breath against my skin but quickly master myself. "Faraine," I say. "Please, my name is Faraine."

He doesn't answer for a moment. Then, "And you will permit the familiarity?"

I wince. How could I have forgotten? The fae hold names as precious and dangerous. To give one's name to a fae can be a deadly mistake. But I can't very well take it back now, can I?

"Yes, please." I hope my voice doesn't betray the tension in my gut. "I've been living away from court these last two years and have grown disused to titles."

"In that case, you must call me Vor."

"I'm not sure I could."

"And why not? If I'm to call you by your name, it is only fair you should grant me the same kindness."

"My . . . my father would not be pleased."

"Your father is not here."

Well, that's true enough. But I feel the distance between me and Beldroth Castle shrinking with every step of this powerful beast I ride. Soon I'll be back under my father's stern and disappointed eye. I'm not sure I'm ready for that.

Hastily, I switch tacks. "And what of your people? How would they feel about such informality?"

"Shocked and horrified," he answers at once. "Which should be a sight to behold, so you really must indulge me."

A laugh burbles from my lips before I can swallow it back. "Very well," I say, trying to recover my dignity. Then add "Vor" for good measure. It's a strange name, so harsh and abrupt. Which doesn't seem to suit him at all.

I lapse back into silence. I really shouldn't be enjoying myself this much. Following the attack on the carriage, the death that surrounded me, the fear and the terror, my mind should be a wreck. Such a deluge of sensation would ordinarily leave me incapacitated for days. Yet here I am, head clear, pain-free. It's strange and incredible. I want to hold on to this feeling as long as possible.

The Shadow King reins his creature to a halt. We've come to a rocky promontory overlooking the valley below. In the distance, just visible under moonlight, stand the high towers of Beldroth. My heart lurches at the sight. I'm not sure whether I feel dread or homesickness or some strange combination of the two. While I miss my sisters, home has always been a place of pain for me. Life at Nornala Convent is lonely and dull, but I've enjoyed relative peace there compared to the turmoil of my father's court.

"Is that our destination?" Vor asks.

"Yes."

"Interesting."

I turn, trying to glimpse his face. He seems contemplative, possibly even a little uncertain. He glances down at me, catching my eye. "This is my first time traveling to the human world," he says. "It seems very strange to me, building a fortress like that out under the open sky. To my eye, it feels dangerously exposed. Tell me, what should I expect upon reaching your father's house?"

I hesitate. I must tread carefully here. "I suppose that depends. What do you expect?"

Once more I get a prickling of uncertainty from him. "Your father has promised me feasting and friendship. His messages have been . . . effusive. We have both stated our hopes of securing an alliance, of lasting peace and brotherhood between Mythanar and Gavaria for generations to come."

Marriage. He's referring to a marriage. He doesn't have to say the word for me to know what he means.

"Well," I continue, choosing to be direct in my answer, "if that is what's promised, I believe there will be plenty of food and drink and merrymaking. I've seen my father host potential suitors before."

"Really?" His tone alters slightly. "I understand King Larongar has three daughters. Has he secured marriages for either of your sisters?"

"Not yet."

Vor is silent for a moment. He spurs his creature back into motion, and the party continues down the mountain road. At length, he says, "Where do you stand in the family? Your brother is the eldest, am I correct?"

His interest is disconcerting. In the space of this ride, he has already asked me more personal questions than Prince Orsan did over our entire monthlong courtship. Part of me wonders if I should be offended or distrustful. Another part cannot help enjoying the attention. I must remember that he's simply gathering information. He's a strategist, and he wants to be prepared before he enters into negotiations with my father. That is all.

So why do I get such a strong sensation of . . . *warmth* from him?

"I am the second-born," I say. "After me are two younger sisters, Ilsevel and Aurae."

"Indeed?" Vor goes silent again, considering. While my gods-gift does not enable me to read another's thoughts, I can almost *feel* him realizing I am the one my father tried to marry off to some suitor in the past. He's probably wondering what's wrong with me that the marriage did not succeed.

I swallow hard and quickly say, "You have a great pleasure ahead of you in meeting my sister Ilsevel."

"Is that so? And why is that?"

"She is widely considered the most beautiful woman in all Gavaria. To that virtue, she adds many accomplishments: dancing, riding, hunting, fine needlework. Her wit is unmatched among the ladies of court, and she is peerless in both humor and charm."

"You seem very proud of this sister of yours."

"I am. She is the darling of my heart."

"High praise, I'm sure."

"The highest I can bestow." I look down at my hands, at the strands of black mane twisted between my fingers. "And, of course, there's her gods-gift to consider."

"Gods-gift?"

"Yes. Did you not know? The children of King Larongar were all blessed by the gods with extraordinary gifts on the day of their christening. Ilsevel was bestowed the gift of song. There is no voice in all the kingdom that can rival hers, and she plays all instruments brilliantly."

"In that case, I look forward to many enjoyable performances." Vor goes silent. I try not to but can't help reaching out with my senses to discern what he's feeling. His emotions are complicated. I'm not certain I could name them.

"If you don't mind my asking," he says suddenly, "what gift did the gods bestow upon your brother?"

"Oh, couldn't you tell?" I grin. "His gift is *beauty*."

Vor is silent for several paces. Then, "I can't decide if you're teasing."

I laugh outright at that, drawing a few suspicious glances from the riders around us. "No, indeed! Among our kind, Theodre is considered quite devastatingly beautiful. He always has a string of doting lovers sighing after him wherever he goes. I understand my father hoped he'd be given a war gift, which would have been more useful to the crown. But my brother definitely enjoys his gift to the fullest."

A low chuckle rumbles in the Shadow King's throat. The sound sparks against my senses, heady as a sip of strong wine. "You'll forgive me, but I struggle to imagine that."

"Well, you've not yet seen my brother in his element."

"True." I can feel the next question rising to his lips. He holds on to it for some while, but I know it's coming and brace myself. "If I may be so bold," he says at last, "to ask about *your* gods-gift?"

"You may ask."

Another moment's hesitation. Then, "But you won't tell me."

"No."

"In that case, I will hold my tongue."

We continue in silence for a little while. The rolling gait of the king's monster steed is almost soothing beneath the starry sky. It's a far more comfortable mode of transportation than the carriage. If I close my eyes and let myself forget the hideous appearance of the creature on which I ride, I could almost imagine I was carried on a warm and gentle wind. Combined with the inexplicable calm radiating from the Shadow King, I find myself lulled and peaceful.

I could almost drift off into sleep, my head cushioned against a firm, broad shoulder.

"Gods damn and blast!" Theodre's voice erupts suddenly, disturbing my calm. "Your hilt is digging into my stomach! Gods save me, I *cannot* be expected to ride all the way to Beldroth in such a fashion! I demand you pull this beast up at once and adjust your weaponry, woman!"

A low chuckle rumbles in my ear once more. "*Beauty*, eh?"

I smile. "Well, beauty is in the eye of the beholder, after all."

"Not troldefolk beholders, I fear."

Heat creeps to my cheeks. For a moment, I can't say if it's embarrassment on my brother's behalf or . . . something else. The question suddenly springs into my head: if this majestic and otherworldly king doesn't consider my gods-gifted brother beautiful, what must he think of *me*? I've never been much concerned with thoughts of my own attractiveness. Standing between Theodre on one hand and Ilsevel on the other, I know myself to be rather dull and pale. Worse still, my physical limitations keep me from venturing out in company more than absolutely necessary, so I've had little opportunity to develop either charm or wit. Whenever Prince Orsan tried to lead me into a bout of flirting, my senses were always so overwhelmed, it was all I could do to make any sense of his words. I never did learn the knack of a well-timed barb or a mischievous toss of the head. Not that it mattered. Orsan pursued me for my title and position. And even that wasn't enough to win him over in the end.

As for this man? This king? He's meant for better than the likes of me. So why should I care what he or his kind think of my appearance?

"*Troldefolk*," I say, latching on to a chance to shift the conversation elsewhere. "You've said that word before. Is it the proper name for your people?"

"Yes," Vor answers. "It is what we call ourselves. Why? Did you think we were *trolls*?"

His tone is teasing, but I sense a hint of disdain. I wince, remembering my brother's blatant use of the word. "I'll admit," I say, "I was told the King of the Trolls was on his way to pay his respects to my father."

"And you've been envisioning a big slab of knuckle-dragging rock, no doubt."

"Well, a few of your party *do* rather meet that description."

"True, true." For a moment, I fear I've offended him. When I search his feelings, however, I don't detect any irritation. Instead, there's an undercurrent of sorrow I don't understand.

I'm still trying to decide if I dare ask more searching questions when he continues in a heavier voice than before: "Over the last few generations, a change has occurred among my people. More and more trolde children are born with rock hides. As though the stone from which we were carved in the Dawning of Time seeks now to reclaim our flesh and souls."

I glance sideways at Captain Hael, who has shifted my brother to sit in front of her and has her arm wrapped around his waist. She's so tall and powerful, he looks positively childlike by comparison. For the most part, she boasts the same pale beauty as most of the others in this party, but I'd not failed to notice the hard, gray, lumpish skin which creeps up her neck, partway up her jaw and the right side of her face. Her right hand is similarly rough-hewn and twice the size of her left.

"Does anyone know what causes it?" I ask, hoping Vor will take my question as interest, not rudeness.

"No one knows for certain," he responds. "But there are theories. Our priestesses call it the *dorgarag.*"

"What does that mean?"

He considers. "It's difficult to translate into your tongue. Perhaps the best word would be *the return*. In trolde lore, our god is *Morar tor Grakanak*, the God of the Deeper Dark. We believe he carved the original trolde man from a slab of obsidian and the original trolde woman from a black diamond. When he breathed life into them, the stone fell away, revealing the supple flesh beneath. But their hearts were still stone, and to stone they must someday return. Thus our priestesses believe the Deeper Dark is stirring, summoning all troldefolk to return to their true and original state of stone."

His voice is heavy, ominous. Whatever his priestesses may teach, he does not sound like a man of faith speaking of hoped-for salvation. "And what do you believe?" I ask softly.

I feel the swell of his broad chest at my back, then the gust of air as he releases the deep breath from his lungs. "It doesn't matter what I believe. I am Lord Protector of the Under Realm. It is my sacred duty and honor to defend my people."

For just an instant, a strong emotion emanates from his core: *fear.* It's sharp and quick, like the swift stab of a knife. Ordinarily, such a stab would cause me to cry out and crumple over into myself. This time, however, though I sense it with perfect clarity, it does not hurt me. Strange.

I turn my head, trying to catch another glimpse of the Shadow King's face. It's hard to see much from this angle and under moonlight. What does he fear exactly? My first impressions of him in the midst of battle were of total confidence and unshakable conviction. But something must be driving him to leave his own world and seek this alliance with Gavaria. What does he think my father might give him? Because I can't imagine he's traveled across worlds for the sole purpose of pursuing a human bride. There must be something more at stake, something I don't understand.

The road before us begins to level out. We're already leaving the mountains behind. How many miles have we traveled in such a short time? The monsters move so smoothly, I'd not noticed their speed until now as we spill out into the open plain. Beldroth Castle stands a good two miles distant, perched on a rocky promontory.

Ripples of unease disturb the atmosphere around me. I glance at the other troldefolk riders, all of them wide-eyed and tense-shouldered astride their great steeds. I brace myself, prepared for the pain that usually accompanies such strong emotions, but none comes. I feel it, yet it seems to pass through a filtering fog that dulls the intensity before it reaches me. I'm so surprised by this unexpected blessing that it takes me a few moments to realize the king himself is as disturbed as his companions. His jaw is tight, and I can hear his teeth grinding. "Are you well, Vor?" I ask.

He blinks, and his brow puckers with faint surprise. "Ah, yes. Of course." After a moment, he adds, "It's the sky. While we traveled in the mountains, it was easier to ignore, but now . . ." He shudders, the cords of his throat standing out starkly. "I find it deeply unsettling."

I glance up at the star-strewn arc of night overhead. It's lovely and clear, and the early spring constellations are on proud display. "Why does it bother you so?"

"Did you not know?" He catches my eye again. "Mythanar is a subterranean kingdom. By and large, troldefolk prefer to dwell under stone with a good, solid ceiling overhead."

My brow furrows as this information sinks in. A subterranean kingdom? I hadn't considered that possibility. It's not good . . . not good at all. When I think about Ilsevel, my sweet, spirited sister, I think of sun and sky and wide-open spaces. She was born for the saddle, born for the far horizon. How would she fare as queen of a dark, underground realm?

I shake my head, driving this thought away. No point in dwelling on things I cannot help. Instead, I turn my attention back to the rising unease in Vor. It increases with every passing moment until I feel it with every shuddering breath he takes.

I chew the inside of my cheek, considering. This probably isn't a good idea. I should mind my own business, leave well enough alone. My world is fraught with forces about which I can do nothing. But here, in this moment . . . I am not without power.

Releasing a handful of dark mane, I slip my hand under my borrowed cloak and find my crystal pendant on its chain around my neck. I close my eyes, let my breath level out, and feel the thrumming pulse down in the heart of the crystal. My heartbeat slows to match that pulse until my body hums in synchronization.

Then, letting go of the crystal, I reach out from under the cloak and very gently place my fingers on Vor's wrist. The moment my fingertips brush his skin, something sharp sparks between us. Ribbons of energy run up my arm to burst in my head. That first shock is painful, but as the sensation cascades down my spine and flows through the rest of my body, the pain melts away into something strange and wondrous.

Vor lets out a long exhale. Surprise flows out from him, carrying with it that simmering anxiety. In its place there is only calm.

I lift my hand from his wrist and grab a tangle of monster mane. We ride in silence, and I keep my gaze fixed on the looming towers of Beldroth. After what seems a long time, Vor's voice rumbles in my ear again. "Did you do something?"

I blink, surprised. Was it that obvious? "Yes," I answer softly.

A breath. Then, "If I ask you what, will you tell me?"

"No."

"Ah."

Beldroth is closer now. Soon, guards along the battlements will sound the heralding trumpets, alerting the castle denizens to the Shadow King's approach. Soon after, I'll be back within my father's house—back in that realm of existence where I've always been little more than an inconvenience, a bother, a disappointment. Even a liability. And the only good I can offer is to try to convince my sister to marry this otherworldly man with whom I now ride.

For some reason, I find that notion even more disturbing now that I've met Vor. Perhaps it's the knowledge of the underground world from which he hails. I know Ilsevel will be unhappy buried so far from the sun and stars.

But if I'm honest, that's not the only reason for my unease. Something else stabs at my heart, a bitter thorn I hardly dare name: *jealousy.*

But no. That's foolish. Ridiculous! Ever since my disastrous experience with Prince Orsan, I've learned to be grateful Father sent me away to Nornala Convent; grateful I would never again face the terror of an arranged marriage to an unknown groom. While life in the convent is certainly lonely, at least I can live there as my own person. I won't let a chance encounter with a handsome stranger—not even one who saved my life—make me feel unhappy with my lot. I am resigned. I know my place. And when I get home, I will do all I can to comfort and prepare Ilsevel for the life ahead of her.

Drawing Vor's cloak a little closer, I sit very straight in the saddle, determined not to rest back against the king's chest. I grip my crystal again. The pulse in its center is faint, but when I close my eyes and focus, I can just find it. I concentrate on that pulse, drawing deeply inward.

But I cannot fully block out the sensation of those strong arms wrapped around me and the warmth of breath against my ear.

4

Vor

We ride swiftly across the open plain beneath an agonizingly vast sky alight with a million stars. I sense the quiet terror in the hearts of my people riding beside and behind me. Terror I shared up until a few moments ago. Now, it seems like a faraway memory. I'm full of both calm and confidence as the distance to the human castle slowly shrinks.

I surreptitiously study the young woman seated in front of me. Something about her makes me feel unexpectedly centered. I'm uncertain how to express it, even in the privacy of my own thoughts. Closing my eyes, I inhale gently. Her soft hair, though tangled and snarled, gives off a sweet, delicate scent. It's a strange perfume to my nose, but not unpleasant. Perhaps if I were full-blooded trolde, I would find her repellent. As it is, it's definitely not repulsion I feel.

I've always known I would have to marry for the sake of the kingdom. My own father did—twice. And his first wife, my mother, was human. A fact that has only made my life more difficult. While

I look trolde and live my life according to troldefolk ways, there are those who will not forget my half-blood nature. There was even talk, upon my father's death, about passing the crown to my full-blooded trolde brother rather than to me.

If I go through with this alliance—if I take a human wife—my children will bear more human blood than trolde. I wonder if my people will ever accept such offspring as legitimate heirs to my kingdom.

Then again, there will be no kingdom if I don't make this alliance. No kingdom. No crown. No Under Realm.

This bleak thought draws my attention away from the young woman and on to our destination. That great grim castle standing atop a high promontory above a sprawling town. Six tall towers rise like teeth to tear at the sky, and the walls are high and forbidding. It's a gruesome sight: so many dead stones hauled from their natural settings and piled one on top of the other in such a fashion. This is not the way troldefolk create our dwellings. We would never treat the stone so cruelly.

I squint, focusing my gaze, and count the guards standing watch along those walls. No fewer than twenty, probably more that I cannot see. What's more, I detect a glimmer of magic surrounding them.

Sul rides his morleth close to my side. "Do you see what I see?" he asks in troldish.

I nod. "Miphates spells."

My brother flashes a diamond-hard smile. "Are we going to ride straight into their clutches, oh wise and worthy King? Is this one of those glory-and-honor moments I've heard sung about?"

"What?"

"You know—one of those ballads wherein the hero forgets all reason for the sake of a pretty face and rides recklessly to certain doom, dragging everyone else down with him in the process. All very romantic, I'm sure."

I growl low in my throat. "Watch your tongue, brother."

"Certainly." His smile only grows. "I'll watch my tongue so long as you watch your step." He eyes Faraine, letting his gaze run up and down her figure in a way I don't like. As though he can see right through the folds of cloak shrouding her.

I turn my shoulder slightly, wishing I could hide the girl from his view. "Shall I remind you that the human king has promised us a warm welcome?"

"King Larongar has promised, eh? Yes, I'm sure we'll be warmly welcomed once those Miphates spells start flying and we're all burnt to cinders."

At the sound of her father's name, Faraine stiffens. She faces firmly forward, her shoulders shrugging up to her ears. How much does she understand? She doesn't know our tongue, but she's sensitive to tone. I feel the ease between us vanishing, and she sits like dead stone before me.

I spur Knar a little faster, putting some distance between us and Sul. "You must pardon my brother's suspicious nature," I say, switching to her language and speaking low in her ear. "We did not expect to see overt signs of Miphates magic so soon upon arrival. Your father boasts impressive defenses."

A little shiver rolls down her neck. "Of course. We have been fighting the fae these last many years."

It's a fair point. Faced with the likes of the Licornyn Riders, Larongar is wise to make use of his Miphates mages to defend his own household. Those cold, dead stone walls wouldn't offer much protection against a determined fae host, after all.

Still, human magic is mysterious. And dangerous. I've heard

many tales of the Miphates magicians and their miraculous powers. Tales I hope will prove true, for I have grave need of a miracle. But I don't like to put myself at the mercy of such a force.

"Faraine," I say, "may I ask an impertinent question?"

She shoots me a quick glance from those strange eyes of hers. "Only if you can bear an impertinent answer."

My lips quirk to one side. "I can bear any amount of impertinence so long as your answer is honest."

"In that case, ask away."

"I'm only wondering how great the chance is that I am even now leading my people into an ambush."

She does not answer at once. Have I insulted her? I don't think so. She seems to possess a fair and straightforward sort of mind that would appreciate candor. Then again, I've not known her long enough to form a clear picture of her character. For all I know, I've just overstepped myself rather badly.

"Whatever chance there was," she says at last, "has been drastically decreased by the simple fact that you have my father's firstborn and heir in your keeping."

I chuckle dryly. "A happy turn of events for me. But I hope there is no need for our little rescue to turn into something so unsavory as a hostage situation."

"From your lips to the gods' ears."

Her spine is as straight as a spear shaft. I wish I could say something to relieve her tension. I would like for her to trust me, to believe I have no desire to put her at risk. But my foremost concern must be for my people.

We are now near enough to Beldroth that I can hear the shouts going out as watchmen alert the castle to our approach. Hael rides her morleth up beside me, with Theodre clinging to the pommel of her saddle and looking positively ill beneath the pale starlight.

"My king," Hael says, speaking loud enough to be heard over the human prince's grumbles. "Let me go ahead with the prince. It would be wise to let the humans see him first."

I nod, and Hael takes the lead. She is an intimidating figure, even among troldekind. A valiant, unselfish soul whom I would trust with my life. I know how hard it is for her to continue on this mission while her brother's fate remains uncertain. But she would never falter in the face of her duty.

She approaches the gate. "Halt!" a human voice calls out, not quite able to disguise a nervous quaver. "Who goes there?"

"King Vor of Mythanar," Hael replies, "come at the invitation of Larongar Cyhorn, King of Gavaria. We met with your own crown prince on the road and offered him escort."

"The prince?" the human voice says, rather doubtfully. I forget sometimes that humans cannot see well in the dark. "Prince Theodre is with you?"

"Yes, I'm with the trolls, gods damn it!" Theodre bellows, cupping his hands around his mouth. "Open the gates, man. It's spitting cold out here!"

A moment of silence punctuated by low murmurs. Then, with a heavy creak of levers and chains, the portcullis rises. Sul catches my gaze. He raises an eyebrow. This is the moment of truth. Once we're through those gates, we'll be at the human king's mercy. I've been so certain of my path all this time, but now we've come to it, I wonder if I'm truly willing to risk the lives of these brave men and women who've followed me into this strange, cold world.

As though sensing my unease, Faraine turns suddenly and looks up at me. She's so near, I can see the little flecks of green present in both her gold and her blue eye. They're unexpectedly lovely, and I find myself wanting to look more deeply still, to search after the soul revealed behind those colored orbs.

"Don't worry, Vor," she says softly. I like the way my name sounds coming from her lips. She speaks it with a human accent, lilting and gentle. "My father desires this alliance. He's willing even to give up his favorite daughter to secure it."

His favorite daughter. She's not referring to herself. She means Ilsevel: the incredible Ilsevel she's mentioned several times now. Larongar mentioned none of his three daughters by name in any of our correspondence. While we danced around the topic of a marriage, neither of us speaking of it save in hints and implications, I'd assumed when the time came, I would have my pick of the human princesses. Is this not to be the case?

I shake my head. Now is not the time to worry over such details. Faraine's words are all the assurance I need. Larongar wants this alliance. I needn't fear an ambush. Not tonight at any rate.

Hael turns in her saddle. "My king?" she says. I nod, and she spurs her morleth forward, leading the way through the open gate. I follow just behind her, and the other ten members of my party fall in line at my back. It's a comfort to be once more surrounded by stone—even dead stone like these rough-hewn blocks shoved together by unloving hands.

Humans surround us. The smell of them is nearly overwhelming—the stink of time-bound beings, their bodies given over to swift decay. I surreptitiously scrutinize the figures lining the walls. King Larongar is taking no chances. Not even with a prospective son-in-law.

"Get me off this monstrous thing!" Prince Theodre's voice rings out loudly. I turn to see him scrambling to get down from his mount's back. Hael manages to catch him by the collar of his shirt and holds him squirming several feet above the paving stones.

"Put the prince down, Hael," I speak sharply in troldish.

Her lip curls disdainfully. But she opens her hand and lets Theodre drop in an unsightly heap. He picks himself up hastily, straightens his garments, smooths back his long, oiled hair. He staggers a few steps, his legs bowed from the long ride on morleth-back, and very nearly sits down hard right there in the middle of the courtyard. With a little shake, he regains his balance.

Then he whips his head around, shooting a glare directly at me. "Unhand my sister, troll king."

Were I not in such desperate need of making this alliance, I would smash his nose in and see what that does to his gods-gifted beauty. My arm unconsciously tightens around the princess's waist. Am I mistaken, or has her straight spine relaxed, allowing her to lean back against me? No, I must be imagining it.

Hastily, I swing down from the saddle. "Allow me to help you, Princess," I say, forgoing the informality of her name even as I place my hands around her waist. She grips my shoulders, and I lift her down, setting her on her feet. She staggers like her brother, unused to such long hours in the saddle. For a moment, she leans into me for support. My heart makes a peculiar leap to my throat.

She draws away, pulling my cloak close around her body. I feel a cold space in the air where she had stood before, an emptiness that I do not like. She blinks, looks down at herself, then begins to remove the cloak from her shoulders. "No, please," I say quickly, putting out a hand but not quite touching hers. "Keep it. You can return it later."

She gazes up at me, eyelashes fluttering softly. Her lips part, and I tilt my head, eager to catch what she might say.

"Vor! My friend!" The voice booms against the stone walls, causing the morleth to toss their heads and growl. "Is that you at last? We've been anticipating your arrival since sundown. And who are these ragamuffins you've picked up on your journey?"

I turn to face the wide stone stair leading up to a massive front entrance. A man stands framed in the open doorway—a great, square warrior with enormous hands meant for hefting battle-axes, and a once-handsome face now disfigured by a great red scar and an empty eye socket. King Larongar, I presume.

Movement behind him draws my gaze. Three bearded men in elaborately embroidered robes stand just behind the king. I struggle to discern differences among human faces, but the foremost of them has a long white beard while the other two are dark. All brim with unmistakable magical potency. I know at once who they are: the King's Miphates. They trail a few paces behind Larongar as he descends the steps to us.

Theodre, bowlegged and stiff, wobbles over to meet his father, offering a perfunctory bow. "How now, boy," Larongar says, turning to him without much interest. "You look like something the dragon chewed up and spat back out again. What have you been up to?"

His son scowls. "It's not my fault, Father. We were set upon by unicorn riders in the Ettrian Pass. The bastards slaughtered most of our guard. The rest scattered, leaving us to our fate."

Larongar's mustache curls, either with mirth or disdain, I can't quite tell. "Well," he says gruffly, "a bit of adventuring does a man good. And I'm sure you made a decent show of yourself with that sparkly sword of yours, didn't you, my boy?"

Theodre runs his fingers through his shining hair and pulls himself a little straighter. "I did what I could to defend my sister," he declares staunchly. An interesting revision of events. I'd seen the prince abandon Faraine in the carriage in his bid for escape.

Larongar grunts, unimpressed. "Your sister, eh? And where is she?"

"Here, Father," Faraine says, stepping away from me. My gaze follows her as she approaches the king and sinks into a deep curtsy.

Larongar looks from her to me and back again, his expression all too keen. "Well now, Faraine," he rumbles. "Good to have you home again. All in one piece, I trust?"

"Yes, thank you, Father."

"Excellent." He hesitates. Then, as though following some predetermined script, he reaches out and pats her head. "Your sister is in the east tower. Go ahead and, erh . . . help make her ready to meet our guests. You know what to do."

"Yes, Father," Faraine says with another curtsy. She starts for the stair, pauses. For a moment, I wonder if she'll turn and look back at me. I don't know why, but I would like very much to catch a last glimpse of her pale, earnest face. But she doesn't turn. Her hands merely grip the cloak a little closer as she slips up the stair and vanishes into the castle.

"Well, my friend," Larongar says, drawing my attention back to him. "We meet at last, face-to-face. Come! Embrace me!"

He closes the distance between us with a few swift strides and grips me by the shoulders, pulling me into a bear hug. I break his hold as soon as I can without seeming rude, taking care not to stare at the gaping hole where an eye ought to be. This man has made a name for himself with his campaigns against the fae. Over the last two decades he's fought to drive them from his lands, and there are some who believe Larongar might be the man to oust the fae from the human world entirely. Gazing now into his one good eye, I behold in its depths great strength, conviction, pride . . . and malice.

"So, I owe you thanks for the safe return of my children, do I?" he says. His tone is wary. He, like his son, is reluctant to be indebted to one of the fae.

"It was my pleasure to render assistance," I say quickly. "My people and I have faced Licornyn Riders before. They are a deadly band."

"Aye, and they've caused me no end of grief this last season since pledging their service to Prince Ruvaen. Pretty bastards, one and all." He turns then to inspect the rest of my party scattered around the courtyard. His eye widens as he takes in our mounts, particularly my big Knar, standing close at hand. "Here now, this is quite the mighty steed you've got, my friend. Is this what passes for a horse in your world? It looks as though it likes the taste of red meat!"

"Indeed, morleth have been known to feast upon their gentler kin," I reply, casting a fond glance Knar's way.

"You don't say?" Larongar pales beneath his beard. "I fear our stables might be a bit cramped for such a herd."

At this, I laugh. I try not to, but the idea of crowding morleth into a stable with mortal horses is painfully amusing. "Not to worry, friend Larongar," I hasten to reassure him. "So long as the shadows are deep enough, our morleth shall fold inside them and rest comfortably."

Larongar's single eye blinks blankly. He turns to the white-bearded Miphato hovering at his elbow. "Is there something I'm missing here?"

The Miphato inclines his head. "It is my understanding, Majesty, that morleth are interdimensional beings."

"What now?"

"They're magic. Don't worry about it."

"Ah!" The king shrugs and turns back to me. "Well, that settles it. I've always found it best to leave the magic to the Miphates. I quite depend on old Wistari here, my head mage and vizier. What he says is as good as law in these parts."

I shoot a studying glance at the old Miphato, who meets my eye with deceptively placid calm. There's no doubt in my mind: this is the very man I need to save my people from disaster. A knot tightens in my gut. This alliance must work. There is no other alternative for Mythanar, for all of the Under Realm. I must have the might of the human mages on my side. Or we're all doomed.

"Well, Vor, I trust you are hungry," Larongar says, wrapping an arm around my shoulder and guiding me toward the stair. "I've arranged rooms for your people and meals to be brought at once. It'll be dawn soon enough, and I understand your folk prefer to sleep through the day. I hope you'll take your ease, then join us at sundown. I've prepared a little reception to introduce you to my court."

"I look forward to it. And will your daughter Ilsevel be present?" I watch him closely for a reaction.

Larongar's cheek twitches. It's a small enough tell, but informative. "Ah, so you're keen to meet my Ilsie, are you? Word of her travels far and wide, I know. She's as spritely a little thing as a man could ask for. A beauty too, like her mother before her, but with my spirit and strength of will. I defy you to find another maid her equal."

"Indeed?" I force a smile into place. "In that case, I am eager to make her acquaintance."

5

Faraine

I pause within the shelter of the doorway to look back down into the yard. The Shadow King stands close to my father, so tall and solemn and beautiful.

I'm suddenly reluctant to leave his vicinity. For the last few hours, I've luxuriated in the calm of his atmosphere, so inexplicable and so welcome. Now, parting from him, I reenter the world I've always known—a world of dissonance and pain.

So, my gaze lingers. Longer than I should allow it to. He wears a chain mail shirt after the fashion of his people, bright silver with sharp points that give an impression of dragon scales. It fits him perfectly, emphasizing the breadth of his shoulders, the narrow taper of his waist. Tall boots hug his legs up to the knee. He is all muscular athleticism mingled with eerie beauty.

How strange he looks, standing here in the setting of my childhood. The familiarity of these surroundings emphasizes his otherworldliness, and he holds himself with such dignity, a commanding presence. The contrast with my father is stark. King Larongar's life is defined by constant striving. He won his throne by blood and battle and has held on to it with the tenacity of a bulldog. He is a powerful man, impressive and deadly.

But Vor . . . his whole bearing is different. I've seen his prowess in battle and don't doubt he is my father's superior when it comes to pure brawn. But unlike my father, he has nothing to prove. He carries himself as one who was simply born to command.

My mouth is dry. I swallow hard, forcing a lump down my throat. Gods, what am I doing, standing here in the shadows, admiring this stranger? A stranger who, if my father has his way, will very soon wed my sister.

My sister.

Enough dawdling. I have a job to do.

Pulling back from the doorway, I gather the Shadow King's cloak close around me and hasten through the familiar passages of Beldroth. It's quite dark at this hour of the night, with precious few torches lit to guide my footsteps. But I grew up here and know the way so well, I could walk it in my sleep. I meet no one. Those of the household who are awake are busy with last-minute preparations for the king's guests. Thus I proceed unheeded and unhindered to the east tower and open the door to the stairwell.

A ringing voice echoes down to me: "I don't care if he's the son of the Goddess of Love sprung to life! I'm *not* coming out of this room until he's *gone*."

I press my lips together. Apparently, someone has carried word to Ilsevel of her prospective bridegroom's arrival. I'd hoped to be able to break the news to her myself. Oh well. Nothing for it now.

I pluck the hem of my skirt out of my way and climb the spiral stair. My legs and back are so sore after the long ride on the shadowy monster steed. These last two years of quiet life at Nornala Convent have left me sadly out of condition. But, puffing and panting, I make my way to the top of the tower and the little landing outside the topmost chamber door. Lantern light gleams, and I shield my eyes against its glare, squinting to discern the two figures standing before me.

One of them turns to me and lets out a little gasp before flinging herself into my embrace. "Oh! Fairie! You came!"

"Aurae, darling, is that you?" I pull back, trying to discern the face of my youngest sister in the combination of shadows and lantern glow. Enormous fawn eyes gaze up at me with hopeful anxiety. "Gods above, how you've grown!" When I left Beldroth two years ago, Aurae was a gawky girl of fifteen, stick thin and all elbows and knees. Blossoming womanhood has softened her frame just enough that one can see the beauty she truly is, with her thick chestnut hair and heart-shaped face.

Aurae holds my hand tightly, refusing to let go even when I surreptitiously try to shake her fingers free. Fear and concern ripple up my arm, mingled with a sudden burst of unexpected relief. "I'm so glad you're here," she says. "It's been awful, you don't even know! Father told Ilsevel she would have to marry the troll king, and Ilsevel yelled at him. In front of the entire court! I thought I would die. Then she tried to run away. Took a horse and left in the dead of night and got all the way to the Cornaith border before they caught her. They dragged her back, but then she locked herself in this tower and has refused to come out. That was a week ago now."

"In other words, typical Ilsevel drama." Another voice speaks from behind my sister. Another woman. Like Aurae, she is clad only in a nightgown with a thick shawl wrapped around her shoulders.

She holds a lantern in one hand, and its light gleams on her spun-gold hair, highlights her high cheekbones and the bridge of her dainty nose.

Her mouth quirks to one side. "Welcome home, Princess," she says, and drops a curtsy as elegant as though she wears courtly finery. "How was life in exile? Did you do penance for failing to snatch that greasy Prince Orsan? I heard all about it in Hagmer. It was the talk of the season! Never thought of you as a scandal maker. You gave us all a nice surprise."

My brow puckers. "I'm sorry, do I know you?"

"How silly of me!" Her smile grows broader and colder, her pale eyes like chips of ice. "Of course, why should you remember? Lyria Arakian, at your service."

Oh. A stone drops in my stomach. I recognize her now. This golden-haired beauty is officially the daughter of Lord Arakian, one of the preeminent members of my father's council. She looks very like her mother, the beautiful and vivacious Lady Fyndra, quite a favorite at court. In fact, she would be the absolute picture of her mother. Except for her eyes. Those she gets from Larongar.

It's common knowledge that Fyndra has been the king's mistress these past twenty years at least. I'd heard rumors that Lyria was not Lord Arakian's natural child, but as Lyria herself was sent away from Beldroth at a young age, there was no way to prove the claim one way or another. Now, seeing her for the first time as a grown woman, I cannot deny the connection. She is my father's daughter. My half sister.

Our gazes lock in the flickering lantern light. We'd been friends once, long ago, when we were both very small. In this moment, however, I feel nothing of that old friendship between us. Her eyes spark with animosity so vicious, I half wish I could turn and flee back down the stair.

Instead, I stand my ground. "Ah yes. Of course, I remember you. And when did you return to court, Lyria?"

She shrugs. "Oh, hadn't you heard? Following your disastrous little dalliance with Prince Orsan, no one from Gavaria is welcome in Cornaith. They tossed me out on my ear! King Gordun has withdrawn aid from the south border, and the fae are sweeping in unchecked. That's why Larongar is rushing this alliance through with the trolls. He needs fresh support and soon, or we're done for. Which means our Ilsie is going to have to get over her quibbles and marry this troll king, like it or not."

"Do you think you can help her, Fairie?" Aurae breaks in. Her eyes are so large, so anxious and soft. "Ilsie's only opened the door three times in the last week, and that's just to let me in with a little food and a spare chamber pot. She dropped the first pot out the window on the heads of the guards Father sent to bash the door in. Now Father won't let me bring her anything."

"How long since she last ate?" I ask.

"Two days. She says she'll starve before she comes out."

I catch Lyria's eye. One of her fine-shaped eyebrows rises slowly. "I fear," she says, "the princess suffered under the delusion that because she's the king's favorite, he won't use her for his own gain the same as the rest of us."

"Lyria!" Aurae gasps.

"What? We're all thinking it. I'm just the only one not afraid to say it." Another wave of resentment rolls out from her, hitting me hard. I can feel a headache coming on fast. I need to get through this quickly before I'm completely incapacitated.

Pulling free of Aurae's clutching fingers, I approach the door. Lyria steps to one side, swinging the lantern and making our shadows dance about the small space. I stand for a moment, my lips pursed, then press my ear to one of the panels and close my eyes. Even through the wood, I can feel Ilsevel's roiling rage.

"Ilsie?" I call softly. "Can you hear me?"

"I'm not coming out, Faraine," Ilsevel's voice growls just on the other side of the door. "I'm sorry they dragged you all this way for nothing. I'm not coming out, and you can't make me."

I glance back at Aurae and Lyria. They watch me closely. Aurae's brow is puckered. Lyria's mouth quirks in a half smile. I chew the inside of my cheek, then face the door again. "Why don't you let me in, Ilsevel? We can talk better face-to-face."

"Don't try that on me!" Her voice snaps like a guard dog defending its porch. "I know what you're thinking. You'll get hold of my hand, and you'll make me feel all warm and calm and peaceful, and I'll start thinking, *Oh, why have I been so resistant to letting myself be bartered off like a piece of livestock all this time? How insensitive of me!* The next thing I know, I'll be married to a gods-spitting troll and dragged away to his lair, wondering how in the seven secret names I let myself be talked into it."

I blink. After all, that's exactly what my father is hoping will happen. It's the very reason Theodre came to fetch me personally from Nornala Convent. "If you let me in, I swear I won't touch you. We'll talk. That's all."

Silence.

"Please, Ilsevel. I'm here to help you. I've met the Shadow King, you see. Just last night, on the way here. Our party was attacked by fae, and he and his people saved us. I've spoken to him, and he's not at all like what you're imagining."

More silence. Then, "Are you saying he's not a lurching rock monster inclined to devour young maidens for breakfast?"

"Hardly! In fact, he's . . . well, he's rather handsome."

"*Rather* handsome? Spare me these effusions, Fairie!"

"All right. Fine. He's beautiful. Stunningly beautiful, with a physique like a demigod, eyes like distant stars, and a voice so warm it would melt even a heart of stone. Does that sound more to your liking?"

"You're exaggerating."

"I swear, I'm not! I don't have the imagination."

"That's true. You always were rather a dullard."

"The dullest of dullards. Poetry leaves me positively cold, and I fall asleep when the minstrel starts singing."

I wait, counting my breaths. Just as I reach seven slow exhales, my sister speaks again: "If I let you in, you swear you won't touch me? I won't have you gods-gifting me into submission."

"I swear it, darling. Please, I'm going hoarse shouting through the door like this."

Another five breaths. Then, to my relief, the sound of a heavy bolt lifting. From the corner of my eye, I see sharp movement from Lyria as she prepares to dive into action. I motion with one hand, shooting her a stern glare. Aurae quickly grips Lyria's arm, holding her in place.

The next moment, the door opens. Ilsevel peeks out. "You're alone?"

"I am," I say, motioning for Lyria and Aurae to stay back.

Ilsevel opens the door just a little wider, catches me by the shoulders, and pulls me inside. She shuts the door and drops the bolt before whirling and leaning her back against it, breathing out a long sigh.

I look around the chamber. It's a sparse space with a simple pallet bed, a fireplace with no fire, a chamber pot, and a few other odds and ends. "I see you've made yourself nice and cozy up here."

My sister shudders. "It's gods-spitting freezing. I ran out of fuel three days ago, and Father won't let Aurae bring me more. Now he's refusing to let her bring food either. Thinks he can starve me out." Her eyes are deep, shadow-ringed hollows, and her cheeks are pinched, her skin tight with cold. She's still lovely, of course—it would take more than three days of hunger to deprive Ilsevel of her natural beauty. But she doesn't look well at all.

"You know you're going to have to relent eventually," I say.

"Am I?" Fire flares in her eyes. "I'm not going to let him do this to me, Fairie. Do you hear me?"

I sigh and take a seat on the one little chair by the cold fireplace, wrapping the folds of Vor's cloak around me. I close my eyes and breathe in his scent—the aroma of deep earth and a heady spice that momentarily clears some of the pounding from my temples. Funny how even that scent is enough to bring back some small measure of the calm he instills.

I shake that thought away quickly. Raising my chin, I catch my sister's gaze again. "There's no use playing the martyr, Ilsevel. We've known all along what our lives would be. We are servants of the crown, same as everyone else. We marry for the good of the kingdom."

"You didn't."

"I would have."

Ilsevel narrows her eyes. "You know, you've got a point. Best to make it seem like it was *his* idea to back out. Do you think you can smuggle a handful of pukeweed up here? If I take it at the right time, I'll vomit during the reception tomorrow night. I'm sure I could aim for my prospective groom."

I give her a look. "Don't tease, Ilsevel."

"I'm not! I've never fully given you credit for how neatly you slipped the noose two years ago. Tell me, is convent life so bad as all that? Do you think the nuns would still let me ride?"

Folding my hands, I draw a steadying breath and hold my sister's gaze. "You know I love you, don't you?"

"I believe you've had moments of fondness for me over the years, yes." Ilsevel sighs and goes to her pallet bed, sinking down onto it in a puddle of skirts. "Is this the part where you tell me you have my best interests at heart?"

"No. This is the part where I tell you you're making a mistake."

"Right. Because you've met the Shadow King, and he's gorgeous. So I should just submit to being treated like a brood mare."

"It is a sign of maturity to accept one's fate with grace and then to make the most of it."

"Well, everyone knows you're the mature one, Fairie. I'm the spitfire; Aurae is the darling. And our other sister, the one no one talks about . . . she's the devil." Ilsevel smiles sadly. "We all have our parts to play, don't we?"

Fear roils beneath her bantering words. She's doing her best to disguise how terrified she actually feels, but she can't hold back the tide much longer.

"You know you have to meet him," I say after a few silent moments.

Ilsevel drops her gaze. "I do." She curses bitterly. "Much as I like to pretend otherwise, I'm not really the heroine-of-ballads type. I don't have it in me to die for a cause." She sniffs and rubs her nose, blinking back tears. "I am a coward after all."

"No, Ilsie."

"I am, though! When I heard your voice outside the door, do

you know what I thought? I thought, *Oh, thank the gods! Faraine is here now. She'll talk sense into me.* I think I've been waiting for you all along. You're my excuse to give up."

I frown. "Dearest, I want you to be happy. And I . . . I think once you meet the Shadow King, you'll be surprised. I know I was."

"*You* marry him, then."

Warmth rushes to my cheeks. It's not as though the thought hadn't occurred to me once or twice during the ride to Beldroth. What would it be like if I were Vor's choice? What if I were to spend the rest of my days at the side of such a man? The notion is not unappealing. The calm of his presence, even in the midst of battle, was extraordinary in itself. And during that ride, I'd found his manners and speech very pleasing. I can't help thinking that, given time, I could come to . . . to care for such a man. Very deeply.

I play with the edge of his cloak. I'd not noticed before the fine embroidery decorating its edge. Now that I look more closely, I see a stylized rendering of a dragon, its coiling body snaking all around the hem and border. It's fine, delicate work. Not at all what I would expect for a troll. But then, they aren't trolls at all. They're troldefolk. A fascinating people from a fascinating world. A world I would like to learn more about.

I shouldn't indulge such thoughts. They'll only lead to disappointment.

"I'm sorry, Faraine," Ilsevel says, misinterpreting my silence. "I didn't mean that. You know I didn't mean it, right?"

"Of course." I smile at my sister and try to make my voice teasing, careless. "After all, it'll be *his* choice, won't it?" Then, before she can read more into my words than I want her to, I hurry on. "Please, Ilsie, will you at least come meet him at the reception? If you don't like him, I'll lock you back in this tower myself and swallow the key."

"Promise?" Ilsevel eyes me closely.

"By the Goddess Nornala herself." I make a solemn sign with my right hand. "May I suffer the indigestion of a thousand lifetimes if I fail you."

Ilsevel picks herself up off the bed and approaches slowly. As though suddenly too exhausted to continue, she sinks to her knees and places her head in my lap. I close my eyes against the sudden flood of her emotions washing over me. Steeling myself, I touch my crystal, reaching for the vibration deep inside. With my other hand, I stroke my sister's forehead. Slowly, I let some of the vibration from the crystal travel through my fingertips into Ilsevel.

"You're doing it, aren't you," she mutters into my lap. "Your gods-gift."

"Shhhh." I push hair gently back from her eyes.

"I do feel more peaceful. Gods blight you." She lifts her head, catching my gaze. "You'll come to the reception tonight, won't you? Only, I'm not sure I can bear to meet the Shadow King without you there."

"I'll be there," I promise. Though I know the crush of people at such an event will overwhelm me, leaving my body and mind wracked with pain for days. I can't abandon my sister. Not now. "I'll be there," I repeat.

And maybe, I tell myself in the privacy of my own mind, maybe it'll all turn out. Maybe Ilsevel doesn't need to be frightened. Maybe . . .

Maybe Vor will choose me instead.

6

Vor

"This place is positively barbaric! Do you know they actually expect me to hang my garments in the *garderobe*? Have you ever heard of anything so ghastly?"

I turn as the door to my private room bursts open and my brother saunters in. He tosses himself across the bed. The rope frame creaks ominously beneath his weight, and I half fear the four wooden posts will topple like felled trees. Sul flings an arm across his face in an attitude of languishing woe and groans. "No running water either. I tell you, brother, I don't know how we're going to survive!"

"Watch your tongue, Sul," I growl, not for the first time and certainly not for the last. Fingers fumbling, I fasten the jeweled collar that rests across my shoulders and collarbone above a loose, shimmering tunic of *hugagug* silk. "They're only human after all. We knew all along their society was not particularly advanced."

"Not advanced?" Sul lifts his hand enough to catch my eye. "We've traveled back to an age so primitive, they wouldn't have discovered fire yet if the gods hadn't dropped it on their thick heads."

"You're comfortable enough. I saw you eating well from the meal provided. And you slept like a babe through the daylight hours. I could hear you snoring right through the wall."

"Yes, well, torturous rides beneath empty sky following life-or-death battles do tend to take it out of a fellow." Sul sits up, crossing his legs and leaning his elbows on his knees. "Tell me, brother, can you really intend to make one of these creatures your bride?"

I narrow my eyes at him. Sometimes I have to wonder if my brother's stubborn refusal to acknowledge my own human bloodline is meant as an insult or kindness. Possibly both. Or neither. Sul is a slippery sort.

Leaving his question unanswered, I wrap a gold braided belt around my waist, securing it on the side after the fashion in Mythanar. There's no mirror in the room, and I did not bring a servant with me, so I must hope I can pull myself together for the reception. Sul has already donned his own tunic, collar, and belt. He wears the three-braided belt that denotes him as a member of the royal house. My belt is four-braided and studded with living gems as befits a king.

"Making yourself pretty for anyone in particular?" Sul asks. When I still won't answer, he leans a little more heavily on his knees. "I know what you're thinking."

"I hope not."

"Oh, you can't hide anything from me." He smirks. "Your head's not been set right since you scooped that little mortal miss into your lap. You'd best be careful."

"I'm always careful."

"Ha!" Sul's laugh is a sharp bark without mirth. "That may have been true enough up until recent history. But let's face it, brother, behind that stony façade of yours lies the heart of a poet. You *like* the notion of sweeping that girl off her feet, and the two of you riding off into your own personal Ever After, a pair of gods-fated lovers and all that."

"I don't know, Sul." I cast him a look. "Seems like *you're* the poet. Are you sure you didn't miss your calling? Mythanar could use an official royal bard on retainer. Or perhaps you'd prefer the role of jester?"

"It would never do." Sul sniffs. "I'm the pragmatist of the two of us. I'm happy to enjoy one pretty lass as much as the next." He tilts his chin, fixing me with a narrow stare. "You'd be wise to follow my example."

"I don't know what you're talking about."

"Oh, don't you?" Sul draws breath to continue, but to my great relief, the door opens and Hael steps into the room. She wears a shining silver gorget around her throat, collarbone, and shoulders, and fitted faulds wrap her hips, emphasizing her curves. Other than these pieces of armor, however, she's wearing shimmering silk draped in long and luxurious folds, glinting with chips of diamond.

"It's time, my king," she says. "The reception has already commenced, and you are due to appear."

Before I can say anything, Sul springs from the bed, his eyes suddenly alight. "Why, Captain Hael!" he declares, looking her up and down. "What's this? It couldn't possibly be the stalwart warrior we all know and love. Why, from certain angles, you're positively ravishing!"

I wish I could take my brother's head in my hand and dash it a few times against the dead stone wall. Glancing at Hael, I can see she didn't miss the thinly veiled insult . . . the reference to the stone covering the right side of her body and face. The deformity is difficult to look past to see her otherwise strong and striking features. Hael has been in love with Sul since we were all children together, but my brother has only ever chased after the great beauties at court. He treats Hael with a brotherly sort of affection mingled with disdain, which I find appalling. I hope he is simply unaware of her feelings for him and not as callous as he seems.

Sul bows and gallantly offers Hael his arm. "May I have the honor of escorting the lady down to supper?"

She eyes his arm as if he's just offered her a wurm larva. "I'm working tonight," she says shortly, then turns to me. "Are you ready, my king?"

"I am." I make a last adjustment to my belt and straighten my shoulders. "Lead on, Captain."

I follow her out from my private chamber into the receiving room. Larongar has given me and my people a suite of rooms in the west wing of Beldroth, set a little apart from the rest of the household. I give him credit for attempting to make the space welcoming to my kind. I see the gifts I have sent to him over the last cycle proudly displayed: tapestries of woven *hugagug* thread hung on the walls, *varthur* wolf pelts slung across the backs of chairs. A dragon scale sits on a stand in the center of the room, a small fire built in its curved base. The warmed scale radiates a glow in the room that is both familiar and strange. Back in Mythanar, we would burn only moonfire in such a scale, and the light it cast would be pure and white. But this is close enough.

My people stand around the fire, dressed in finery for the reception. Umog Zu, our priestess, has donned a headdress of mothwings and skulls, and looks positively ferocious. The others wear rather more subdued fashions of tunics and belted gowns; the cloth and cut are extremely fine, but the overall look is simple. Only Hael wears armor and, I suspect, weapons strapped to her thighs and upper arms.

I find my gaze searching for Yok among the rest. Sorrow pricks my conscience when I remember why the boy is not with us. If only there were some way to get news of him.

"Well, my friends," I say, surveying the others solemnly. "Once again, let me thank you for making this journey with me. We have faced trials already, and what remains for us to do over the coming days, possibly weeks, will test our resolve. Only try to remember, it's all for Mythanar." I place a hand over my heart. "I am proud to have such noble souls at my side for what is to come."

"Gods, brother," Sul says, crossing his arms and leaning against the wall. "It's not like you're stepping into the dragon's throat! It's a little wine and a dance or two. How bad can it be?"

"I thought it a good speech," Hael growls. "Inspiring."

Sul shoots her a sweet smile. "Boot kisser. Though, so long as you're wearing that dress, you can kiss me anywhere you like."

"Enough!" I quickly step between the two of them, blocking Hael's deadly glower. "It's time to go."

A page waits for us in the passage just outside our suite. The poor lad nearly starts out of his skin at the sight of us. He quickly bows after the awkward human fashion, his feathered cap falling from his head. He catches it and crams it back on his skull, all while babbling, "If you'll follow me, great King! My lords!"

Sul snorts. I ignore him and fall into place behind the trembling boy. He leads us down a series of stairs and passages. Soon enough, I can hear the murmur of voices and the unfamiliar lilt of human musical instruments playing a rather screeching melody on strings and pipes. If that's an indication of the entertainments to come, it will be a long night.

We emerge at one end of a long gallery lit with copper braziers full of very red, glaring flames. The light they cast gives the whole space a hellish glow to my eyes, accustomed as I am to moonfire. Humans mill about the space, adorned in many layers and ruffles, voluminous sleeves, and towering headdresses that dwarf even Umog Zu's creation. The stink of mortality hits me rather harder than I expect, and for a moment I wish I'd applied more of the *jiru* nectar perfume I'd brought with me just to drown out the stench.

The page boy tugs on the sleeve of a man in white livery. The man peers at us through heavily lidded eyes, his expression unreadable, before turning to the room. "King Vor of Mythanar, Lord Protector of the Under Realm," he announces in a booming voice.

There's not much of a response. A few of those nearest this end of the gallery turn and look warily our way. Ladies whisper behind their hands, while men overtly sneer. Not quite the welcome I expected.

I catch myself searching for a certain pale face amid all these staring strangers. Surely she will be here tonight. As a princess of the realm, she would be expected to present herself at such a gathering. But I don't spy her right away.

I do spy Larongar, however. He's halfway across the room, whispering in the ear of a stunningly voluptuous woman with bounteous golden curls. The queen? If so, she's not at all how I would have pictured Faraine's mother.

The woman catches my eye and smiles archly. The king scowls and, turning to follow the trajectory of her gaze, spots me standing in the entrance. His face breaks into a grin. "Vor!" he cries. "My friend! Come, come and meet everyone."

I adjust the set of my shoulders. Time to make the plunge into this sea of humans. Larongar grabs me in another disconcertingly familiar embrace the moment I'm within reach. Humans are certainly a lot more demonstrative than I anticipated. "I hope you're rested, dear boy," he says. "We have a whole night full of pleasures in store for you. And here, first among these, allow me to introduce the Lady Arakian."

I turn to the king's companion and accept the hand she offers me. Bowing over it, I murmur, "A pleasure, madam."

"Oh, sweet King!" She touches her heart, drawing attention to her heaving breast and the low cut of her gown. "I hope the pleasure will be all mine!"

The look that accompanies this statement is enough to make my blood boil. I hastily release the lady's hand, even as Larongar growls, "Here, none of that now, gem of my heart," and pinches her. Lady Arakian giggles and slaps his hand, tossing her curls. Looking from one of them to the other, it dawns on me suddenly who and what this woman is. Definitely *not* the queen.

Larongar turns abruptly and calls through the crowd, "Theodre! Get over here, boy, and greet your rescuer, why don't you?"

The crown prince lounges at a table, a cluster of young ladies and gentlemen gathered around him. He's resplendent in gold velvet nearly the same shade as his gleaming hair, draped in jewels and a fur-trimmed cape. He makes for a stunning picture and looks as though he knows it.

He casts me a bored look. "Hullo there, troll king. My sisters will be down shortly, I'm sure. Care to wager that belt of yours in a round of jackanapes?"

I open my mouth to coldly decline, but Larongar interrupts. "Not everyone wants to lose their shirt and shoes at the gaming tables like some young wastrels I could mention!" He turns to me, shaking his head heavily. "That boy will be the death of me. Blessed with beauty by the gods! But the gods never give gifts without taking something in exchange. They took that boy's brains and left him the prettiest oaf in the realm. What I wouldn't give for a proper son at my side in these dark times! But here," he adds with a significant look, "mayhap the gods have heard my prayers after all. Tell me, Vor, do you care for dancing?"

"Indeed, I do. Though I fear I know few human dances."

"That's no problem. We'll find you a pretty teacher in no time! And perhaps you can teach us a thing or two about troll dancing, eh?"

I wince inwardly at the slur so casually spoken. Sul, standing at my elbow, leans in close and whispers in troldish, "If someone uses that word one more time, so help me, I'm going to start bashing skulls and ripping limbs and beating my breast with both fists."

"Let it go, Sul," I hiss in response. "They don't realize what they're saying."

"Are you sure about that?" My brother raises an eyebrow significantly.

Before I can respond, the herald's voice fills the space again: "Queen Mereth and the princesses, Ilsevel and Aurae Cyhorn."

My gut twists. Gods on high! I'd promised myself I wouldn't be nervous. It's not as though it really matters what I think of the princess, whether I find her attractive or witty or even remotely interesting. It's her father and his Miphates I've come here to win, not her hand or heart. Yet I cannot help the sudden lurch in my chest as I turn sharply toward the arched entrance, my neck craning as I seek my first glimpse of Ilsevel.

Three figures stand just inside the doorway. The first and foremost is older than the others, a refined and delicate dame. I know at once she must be Faraine's mother. Her silver-streaked hair is wound in thick coils over each ear, and a dainty crown and veil perches on her head. Her eyes are very solemn, a little sad.

It's the second woman who draws my attention, however. Clad in red and white, she is a startling beauty with abundant dark curls. She's the tallest of the three and holds her shoulders back and her spine very straight, as though she's preparing to dive into battle. Though I cannot begin to picture such a fine-boned creature wielding a sword, that first glance tells me she would try if she had to. There's a subtle air of ferocity about her.

The next girl, standing just behind her, is a pretty little thing in blue, rather young and shrinking, with enormous, frightened eyes. Definitely not the spirited creature her sister is. I cannot imagine making a bargain for her hand; she's scarcely more than a child.

They enter the hall sedately, eyes downcast, hands demurely folded. A cluster of ladies follows, some young, some old. But the face I seek is not among them. Where is Faraine? Is she too fatigued from last night's journey to attend the festivities this evening?

I spy her at last, keeping to the shadows behind her sisters and their ladies. I almost miss her, for she is clad in a quiet gray gown with a white veil over her hair, her head bowed. As though feeling my gaze upon her, she looks up. Catches my eye for an instant.

My heart makes a strange, juddering beat.

Someone grips my arm. "Come, Vor!" Larongar bellows rather too close to my ear. "It's high time you met my womenfolk." With that, he drags me forward, and the crowd parts before him. "Here she is," he declares grandly with a sweep of one hand, "the keeper of my heart and mother of my heir, Queen Mereth. Merrie, my love, meet King Vor of Mythanar."

The queen's small rosebud mouth opens into a brief smile.

"Greetings, Your Highness," she says smoothly. "Welcome to Beldroth."

I murmur something I hope is appropriate but scarcely get the words out before Larongar takes the hand of the tall, dark-haired girl in the crimson gown and pulls her forward. She flashes me a smile like a dagger. "This is Ilsevel, my thirdborn," Larongar says fondly as the girl sinks into a deep curtsy. "A father's not supposed to have favorites, I know. Let's just say, I defy you to find a prettier face anywhere in the worlds! But if one was to give her a run for her money, it's my youngest, Aurae."

At this, he draws the girl in blue forward. She offers a curtsy as well, very graceful and correct, though she does not have the courage to cast more than the briefest of glances my way. I try to offer a kindly smile but suspect it only frightens her more.

I turn then to Faraine, still standing at the back of the throng. Shouldn't she be with her sisters as they are presented? I open my mouth to speak some greeting, but before the words can form, Larongar drags my attention back to the girl in crimson. "Perhaps, Ilsevel," he says, "you would be so good as to sit with King Vor tonight. He could use a companion to inform him of our customs and perhaps to steer him away from the hog's foot jelly."

The courtiers around us titter softly. I can't tell if I'm being made the butt of some joke or not. I glance at Sul and Hael, both standing close at hand. Sul's face has gone completely granite, unreadable, but Hael raises an eyebrow and nods encouragingly. She wants me to keep going, to play the charming wooer.

Bracing my shoulders, I address the dark-eyed princess. "I would be honored indeed to enjoy the company of so fair a dinner companion."

She blinks at me, her lips parting ever so slightly. "Oh! I didn't . . . That is . . ." A blush stains her cheeks, and she glances at her father.

"Go on," I say, hoping my voice sounds gentle. "Don't be afraid. Did I say something amiss?"

"No indeed, great King." The girl meets my gaze again bravely. "It's just . . . I did not expect you to speak our tongue so fluently."

I chuckle. "Yes, well, I know most humans think of troldefolk as great lumbering rock monsters who communicate only via growls and grunts."

Ilsevel's flush deepens. It's unusual to my eye. My kind do not change color so easily. But it's pretty. "I fear I have embarrassed you, Princess," I say quickly, hoping to put her at ease. "Do forgive me. You may find my knowledge somewhat lacking when it comes to human modes and manners. However, I hope I may prove myself a willing student to a patient teacher."

It's not a bad line so far as flirtation goes. I watch it work the desired effect on the girl. She smiles at me, this time more sincerely than before. Perhaps I can manage to navigate the complexities of this evening after all.

"Now then, Ilsevel," Larongar says, eager to hurry things along, "do take our guest to find his seat, will you? He traveled far to pay us this visit and is surely famished!"

"Of course." The princess holds out her hand to me. "If you will, good King?"

I know I should show myself to be pliant and pleasing. But something stops me from taking her hand.

Instead, I turn to her older sister. "And you, Princess Faraine?" I say, addressing her over the heads of several watching ladies. "How do you fare after our journey? I know from experience how tiring a long ride on morlethback can be."

She looks up, startled. Her eyes flicker with some emotion I cannot name. Surprise, yes, but something else as well. Could it be pleasure? Or am I only reading what I hope to see? "I am quite recovered, thank you, Your Highness," she says. I feel only a little pang that she does not use my name. We are in public, after all; the ease of formality we enjoyed on our night ride would be inappropriate in this setting. A little smile pulls at her lips. "The morleth ride certainly made me aware of parts of my anatomy I'd not previously known existed!"

"I'll bet it did," Sul mutters in troldish at my back. With an effort, I keep a straight face.

"Now, Faraine," Larongar says, pushing a step between me and her. "Don't you bother the troll king. Are you planning to stay for the feast?"

Faraine opens her mouth, but Ilsevel chimes in first. "I asked Faraine to stay." Her eyes catch and hold her father's gaze. "If she goes, I go too."

The air between them sparks in a silent battle of wills. I draw back a half step. What exactly is going on here between the king and his favorite daughter? By the look on Larongar's face, I wouldn't be altogether surprised if he lashed out and struck her.

At last, however, Larongar smiles. "Of course. Faraine is welcome to stay as long as she likes." With that, he calls out for someone to set a place for his eldest daughter at the high table. Then he turns to me and slaps my shoulder. "Never mind her! She's a strange one, that Faraine. We mostly don't have her at court, but if Ilsevel wants her, what am I to do? It's a rare day I can refuse my pretty poppet anything she desires! Surely you understand that already, eh, my boy?"

I make a polite sort of sound and offer my arm to Ilsevel as I am clearly expected to. The next moment, I'm led across the gallery into the gathering. Before I've gone five paces, I look back over my shoulder. And for a brief flash, I catch a glimpse of odd, mismatched eyes. Then the crowd closes in and blocks them from my sight.

7

Faraine

My place is set at the end of the family table, farthest from the light and closest to the nearest exit. Not exactly a place of honor for the king's eldest daughter. But I'm grateful. If need be, I can slink into the shadows, observing but unobserved.

My dinner companion is a second cousin of my mother's, nearly eighty years old, and not at all interested in making conversation with me. He asks me if I like my pretty dress, then busies himself with his meal and cup, leaving me to my own company. I eat little. My stomach churns, and my temples already throb with the pressure roiling in the atmosphere of the banquet hall. I won't be able to stand much of this. Though I grip my crystal with all my might, I can scarcely feel its pulse through the dissonance.

Whispering a swift prayer for strength, I lift my gaze to the head of the table where the rest of my family sits. My father takes precedence, of course, with Vor on his right hand and Ilsevel just beyond.

I try not to let myself look too closely at the Shadow King. But in truth, I find it difficult to tear my gaze away. Once again, I'm struck by his strange beauty. No longer clad in chain mail or riding boots, instead he wears a light loose tunic, which opens to reveal rather a lot of his chest. This must be the trolde fashion, as the other men in his party are dressed similarly. A wide belt wraps his waist, and a golden collar drapes across his shoulders, emphasizing the wide V of his build. Pale hair spills across his shoulders and catches the light. What would it be like to run my fingers through those silky strands?

Stop it.

I clear my throat and look down at the untouched meal on my plate. Gods, what am I doing? Ogling the beautiful king like some hound drooling over a cut of meat! What would the nuns think if they could see me now? I press my lips into a rueful smile and shake my head. While I may not control much about my life, I can control what goes on inside my mind. I will not indulge in foolish dreaming. Not now. Not ever.

When I raise my gaze once more, it's Ilsevel I seek. She sits very straight, her shoulders back, her chin up, taking small bites from a piece of meat skewered on the end of a jeweled knife. Vor leans to one side to speak to her, and she nods. Then, to my surprise, she laughs and flashes him a quick smile.

I chew my lower lip. Gripping my crystal a little harder, I try to catch a sense of my sister's feelings. Is she finding this evening more pleasant than she'd anticipated? Are her defenses breaking down in the face of Vor's undeniable charm and beauty? Is she . . . ? Could she . . . ? But no. I cannot find her. The crush in the atmosphere is too great to discern any single feeling with clarity. The more I try, the more the pressure in my head mounts.

I drop my gaze again, drawing steadying breaths and letting

my senses sink into dullness. If only I could slip from the hall! But I promised Ilsevel I would stay through the end of the meal. I'm not sure what comfort I can offer, seated this far away in the shadows. But I won't go back on my word.

Suddenly, my skin prickles. Unsettled, I turn . . . and find a pair of ice-blue eyes fixed upon me. Lyria, seated at one of the lower tables with the other ladies-in-waiting, catches my gaze. She smiles slowly, like a cat with a secret. Tilting her head, she lifts her goblet in salute. I look down at my hands in my lap. There's something deeply disconcerting about that girl.

"You there! Minstrels!" Father's abrupt bark echoes to the rafters overhead. Several faces appear from the minstrels' gallery as the lilting strains of background music continue to rain down from above. "Enough of that lilly-laying. It's time for a dance!" Father leans an elbow on the arm of his chair and rolls his head toward Vor. "What say you, my boy? Why don't you take this daughter of mine and fling her about the floor a little, eh? She'll give as good as she gets, I promise you that!"

Ilsevel narrows her eyes ever so slightly. Though her brow remains smooth, I can see the storm clouds gathering. Before she can speak, however, Vor says, "While I would indeed be honored to stand up with Princess Ilsevel, I'm afraid I am not yet familiar with your human dances."

"That's no trouble." Father shrugs dismissively. "Ilsie will teach you what you need to know. The rest you can make up as you go. That's always been my way, and I get by well enough, isn't that right, my dear?" He turns this last question on my mother.

She gives him a half-lidded glance. "Quite."

"There, you see? Nothing to it."

Vor's smile is thin lipped. "Thank you, friend Larongar. But for the moment, I would simply enjoy the pleasure of watching the dance."

Much to my relief, Father doesn't force the issue. "Suit yourself," he says instead, then, "Tramyar!"

A knight seated at the opposite end of the table from me starts in his seat and half rises. "Your Majesty?"

"Take my daughter out on the dance floor and show off her paces. Minstrels, what are you waiting for? Play, gods blight you!"

A spritely tune commences, and Sir Tramyar hastens to my sister's side, bowing and offering his hand. My sister takes a precise bite of her meat, chews slowly, swallows. Only then does she set her dagger aside and, after thoroughly wiping her hands on a cloth, accepts Tramyar's hand. All this without so much as a glance for either Vor or our father.

Various other young people move to the floor between the lower tables, filling up the space in long straight lines. Aurae's hand is claimed by a widowed duke some twenty years her senior, who positively dwarfs my sister in size. Another knight offers Lyria his hand, and I watch her take a place several rows down from my sisters, who stand at the head of the line.

The dance begins, and the couples start their first turns. Their feet are light, their arms upraised and graceful as they pace in and out of the patterns. Ilsevel is certainly elegant enough at the front of the line, but it's Aurae who lights up the floor. Her shyness seems to melt away as the music washes over her. Her body moves to the rhythms like a swan gliding on a crystal lake. It's not difficult in moments like this to guess what her gods-gift is.

I watch the dance through several turns before movement draws my attention back to the head of the table. Lady Fyndra approaches the king's seat and sinks into a deep curtsy that prominently displays all that her low-cut gown has to reveal. Father's smile is voracious. My mother, however, coldly looks the other way. "Beloved King," Fyndra says, holding out her hand, "it is only right that you show your guests the way, is it not?"

Father chuckles and leans over to Vor, saying something I cannot hear. Vor's face is a study, closed to all interpretation. My mother, however, leans over and says sharply, "Larongar! For gods' sake."

"What?" Father laughs and pushes back his chair. "It's not as though *you're* going to dance with me, are you?" With that, he takes Fyndra's hand and allows himself to be led to the floor. The two of them assume the lead position, flowing into the pattern of the dance. Fyndra moves with practiced grace, while my father clumps and stomps his way across the floor as he might a battleground. He laughs lustily with each turn that brings him close enough to pinch or caress his lady, who shrieks and bats his hand in response.

I grip my crystal hard. The pressure in my head grows by the second. I wonder how much of it stems directly from my mother, sitting in rigid silence, her face a mask. One would think, after all these years, she'd have grown used to Father's ways. Somehow, however, he still contrives to hurt her.

The first song ends, and another begins right away, another spritely little tune that makes the feet want to skip. For the first time since entering that hall, the pressure in the atmosphere relaxes somewhat. No one listening to that song can help but feel uplifted. I sigh, leaning back in my chair. My fingers drum on the edge of the table in time with the beat. I used to take lessons as a child. I remember being paired with Lyria, and we'd giggle like little fiends, ignoring the dance master's stern demands for decorum. What a long time ago that was! Back before my gods-gift had manifested. Back when I was still able to participate in ordinary life.

"Do you not enjoy dancing like your sisters?"

I start at the sound of that deep, rumbling burr. Turning in my seat, I look up into the pale eyes of the Shadow King, who stands just behind my chair. Somehow, he'd slipped from his place at the table and made his way to my end without my noticing.

He smiles. But while his expression is warm, the intensity in his eyes makes my breath catch and heat flood my cheeks. I feel suddenly exposed, despite the demure cut of my humble gown. My fingers grip my crystal a little tighter out of habit, though there's hardly any need. Now back in his proximity, the stresses of the room seem to melt away.

Realizing I've not answered his question, I hastily say, "Oh, I do! That is to say, I'm fond of dancing, yes. But I rarely have the opportunity."

"And why is that?" Vor leans an elbow on the back of my chair. "I understand Larongar is known for his lavish banquets. Beldroth is quite the center for gaiety in your world, is that not so?"

"Indeed, it is. But you see, I spend most of my time away from court. At the Convent of Nornala in the Ettrian Mountains."

"Ah!" Vor considers this information. "Then, were you traveling from the convent when I met you last night?"

"Yes."

"So Beldroth is not your home."

"No. Not anymore."

He is silent some moments, his attention seemingly focused on the dance floor. Then he asks in a musing tone, "Which goddess is Nornala again?"

I smile. "The Goddess of Unity."

"Ah! That seems apt, under the circumstances. And—if I may

be so bold as to ask—do you intend to devote your life to Nornala's service?"

Once again, heat climbs my neck and floods my cheeks. "Yes. I do."

"By taking the holy vows?"

"There are many ways to devote oneself to the cause of unity. I have not yet decided on mine."

"I see." I feel his gaze on the side of my face but can't bring myself to look at him. For a moment, I think he will not speak again but will simply move on, find someone livelier to converse with. Instead, he says, "I fear I have embarrassed you with my questions, Faraine."

A butterfly unfurls its wings in my stomach. I'd not realized until that moment how much I wanted him to speak my name again. For a moment, I am transported back to that ride on the monster's back beneath the star-strewn sky. I open my mouth, wanting to speak his name in return.

But no. This is dangerous. After all, he's come to my father's house for a very specific purpose. I must take care to guard my heart.

"You've not embarrassed me, good King," I say, keeping my tone friendly but distant. "It's only . . . Well, the men I know would not ask a lady such questions."

"No? And why not?"

"Because her answers would be beneath his interest. Or concern."

"Indeed?" He raises an eyebrow, his expression incredulous. "Do human men not cultivate friendships with women, then?"

"Rarely, I'm sure. Perhaps not ever."

Vor looks surprised. "That's . . . Well, you'll pardon my saying it, but that's absurd."

I can't help laughing at this. He sounds so sincerely dumbfounded. "I suppose it's different among troldefolk?"

"Quite different, I assure you." He coughs and runs his fingers through his shining silver hair. "I beg your pardon. I don't mean to sound so critical of your people."

"Not at all." I let my smile linger. "As someone who has grown up in this society, I suppose I'm used to the way things are done and never thought to question it. So, tell me about trolde women. Are they . . . are they considered the *equals* of men?"

The chair next to me is vacant, as my mother's elderly cousin has long since abandoned the party for bed. Vor pulls it back, turning it a little toward me, and takes a seat. He's so tall, it's a wonder he can make himself fit so gracefully in such a small chair, but he angles his long legs and rests his elbows on his knees, contriving to look perfectly at ease. "The *equals* of men, you ask?" He considers the idea, his eyes bright in the candlelight. "A peculiar question. Are we not all trolde—both men and women alike? We cannot very well exist one without the other, so how could one be deemed superior to the other?"

"I've heard it argued that because men are physically stronger, they must naturally take on the dominant role as protectors and providers." I raise my goblet, swirling the wine idly, leaving the unspoken question hanging in the air between us.

Vor's mouth quirks in a half smile. "Are your human men strong enough to endure the hardship of birthing?"

My hand slips. Wine sloshes over the edge of my goblet. Hastily, I set it down on the table.

Vor chuckles. "I see I've embarrassed you again. Forgive me. I take it childbirth is another topic not discussed among your people."

"Well, no, actually." I clear my throat and place both hands in my lap. "All of *that* business is kept firmly behind closed doors."

"Ah! That explains it."

"Explains what?"

"How your human men may pretend they are stronger than their women. If they acknowledged what women endure simply to bring life into the world, they would necessarily have to adjust their thinking."

I stare at him. I cannot help it. Never in my life have I heard a man speak as he does.

His smile grows. "You think me very strange, do you not?"

Another butterfly awakens and flutters its wings in my belly. Gods, what that voice of his does to me! "Yes," I admit. "Very strange." Then, realizing what I've said, I hastily add, "I do beg your pardon, good King. I don't mean to be rude."

"Is it rude to be honest?"

"Sometimes!" Now it's my turn to smile. "A little honesty may indeed be the worst vulgarity around here. One must take care not to let the truth be too widely known."

Vor's smile fades slowly. His expression grows thoughtful. "I see," he says.

"What do you see?"

"You do not live at the convent because of your devotion to Nornala. *You* are the truth that must not be known."

My eyes widen. I blink, breaking his gaze, and stare down at my folded hands. My heart beats an uncomfortable rhythm, and when I clutch my crystal pendant, I find it pulses to the same erratic beat.

Vor leans in a little closer. "Am I wrong?" His voice, dropped an octave, warms my already burning ears.

"No." I bite my lips hard. "No, you're not wrong. I am . . . It's best for my father if I remain out of sight."

I feel his gaze on the side of my face. I cannot bear to turn and look at him, cannot bear to see what he might make of this statement. He maintains his silence for a long, contemplative moment.

Then: "Only weak men feel the need to hide such strength behind closed doors."

I flash him a sidelong glance. "If you want this alliance to succeed, you'd best not let the king hear you refer to him as weak."

Vor inclines his head politely. "As you say, a little honesty may indeed be deadly."

The bright, lilting melody ends, and the dancers laughingly take each other's hands and leave the floor. A new song begins to play—this one a soaring and plunging melody underscored by deep-bellied kettledrums. The beat rolls in my gut, a thrilling pulse that moves through my blood.

"Ah!" Vor sits upright in his chair. "I know this one!"

I blink up at him. "You do?"

"Yes. It's the Phoenix Flight. My mother used to sing it to me and taught me the steps when I was young."

"Your mother?" I couldn't be more surprised. Why should his mother know a human song, much less teach it to her son?

Before I have time to consider this question further, Vor rises from his chair and, turning, bows and extends his hand. "As this may be the only human dance I know with any proficiency, I feel I must take advantage of this opportunity. Will you dance with me?"

"Oh! But I couldn't."

"And why not?" He raises an eyebrow, and his mouth quirks in that devastating half smile. "You did say you were fond of dancing."

"I am, yes, but . . . but Ilsevel . . ."

Vor looks out across the table to the dance floor. "Your sisters appear to be engaged to dance already."

He's right. Ilsevel and Aurae have both been claimed by partners and even now perform the first steps of the Phoenix pattern. Their wide sleeves whirl like wings as they twirl, and their dainty feet flash beneath the rippling hems of their skirts.

Vor could assert himself, of course. He could step in, request that Ilsevel's partner hand her over, and it would be done. If he means to dance at all tonight, it ought to be with her. He knows it. I know it. Everyone in that room knows it.

But his hand is still extended. And when I dare to look up, he holds my gaze.

"Come." His smile broadens. "You wouldn't want to insult your father's guest, would you?"

I wait to see if some excuse springs to my tongue. But nothing comes. So, I slip my hand into his. Allow him to pull me to my feet.

He leads me around the table and out from the shadows, down the steps to the lower floor. I feel all the eyes of my father's court fixed upon me, hear the collective whisper rippling around the room. My father's gaze burns into the back of my skull, but I don't have the courage to look his way. I don't have the courage to look anywhere save at Vor himself. I gaze into his eyes like they're my lifeline. If I dare look elsewhere, I'll crumble into pieces.

The dancers have all drawn away, no longer twirling in time to the music, but staring at the tall Shadow King as he approaches. The minstrels in the gallery, unaware of the change below, play on. The strains of the Phoenix Flight twirl around me, like visible motes of light on the edges of my vision.

Vor takes a stance across from me. He bows, and I curtsy in response, still holding his hand. We turn, performing the opening steps. He's surprisingly light on his feet for such a tall man. He shifts his grip on my hand so that he may place his other hand on my waist, leading me into the first turn.

The turn ends, and we face one another. I know my cheeks must be crimson by now. The burning stares are going to melt me where I stand. I should never have agreed to this, should never have allowed any attention to be diverted from Ilsevel.

The music builds. The deep rumble of the kettledrums, soft but swelling, growls like a storm rolling in. Vor steps toward me, slips his hand around my waist once more. Only this time, he does not rest his hand lightly. He catches hold of me. The melody soars, and I just have time to grip his shoulders before he sweeps me off my feet and spins me in a full circle.

The crowd gasps. Someone screams. The minstrels, finally aware that something is happening below, break off their playing in a series of strangled squeaks and groans.

Vor sets me down lightly. I stagger and would fall were it not for his arm around me. Catching my balance, I wrench away and back up several paces, staring at him. A hundred shocked and churning emotions batter at my head at once, but I'm only vaguely aware of them. I'm caught in his gaze. He looks both perplexed and faintly amused. "Princess?" he begins.

Before he can say anything more, my father is there, standing between us. "How now, King Vor!" he barks, a dangerous light in his eye. "Is this some troll practice wherein you maul a man's daughter right before his eyes?"

Vor's expression is impossible to read. "Your pardon, friend Largongar," he says with an inclination of his head. "I was taught this dance as a child. This is how we dance it in Mythanar."

Father's wrath swells. I can almost see it, a red aura churning in his core. My head throbs. I want to turn, to run, to hide. To escape the pain that I know is coming. But what about the alliance? What about Vor himself? The next breath could spell the end of everything, unless . . .

I take a quick step forward, drawing my father's attention. Immediately, I wish I hadn't. The moment his single eye turns to me, I get the full blast of his fury, and it's enough to make my head spin. Bracing myself, I draw back my shoulders and force a smile on my face. "Father, is this not exactly why we have opened our gates to the folk of Mythanar? To learn of their ways, both how they are similar to and how they differ from ours?"

Father looks from me to Vor again. His brow is dark, and for a moment that red aura pulses strong.

Then, with the abruptness of sunlight breaking through storm clouds, his expression clears and his mouth breaks into a smile. He throws back his head and laughs. "Come, my friend! You must teach us all to perform such feats of manliness! I'm sure our women are as brave as any troll dame. Fyndra!"

"Yes, my king?"

"Come here and let me toss you around a bit, will you?"

"Willingly, my king!"

With a shout for the minstrels to begin again, Father takes Fyndra's hand and leads her to the center of the floor. Vor reaches for me. But Father is too quick. "None of that now!" he barks. "We need to find you a worthy partner for your athleticism. Ilsevel, my sweet! Come show our new friend how well you fly."

Ilsevel obeys, stepping away from her partner and approaching Vor. She doesn't look at me. She doesn't have to—I feel the wave of resentment rippling off of her. Is she angry with me? Does she think I was trying to steal her suitor? Vor's eyes are still upon me. I fear he's going to protest, make a scene. But that I can't bear.

Grabbing my skirts, I turn and dart straight into the crowd, using their bodies to hide my getaway. The sudden pressure of their emotions is enough to make me gag. I press the back of my hand to my mouth and shove my way through, using my elbows where necessary. I make it to the end of the hall and up the stairs to the door. Already there is some relief as I put distance between myself and the dancers.

Just in the doorway, I pause and look back. The music swells. Dancers fly. In the very center of the floor, Vor lifts Ilsevel and spins her in a flurry of crimson skirts. She's smiling enormously, laughing at the wildness of the dance.

I'm glad she's happy. I'm glad she's enjoying herself. I'm glad she's not locked in a tower, starving and frightened and cold. She deserves all the good things this life can give her, that sweet sister of mine.

I flee into the darkness of the gallery beyond. The cold air bites my cheeks, almost sharp enough to make me forget the warmth of Vor's hand where it rested on my waist, or the thrill in my heart when he lifted me off my feet.

8

Vor

The last brilliant notes of the Phoenix Flight resolve as I whirl Ilsevel in a final turn and set her lightly on her feet. She is breathless, panting, and places a hand on her heaving chest. Her eyes flick up to meet mine, full of vibrant laughter. She is undeniably charming.

I smile down at her. "Did you enjoy your flight, Princess?"

She tosses her head and spreads her arms, her long sleeves wafting on either side of her. "If only I had proper wings, I feel I could rise straight into the sky!"

I repress a shudder. How anyone could speak so casually of that hideous expanse is beyond me. Taking care not to let my smile shift, I offer the princess my arm. "That would be a shame. This court would be deprived of one of its chief beauties should you make such an escape."

She shoots me an arch expression and gently rests her fingers on my forearm. "Do you prefer your birds in cages then, King Vor?"

There's something about the way she asks the question, something behind that playful, flirtatious tone. Is that fear I see simmering behind the defiance in her eyes? My stomach clenches. In the press of my own needs—my concerns for Mythanar, the complexities of negotiations with Larongar, the constant balance of expectation and desperation—it's all too easy to forget there is another person on the other side of these dealings.

I pat her hand lightly as I lead her from the dance floor. "It is my belief that no thing of beauty should ever be caged, Princess. I would only hope that even a wild bird might be convinced to remain of its own free will. And a man who truly cared for such a bird would be honored to do everything in his power to convince it."

She narrows her eyes, considering me closely. "Well spoken, King." With a bobbing curtsy, she releases my arm and slips into the crowd. I can only hope I said the right thing, that my words offered the princess some peace of mind.

I turn in place, searching for Faraine. Now that I've satisfied Larongar by dancing with his younger daughter, I should like to find the elder and resume our conversation. The crowd is dense, and with all those human faces and garish colors mingled beneath the orange glow of the lanterns and braziers, it's difficult to discern one face from another.

A heavy hand claps my shoulder. "That, my boy, was the most fun I've had in an age!" I turn to meet Larongar's wide grin, his face red and glistening with perspiration. "I hope you have more such dances up your sleeve to teach the sleepy folk of my court. We could all do with a little shake-up!"

I grin and try to surreptitiously slip out of his grasp. "Most trolde dances would be rather difficult to teach," I admit. "And possibly dangerous in such a setting."

Larongar laughs. "We like a bit of danger around here. Don't we, my Lady Fyndra?"

"That we do, sweet King!" Fyndra responds, leaning heavily on Larongar's arm but training her smile upon me. "I'd give anything for a proper thrill for once."

"What, am I not thrilling enough for you?" Larongar angles her away from me, then takes hold of my arm. "Keep your dangerous dances to yourself for now, my boy. I've got something else for you. Call it a gift."

"Indeed, friend Larongar, such a fine meal and equally fine company is gift enough."

"Nonsense! I intend to make a good impression on my Mythanar brother, and I won't let anyone stop me. Come!"

So saying, the king leads me back to the tables. The meal has been cleared away, leaving only wine and bowls of sugared fruits. Larongar sends Fyndra away, telling her to fend for herself, and takes his seat beside his queen. I cast one last look around the great hall for a glimpse of Faraine, but spy only Hael and Sul standing on the fringes—Hael with her arms crossed, Sul lounging languidly against a pillar. My other people are positioned similarly, keeping to themselves in clusters of two or three. They're leaving the socialization to me. After all, I'm the mad fool who's determined to take one of these humans for a wife.

There's no sign of Faraine anywhere. Did she leave the banquet already? Did I insult her when I unexpectedly spun her in the dance? It never occurred to me that humans might dance that song differently than the way I was taught. And coming from the convent, Faraine must be far less used to the gaieties of court life than her sister.

Still, she was quick to defuse the situation when her father took offense. She successfully mitigated his anger and salvaged what could have been sudden disaster for both me and my people. If I did somehow wound her, she rose to my defense anyway. Gods, I wish I'd been quick enough to—

"Ah! There she is." Larongar's booming voice breaks my train of thought. "Ilsevel, child, come make your father proud, why don't you?"

I look down to the dance floor, now cleared. Ilsevel is there, standing alone in the center, a lute in her hands. A servant brings a chair, and she sits, her red gown pooling around her. Firelight plays on the folds of fabric, making her look ablaze. It's suddenly difficult to look anywhere else.

"Now," Larongar says, leaning to whisper loudly in my ear, "*this* is worth traveling across worlds for, trust me."

The princess begins to strum her instrument. The chords are simple, but ring out so clear and true, they strike my senses like shards of pure light. Then she opens her mouth and begins to sing. Low, soft. A crooning lilt without words, but full of far more meaning than mere words could express. All other awareness is swallowed up in the sound of her voice. Magical and rich. Haunting and sad. At first, I feel nothing but sound, pure, almost holy.

Then, slowly a sensation comes over me—an impression of far-off home. Known, but never before seen. Longed for with a broken heart. A home that may never be found unless the heart is healed, but the heart cannot heal until it finds rest. A painful, endless, glorious dichotomy.

Her voice, the song, enraptures me. I'm transported from this hall of smoke and humanity into a world I never knew existed. I've always known where I belong: at Mythanar, in the Palace of Living Stone, raised to sit upon my father's throne. It is my place, my purpose. I've never wanted more.

But now I taste *longing*. Not the stirrings of lust that every young man knows as he reaches a certain age. Not the unsettled discomfort in the blood that urges for action and adventure. No, this is true longing. An ache in the soul. A realization that my heart is not whole and won't be until somehow, somewhere, I find that missing piece.

Who would have thought so much personal revelation could be brought about by a song?

The melody comes to an end. I become aware of applause filling the air. King Larongar elbows me in the arm. "Well, my boy? Have you ever heard anything more lovely? The girl was gods-gifted at her christening, as all my children were. Ilsevel's gift is by far the most valuable."

Are those tears I see in the king's eyes as he speaks of his daughter? "She really is extraordinary," I admit, and realize there are tears on my own cheeks too. I hastily dash them away.

"Perhaps," Larongar says, "we will speak more on the subject of Ilsevel's extraordinariness on the morrow, eh? But for now, more wine!"

Dancers are summoned; jugglers, tumblers, and other performers to gad about and make themselves amusing for the king and his guests. But I cannot get Ilsevel's song out of my head. Only, it's strange . . . Though it's her voice I hear, echoing and sweet . . . when I close my eyes, it's another face I see in the darkness behind my lids. Gazing up at me with strange, earnest eyes. One blue. One gold.

. . . .

"Deeper Dark devour me, I thought it would never end!"

Sul collapses on my bed and stretches hugely as he utters a

yowling yawn. I yank the pillow out from under his feet. "I'd prefer not to smell the grime off the soles of your shoes while I sleep today, brother."

"A better aroma than anything else you'll find in this death-stinking world." Sul angles his head to leer at me. "At least that ghastly Larongar has given you a decent-sized room. Mine is nowhere near this large. Hael's is basically a cupboard."

I turn to my captain, who has taken a seat at a little table near the fireplace and pours herself a goblet of wine. She took no drink during the banquet as she was officially on duty, and only now allows herself any refreshment. "Are your accommodations insufficient, Hael?"

She gives me a look. "I didn't journey to the human realm with the hope of luxury in mind. I, at least, am on a mission."

"Sweet Hael," Sul says, rolling over and propping his chin in his hands, "let me assure you, the mission is forefront in my mind. Didn't you see me making nice to the grisly human wenches throughout the evening? I suffered hard for the sake of the crown!"

Hael casts him a scathing look before addressing me. "What did you make of our host and his daughters?"

"Of our host, I think rather little." I accept the cup she offers me. "He is what I expected. I wouldn't turn my back on him in the dark. Of his daughters, however . . ." I take a gulp, leaving the thought hanging.

Sul sits up on the bed. "His daughters are unexpectedly toothsome morsels, aren't they? Especially that Ilsevel. I've never been particularly inclined toward humans before, but looking at her, I begin to understand the mountain troll penchant for devouring human maidens." He runs his tongue lasciviously over his teeth.

"Watch it," Hael growls. "You'll get drool on your shirt." She turns back to me. "And you, my king? What was your opinion?"

"I'll admit they are . . . rather more than I anticipated." I stroll to the window, gazing down on the courtyard below. Clouds have rolled in to cover the stars, and I find the sky more bearable from under their canopy. It's still several hours before dawn. I should try to get some sleep, for humans go about their business by daylight, and I will need to act accordingly. Now all the initial niceties have been gotten out of the way, negotiations will begin in earnest. I hope to have the matter settled in a few days.

"So, you will pursue the alliance?" Hael persists.

I face my friends, swirling the drink in my cup. "I'm not sure I have much choice. Up until now, Larongar has been firm in all his correspondence—he will not send his Miphates to us until he can be sure the threat of Prince Ruvaen has been dealt with. We must give him what he wants before he'll give back."

"Then why should we deal with him at all?" Sul demands.

"Do you have some other trick up your sleeve to save Mythanar?"

Neither my brother nor my captain answer. They exchange glances, then look away quickly. I continue, saying what they both already know too well: "The prophecy is going to come about. One way or another, sooner or later. But all signs indicate sooner. Unless drastic action is taken, all the Under Realm is at risk. Fae magic can do nothing against that which stirs in the darkness. We *need* the power of the human mages. We *need* the Miphates."

Even Sul's expression melts into one of solemn study. He cannot deny the truth I speak. Our circumstances are too dire for his habitual mirth.

"But Vor," Hael says, forgoing my title and slipping back into the familiarity we once knew as children, before I became her king and she, my captain. "Do you need to make a marriage bargain? Why can we not simply trade—our warriors for Larongar's Miphates? Why does a marriage need to be entered into?"

Sul snorts. "Have you met the human king? He positively reeks of duplicity."

"Sul is right."

"What was that?" My brother cups a hand around his ear. "Did I hear those sweet words correctly? Or were they but a dream?"

Ignoring him, I look down at the last of the wine swirling in my cup. "Larongar is not to be trusted. Not even to honor a signed agreement. Written bindings do not bind humans as they do our kind. The magic of the written word doesn't affect them in the same way. But if there is a marriage, Larongar might be compelled to honor his word if the safety of his own daughter is in question."

"What you need is a hostage, not a bride."

Hael's statement sends a stone sinking in my gut. She's not wrong. "It cannot be helped. And I will . . . I will do what I can to make the arrangement agreeable for the girl."

"Oh, no one doubts that, brother mine." Sul smirks. Hael shoots him a warning look. "What?" he demands. "Have you *seen* what passes for men around here? Our dear Vor is positively magnificent by comparison! Surely his blushing bride will be more than happy to be the recipient of his *largess*."

Hael sets her goblet down on the table. "But are you certain, my king, truly certain? Will such a marriage not be too great a burden to bear for a lifetime?"

I smile dryly. "So, you weren't charmed by the pretty Ilsevel, I take it."

"The question is not whether *I* was charmed. You're the one marrying her. And, correct me if I'm wrong, but I thought perhaps you found your attention drawn a different direction."

"Indeed?" Sul rubs his hands together. "Please, tell me it wasn't the king's mistress! Or rather, tell me it was. I beg you."

"Shut up, Sul." Hael growls.

My brother snickers and slips off the bed. He saunters to the table, takes the seat opposite Hael and pours himself a measure of wine. "I will seal these luscious lips of mine, sweet Hael, but only after I've made one last point: if our king is indeed determined to shackle himself to a human till death doth sunder all spousal ties, he'd best be sure he picks the right bride."

"And what does that mean?" I ask sharply.

"I think you know what I mean." Sul takes a sip, looking at me over the rim of his cup, then lowers it and wipes his upper lip with the back of his hand. "If it's a hostage bride you need, we must be certain Larongar actually cares for her well-being."

"A father would naturally care for his daughter."

"To be sure. But most fathers don't seat their eldest daughters at the far end of the table, nearly out of sight. Or keep them shut away in convents far from court. Or constantly push the younger daughter to the forefront."

"So, what are you saying?"

"You know very well what I'm saying."

"Pretend I don't. Spell it out for me. Exactly."

Hael's voice, quiet and rock hard, interrupts whatever snide remark Sul is about to make. "You need to choose Ilsevel. Not Faraine."

I lift my cup to my lips only to find I've already drained it. I scowl at the dregs.

"You've said it yourself," my captain continues. "Written

agreements do not bind humans as they bind us. You must have adequate collateral. We cannot send our warriors to give their lives pointlessly in another man's war."

"They'll give their lives for Mythanar," I say. "We all would die for Mythanar."

Sul tilts his chair back on two legs, balancing precariously. "Picture this, brother mine: Say you lead us all in glorious battle, and we pour out our blood upon these human fields. What happens when you return? When you summon Larongar to send his Miphates? What happens when he answers, *Thanks, friend Vor, for all those bodies you sent to fertilize my crops. But I'm keeping my mages safe and close*? What then?"

"Then we remind him of his promises."

"Promises which mean nothing to a human."

"Then we bid his daughter to compel him."

"The daughter he loves and cares for? Or the one he obviously despises?"

I put my back to them, scowling out the window. All is very still and cold on the other side of the leaded glass.

Then, suddenly, movement. It draws my gaze to a building on the far side of the yard. A door opens, and out steps a little figure, cloaked and hooded.

"Come, now," Sul says. "You're not going to try to convince me you've *fallen in love*, are you? After one short ride and one small turn of a dance?"

The figure passes beneath a torch. Flickering orange light gleams against the silver threads decorating the cloak's hem. Even from this distance, I recognize that pattern: the coiling dragon.

"Vor? Don't leave us in suspense like this." Sul snaps his fingers several times. "What's your answer? Will you take the scrumptious little Ilsevel and save us all? Or will you doom us to prophetic oblivion? I mean, I understand it's difficult to think about doom and salvation and all those unpleasantries when you're following the inclinations of your—*ahem*—heart."

"I'm going out." I turn abruptly, facing the two of them. They watch me too closely, Sul with that knowing smirk of his, Hael with her grim, stern brow. "I need air." Before they can protest, I stride for the door, fling it wide, and escape the room, tossing back over my shoulder as I go, "And if either of you tries to follow me, I'll grind your bones to fine powder."

In four quick steps, I cross the receiving room, push open the door, and step out into the dark passage beyond. Sul's voice trails behind me: "Good talk, brother! Can't wait to find out if the whims of romance mean us to live or die!"

9

Faraine

The pressure feels as though it will crack my skull in two.

I roll onto my side, clutching bedclothes to my chest, drawing deep breaths and holding them as long as possible before letting them out in long gusts. It helps. But only a little. Gods, I should have known better than to linger so long at the feast! The accumulation of all that emotion has left me weak, trembling. I've already vomited up everything I ate. My throat burns and my mouth tastes foul, and still my body is wracked with dry heaves.

A little knock on the door. "Fairie?"

It's Ilsevel.

I cannot answer. I can only lie here, holding my breath, hoping she will go away.

The door creaks behind me. Just a little. I feel my sister's hesitation as she peers into the dark chamber, lit only by near-dead coals on the hearth. "Fairie," she says softly, "are you awake?"

I close my eyes, counting my heartbeats. Hoping, praying.

"I just wanted to thank you. For being with me tonight." She's silent for a few moments, as though considering her next words. "You were right. The Shadow King wasn't as bad as I feared. Maybe . . . Maybe it will all be . . ."

She leaves that last thought unfinished. A moment later, the door clicks shut again. The pressure of my sister's feelings leaves the atmosphere, and I let my breath out in another long, shuddering exhale. At least now I know that whatever resentment I'd felt from her in the banquet hall wasn't directed at me. Thank the gods. I would hate to cause my sweet Ilsevel pain.

Groaning, I roll over and stare up at the canopy of my bed. For some moments I simply lie there, waiting for I'm not sure what. For the pain to pass. For sleep to claim me. For the feelings whirling in my head to still.

For the image of silvery pale eyes set beneath a broad, noble brow to fade.

With another groan, I push back my blankets and sit up, swinging my legs over the edge of the bed. A wave of dizziness passes over me. I brace myself until it rolls on by. My limbs feel weak and shuddery, but I rise, stagger across the room to the wash basin. The water inside is filmed with ice. I break it with my elbow, then splash cold droplets on my face, rubbing my eyes. It doesn't help. Nothing helps. My skin crawls, my stomach churns, my limbs ache. When one of these fits takes hold of me, there's nothing to do but ride it out. I'm trapped. A prisoner in my own body.

Oh, how I long for the cold mountain air of the convent! For the relative peace and calm of that life, separated from all the intrigues of court. "Soon," I whisper, my breath puffing out in white vapors. "It will all be settled soon. Then you'll go back where you belong, and all this will be nothing but a memory."

A memory . . . A beautiful, almost illicit memory . . .

My gaze catches on a mound of fabric draped over the back of a chair. I don't recognize it at first. Then it comes to me: Vor's cloak. I stare at it for some moments, chewing my dry lower lip. On impulse, I snatch it up and wrap it around myself. Pulling a fold of cloth over my face, I breathe in deeply. That scent of dark earth and sweet spice fills my nostrils, creeps into my head.

The fog clears; the pain dissipates. Not entirely. But enough.

"Oh!" I sigh, sinking into the chair. "Oh, gods, thank you!"

I sit there for I don't know how long, inhaling his scent, exhaling relief. When my mind is finally clear, I pull back the cloth and look at my bed once more. I should try to sleep. Tomorrow will be another long day. I need whatever strength I can gather.

Instead, I rise, pulling the cloak a little tighter around my body. It's the work of a moment to find a pair of tall boots. Then I'm slipping from the room, making my way through the cold, dark passages of Beldroth. No torches are lit or lanterns hung at this hour of the night. I meet no one as I go. The whole castle seems to be caught in a dreamlike stillness.

I find the door I seek and step out into the courtyard. The night sky is heavily overcast, and the air holds the scent of snow. Brisk winter winds pinch my cheeks, but Vor's cloak is warm. I pull the hood low over my face and hasten across the paving stones, making my way to a small door set in the far wall. It is unlocked, and I pass through into a garden sheltered within the walls of the castle itself. It's not expansive—a low hedge maze, a series of pale stone walkways, a few fruit trees, now dormant. A pond in the center is frozen over with a dark glaze of ice.

I make my way to the pond and take a seat on a stone bench. Down under the ice, turtles and fish lie slumbering in hibernation. There's a sleepy sort of peacefulness in the air. The shrubs and trees around me are skeletal and stark, their branches edged in frost. They look dead, but if I close my eyes, I can almost feel the life in their centers, just waiting for the call of spring to summon them awake.

I tuck my arms around myself. "Goddess," I whisper through gritted teeth, and lift my gaze from the dark, frozen pool to the sky above. Heavy clouds limned with moonlight roll by overhead. "Nornala, Goddess of Unity, giver of life and love . . . what am I to do?"

I wait. In silence. In expectation. In hope.

But I already know the answer. There can be only one answer for the likes of me. I will support Ilsevel. I will serve my king and my country. And when I've done all I can with my limited abilities, I will return to the convent and live out the rest of my life in seclusion. My gods-gift will have fulfilled its purpose: calming Ilsevel long enough for her to realize the Shadow King is a good match for her. Beyond that, I'm no longer necessary. Not here. Not anywhere.

Is this then to be the sum total of my existence? Hiding? Trying not to cause trouble? Trying not to get in the way; to be an inconvenience to those who feel obliged to care for me? What kind of life is that? Gods above, I feel as though my skin is crawling with my spirit's need to break free! To fly, to soar. To escape.

I sit on that bench, gazing up at the sky. My chapped lips move, breathing out strands of frozen air. "Like a phoenix," I whisper.

"Faraine."

My heart leaps to my throat, pounding hard enough to choke. I whirl in my seat, the hood falling back from my face. A tall, pale figure stands on the path behind me.

"Forgive me," the Shadow King says. "I do not mean to intrude upon your reverie."

"Oh!" I let out my breath in a rush. My heart seems to drop

from my throat to my gut, thudding hard. With an effort, I find my voice. "Oh, no! You're not an intrusion. Not at all."

There's just enough moonlight to illuminate his smile. He takes a few steps nearer. "May I sit?"

I nod and slide to one side, making room on the bench. He perches on the edge, his hands on his knees. He's still wearing the open-fronted tunic from the feast, with the metal collar across his shoulders and the braided belt at his waist. The silk front gapes, offering a clear view of his muscled torso. I realize I'm staring and look away quickly. Instead, I focus my gaze on his hands, on those surprisingly long, graceful fingers.

"Are you cold, Your Highness?" I ask abruptly. "I . . . I did not mean to steal your cloak. Would you like to have it back?"

He turns another smile my way. His eyes are strangely bright, glowing with their own inner light. It would be disconcerting if it wasn't so beautiful. "I don't feel the cold," he says. "And I'd rather you didn't freeze on my account. But tell me, Faraine: are we no longer the friends we were?"

"Your Highness?"

"There. See? You've done it again." He tilts his chin, looking at me from beneath his puckered brows. "My name is Vor. Remember?"

"Oh." I turn away quickly, focusing my gaze on the ripples frozen into the surface of the pond. "We are no longer travelers on the open road. Here in Beldroth, certain decorum must be maintained."

"Even when there's no one around to care?"

"Especially then."

"Ah." He goes silent, considering. Then: "Very well, Princess."

We say nothing for some moments. I wonder if I should rise, make some polite excuse, and leave. But what kind of excuse can I offer for being outside in this frigid air at this hour of the night?

Everything I come up with sounds foolish in my own head. So, I hold my tongue.

"It's more barren than I anticipated," the king says suddenly. He waves a vague hand. "I'd heard tell of human gardens and their bountiful colors and aromas. This isn't what I'd envisioned."

A small laugh springs to my lips. "It is winter, after all."

"Is that right?" He looks curious. "I seem to remember something about that. About . . . seasons."

"Do you not have seasons in Mythanar?"

"No. Beneath the earth, we are not subject to the whims of weather or the turning of the sun. We organize our lives according to the cycles of *Vagungad* instead."

"And what is . . ." I hesitate before making an attempt. "What is *vah-goon* . . ."

"*Vagungad*? It is the holy cycle of our god. When the cycle is at its lowest, my people spend periods of time in deeper darkness, near to the stone from which we sprang. When the cycle is at its peak, however, we live closer to the light and are more *animated*, as it were."

"Is there any light underground?"

"More light than you can imagine. More light, more color, more life. More everything."

The passion in his voice stirs my blood. Even my frozen fingers and toes are suddenly warm. "I struggle to imagine it. When I think of being underground, I think of . . ."

"What?" His tone is encouraging.

"Well," I admit slowly, "I think of a tomb. Cold. Dark. And dead."

He is silent for a few breaths. Have I insulted him? I should say something, find some way to take back my ill-thought words. Before I can gather my wits enough to speak, however, he says, "I wish I could show you Mythanar. At *urz-va*, the high point of the holy cycle. Then the *jiru* blossoms are in full bloom, and the *urzul* crystals sing, and the Living Light is at its peak. Troldefolk love the dark, but . . . well, I am not pure trolde blood. I carry human blood in me as well, so perhaps that is why I love the *urz-va* more."

His words paint such sensations in my head. Not visions, for I have no way of envisioning the strange things of which he speaks. It's more like color and music, all blended into one, weaving together in impossible patterns. I close my eyes and let myself revel in the feeling, the sweetness of tantalizing longing it instills in me.

Then I frown. "You have human blood?" I open my eyes and catch his gaze on me.

"Yes." He blinks. "Did you not know? My mother was human."

"Oh! Then marriage to a . . . a . . ." I stop, uncertain I should continue.

He finishes for me. "Marriage to a human is not so strange to me after all, no. Though I confess, I find this manner of bartering for a bride more than a little unsettling."

I manage a small smile. "Is marriage bartering not a trolde pastime then?"

"No, indeed. Traditionally, marriage matches are made during the *marhg*."

"And what does that mean?"

"The hunt."

I draw my head back and raise my eyebrows. Vor laughs outright. "It's not what you're imagining! Loving pairs who desire to wed participate. Back in the First Age, there was perhaps an ominous twist to it all, and in the wild, troldes practice a more feral version of the *marhg*. But in civilized Mythanar, it's all much more polite. Men arm themselves and give their desired brides a head start into the tunnels outside the city. At the sound of the *zinsbog*, the chase is on. A couple that comes together too easily is said to be weaker. The longer and more arduous the hunt, the more successful the marriage match. At least according to tradition." His teeth flash in the pale moonlight. "Somehow, no bridegroom ever *fails* to chase down his quarry. And it's all highly entertaining to observers."

I snort. "I suspect Ilsevel would be better suited to such a form of courtship."

"Yes, I did get that impression of your sister."

We lapse back into silence. As though the image of Ilsevel has suddenly come to sit between us on that little bench. I clear my throat softly. "I trust Ilsie sang for you this evening. Did you enjoy her performance?"

"Why, yes. She did." Vor adjusts his seat as though he's suddenly uncomfortable. "She took me by surprise. You'd told me of her gods-gift, of course, but I wasn't aware how such a gift could manifest."

"Are there no gods-gifts among your people?"

"No, indeed. Not among troldefolk nor any of the fae, as far as I know. If I understand it right, gods-gifts are meant to be a pacifier from the gods to humans, whom they made less magical than their fae counterparts."

"I suppose that's one way of looking at it."

Vor chuckles. "I'm afraid I've insulted you. Please, take no offense. It is a simple fact that fae are born with magic in their blood, whereas humans are not. So, the gods-gifts are more unusual and more powerful as a result."

I duck my head, hoping he cannot see the flush staining my

cheeks. Heavens above, but his laugh is such a dangerous thing! I could so easily learn to crave the sound. "I thought trolde were not magical like other fae," I say hastily to cover my embarrassment.

"Not *like* other fae," he acknowledges. "But we have magic of our own, make no mistake. We are not for *glamours* so much as for *influences*. And unlike the rest of the fae, we can *make*. We have our own forms of art and craft, and in that respect, we are more like humans. Some speculate that original troldekind were the turning point of creation—the pivotal moment at which the gods turned from creating fae to creating humans. Or vice versa. No one really knows which came first, only that troldefolk are in the middle."

I soak in the information he imparts. My education has been so limited, my knowledge of the fae mostly composed of rumors I've picked up, all pertaining to their viciousness, beauty, and cunning. Of the troldefolk I've heard next to nothing, and most of what I have heard has proven inaccurate.

"Your people and your ways sound fascinating." The words slip unguarded from my lips. "I wish I could see it. Mythanar, I mean."

"You could."

I look up, meet his gaze.

"If all goes well with the negotiations tomorrow," he persists. The dark pupils of his eyes dilate, becoming deep pools of midnight filled with the light of distant stars. "Would you come?"

Is he saying what I think he's saying? Surely not. Surely I'm imagining that earnestness underscoring his voice. But oh! I long to respond to it! How can it be that a mere two days have wrought such an unexpected change in my heart? Filling me with hopes and dreams I have no business indulging.

But he's here. Beside me. I feel the radiating warmth of his soul, clearer to my gods-gifted senses even than the beauty of his face or the timbre of his voice. I know exactly what he's asking. My mouth opens, my lips move. My answer rests on the very tip of my tongue.

Instead, I find myself saying: "What do you hope to gain in coming here, Vor?"

He blinks, surprised at my tone perhaps. He'd leaned in toward me but now draws back a fraction. "I should think that was obvious. I hope to gain a wife."

"Yes, but why? Why have you come seeking here, in this world? No doubt any number of trolde women would gladly become your queen. You have another purpose in knocking at my father's door."

He turns from me, leans his elbows on his knees, and gazes across the winter-wrapped garden. His chest expands in a sigh. "It's the Miphates," he says at last. "I have a . . . a need back home. A difficulty that requires a magical solution. Fae magic won't do, nor trolde. This requires something different. Human magic, but on a scale as yet unseen in this world or any other."

There's something in his voice, in his soul. A darkness which I now realize has been there all along, but which I had not recognized until this moment. It's like a great, clawed creature, clinging to his shoulders, weighing him down. Crushing him beneath its weight.

I nod slowly. Now I understand. Not everything, perhaps. But enough. Enough to know what answer I must give.

"If you take my sister as your bride, my father will honor his agreement."

Vor looks up sharply, his eyes seeking mine. I duck my head, focus on my folded hands. Am I betraying Ilsevel by telling Vor this? Am I securing a fate she would not choose for herself? Perhaps.

I continue, nonetheless: "My father does not love easily. But he loves Ilsevel."

Vor is silent for some time. At long last, he lets out a breath. "I understand."

I feel the abrupt shift in his spirit, feel how he pulls back from me. Only as he retreats do I recognize just how close he'd drawn. So, I wasn't mistaken. He was offering me something . . . something I very much want to accept. Something I must refuse. For his sake.

We are silent for a little while. Then Vor rises. I close my eyes a moment before tilting my head to look up at him. "I will leave you now, Princess," he says, offering a short bow. "I trust I will see you again before my visit here is done?"

"Yes, thank you." I tip my head politely. "I'm sure we shall meet."

Without another word, he turns and starts back across the garden, following the path. I watch him go. I tell myself not to let my gaze linger. But somehow, I cannot resist what feels like my final glimpse of this stranger who has, in so short a space of time, worked such a change in my heart.

He reaches the door in the wall. Shadows close around him, obscuring him from my view. The next moment, he's gone.

When we see one another again, he will be a different man entirely. A man who belongs to my sister.

10

Vor

"How does this go on exactly?"

I look up from where I sit, trying to stuff my feet into a pair of too-tight boots, to see Sul pluck a human garment from where it lies on my bed. He holds it upside down in front of him and flaps it a few times.

Hael grunts and snatches it out of his hands. "It laces up the front. Here." She holds it right side up, but her brow tightens. She turns it around, murmuring, "Or perhaps it's up the back?"

"Hand it over," I growl. Hael shrugs and tosses the garment to me. "A little privacy, if you please?"

She politely turns her back, but my brother maintains his place, seated backwards on a chair, his arms folded over the back, his chin propped. He smirks as he watches me struggle into the shirt. It's much too tight across the shoulders, and the armholes pinch. I try to adjust. A seam rips somewhere. Grimacing, I search for a hole, but find nothing. I fumble with the front ties.

"Do you plan to adopt human garb from this day forth?" Sul asks. "Does your bride's delicacy require this sacrifice?"

I shoot him a look, rolling my shoulder and causing another disconcerting rip. "I agreed to wear the customary garments for a human heartfasting today. In turn, my bride will don traditional trolde apparel for the wedding ceremony. It seemed a fair exchange at the time."

Sul makes a face. He plucks a circlet from the bed. It's gold and set with green jewels. Dead and lifeless jewels, for there are no living gems to be found anywhere in this world. He turns it round with obvious distaste before tossing it aside. "Let me be sure I've got this right," he says, setting his chin back on his arms. "Today's little event isn't a *marriage* ceremony?"

"Haven't you been paying any attention?" Hael scoffs, still facing the wall.

"Very little. I try not to listen when humans are talking. I find it better for my sanity on the whole."

I shoot him a look. "Need I remind you, brother, that I myself am half human?"

"Yes, my king." Sul grins, showing too many teeth. "And we have all forgiven you for this defect in your person as you so magnificently make up for it in all other respects."

I narrow my eyes slightly. "You may laugh and jest as you like today, brother. But you'd best learn to curb your tongue. Any such speech made about *my wife* will not be tolerated. And any such speech made against my future children by that wife will be taken as treachery against the crown itself."

Sul sits up, hands gripping the back of the chair. The smile melts from his face, and his eyes are suddenly hard. "Be serious, Vor. Do you truly intend to go through with this madness?"

"I do. And you will accept it, brother. And when you cannot accept it, you will hold your tongue. Do you understand me?"

For a long moment, Sul says nothing. His eyes search my face for some sign of weakness. I give him none. I match his stare—hard, unflinching.

At last Sul rises. He offers a slow, almost languid bow. When he rises, he says only, "My king."

He leaves the room without another word, leaving me with Hael and Umog Zu. The priestess sits cross-legged in the middle of the floor, caught up in a long and involved prayer. Her pale skin has turned gray and hard as she sinks into her *va*, becoming one with the stone. She's nearly naked save for her ornamental headdress, and her voice provides a background drone to the atmosphere.

I return to fumbling with the laces of my garment but see from the tail of my eye when Hael turns, her gaze heavy upon me. "What?" I demand at last.

"You know Sul is only concerned for you. For your future happiness."

"Sul has never fully forgiven me for being born first. And born of a human mother."

"Perhaps. But he's never allowed that resentment to color either his love for you or his loyalty to your crown. You know that, don't you?"

I do. I've fought side by side with Sul on many occasions and would trust my half brother with my life. I know that, even now, some among my own council would prefer to see Sul seated on the throne of Mythanar. After our father's death, many urged Sul to demand the Rite of the Thorn and fight me for crown and kingdom.

Instead, Sul knelt before me and pledged his life, swearing the Unbreakable Oath. For all his viper's tongue, Sul would never dare go back on such an oath. He is, in his own way, quite devout.

But loyalty to me will not necessarily translate to my wife.

"Sul must understand that when I take a wife, the two of us will be made one. Whatever devotion Sul feels for me, he must in turn impart on my bride. There can be no division." Finishing up the shirt ties, I complete the rest of my clumsy efforts to dress, setting the gold circlet on my brow last of all. "Is all made ready for our departure?" I ask, straightening the front of the strange, ill-fitted shirt.

"Yes, my king," Hael responds. "We are to set out for Mythanar tomorrow." She sounds ready to escape this place. And I know she is eager to get home and seek out word of her brother. I'm scarcely less eager myself. Upon our return, I will have approximately two weeks to prepare for my bride's arrival. It is the custom in Gavaria following the heartfasting ceremony for a bride to make her Maiden's Journey, sacrificing at certain altars and praying before certain shrines. Until the Maiden's Journey is complete, she and I will not be permitted to see one another. Thus I will return home and plan for her coming.

And that should give me ample time to get the image of her sister out of my head.

I wince and swiftly turn away from Hael, pretending to adjust the set of my belt. Three nights have now passed since I met Faraine in the still, cold garden by moonlight. Larongar has hosted elaborate feasts every evening since, but though I've looked for her, Faraine has not been present.

Is she avoiding me? Perhaps. Perhaps it's just as well. I've made my decision. And I'm determined to be a good husband to Ilsevel. Which I cannot be if I'm thinking about another woman.

Still, I wonder if Faraine will be present to observe the heartfasting. I hope so. I should like a chance to prove to myself that I don't feel anything. That the sight of her has no power to move me. That I'm truly ready to put those feelings to rest.

Ilsevel will be my wife.

Ilsevel.

I close my eyes, calling to mind an image of her pretty face; her flashing eyes; her rich, dark hair. We've been given very little time to interact. The last three days have been consumed by hard negotiations with Larongar and his council. In the evenings, I have dined beside and danced with Ilsevel, exchanging pleasantries all under the watchful eyes of the Gavarian court. Just last night, Larongar declared before all that an agreement had been reached and the heartfasting would be held on the morrow.

Soon after, I led Ilsevel to perform a simple and sedate human dance I'd learned specifically for the occasion. In that short interval, as I took her hand and guided her from the table down to the floor, I leaned in and whispered: "I feel I should officially ask you: will you accept my hand in marriage, Princess?"

She gave me a sharp look. "Do I have any choice in the matter?"

I hesitated. After all, I need this alliance. More, even, than I dare admit. But I could not bear that expression in her eyes. "Yes," I assured her. "You have a choice. Say the word, and I will gather my people and leave your father's house at once."

She didn't return an answer right away. The music began, and we assumed our places on the floor, bowing and curtsying respectively. I concentrated on my footwork, gliding with her through the first pattern of the dance. When we came to the end, we stood before each other, scarcely a foot of space between us.

She looked me in the eye. "I will accept your hand, King Vor," she said.

That was it. Nothing more. Nothing less. We completed two more turns of the dance. The music ended. I guided her back to her place at the table.

We did not speak again.

Now, drawing a long breath, I turn and face Hael. "How do I look?"

She blinks slowly, her lips pursed. "Very, um . . . human."

"Thanks for the confidence." I shrug and roll my shoulders one last time, causing a final disconcerting rip somewhere. "Shall we, then?"

11

Faraine

I divide my long hair into three parts and plait each part separately. Then I weave the three long plaits together into a single long rope down my back, my fingers deft and confident. I've grown used to caring for my own needs over the last two years at Nornala Convent. While Ilsevel has several times offered to send over one of her ladies to tend me, I've staunchly refused. I can't quite bear the idea of letting a stranger touch me, even the trace contact of fingers in my hair. It's more than my strained senses can bear.

So, I finish the long plait, tie the end, then arrange a gauzy veil in place, securing it with a delicate silver circlet. I have no mirror to inspect the results. What does it matter? No one will be looking at me at the heartfasting today. If I'm lucky, I'll be able to get through the ordeal without anyone noticing I'm there. I touch the crystal pendant resting against my heart. Slowly, I draw in a breath, hold it, let it out again.

I can't avoid him any longer.

Closing my eyes, I drop my chin, striving to still my mind. It's too late. Now that I've let thoughts of Vor intrude, I cannot stop the mental image that springs so vividly to mind—the expression in his eyes beneath the moonlight when he voiced those simple words: *Would you come?*

A sharp breath escapes my lips. I sit upright, open my eyes, and stare into my flickering fire, concentrating on the dance of flames. I've taken care over the last few days to avoid even a chance glimpse of the Shadow King. I've kept to my rooms, interacting with no one but Ilsevel and Aurae. Ilsevel has begged me to join the evening revels, but I've firmly put her off, citing illness as my excuse.

It's hardly an excuse. A single evening back in Beldroth was enough to drive me to desperate pain. I cannot bear more. Ilsevel's tumultuous emotions are enough for me to manage. Goddess save me! I must return to the convent soon. To peace. And quiet. If I hadn't promised Ilsevel I'd remain through the heartfasting, I would have begged Father to let me go already.

My door creaks open. "Fairie?"

Surprised, I turn in my chair. "Come in, Ilsevel."

My sister stands in the doorway. She wears the traditional heartfasting gown—a long column of soft white with a deeply plunging neckline. A cloak fastens at her throat and falls over her shoulders, embroidered with gold threads in the sacred patterns of Nornala and holy unity. Her hair is gathered up in a gold net, and she holds a heavily beaded veil in both hands. Her eyes are wide, shadowed.

"Fairie," she says quietly, "are you alone?"

"I am." A frown puckers my brow. "Dearest, what's wrong?"

She steps into the room and draws the door shut behind her. Then, in a few quick strides, she crosses to me, kneels, and places her head in my lap. I freeze in place as the wave of her emotion rolls over me. For a moment I fear it will pierce my small defenses and leave me gasping. I grip my crystal, count my breaths, and maintain a steady pulse in time with the stone's heart.

Ilsevel lets out a ragged sob. "I'm not sure I can do this."

My heart twists. Though I can already feel the beginnings of a headache, I push it back and rest my hand on top of Ilsevel's head. My fingers brush the gold threads of her hairnet and the jeweled pins holding it in place. "Can't do what?" I ask softly, though I already know the answer.

Ilsevel lifts her head, her eyes gleaming. "This absurd pantomime. This playacting of *true love* and *eternal devotion*." She tries to smile, but a tear escapes down her cheek before she can wipe it away. "I don't think I was meant for the stage. I'm not that good of an actress."

I chew my lower lip, taking care what words I choose. "Is . . . is it King Vor? Is he . . . ? Do you think . . . ?" I can't finish the question. I'm not sure what I'm trying to ask.

Ilsevel shrugs and rests her head on my knee again. "King Vor has been kind enough. At least, as kind as a man like him can be."

"Have you spoken together in private? About the marriage, I mean."

"In private?" She laughs bitterly. "As if Father would stand for it! He's much too afraid I'll say the wrong thing, mess up his precious negotiations."

I nod slowly, my lips pressed tight. This is not a conversation I want to be having. Not now. Not ever. But my sister's distress is so potent, it doesn't take a gods-gift to feel it. "I got the impression the Shadow King wants to do right by you."

Ilsevel turns her head just enough to glare up at me. "How in the seven gods' names could you form any such impression, hidden away in your rooms like this?"

Heat rushes to my cheeks. I turn away quickly. The last thing I want is to tell Ilsevel about my chance meeting in the garden with her intended. If I try, my voice will surely betray . . . something. Something I'm not certain I can define even for myself. Something I'm not at all prepared to explain.

Instead, I answer softly, "I'm sorry I wasn't there for you, Ilsie. These last few days, I mean. I hope you know how I wanted to be."

Ilsevel sits back on her heels and studies my face. Is she reading the feelings I've been striving so hard to suppress? Are they as evident in my eyes as I fear?

At last she sighs, her shoulders sagging. "The truth is . . ." Her lips twist to one side as though what she's about to say is particularly distasteful. "The truth is, the troll king terrifies me."

I wince, repressing an impulse to correct her word choice. Now is not the time. Ilsevel continues all in a rush, as though she has to get the words out now or never. "The idea of being a wife, of . . . of everything that means! Fyndra has been to see me, you know. Father sent her to give me *instruction*." She wraps her arms around her stomach. "She told me what I'm meant to do, the duties of a wife, and I . . . I can't bear to think of it. Not with him. He's so big and stern and terrifying and . . . when he looks at me, I can't help thinking he's already disappointed. How can I help but disappoint him more? I'm not what he wants any more than he's what I want. So how can we ever make each other happy?"

Her despair is so potent, it hits me like a slap. I close my eyes, riding out the worst of it, even as I force my own seething emotions into place. I don't have time to wrestle with jealousy, with resentment. I don't have time to wish I could switch places with my sister, to even consider the possibility that *I* might have what it takes to please *her* future husband. Nothing about this situation is fair. Nothing about it is right. But we don't get to choose the trials fate sends our way.

I take one of Ilsevel's hands. Her skin is cool and dry, and the touch sends a jolt right up my arm and into my head. I grimace, but grab hold of that pain, use it to steady myself. When I speak, my voice is surprisingly calm. "Is there anything I can do, Ilsie? Any way I can help you?"

My sister's tear-brimming eyes flash to meet mine. "Yes!"

The force of her response startles me. "Really?" I shake my head and lean a little closer. "Tell me."

"You can take my place."

"What?"

Ilsevel grips my hand in both of hers. "You can take my place, Fairie," she says, her voice low and eager. "Not for . . . for all of it, of course. I just mean for today. You can stand in for me at the heartfasting."

"No, Ilsevel. I couldn't—"

"It's all perfectly legal!" My sister cuts me off quickly. When I try to withdraw my hand, she holds on tighter, her fingers digging in hard. "So long as one of my own blood stands in my place and speaks the vows in my name, the heartfasting is binding in the eyes of Nornala. It's done all the time when securing long-distance alliances. Remember when Uncle Hamon married that countess from Vaalyun? Remember when the lady's brother stood proxy at the heartfasting, and uncle had to swear all the vows to him instead? We giggled so hard, Mother sent us away and had us whipped with willow rods afterwards."

She's so earnest, she cannot seem to see how hard I'm shaking my head. "But what good would it do?" I protest when she lets me get a word in. "Even if I were to stand in for you today, I cannot take the burden of this marriage from your shoulders."

Ilsevel wilts and finally lets go of my hand. She sinks into her white skirts, so close to the hearth I fear she'll dirty the hem. "I still have the Maiden's Journey," she says, looking down at her hands. "I've got a little time while making the sacrifices. Time to prepare my mind. To say goodbye to . . . to everything. To fresh air and sunshine and rolling green hills. Everything." She lifts her gaze, and the expression in her eyes is enough to break my heart. "Once I've said goodbye, I think I'll be ready to do this. To enter into this entombment Father has chosen for me."

"Ilsie—"

She rises and strides to the window, standing in the sunlight. I've always thought my sister so fierce, so fearless. But looking at her now, I can see little of that girl I know.

"When I think about the future," she says, gazing up at the clouds rolling by in the cold blue sky, "of living in *his* underground world, of never seeing the sun again . . . of being bedded by this monster, expected to bear his enormous, inhuman children . . ." She shudders and turns to me. All the terror she's been trying to hold at bay stains her face in vivid hues. "I feel like an offering. Like the marriage altar is no better than a sacrificial slab. And I am the lamb Father has chosen. Mine is the blood that will be spilled for the sake of our kingdom."

What can I say? What comfort can I offer? Any words of mine will sound so dismissive in the face of her fear.

"Please, Fairie," Ilsevel continues, her hands folded in pleading. "Please, stand in my place today. Just today. You'll be wearing the veil anyway. King Vor won't even know the difference. Please."

She doesn't know what she's asking. She's so lost in her own fear, she cannot begin to comprehend what her words are doing to me. I fix my gaze on the ceremonial veil she left lying on the floor. It's made of gold lace and heavily beaded. A perfect disguise. My head throbs with the force of my sister's fear. It throbs as well with my own pain, my own unspoken longings and fears. I feel so helpless, so hopeless. For Ilsevel. For me. For Vor.

But perhaps in this moment, I can offer some small measure of relief.

I rise, smoothing out the folds of my gown. Then I move to my sister, take both her hands in mine. "Do you think that gown will fit me?"

Ilsevel gasps. "Then you'll do it?"

I nod.

"Oh, Fairie!" The next moment, her arms are around me. "Thank you!"

My gift does not allow me to take away pain, only to feel it. But in this moment, my sister's relief is so great, it almost seems as though I could. And maybe that's enough. Maybe the knowledge that I could help her in this small way will be sufficient to carry me through this ordeal. Goddess help me.

Ilsevel takes my hand. "Hurry," she says. "We need to change. They'll be coming for me soon."

12

Vor

The heartfasting ceremony is held at sunset in a small courtyard set apart from the rest of the gardens. I've not been permitted to see it in advance. It is a sacred place, or so I'm told.

My people walk with me through the Beldroth gardens. Umog Zu leads the way, her head bowed, her heavy staff striking the gravel path with every step she makes, her voice muttering. She has forgone her headdress for a heavy robe, the hood edged in uncut gems and pulled so low her face is hidden. She won't play a role in the ceremony to come, which is a human tradition, not trolde. But she is determined to make certain my path is clear, so she walks before me, uttering prayers to ward off evil spirits and trickery.

Hael and Sul walk in my wake, side by side. Hael reluctantly agreed to bring no weapons, though I know she feels naked without them. Sul refused to don the human garb offered him for the ceremony, saying if I chose to make myself look ridiculous I was welcome to, but I couldn't drag him down to such a level. I know he would prefer not to be present at all. But I'm glad to have him at my back.

The rest of my party trails behind, all come to witness this first and vital step in bringing the alliance to fruition. Not that they will be permitted into the sacred garden. I'm told they will observe through a hidden screen, but that Ilsevel and I will be, to all appearances, alone.

My heart pounds as we make our way through the winter-still garden of Beldroth. Almost against my will, I glance toward the quiet bench by the pond where I sat only three nights ago. I must not think about that night, must not think about the young woman whose company I shared. The time for such thoughts is past.

I focus ahead. An ivy-covered wall stands at the far end of the garden. A door set deep into the wall is just visible beneath the greenery. Larongar stands there waiting for me, flanked by his people. Three priests wait before the door. One holds a silver ewer; the next holds a basin; the third, a towel.

This is all very different from marriage ceremonies among my own people. But then, this isn't a marriage ceremony. It's a ceremony of intention—a sacred declaration of my promise to take Ilsevel as my wife.

My mouth goes dry. I've had so little interaction with the young woman. A few dances, a few public meals. That's it. Once I asked Larongar if he would permit a private audience with the girl but was denied. Larongar told me I could speak to her as much as I liked once she was mine in the eyes of Nornala and holy unity. Until then, no. She would remain untouched.

I was shocked at his response. Did the king really think I intended, in a moment of privacy, to violate the girl in some way?

And if he thought me so uncontrolled in my passions, how could he agree to give his daughter over to me? But I chose not to press the issue. And Ilsevel herself scarcely looked at me without a beaming and altogether false smile on her face. A smile which I'm sure masked unspoken dismay.

Gods above, am I really supposed to take her in my arms and make her mine? I must hope her Maiden's Journey will give us both the time we need to settle into the idea.

I was versed ahead of time in the protocol of this ceremony. I'm to be cleansed here at the door, then must enter the sacred space alone. I incline my head to Larongar as I draw near. He offers a curt nod but says nothing. This ritual is a silent one. Even Umog Zu has ceased her muttered prayers and lapsed into stoic stillness.

I roll back the long, loose sleeves of the ill-fitting shirt and hold my hands over the basin. The first priest pours a stream of water from his ewer, and I quickly perform the handwashing as I was told—a single brush to the top and bottom of each hand, a single shake to scatter the droplets. I'm told this symbolizes how, whatever my past may have been, I am now ready to make myself pure and clean of both body and soul, to be given only to my bride and no other.

No other.

Ilsevel.

Ilsevel.

Only Ilsevel.

I hold my hands out to the third priest, who wipes them with care. Not a word is spoken, not even a prayer. The silence is unsettling. Though I know Hael and Sul are watching me, I refuse to glance their way as I turn to face the door. For a moment I stand frozen. Once I open that door, there is no going back.

But the truth is, I passed the point of no return a long time ago.

I take hold of the latch. The door swings outward when I pull. I step through into the silence of the garden beyond. Someone shuts the door behind me, and I am alone.

The sun is setting heavily now, streaking the sky with orange and purple. I've been informed that the heartfasting is ordinarily held at sunup, but Larongar agreed to make a concession, much to my relief. My eyes are better suited to the dimness.

The garden itself is as barren as the larger garden beyond the wall. Here and there I see little green buds on gray twigs. Signs of the turning season, perhaps. In a few weeks, what will this space be like? Will it be the bounty of greenery and aromatic blossoms my mother once described to me? I hope so.

In the center of the garden stands an ornate basin filled with sparkling water from which a statue rises. The deadness of the stone is unappealing to me, but a sculptor has shaped it with loving care. It's an image of a man and a woman, naked, locked in an embrace. She stands with her back to him, turning her head to accept his kiss. One of his hands holds her jaw, gently drawing her to him, while the other hand cups her breast. It's a tender embrace, both loving and sensual.

Troldefolk do not carve stone after the fashion of humans. I've never seen anything quite like that statue. Warmth floods my body, pools in my gut.

A door opens across the garden, drawing my attention. Through a veil of trailing vines steps a veiled figure in white and gold. *Ilsevel.* The door shuts behind her. She stands in place, and I count my breaths, waiting for her to make the first move. I can feel her looking at me through the heavy beading of her veil.

My throat thickens, making it difficult to breathe. This is much harder than I'd anticipated. But I must try to find some way to put her at ease. I lift my hand, offer a smile. Gods, but it's grossly unfair that she should be given a veil to wear and I not! I have no idea how she reacts.

When I take a step toward the basin, however, she steps as well. That's a good sign. I take another step, and she responds, staying in time with me. I make certain I keep my strides short, for we are supposed to make an equal number of paces to the center, meeting at the water. Our progress is painfully slow, but my heart races as though I sprint at full tilt. Slowly, slowly the space between us shrinks.

At last we stand together, the water on my right, Ilsevel a half step in front of me. I gaze down at her, trying to discern her face through that veil. The beading and embroidery are far too elaborate. Can she see me any better?

"Ilsevel Cyhorn, Princess of Gavaria," I say solemnly.

She hesitates but a moment. Then, her voice muffled through the thickness of the veil, she answers, "Vor, King of Mythanar, Lord Protector of the Under Realm."

I draw a long breath. The words I am about to speak are strange to me; I learned them less than an hour ago. But when I speak, I want her to hear truth in my voice. So I must not falter. I must not stumble.

"By the Blade of Tanatar shall I spill my blood for your protection," I say, my voice low but earnest. "By the Darkness of Lamruil shall I reveal and discover those secrets which are to be ours alone. By the Spear of Tanyl shall I provide for your needs. By the Amulet of Elawynn shall I seek your mercy and your grace. By the Knot of Nornala shall I bind myself to you, unbreakable and true.

By the Eye of Aneirin shall I hold myself to these vows, from this day until the sundering of death. Will you accept them, Ilsevel?"

I wait. For a terrible breathless moment.

Then, very softly, she answers, "I will."

My hands tremble as I reach for the front of her gown. One by one, I unfasten the buttons securing her cloak across her bosom. It comes apart, revealing the low-cut dress beneath. The neckline plunges nearly to her navel, and the white fabric clings to the curves of her breasts. She's quivering like a leaf.

I take care not to let my gaze linger on her body but focus on the impression of her face through the veil. Leaning to one side, I dip my hand in the water. Then I rest two fingers at the hollow of her throat.

"By the seven gods," I say, and draw a line down her breastbone. "By the seven names." I trace a circle. My fingertips burn at the touch of her bare flesh. Her pulse is racing wildly. "I pledge my heart to thee." Droplets trail down her skin as I draw the second circle and finish with a line between the two. The heartfasting sigil.

Slowly I withdraw my hand. And wait. Anxious, though I cannot say why.

She takes a long, shuddering breath. Is she frightened? Or am I mistaken in thinking there's something else in her tone? Something much warmer than fear.

Something that calls to my blood.

She reaches out to me, her hands working the laces of the strange, tight-fitted shirt I wear. She pulls the laces apart, baring my chest. Her hands tremble as hard as mine did. For some moments she does not speak. Is she looking at me? Taking in the sight of my exposed torso? Does she like what she sees? My blue-gray skin is so different from hers. Among my own kind I am considered handsome, and I have never lacked for female admiration. How must I look to her human gaze?

I wish I could speak to her; wish I could offer her some sort of comfort or reassurance. But I feel the unseen eyes watching us from hidden spyholes. I must maintain the dignity and solemnity of this ceremony.

"By the Blade of Tanatar shall I spill my blood for your protection," she says at last, in that same low tone that doesn't quite sound like Ilsevel. Perhaps her nerves are making it difficult for her to speak. "By the Darkness of Lamruil shall I reveal and discover those secrets which are to be ours alone."

She continues through the names of each god. And when she asks if I will accept her vows, I answer solemnly, "I will."

My bride-to-be turns slightly to dip her hand in the water. "By the seven gods," she says, placing her two fingers at the hollow of my throat. A spark like fire ignites in my body at her touch and runs in a line of heat as she trails her fingers down my chest. "By the seven names." She paints the sigil: the two circles and the line. "I pledge my heart to thee."

She lifts her head. I feel the force of her eyes meeting mine through the fabric of that veil. An almost overwhelming urge comes over me to lift that veil, to look upon her face. To see and to know this girl to whom I have just made such solemn vows. Because something is here, between us . . . something not quite what I felt when I danced with her only just last night. Something in this moment, this solemn moment of oath-making that makes me think of . . . of . . .

No.

I give my head a single sharp shake. My bride, startled, draws back a step, catching her breath. But it doesn't matter. The deed is done. The pledge is made.

We stand a moment longer, looking at each other. Ought I to say something? Offer some word of . . . thanks, perhaps? But how foolish that would be. How can I thank her for being a pawn in the games of kings? Particularly when I myself am one of those kings.

Instead, I simply bow from the waist. She answers with a curtsy. Without a word, she turns and flits from the garden, vanishing through the far door. I won't see her again until she has completed her Maiden's Journey and joins me at the Between Gate for the trek into the Under Realm.

By that time surely I will have managed to purge the strange bicolored eyes of her sister out of my head.

I touch the damp place on my chest where the invisible sigil rests. I can still feel the trembling warmth of her fingertips. A growl rumbling in my throat, I turn and retreat from the yard.

13

Faraine

For once in my life, my head is so full of my own storming feelings that I'm only faintly aware of the emotions surging in the atmosphere around me.

Aurae gives me the strongest impression. My youngest sister holds my hand tight, and ripples of concern and care and love communicate directly from her palm into mine. Lyria, walking ahead of me, gives off a faint buzz, but whatever she's feeling is not strong enough for me to discern with any clarity. I'm glad. I can't bear to deal with other people's emotions just now.

We make our way back through the garden paths, leaving the sacred grove behind. Vor and his people will take different paths to make certain we do not meet one another. It is against the sacred laws for him to see his heartfasted bride until the Claiming. The vows we've spoken are still too new and need time to solidify.

Only, how can they ever be strong enough when Ilsevel neither spoke nor received those vows in person? The sigil of heartfasting doesn't even now burn upon her breast along with the memory of Vor's touch.

I close my eyes, allowing Aurae to guide me for several paces. Gods on high, when I agreed to stand in as blood substitute, I hadn't realized just how painful, how confusing, how glorious it would be! I never should have agreed to it.

My mother stands at the top of the garden, flanked by three of her own ladies-in-waiting. She watches our approach with a cool, calculating gaze. She didn't observe the heartfasting herself, for which I am thankful. "Is it done?" she asks as we draw near and genuflect before her.

I cannot bring myself to answer. Mother will recognize my voice no matter how I try to disguise it. I can only stand there, letting the awkward silence grow.

Aurae finally steps in to save me. "It is done, Mother," she says, her voice clear and innocent.

Mother narrows her eyes. For a terrible moment, I fear her gaze will burn right through my veil. She knows Ilsevel well enough to be suspicious. Ilsevel would never ordinarily allow anyone to speak for her. At last, however, she says simply, "Gods be with you on your Maiden's Journey, Ilsevel." With that and nothing more, the queen turns and retreats into the castle, trailed by her three ladies. She's never been much of a one for shows of maternal affection.

"Ilsie?" Aurae asks softly. "Are you all right?"

Hastily, I nod and squeeze Aurae's hand. Reassured, my sister leads me into the castle and down the passage toward Ilsevel's set of rooms. When we reach the stair, however, I stop. Leaning close to Aurae, I whisper in her ear, "Send the others away. Tell them to finish whatever preparations they need for the journey. I want to stop in Faraine's room before it's time to leave, and I don't want them with me."

Aurae starts. Her eyes widen. I stare at her through swirls of gold lace and beads, watching her expression, fearing she's about to speak out and reveal my identity.

To my relief, however, she gives a little nod. Then she turns to the others, speaking a few swift commands. Lyria looks closely from Aurae to me, and I can almost hear my half sister's shrewd mind making connections, drawing conclusions. Whatever she thinks she knows, she merely curtsies and departs with the other ladies.

When it's just the two of us again, Aurae turns to me. "Ilsie? Is that . . . is that you?"

"Go with the others, Aurae," I whisper. "The company will depart on time, I swear. But I need to go to Faraine's room now."

Aurae presses her lips in a line. Then she nods. "Please be sure Ilsevel is ready to ride," she says softly, and slips away before I can respond.

I breathe a little easier now that I'm on my own. Gathering handfuls of white skirts, I turn to the stair and climb swiftly. I make it up two flights before I'm out of breath and pause to lean against the rail. Squeezing my eyes shut, I touch the place on my bared breast where Vor's fingers had lingered. That place where even now I feel the invisible sigil burning. In my mind's eye, I can see him as he stood before me: his shirt open, his broad, muscular chest displayed to full advantage. He was so great, so intimidating, so . . . so . . .

I bite my lower lip. This man—this king—is pledged to my sister. It doesn't matter which one of us stood before him receiving those solemn words. It was Ilsevel's name he spoke and to Ilsevel he vowed. He is hers now, body and soul.

Drawing a sharp breath through my nostrils, I grip the stair rail and climb again, faster. I reach the floor of my own room and all but run to the door. It's locked, but when I knock in the signal we prearranged, Ilsevel opens it. She steps back, allowing me to hurtle through, and shuts the door behind me, dropping the bolt into place once more.

"Fairie?" she asks, her voice small and a little tight. "Did you do it?"

I turn to her, throwing back the veil and gazing into her pale, drawn face. "It's done. I . . . I don't think anyone guessed."

Ilsevel nods. She grips her own upper arms tight, as though she's trying to hold herself together. "Out of the dress then," she says. "I've got to put that awful thing on before I head downstairs. Father's probably already raging at my tardiness."

I hastily yank the veil from my head, followed by the cape and then the revealing, low-cut gown. I shimmy out of it, leaving it in a puddle on the floor, and wrap a dressing gown around my body. I'll dress properly later, but first I need to help Ilsevel back into her ceremonial finery. I tie the laces of the gown, button the cape over her shoulders, stuff her dark locks into the gold hairnet. Last of all, I drop the veil over her head.

Ilsevel lifts the edge of the veil. Her eyes swim with tears as she looks at me. "I'm never going to see you again, am I, Fairie?"

It's true. This moment, right here and now, is probably the last we will spend in each other's company. The Maiden's Journey will end when Ilsevel reaches the Between Gate and meets her betrothed. From there she will travel into his world. The likelihood of her returning is small. Even if she does, she won't be traveling out to remote Nornala Convent to visit me in my seclusion.

"I'll write to you," I say in lieu of an answer. "Every day."

Ilsevel's laugh is thin and brittle. "And how will you come by a post rider willing to journey to Mythanar? Or perhaps you hope to outfit someone with a morleth to go back and forth between worlds."

"I'll send my letters to Beldroth. Surely there will be concourse between Mythanar and Gavaria following the marriage. You should prepare yourself to receive a whole satchel full of letters in one fell swoop."

Ilsevel laughs again. "A whole satchel full? How in the gods' seven names will you find so much to write about from that frozen convent of yours?" I can see regret in her face the moment the words leave her mouth. "I'm sorry, Fairie," she says at once, her brow puckering. "I didn't mean—"

"No, no." I hold up a hand. "Don't apologize, darling. It's true! But I'm sure I can eavesdrop on enough nuns' gossip to make for a handful of interesting pages anyway."

Ilsevel shoots me a weak smile, holding the veil up out of her face. "I'll enjoy every word."

She looks so desperate. So lost and forlorn. So little like my spirited sister, as though that veil on her head weighs a thousand pounds and will surely crush her. I take a quick step forward and wrap my arms around her. She squeezes me back, hard. Her lips graze my cheek ever so briefly, and I wince at the shock of pain such a touch inevitably brings me. This time, the pain isn't fear, however. It's sorrow. Real sorrow. For perhaps the first time, I realize just how much my sister loves me. Part of me believed our bond had faded over the last few years since my sickness grew so bad and drove me to avoid both her and Aurae. But no; the old ties are still there. Ilsevel still sees me as her older sister, her protector, her shield—though Ilsevel herself is far braver than I could ever be.

Her sorrow and her love stab me like a knife through the temple. But I hold on just a little longer. If only I could take this moment and bottle it up, keep it forever. Instead, I let out a breath and step back two paces. "Go," I say, holding my sister's gaze. "Find love. Find life. Find adventure."

She chuckles tearfully. "Careful what you wish for!"

14

Vor

I stand across from Larongar in his council chamber. He bends over the table, the plume of his quill pen wafting as he signs his name in triplicate.

Part of me is appalled at the ease with which he does it. How almost carelessly he makes those signs which attach his name to the agreement between our peoples. I know where this ease of his stems from, however. He is human. The written word, though valuable to him, does not compel him. He can break his word at any time and not suffer any dreadful consequence. Not in this life, at least.

As for me? I am of Eldria. I am trolde. I am fae. Yes, I am also human, but that part of my blood is not strong enough to make me immune to the power of written magic. Once I put my name to that agreement, I will be bound unto death. Should I attempt to break that binding, I shudder to think of what would happen.

We've established safeguards, of course. For instance, should something happen to my heartfasted bride before the marriage can be consummated, the terms of the alliance will be rendered null.

The same shall be true should the marriage go unconsummated for a full lunar cycle. So many lives hang in the balance of that consummation.

A shiver quickens my blood. For the barest instant, I recall the touch of my bride's skin beneath my fingertips when I traced the heartfasting sigil against her breast . . . But no. Now is not the time to dwell on such things. I have two weeks before Ilsevel and I will speak our marriage vows. Perhaps while she performs her Maiden's Journey, I, too, will have time to prepare in both mind and body for our fateful wedding night.

Larongar turns the three scrolls detailing our alliance around to face me. I see the scrawl that serves as his name mark and the dotted line where my own mark is to go. "There you are, my friend," Larongar says, fixing me with his cat's smile. He offers me the quill, wafting it ever so gently in the air between us. "Let us sign and be brothers henceforward."

Standing in the shadows behind me, Sul snorts. "Since when do brothers wed each other's daughters?" he mutters in troldish.

"Shut up, Sul," Hael hisses.

I hold Larongar's gaze for a long moment. I cannot shake the feeling I've missed something, that this sly viper of a man has somehow slipped some subtle phrase into the agreement, some twist of the words that will entrap me to his will. That by signing, I will condemn my people to die in his wars, and Mythanar will be left undefended.

I cannot hesitate. I cannot show weakness.

I take the pen. It is many years now since my mother first taught me the scrawling lines that form my name, and I have had no opportunity to practice since then. But it comes back to me well enough. I write the three simple marks. Behind me, I feel the collective breath drawn by my people as they watch me perform this simple spell. A magic so different from their own. So powerful. So dangerous. That I should even be able to perform such a feat will always render me a little strange and terrible in their eyes.

I come to the end of the word—my name—and lift the pen from the page. Power simmers in the air. The power of human magic. Of written magic.

Gods on high, what have I done?

I've risked everything to save Mythanar.

I can only pray the risk will prove worth the reward.

"And here," Larongar says, pointing to the copy. "And here." I sign the duplicate copies. Then, setting the quill aside, I offer my hand. Larongar takes it, putting power into his grip, his grin wide and full of teeth. I respond with a thin-lipped smile of my own and apply a fraction more pressure. Larongar's smile hardens, and his one eye widens. But he doesn't let go. "Good dealings, my friend," he says. "I look forward to the day when I may call you *son*. I've always wanted a proper son to fight by my side in these dark times." He casts a glance Theodre's way. "No offense."

The prince of Gavaria lounges in a chair close to the hearth, his feet propped on a stool. "Oh, none taken, Father," he sneers. "I much prefer to be an *improper* son."

"You're an imbecile, is what you are." Larongar turns back to address me. "And will your people stay one more night?"

I release my grip at last, noting the way he surreptitiously puts both hands behind his back, massaging his palm. "I thank you, no. My Master of Beasts is even now preparing the morleth to ride. We will set out as soon as the sun has fully set. Many thanks, Larongar, for your hospitality."

"Hospitality, my arse!" Larongar chuckles and reaches across the table to clap my shoulder. "Thank me for fathering the prettiest little piece of maiden flesh this side of the worlds. I assure you, you'll be doubly glad you made the bargain once you get Ilsevel home and into bed. But enough of that now." He takes a step back from the table, raises an eyebrow, and nods to indicate my people standing behind me. "Perhaps you'll leave one or two of those strapping warriors of yours here. You know, to begin preparing for the spring campaign."

I chuckle but take care to show my sharp canines in a flash. "Once Ilsevel is safely ensconced in Mythanar, then will my people prepare for war. No sooner."

"Aye, of course." Larongar nods. "And once Ruvaen is ousted from that fortress of his, I will be only too eager to send my Miphates to deal with your . . . little problem."

I look from Larongar to his three mages, clad in their richly embroidered robes. Their bearded faces are enigmatic. I catch the eye of the foremost among them, Mage Wistari. The old man holds my gaze, his expression positively serene. So why do I get such a strong impression of unadulterated hatred?

It's a relief to leave that council room behind. We've spent too much time there over the last three days. There were moments when I feared we'd come all this way for nothing, that the tentative structure of friendship we'd labored to build was about to crumble around our ears. Now, at last, the mission is accomplished. I've signed. There remains only to take my bride, make her mine, and seal the alliance upon my marriage bed.

We step into the apartment suite that has been our home these last several days. It feels empty and echoing now, cleared of our gear. "Gods!" Sul says, pulling a chair back from the central table and flinging himself into it. "If I have to hear the word *consummation* one more time, I swear I'll go mad. Don't get me wrong—I consider myself a consummate consummator. But something about that word makes it all sound so sordid. Why can't they simply say, *Once you've given the young lady a right proper* grundling, *all will be complete*?"

"Shut up, Sul," Hael growls, then turns to me. "Do you require anything, my king?"

What I require is space to get my thoughts in order. What I require is assurance that I've made the right decision, that I've not just doomed good men and women to die with the flick of a pen. What I require is a bride I can trust, can bear to spend the rest of my life with.

"Are our people ready to travel?" I ask.

"Soon. Will you come to the courtyard?"

"I'll wait in my room." So saying, I cross the space and step through the door into my personal chamber. "Let me know when all is prepared. I wish to leave the minute the sun has set."

The door shuts firmly, blocking out their faces. I can still hear Sul's voice on the far side. "Have I offended your delicate sensitivities, beloved Hael? Is *grundled* too blunt for you? I'm sure I can come up with a more palatable alternative if given proper inspira—*ow!*"

"Keep your tongue between your teeth, or I'll hit you harder next time."

"I can think of other places I'd rather put my tongue—*ow!* All right, all right! *Juk,* Hael, don't hand me such opportunities if you don't want me to take them!"

Their voices fade as Hael chases Sul from the room, leaving a ringing silence in their wake. I let out a long breath and turn to face the bedchamber. I'm not sure what to do. My belongings are already packed, and I've nothing with which to occupy myself. Would that we were already on the open road! But it's impossible to get the morleth mobile before sunset. So we must wait. Just a little longer. Then we can put this whole gods-blighted world behind us. Until we're summoned back to fight.

I look down at the leather-and-silver scroll holder I carry. My copy of the agreement, to be safeguarded in Mythanar. Physical evidence of the contractual spell that already holds me in its grip. Will it be worth it?

A morleth bray sounds from beyond my window. I stride across the room and peer through the leaded glass. Shadows fill the courtyard below, and I watch people drag our mounts out into open air. They do not like manifesting in physical form in this world and protest mightily, hawing and braying and snarling viciously even as saddles are loaded on their backs and bits shoved between their teeth. Amid all that commotion, I should not have noticed a flicker of movement from the tail of my eye. But I turn my gaze sharply, searching out the same little door I'd seen open four nights ago.

A slight figure steps into view. A figure wearing my cloak.

Faraine.

My heart springs to my throat. I'd thought she was gone. I'd thought she'd already been sent from Beldroth, for I haven't so much as glimpsed her nor heard a whisper of information about her since our last meeting. Yet there she is, her hooded head turned toward the noise and activity on the opposite side of the courtyard. She sidles unseen along the wall, making for the entrance to the garden.

I watch her go, considering. Then, giving in to a foolish impulse, I push my window open and climb out. No one sees me as I descend the outside of the castle wall. No one would even think to look up here, and it's easy enough for me to keep in the shadows as

I make my way down. My fingers and feet find secure holds in the dead stone, and an old vine offers a little support, though I know better than to trust it with the whole of my weight. In less than a minute, I reach solid ground. Taking care not to draw my people's attention, I follow in Faraine's footsteps, sticking close to the wall until I reach the garden door. I duck my head and step through.

It's strange . . . I was just here yesterday for the heartfasting. I walked these same paths on my way to one of the most important moments of my life. Yet somehow today the atmosphere brims with so much more significance. Those skeletal trees casting their claw-like shadows beneath the setting sun are studded with jewellike bulbs of green, ready to burst into bloom. I feel the life in them as I couldn't before. I feel the song of their roots humming in the soil. The air is full of expectation and renewal.

Faraine sits on the same bench where last we spoke. I cannot see her as clearly by the sun's fading glow as I could by moonlight, but I would recognize her form anywhere, even wrapped in the thick folds of my cloak.

I start toward her. My feet seem to choose for themselves to step into the yellowed grass rather than tread the gravel path and alert her to my presence. I don't yet know if I'm going to speak or if I will simply draw as near as I dare before retreating. Wind stirs the trees and shrubs, making the branches rub against one another in a mournful susurrus. She shivers and pulls my cloak a little closer around herself. I stop. I am but a few paces from her. Still she does not know I am here, apparently lost in her own thoughts. Should I call out to her?

No. I shouldn't. Only yesterday, I spoke vows of faithfulness to her sister. I should turn around. Return to my people. Mount my morleth and ride from this place, banish this woman from my memory.

I take a backwards step. My foot lands on a stick, which breaks with a loud *crack*.

Faraine whirls in place. Are those tears streaking her cheeks? Her eyes widen, her mouth gapes. Then hastily she wipes her face with the back of her hand, drawing a shuddering breath as she stands.

"Your pardon, Princess," I say, holding out both hands. Gods, what a cad I am, intruding on her privacy like this! My tongue keeps wagging, filling the silence with my excuses. "My people are preparing for travel, and I chanced to see you from my window. I thought you'd gone already. Back to the convent."

"Oh. No." She drops her chin, her cheeks flushing pink. "No, I promised Ilsevel I'd stay until her journey begins. I leave tomorrow."

"Yes. Of course." I stand there awkwardly. With every second that passes, I feel more the fool. And yet I linger.

Suddenly she looks up. "Your cloak," she says, and fingers the embroidered edge of the garment, her mouth opening and closing with indecision. Then she pushes the hood back, unfastens the clasp, and slips it from her shoulders. Underneath, she wears that same gray gown she wore the night I danced with her. It fits her figure well, modest but not unshapely. I still remember the way the contours of her body felt when she sat before me on Knar's saddle, wrapped in my arms. She takes a step toward me. Cold wind pushes hair back from her face, and she shivers. "Here," she says, holding out the cloak in a bundle.

I place my hand on top of hers. "Keep it, Princess. I wouldn't want you to freeze."

"I couldn't. It doesn't belong here."

She withdraws her hands, and I have no choice but to grab the cloak or let it fall to the ground. I look down at the folds of dark fabric and the silver threads depicting a dragon that forever chases its own tail.

My throat tightens. I look up, almost surprised when I catch her eye. She stands a mere three steps back, her arms wrapped around herself, shivering. But she feels as though she's miles away, out of reach. Yet I must reach her. Somehow. I need for her to understand . . . what?

"Princess," I say, finding my voice with an effort, "I hope you believe me when I tell you I have every intention of treating your sister well."

Those strange eyes of hers hold my gaze. I cannot read the expression in their depths. But my heart twists with sudden pain.

"Ilsevel is . . . She is special," she says. "I don't mean just her gods-gift. She is, in herself, one of a kind. Brave. Loyal. Stronger than she yet knows. She deserves . . ." Her lashes drop, hiding her gaze from me. I watch the way her white teeth bite at her full pink lip. Then, with a little shake, she lifts her head, her expression firm. "She deserves kindness. And respect."

"She will have both. I swear it."

"She deserves love."

I am silent. The words simply will not come, no matter how I try. My pulse beats in my ears, counting away the seconds. Still I have not spoken. And she's waiting. Waiting for my answer.

"By the Eye of Aneirin shall I hold myself to these vows," I say at last, my voice low, almost a growl. "From this day until the sundering of death."

She lets out a tightly held breath, blowing soft white strands of air before her lips. For an instant I hear a note of song humming in the air between us. It's simple and singular, but I feel the underlying complexity, the intricate and infinite possibilities of melody. It calls to me with a longing I've never before felt. I'm hungry for that song, almost desperate to know all that it could become.

Then she blinks. The song is gone. Even the memory of it fades, vanishes. With a nod, she ducks her head and starts up the path that leads past me. She will not speak, not even to say goodbye. She is going, soon will be gone. I will never see her again.

"Faraine."

She stops. She is a mere step away from me now, her gaze fixed ahead on the door in the far garden wall. But I cannot let her go. Not without something, some acknowledgment of what neither of us dares speak.

I reach out and catch her hand. She starts to pull away, but before she can, I bow at the waist and lift her knuckles to my mouth. A ripple of shock rolls out from her at the brush of my lips against her skin. Her head turns sharply, and once more I meet her gaze.

I want to speak her name again. I want to hear her speak mine.

Without a word, she withdraws her hand, tucks her chin, and flees. I cannot pursue her. I cannot call out to her. I can do nothing but watch her go.

"By the Eye of Aneirin," I whisper. "I shall hold myself to these vows. I shall."

She vanishes through the door. It shuts behind her, a loud and final *thunk* in the still, cold air. I let my breath out slowly.

Then, with a swirl of dark fabric, I don my cloak, fasten it at my throat, and pull the hood up over my head. Time to leave this world behind.

15

Faraine

I'm not certain why it had to be Theodre to escort me back to Nornala Convent. I suspect Father needed a reason to send him away from the gaming tables of Beldroth and out of his sight. "Make yourself useful for once in your gods-blighted life," he'd snarled.

"I've already made myself useful *once*," Theodre responded with a toss of his golden hair. "I don't see why I should have to *go on* being useful to everyone."

Father then threatened to cut him off from the royal coffers without a penny if he didn't do as he was told. Thus, I once again find myself in the close confines of a carriage with my brother. I don't believe we've spoken more than three words to each other the entire way.

When we come to the place where our carriage was attacked, I'm almost certain Theodre holds his breath. He doesn't look out the window but sits twirling his rings one after another, almost like a prayer ritual. I pull back the curtain and peer out at the road, now clear. The carriage was long since fetched away, the bodies and weapons removed. I'm not sure by whom. The air still carries the residual emotion of all the deaths that took place here, but it's faded enough not to cause me pain.

I close my eyes . . . and can almost see the Shadow King as he was that night, mounted on his dark beast, his sword curving in a deadly arc. I can almost feel his great arms wrapped around me, the beat of his heart just behind my head. Strange, how a moment of such carnage and fear could also contain some of life's sweetest sensations. A mystery. One I shall never fully understand.

Our journey proves blessedly uneventful, with no sign of unicorn riders or other fae activity. Perhaps word of the alliance with Mythanar spreads already. Even someone like Prince Ruvaen would hesitate to cross trolde warriors. We pass the same burned-out village I'd glimpsed on the way down, and I'm pleased to see signs of restoration already taking place. I hope the people will be able to reclaim their lives and livelihoods; that all of Gavaria will soon recover from the terrors wrought by the fae and enter an age of prosperity.

As for me? I will live my days quietly behind stone walls. Dreaming of silver eyes set in a proud, beautiful face.

"Welcome home, Princess," Mother Norlee says when the carriage rolls to a stop in the abbey courtyard. I climb down the block step, smile in response, and look around at the familiar buildings: the chapter house and refectory, the sisters' dayroom, and the path leading to the kitchen garden. All exactly as I left it a matter of days ago. Why does it feel as though I've been gone for years? Mother Norlee's word choice echoes dully inside my head: *home*. I suppose this is the closest thing I have to a home anymore. Beldroth certainly doesn't qualify. But I can't pretend to feel any particular sense of homecoming.

Sister Maggella helps me carry my few belongings back to my room. She doesn't bother with a greeting or telling me I was missed. I've always maintained a polite distance from her and the other sisters. To allow myself to be drawn into their friendship would be to open myself up to their emotions and the pain those emotions inevitably bring. Nornala Convent is my shelter. It's also my seclusion.

So Maggella drops my belongings on the bed, bobs a brief curtsy, and leaves. I stand just inside the doorway, looking around at the bare little chamber. The bed. The oak coffer under the window. A hutch and chair. There is no fireplace at which to warm my feet or hands. Nothing but a single silver candlestick and a stump of tallow. If I'm cold, I can make my way to the dayroom to enjoy the big fire kept burning there. Usually, I choose to avoid that crush of human interaction, wrap myself in the wolfskin rug, and pray for the weather to turn.

I sigh and sit on the edge of the bed. There's no point in removing my travel cloak—I'll only start shivering and need to put it on again within minutes. My gaze trails idly across each familiar item in the room, then on to the small square window. It overlooks a view of the Ettrian Mountains. If I stand on tiptoe, I can just glimpse the valley of Gavaria far below.

I don't bother looking. My life is here now. And soon the events of the last two weeks will fade into memory, and memory will fade into impressions. Just now, it all feels so present, so near, so real. But it won't last.

I reach under the folds of my cloak, find my crystal, and grip it hard. "There will be a light," I whisper, closing my eyes and seeking the pulse in the crystal's heart. "There will be a light in the end."

It's almost a prayer. But I don't think any god is listening.

....

The days settle back into their old familiar patterns.

I'm not part of the inner life of the convent. I am not studying to take my vows; I remain apart from the hierarchies of the sisters. I attend prayers and services, always keeping well to the back of the chapel. My meals I take in private, and when cold drives me to the dayroom for warmth, I sit behind a little screen that offers at least some protection from the emotions seething around me. Most of the younger nuns think me arrogant and vain because I will not sit with them. Only Mother Norlee and a handful of the older sisters are aware of my gods-gift and the anguish it gives me. But gods-gifts are not spoken of out loud in a place like Nornala Convent.

It's lonely being back here. But I'm thankful for the loneliness. I'd not realized just how much pain built up inside me while back in Beldroth. As the days slip by, one after another, I feel it seeping out of me once more. Along with the pain go other sensations: longing, excitement, eagerness, hope. Such feelings don't belong in a world like mine. Slowly, I sink back into blessed numbness.

One day I wake to realize I've been back for nearly a week. I stare at the ceiling over my head, and I don't feel sorrow. Or resentment. Not even resignation. I feel nothing.

Eventually, I rise. I go about my morning routine. I wash my face and hands. I don my day clothes, wrapping myself in as many layers as I can. Then, while dawn light streaks the sky overhead, I hasten to the chapel, kneel, and pray for my sister as I have done every morning since my return.

I don't think about Vor.

I don't think about the way his mouth curved in quick and ready smiles.

I don't think about the way his hands felt on my waist when he lifted me in the air and spun me in a breathless circle as though I weighed nothing at all.

I don't remember the deep timbre of his voice when he said, *Would you come?*

I don't remember any of it.

Prayers complete, I make my way to the kitchen gardens. Frost laces the ground and crunches beneath my shoes as I walk among the fallow beds. While down in the lowlands, spring is advancing, winter will linger here much longer. In places, dirty, dingy snow still clings.

Something catches my eye.

I turn slowly, almost languidly. A flash of green where there should be only gray and brown and shadow is enough to merit a second glance. There, in the corner near the wall, a long, knifelike leaf unfurls through the mucky old snow, catching a shaft of morning light. I regard it for a moment. Then, because there is nothing else to draw my attention, I step toward it. Slowly. One measured pace at a time. Upon closer inspection, I discover small white blossoms unfurling their faces to the sun. Maiden's Tears. That's what these are called. The earliest flowers to bloom in the higher reaches of the Ettrian Mountains.

Crouching, I gently brush the tip of one finger against the soft petals. The little blossom shivers at my touch. I wonder . . . the thought fades and is gone, then returns slowly through the dull sluggishness of my brain. I wonder how this flower came by its name. Who was the maiden? Why did she weep?

A sudden commotion erupts behind me. I frown and look slowly over my shoulder. Is that the sound of carriage wheels? There's a cry followed by an angry shout. I rise and fold my arms, turning to face the entrance to the kitchen garden.

To my utmost surprise, Theodre appears. I haven't seen him since the day he dropped me here. He left the following morning without saying goodbye, and I fully expected never to meet him again in this life. But here he is. His feathered hat is askew, his cloak spattered in mud and grime, his luscious golden hair in disarray across his shoulders. His eyes dart about the garden. My gray gown blends into the wall and shadows rather well, and I'm tempted to draw back further and avoid his gaze.

Instead, I lift my chin and call out, "Theodre?"

"Faraine!" he barks, his gaze snapping to meet mine. "Thank the gods, I've found you!"

"Found me?" I shake my head. "Where else would I be?"

He doesn't bother to answer. He's already striding toward me. I have only a moment to catch my breath before he's taken hold of my hand. A shock of pure, primal fear thrills up my arm and explodes in my head. I gasp and sway heavily, afraid I'll drop to the ground on the spot. I try to get free, but Theodre holds fast, his voice breaking through the stabbing white light: "None of your fainting fits now, Faraine! Gather your things. Do you hear me? There's no time to waste."

"What?" I shake my head, struggling to see him through the glare. His face is nothing but a phantom shadow, as though he belongs to another world. "What are you talking about?"

Theodre yanks impatiently on my arm, dragging me back across the garden. "The alliance. With the trolls. It's on the verge of collapse. Father sent me to fetch you the minute word reached Beldroth."

"Word? Word of what?"

"Why, the attack on Ashryn Shrine, of course." He gives me a look over his shoulder. "Haven't you heard? I should have thought the news would travel this far by now. Ilsevel's dead. She was killed in the attack. Aurae too, or so we presume. Either way, the fate of the kingdom is in jeopardy, and you're needed home at once."

16

Vor

I land flat on my back.

My ears ring with a dull droning whine that drowns out all other sound as I stare up at the cavern ceiling. Crystals gleam and wink in constellation clusters far above, spinning slowly as my vision reorients.

Pain. Lines of fire across my chest.

Gods damn it. I should have worn chain mail for this.

I drag in a ragged gasp of air and let it out in a rush. My body responds with a painful convulsion. Drawing another breath, I groan, roll to my side. The world tilts; my vision doubles. I shake my head, force my eyes to steady.

A slavering roar bursts through the thickness in my skull, followed swiftly by a familiar voice: "Vor! Brother, are you dead?"

"Not yet," I growl, and spit out a mouthful of grit and blood.

"Then get your sorry arse back over here!"

I shake my head again and turn, zeroing in on the frantic action taking place some ten yards from where I lie. Sul stands with his back against a boulder, his spear up and angled across his chest. He grips the haft with both hands, pushing it into the jaws of a *woggha*.

The cave devil writhes. Its curved claws slash at my brother's head. Sul ducks and dodges, and the beast tears great gouges into the stone instead. Its hind feet scrabble for purchase as its powerful haunches lunge and lunge again. A black tongue wags, spattering saliva and green foam across Sul's face and down the front of his shirt.

The spear haft groans. It's going to break. When it does, the monster will rip my brother's throat out.

My hand scrambles for my own spear. The haft is shattered into several pieces, but I find the blade, grasp it by the socket, and pull myself onto my knees.

Sul screams. I look up just in time to see him go down. For a moment, the terrible gray bulk of the *woggha* blocks him from view. I can still hear him screaming, which means he's alive. "Sul!" I shout.

Then Hael is there. She lunges straight at the cave devil, wrapping her arms around its hideous muscular body, and topples it over with a single heave. It utters a shriek that sets all the crystals overhead singing a baleful echo. Hael rolls free of the beast and gets to her feet. It whirls on her, down on all fours, its awful eyeless head tilted, its long tongue tasting the air. It tries to circle her, searching for weakness. She crouches low, hands out, teeth bared, planting her feet with care. A deadly, synchronized dance.

With an ear-splitting screech, the cave devil surges forward.

I'm already in motion.

My first three steps are staggering, uncertain. By the fourth step, I've got my balance. The last five I take in a full sprint, then launch myself through the air. I land on the devil's bony back and wrap my arms around its neck. It lashes its head, its body torquing unnaturally, desperate to knock me loose. I get one arm free and thrust with a single, sharp, upward motion into that soft space at the base of the skull where the bone plating offers no protection.

The creature shudders, lurches. Its legs bow outward in another few wobbling steps, as though its body cannot quite accept what has just happened. I feel the moment when the life goes out of it like a rush of wind.

It falls.

I stand astride my fallen foe, every inch of my body thudding with the roar of my pulse. Wrenching viciously, I pull my spearhead free. Blood spurts, hot and putrid. A bellow of victory erupts from my throat, and I throw back my head and let it resound to the stalactites overhead.

As the echoes die, slow applause punctuates the air. I turn, still breathing heavily, to see my brother in an awkward heap on the ground. He tilts his head, gazing up at me from where he lies. "Oh, well done, great King! That warlike yelp at the end really finished off a most magnificent performance. I swoon before your prowess."

Wiping sweat from my brow, I step back from the fallen carcass. Sul cannot be too badly wounded if he's still got breath for sarcasm. As for the rest of my party . . . ? There were five of us total at the beginning of this encounter. Word reached me of a *woggha* in Verthurg, a farming community half a day's ride from Mythanar. I didn't want to believe it but couldn't take any chances. So, along with Sul, Hael, and two other brave warriors, I'd set out to investigate.

The people of Verthurg dared not venture out from their cave dwellings to greet us, not even when Hael sounded the *zinsbog* horn announcing our arrival. I'd glimpsed a few wide-eyed faces peering through windows but nothing more. The farming folk are brave enough in the face of voracious rockwurms and the blind ghost spiders that spin webs big enough to catch a small child. Even the giant bats roosting in caverns near here are but an inconvenience to be dealt with firmly. But cave devils? That's another matter altogether.

After a brief search, we found someone willing to speak to us through a door. She told us the last place the *woggha* had been seen. Following her directions, we made our way to this cavern of sharp stalagmites covered in dark green rugs of *wurtguth* moss, from which waxy flowers bloom. I look around the cavern now at all the blossoms destroyed in our little altercation. Hopefully, whoever owns this plot will be so thankful to have the *woggha* dealt with that he won't resent the destruction of his crops.

Grir, one of my men, lies groaning close at hand. The cave devil launched itself at him first of our party. Lur had been quick to defend him. And where is she now? Off to my right, hunched over and clutching her shoulder as blood oozes between her fingers. Hael crouches beside her, asking to see it, and Lur snarls in answer, "I'm fine! I'm fine! I'm fine!" contrary to visible evidence.

Tossing my broken spearhead aside, I make my way to Sul. He sees me coming and holds out a hand. I pull him into an upright position, and he grimaces but quickly turns it into a grin. "Nothing like a little staring down death's ugly maw to make a fellow feel alive again, eh?"

"Are you hurt?" In that terrible moment before Hael reached him, I feared the devil had torn his face off. But he seems none the worse for wear.

He looks down, feels his body, then shrugs. "Seem to be all in one piece. And you? You're adding to your collection of battle scars,

I see." He indicates the stripes across my chest where those razor talons ripped through my shirt and into flesh.

"I'll probably live." I glance the *woggha*'s way again. It's still twitching. But dead. Definitely dead. Gods, but it's been years since I saw one of those beasts this far up from the Deeps! Cave devils prefer absolute darkness. They are colorless, saggy-fleshed creatures with protruding bones and weird hollows where eyes ought to be. Leaving my brother to find his feet on his own, I approach the dead creature and study it. Its lips are twisted back in a perpetual grin full of savage, razor-sharp teeth. A monster stepped straight out of my worst nightmares.

Green foam dries around its mouth and dapples its gray, hairless hide. That doesn't look natural.

Sul appears beside me and nudges the monster with one foot. "Ugh." He shudders. "A fellow like that really should know better than to show his face in polite society."

Cave devils are always dangerous. Hunters who venture into the Deeps must be wary of them. But this one was different. It was savage. As though it had lost all reason. Numerous wounds gape in its shoulder, haunches, and back, and one of its feet is crushed from a hit of Lur's club. But it never slowed. It behaved as though it didn't care about the pain.

I crouch and sniff. My stomach turns over with revulsion. A sour stink clings to the devil's skin. Like rot.

"Didn't you get a good enough noseful when you were clinging to the thing's back?" Sul asks.

"This wasn't just any devil." I turn, meeting my brother's gaze. "This creature was mad."

The faintly mocking expression Sul wears like armor falters. "You think it's true, then? The rumors?"

"They aren't rumors." I rise and take a step back, staring down at that ruinous hulk. "They're too numerous to be rumors."

Leaving my words to hang in the air above the dead beast, I make my way over to where Hael and Lur are helping Grir to his feet. He looks a little worse for wear, but his stone hide gave him some protection against the devil's claws. Hael slips her shoulder under his arm for support. She looks positively dwarfed by his massive bulk but moves without apparent strain.

"Are you all right, Grir?" I ask.

"Seen worse," he growls. "Wish you hadn't spoiled the fun, my king. I wanted a piece of that ugly hide."

I smile and turn to Lur. "How's the shoulder?"

"Just a scratch," she replies bravely through her teeth.

"Good. Then I have a task for you. Get some of the village folk to load up the *woggha* and cart it back to Mythanar. I want Madame Ar to look it over."

Lur grimaces with distaste but offers a half salute and hastens through the ruined *wurtguth* toward the village. I look beyond her to the cave dwellings built into the walls of the cavern. At least twelve folk were slaughtered by the cave devil before a brave farm boy managed to run all the way to Mythanar and beg for help. Possibly more had perished before we made it back here and put an end to the beast. And how many more will suffer the same fate before I can get the Miphates? Before that terrible Mage Wistari and his brethren can use their strange magic to combat the evil waking in the heart of the Under Realm?

In the end, will their powers be enough? Or is it already too late?

"Are you coming, Vor?" Sul's voice pulls me from my reverie. He stands across the field, holding our morleth's reins.

"Yes," I answer. "Coming."

17

Faraine

No one knows if Prince Ruvaen received word of Ilsevel's journey across the kingdom and set out on purpose to kill her, or if my sister just happened to be in the wrong place at the wrong time. It hardly matters. The ambush was swift and brutal. Only one of my sister's guards made it back alive. Ruvaen turned him loose to carry word of the massacre back to my father.

All were slaughtered, he said. Brutally. Without mercy.

Theodre recites everything back to me, relating every gory detail he can remember as we ride down the Ettrian Mountains, surrounded by a much greater escort guard than the last time we made this same journey. I cannot bear to listen to what my brother has to say. Here and there I surface from a fog of agony and try to force my mind to focus, to take in and accept what I've been told. But it's too much, and I sink again.

My sisters.

Ilsevel.

Aurae.

They appear before my mind's eye, two pale ghosts. I see them seated at a table together, sharing a meal. Laughing. Talking. I feel their surge of panic when the first battle cries sound. I watch them scramble to the window, pulling back the curtains, staring, their pulses thudding with mounting terror. Ilsevel grabs Aurae's hand and they run, desperately. My heart beats in frantic time with theirs as all around them the air explodes with dying screams and the thick sound of blades hacking into flesh.

I see them stop. Ahead is a shadow. Massive. Faceless.

Ilsevel flings herself in front of Aurae, a living shield.

The shadow bears down upon them, demonic horns flashing in the light of burning buildings. A notched blade rises, bursts into flame even as it swings.

I choke on a sob. But the vision won't stop. And when it is through, it plays again. And again. And again. I don't know if it's a dream or a glimpse of reality or some bizarre combination of the two. I lose all track of time. The vision has become my own personal hell from which I cannot escape. Or perhaps I don't want to escape. This horror has become my refuge, the dark home where I can dwell and not face a cruel, empty world.

The carriage lurches to a halt. I open my eyes, shivering, my skin slick with sweat. And I realize that the gods have not seen fit to take my life. Not yet. For reasons known only to themselves, they've left me in this cold existence.

"Come on, Faraine." Theodre's voice pushes through the cloud in my head, drawing my sluggish gaze to him. He's already climbed down from the carriage and peers back in at me. The smile he offers is unexpectedly warm. "We're here now. We're home." He holds out his hand.

I hesitate. Part of me wants to resist, to stay curled up in this dark interior with nothing but my ghosts for company. I close my eyes, calling Ilsevel's face to mind. Her brave, fierce, determined face. Would she want me to crumble into myself like a ruin whose foundations have washed away? No. She would urge me to be strong.

You're the mature one, Fairie. Remember? she would say. *So, chin up and be the princess. Go on!*

I draw a quivering breath. Then, though my body feels hollowed out inside, my limbs numb and useless, I take hold of Theodre's gloved hand. He's surprisingly gentle as he assists me from the carriage. I nearly fall when my foot misses the box step, but his grip on my elbow supports me, and I manage to pull myself upright.

I look around, taking in the high, cold walls of Beldroth. *Home,* Theodre had said. As if this stone prison could ever be home now that my sisters are gone.

Someone is speaking. Theodre answers, but I'm too numb to discern specific words. My brother turns me around to face the entrance stair. Both my parents stand in the doorway above. Father's single eye is narrow and hard as he gazes down at me. Mother's face is a mask. No one would ever know she'd just lost her two youngest children. When I reach out with my gods-gift, I cannot find her anywhere. She's far too deeply retreated into herself.

At Theodre's insistent pressure on my elbow, I manage to stagger up the steps and sink into a curtsy. For half a moment I fear I won't be able to rise again, afraid my legs will simply give out beneath me. Somehow I find the strength and pull myself upright once more.

Father's eye roves over me, from my face down my body. He turns to Mother. "She's all bones and shadows. A veritable skeleton!"

Mother offers a placating smile. "Let Mage Klaern do his work. He won't let you down."

"He'd better not. And you, wife, best be sure she's ready for what lies ahead."

My head spins. Shadows close in around the edges. I blink, and when my eyelids rise again, my father is already gone, disappeared without another word. My mother's blurry features swim back into focus. She looks me over, her eyes sharp and critical. Eventually her gaze returns to my face, and she breathes a faint, long-suffering sigh. "So, Faraine. It is to be you after all. How strange are the ways of the gods sometimes." With that she turns and sweeps inside, casting a short "Follow!" over her shoulder.

I have no choice but to obey. My head pounds and my stomach churns with nausea as I find myself surrounded by Mother's ladies-in-waiting. The sheer number of them is enough to push through my fog and stab me with daggers of anxiety. I tuck my chin, gripping folds of my skirt tight in both hands, and hasten through them after the queen. Mother leads me to her private dressing room. A tall mirror dominates the space, the glass so perfectly clear that it must be laced with any number of spells.

Mage Klaern stands before the mirror, his head bent over an open spellbook resting on his arm. He's one of the younger Miphates in my father's service, though his hair already sports a good deal of gray at the temples. He's severe and stern, with a close-trimmed beard that shapes the lower half of his face into sharp angles. His eyes are small and deep set, but their color, a startlingly bright blue, catches one's attention with almost hypnotic intensity.

Those eyes latch on to mine as I'm hustled into the room. His spirit strikes me with a force that makes me want to turn and run screaming.

"Here she is," Mother says, standing aside and nodding at me without quite looking my way. Her mouth is a grim line. "I fear it's worse than we imagined."

Mage Klaern approaches, circling me slowly. I fight not to recoil. This man radiates a sickly aura that makes my stomach knot. He finally finishes his scrutiny and faces me straight on. His lip curls. "It will be a feat of magic worthy of my talents."

A shudder races down my spine. "What's going on?" I turn to the queen, who looks down at her fingernails and buffs them idly on her sleeve. "Mother, please. Tell me what's happening."

Her eyes are heavy lidded and stubbornly bland. "You are to take your sister's place as the Shadow King's bride."

The words strike my ears like stones against an iron gate, ringing out as they glance aside, unable to penetrate. For some moments I can hear nothing but that ringing, feel nothing but that dull vibration through my bones. Then, understanding comes over me in a rush.

"You can't mean it."

"I can indeed." Mother moves across the room and takes a seat on an upholstered chair beside the mirror. "Your sisters are both dead. Ilsevel cannot fulfill her role as bride, and Aurae cannot step into her place. There remains only you, the last blood princess of the House of Cyhorn, who is eligible to make the substitution."

"She favors her sister around the jaw." Mage Klaern speaks suddenly as though he hasn't listened to anything else being said, being lost in his own thoughts. "I'll start there and draw the similarities out as I go."

My gaze bounces from him to my mother and back again. I seem to have lost the ability to breathe. Then with a great gasp, I leap back a step. "Mother, no!"

She tilts her head to one side. "Now, now, Faraine. You don't want to cause trouble, do you?"

I whirl and lunge for the door. Mother's ladies are too fast for me. Two of them catch me by the arms and drag me back, while a third pulls the door shut and stands in front of it. Wrenching free, I leap to the opposite side of the room, trembling like a deer pinned down by the hounds but determined to make my stand. "Tell me I'm wrong." I face my mother, fists balled into knots. "Please, tell me Father doesn't plan to deceive the Shadow King. To pass me off as Ilsevel."

"No, actually." Mother glances down at her folded hands. "The marriage agreement between Gavaria and Mythanar states that Ilsevel Cyhorn shall be wed to King Vor, thus sealing the alliance. There is no caveat for substitution."

Her expression is serene, but for an instant I feel a flash of true feeling from her. Sharp and quick as a pin struck through the flesh: *shame*. It's gone the next moment, leaving behind nothing but a dull throb.

I stare at her blankly. "Then . . . then is . . . ?" I cannot find the words to finish. My gaze slides to Mage Klaern, again studying his spellbook. He turns a page, his brow furrowed. I shake my head slowly. "Ilsevel is *dead*. She *cannot* be married to Vor."

"Not the original Ilsevel, no. But the Law of Appellative Benefaction permits us to pass the name of the dead child onto the head of the living. Thus, the living child, by right of law, essentially *becomes* the dead."

She says it so smoothly. As though it's the simplest, most natural thing.

"This is madness." I shake my head. "Surely it would be better to inform King Vor outright of . . . of Ilsevel's . . . of what has happened."

"And risk letting the entire alliance come undone?" The queen raises her eyebrows. Without another word, she motions to Klaern, who takes a step toward me.

"No, wait!" The words crawl painfully up my thickened throat. I force them out, one after the other. "I am willing to take Ilsevel's place. But not as an imposter. Let me go as myself. Vor will understand."

Mother utters a patient sigh. "It's too late for that, child. The alliance has been signed, and it was your sister's name upon which all has been founded. The fae may not read or write, but they are bound by the power of the written word. It's like a spell to them. If we were to break it, even with an offered substitute, the ramifications would be disastrous. No, no. The Law of Appellative Benefaction must be enacted. We must honor the alliance to the letter. Which means you must take your sister's place, not as a new bride but as *the* bride. You will take her name and, with the help of Mage Klaern here, you will take her face as well."

Hopelessness closes in around me, binding my limbs, my spirit, my will. "I won't do it. I'll tell Vor who I am. I don't care what spells you put on me. I'll make him see the truth."

Mother's eyes flash. "You do that, and you risk *everything*." She rises and approaches me, her stride slow and measured but her expression ferocious. "Small-minded, shrinking creature. You have no idea what's at stake here! You have no idea how desperate your father is to save Gavaria. Those thrice-cursed fae penetrated far deeper than we ever thought possible when they slaughtered your sisters. And they will continue to slaughter unhindered. They will raze this realm, this entire world, unless they are stopped. Here. Now. But Larongar hasn't the means to stop them alone. Not without the Shadow King. Not without his reinforcements."

She grips my face in a viselike hold, forcing me to look into her eyes. "Do you think you're the only one to suffer this loss? Do you think you're the only one in pain? Do you think you're the only one asked to give everything, *everything* for the sake of strangers who will never even know who you really are? Think again, girl."

The wave of her unchecked wrath crashes over me. I've never felt my mother's emotions so clearly. She's always composed, in control. But in that instant, everything inside her hits me like a war hammer. Were she not holding on to me so hard, I would reel away and fall in a pile of quivering bones at her feet.

Then she blinks. And it's gone. All that powerful force of spirit is once more contained. She lets go and slowly wipes her hands. "You will remember what you are: a servant of the crown. You will trust your betters to know what must be done, and when you are called to serve, you will serve. Willingly. Joyfully. Knowing that everything you do, you do for the sake of Gavaria and all those who will suffer the same fate as your sisters if you fail."

She places a finger under my chin, tilts my gaze up to meet hers. "I know it's hard. Ours are lives devoted to duty. Your life is sworn to the service of your father. He has decreed that the Law of Appellative Benefaction be enacted. So you will take your sister's name. You will take your sister's face. You will become your sister and wed her intended. You will see the marriage consummated as swiftly as possible before your husband discovers the truth. Then . . ." She draws a long breath and lets it out slowly. "Then, whatever his reaction may be, you will bow your head and accept it. If you are lucky, he will understand. If you are not, then at least you will know that you have done all in the service of your country."

I shrink away from her touch. I know I have no choice. None. To refuse will mean disaster and exile. Possibly even death. If my father were to declare me a traitor to the crown, what could I possibly say in my own defense? Closing my eyes, I see again that little burned-out village in the mountains. I see again the dreadful unicorn riders with their flaming swords and bloodthirsty, beautiful faces. I see the phantom images of my sisters holding each other, so frightened, so helpless.

Gavaria cannot last much longer against Prince Ruvaen and his relentless conquest.

I've said nothing, made no decision. But when I open my eyes again, I find myself seated in a little chair in front of the mirror. Mage Klaern stands beside me, studying my reflection in the glass as if I were a faintly interesting tapestry or a piece of tooled leather. He pinches my cheek, runs a lock of my hair through his fingers, and grunts. "This will take time."

"Take all the time you need, dear mage," Mother replies. "But hurry."

He snorts. Then, opening his spellbook, he reads aloud in a strange old language. His words seem to spill from his mouth and cling to my skin, dark and wet and cloying. He circles me slowly, and every now and then pauses to dip his finger in a pot of ink and draw strange marks directly onto my face.

I stare into the glass. Slowly, so slowly that I cannot see it happening, my features melt away, replaced by another face. Not one I know, not yet, at least. But one that is certainly familiar and becoming more so with each passing moment.

Tears brim and spill over onto my cheeks. What am I doing? Betraying Ilsevel. Betraying Vor. This cannot be real. It must be a nightmare brought on by the shock of Theodre's revelation. I must wake up, I must!

But I cannot wake. Because this nightmare is living, true.

Whether I will it or not, I am bound to become the Shadow King's bride.

18

Vor

Our healer, Madame Ar, is a strange woman. When I enter her infirmary with the cloth-wrapped body of the cave devil carried over my shoulders, she lets out a little squeal of delight and nearly falls over herself to get to me.

"Put it down over here!" she cries, clearing one of her worktables with a careless sweep of one arm. "Careful!" she qualifies when I drop my burden with a heavy *thunk*.

"It's already dead, *uggrha*." I step back and roll my shoulders. Cave devils are heavy bastards. "I don't think it minds a little rough treatment."

Madame Ar doesn't hear me. She's already circling the table, pulling the cloth back to expose the hideous head. "I've been wanting to get my hands on one of these for ages! Ah, see? Such a fine example of the *hunag* plating, which tells me this is a male of the species. The *gulg* is already beginning to solidify. It's a good thing you got him to me so quickly, and . . . Oh, Vor." She peels the cloth back a little further, exposing the various wounds lacing its hide. "Did you have to go slicing it to ribbons like this?"

Ar is one of the only people outside my immediate family who persist in calling me by my first name. I don't mind. Hers was the first face I saw when she helped my poor suffering mother deliver me on the day of my birth. Though I don't personally remember that moment, I can't help thinking she's earned the right to a certain familiarity.

"It was trying to eat me alive," I offer. The look she gives me clearly states that's the feeblest excuse she's heard in an age. "Truly, Madame Ar, I've never seen a cave devil in a state like this. It seemed incapable of feeling either fear or pain. Can you tell me why?"

"With a little time and a little messiness, I should be able to formulate some theories," she answers, then turns to the door. Hael is even now helping Grir into the room, Lur trailing behind them. Our healer's face sinks. "I suppose you need me to fix all this first?"

"If you would be so kind, *uggrha.* I could use a few stitches myself when you have the opportunity."

She takes in the cuts on my chest and sighs heavily. Though by far the most skillful healer in all Mythanar, she prefers to devote her time to her weird experiments. For the most part it's best to leave her to it. Still, she beckons for Grir and Lur to take seats by the wall and sets to work gathering her salves.

As I sustained lesser injuries, I wander from Ar's workspace to the back end of the infirmary where she keeps the sickbeds. Most are empty just now, but one figure sits in the bed nearest the window. He idly tosses a ball, sending it up among the stalactites in the ceiling and catching it one-handed as it falls.

"Well now, Yok. That arm is looking rather better."

My young friend turns at the sound of my voice. His face breaks into a grin. "Vor! I mean, Your Majesty! I am much better, see?" He sits up, pulling down the sleeve of his robe. A neat row of stitches lines the muscle. The skin around it is still darkly discolored.

"That looks painful," I say, taking a seat on the edge of his bed.

"It's not too bad. Madame Ar initially thought she'd have to cut the whole arm off to stop the spread of poison, but she was able to purge it all in the end. I'm getting stronger every day now. See? I'm doing exercises." He tosses his ball again, obviously proud of his dexterity, though it's a simple enough maneuver. The smile he turns on me is infectious. I cannot help grinning back.

"Looks good to me. You'll be back in the practice yard before you know it."

"I hope to be well enough to ride with you, Your Majesty. When you go to fetch your bride, I mean."

He speaks the words casually, oblivious to the sudden tightening in my gut. It's been several days now since I've spared a thought for Ilsevel. Upon my return to Mythanar, the needs of the kingdom have kept me busy from the moment I open my eyes at lusterling until I finally drop to my bed in complete exhaustion at dimness. And that was before word arrived of a rabid cave devil in a nearby village.

Now Yok's innocent comment brings it all rushing back to me. Ilsevel. The heartfasting. The passage of days and the countdown to her arrival. Time does not flow at the same rate in the human world as in the Under Realm. For all I know, her Maiden's Journey has already completed, and she could even now be on her way to me.

"We'll see when the time comes," I tell Yok, and give his shoulder a quick squeeze. "Meanwhile, you focus on your recovery, agreed?"

I leave the boy with pleadings and promises still spilling from his lips and return to the front of the infirmary. There I wait my turn as Madame Ar patches up Grir and Lur. They both try to protest that the king should be cared for first, but I swiftly put an end to such nonsense. As though I can't handle a little scratch compared to their gaping wounds! When my turn finally arrives, Madame Ar spreads a thick, gluey substance to bind the flesh together and issues stern warnings not to wash it off for three days at least. I agree and, once it sets, pull a shirt over my head and set out for my own rooms. I'm ready for a hot meal and a soft pillow and at least a few blessed hours of oblivion before I must face the cares of my kingdom once more.

I've taken maybe ten steps from the infirmary before a small voice echoes along the corridor behind me. "Your Majesty!"

Suppressing a sigh, I turn. A child dressed in the purple silks of my stepmother's personal staff hastens to me and bows low. "Your Majesty, the queen has requested you wait upon her at your earliest convenience."

Gods. I'd almost rather face another cave devil than deal with my stepmother just now. But I can't very well ignore her. "Yes, very well," I say heavily. "Lead on."

The child scampers back the way she came, and I stride in her wake. Queen Roh keeps a set of rooms in the west wing of the palace. She moved out of the official Queen's Apartment the same day my father died but has maintained the role of queen so long as I have not taken a wife. Eventually, Ilsevel will be expected to take over her responsibilities, and I hope Roh will offer her assistance as my bride learns the ways of our people. I'm not counting on it.

I find my stepmother in her favorite sitting room beside a waterwall. The carefully channeled droplets trickle down the wall in streams, then flow away in a trench running along the edge of the room. The descending water is slowly carving elaborate but natural patterns in the living black stone. Sometimes, I think I can see an image taking shape—a great coiled dragon, its body wrapped in intricate and inextricable knots, its eyes wide and full of furious vengeance. Most of the time, however, it's merely an abstraction of glistening shadows and grooves.

Roh sits amid a cluster of silent ladies, all of whom are hard at work spinning *hugagug* silk into fine, shimmering thread. The queen has never liked to be idle but maintains steady habits of productivity, which she expects to be modeled among her companions.

In stark contrast to the industrious women is a large, hulking shape seated off in the darkest corner of the room. I know who it is at once: Targ, the self-styled Priest of the Deeper Dark. A great favorite of my stepmother, he sits like a lumpy boulder, mostly naked and making no effort to cover himself. It's deeply unsettling.

"Greetings, Stepmother," I say as I enter the room.

She looks up sharply. "Hush!" she hisses, indicating Targ with a nod of her head. Then, beckoning, she holds up her cheek to be kissed. I've often wondered at this perfunctory demand for affection but grudgingly perform the salute nonetheless.

"Is old Targ quite all right?" I ask in a lower voice.

"Of course, darling," Roh responds, waving one of her ladies out of her seat and bidding me take her place. "He's in deep *va* at the moment."

"Why? *Grak-va* is past, and we're well on our way to the high point of the holy cycle. There's no need for him to spend so much time close to the stone."

"*Need?* What is *need* to a man of faith?" Roh blinks innocently as she goes on winding *hugagug* fibers into her stone spindle. "A true man of the Deeper Dark would prefer to spend all his time in *va*. You would understand if you were more *devout*."

More *trolde* is what she means. Roh will never quite forgive me for my human blood, which prevents me from entering into the deep *va* state. Or, in her mind, from ever being a true king of the troldefolk.

"Well," I say, leaning back in my seat, "it would be difficult to rule a kingdom if I sat around like a lump all the time. Though I won't lie, sometimes I'd much prefer to sink into a nice long nap."

"The *va* state is not restful," Roh snaps. "It takes intense concentration of mind, body, and soul. Again, not something you could comprehend."

I repress a sigh. Best to put this little audience to an end, the sooner the better. "I understand you wanted to see me."

Roh spins her thread, watching the heavy whorl of the spindle gyrate. "A messenger arrived while you were gone." She glances at me again, watching the effect of her words. "From Lady Xag."

My stomach drops. Lady Xag is mistress of Dugorim, the town closest to the Between Gate. It is her responsibility to pass on all messages traveling to and from our world. I know without asking what message she has passed on to me. But I need to hear the words nonetheless. "Go on," I say.

"It would seem Princess Ilsevel Cyhorn—such a name!—has completed her Maiden's Journey, whatever that is. She is even now on her way here and will reach the Between Gate at dusk in three days' time. Three *human* days, I presume. King Larongar bids you welcome her according to the agreement signed between you."

Blood rushes in my ears, rolling around inside my head. *Ilsevel.* Part of me had honestly not thought it would ever come about. Not really. But now it's happening. My bride is on her way. Sent from her world of open skies to enter into my shadowed realm. Will she wither in the darkness of Mythanar, like one of her frail Upper World flowers, starved of sunlight?

Will I be able to keep my promise to her sister?

Gods damn it. I've been trying so hard not to think that thought. As time passes, and the hour of my wedding approaches, I must focus on she who will be my bride. Ilsevel. Only Ilsevel.

But despite my best efforts, the image of Faraine creeps back in. Though I hate to admit it, I can recall the details of her face with much greater clarity than those of her sister. Will I ever be able to truly forget?

"I put the messenger in your receiving room," Roh says, dragging my attention back to her, "and ordered refreshments be served."

"Thank you, Stepmother." I start to rise. "I don't know why you felt the need to bring me here just to tell me that. I'll take my leave—"

Her eyes flash, quick as two *virmaer* blades. "Don't be foolish. I brought you here to try to make you hear reason one last time. I know I have little sway with you, hard-hearted as you are. You've always resented me for being your father's wife, refused to accept all I might offer you as a mother and an elder. But I cannot in good conscience allow what is about to transpire without knowing I've done everything in my power to prevent it."

"Prevent what?"

"This unseemly marriage of yours, of course."

I lean forward in my seat, elbows on my knees, fingers interlaced. "Let me stop you right there. The council has already voted. Months ago. They agreed by majority rule on this course of action. For me and for Mythanar. For all the Under Realm."

Roh stops her spindle abruptly, gripping it tightly with one strong hand. “Are you king, or aren’t you?”

I cannot let this woman goad me. “Thank you for your concern, Stepmother,” I answer, my voice level, my expression calm. “But it is needless. My course is decided. I will take my leave of you now.”

I rise, and she tilts her head back, narrowing her eyes up at me. “We do not decide our own paths, Stepson. It is the gods who direct our steps. Which god will you seek to guide yours?”

“I suppose I’ll let the gods figure that out amongst themselves.” I smile coldly. “Meanwhile, I’ll just have to keep doing the best I can.”

19

Faraine

"I can do nothing for the eyes. They defy magic."

Mage Klaern's voice is almost petulant as he surveys his work in the glass. I stare into my own eyes, holding their gaze for a long moment. One blue. One gold. I still faintly remember a time when they were both blue. Before my gods-gift manifested. Before the pain came.

At least they're mine. Unlike the rest of the face in the glass. A face that is not quite Ilsevel's. Klaern has been hard at work for some hours now, pausing here and there to write new spells into his book before speaking them into being. The jaw is nearly perfect—I would recognize that firm, determined line anywhere. The shape of the mouth is nearly exact as well, wide and full and bow shaped. The ears are a little off, however, sticking out rather more than Ilsevel's. The cheekbones are too wide as well, the bridge of the nose too long. Still, only someone who knew Ilsevel quite well would be able to tell the difference.

The eyes, though . . . that's where the illusion falls apart.

Mother stands behind me, studying Klaern's work in the reflection. Her brow is tight; the lines around her mouth are deep. "I suppose it can't be helped." Her gaze moves to meet mine. "You must take care not to remove your veil, Faraine. Not even for the consummation. The minute Vor recognizes the deception, the entire glamour will melt away. You must see the marriage sealed before then." She tilts her head forward, her expression stern as her hands grip my shoulders and squeeze painfully. "Do you understand?"

Trembling, I nod.

"I said, *do you understand,* Faraine."

"I understand."

"If you do not succeed," she continues relentlessly, "Vor may very well have you killed. While what we are doing is perfectly legal according to Gavarian law, the trolls may not see things the same way. Until the consummation is complete, you are not safe."

My stomach knots. I glance at that stranger's face in the glass, then stare down at my hands. Mother's voice drones on, informing me that following the Benefaction ceremony, I will begin my journey to the Between Gate. My party will include Mage Klaern, Theodre, and two other dignitaries of Father's court.

"And, of course, your sister will accompany you."

"My sister?" I look up, surprised.

Mother's face is stern. She opens her mouth, but before she can answer, another voice speaks from behind her: "I presume she means me."

Lyria leans against the doorway, her arms crossed, her head tilted, her mouth curved in a smile. She's nowhere near as beautiful as either Ilsevel or Aurae, but she possesses a dangerous feline quality that both fascinates and unsettles by turns. She gives me a narrow-eyed stare.

"It's tradition," Mother says, drawing my attention back to her. Her lip curls as though she's smelling something rotten. "A bride must take a young woman of her own blood into her bridegroom's house to bear witness to the ceremony and what comes after."

I glance at Lyria again. Not once have I heard her overtly referred to as my sister or any kind of relation. Only truly dire straits would convince my mother to do so now.

Lyria pushes off the doorpost and saunters into the room. Arms still crossed, she looks me up and down, shaking her head and clucking thoughtfully. Then she turns to the mage. "Your little glamour is weak. Anyone who's looked more than twice at Faraine will recognize her in a heartbeat."

"Let us be thankful the Shadow King has not spent significant time with the princess," Klaern snaps back.

Lyria's mouth crooks. "Are you sure about that?" She addresses my mother. "Does the king not have a more skilled magic-spinner on hand? Where's old Wistari?"

"Insolence!" Klaern bristles like an angry terrier. Even his well-trimmed beard seems to stand on end. "Mage Wistari has not my skill for glamorization. I have made it into an art form like no other, and I will not stand for—"

Lyria reaches out one long finger and deftly draws a shape directly into my cheek. I gasp at the biting spark and draw back sharply. But then I turn to the mirror. The right side of my face has changed. "Oh," I breathe, and holding up one hand, cover the left side. What remains visible is suddenly much more like Ilsevel than it had been a moment before. Painfully like. My heart twists.

"What?" Lyria says, standing behind me and meeting my gaze in the glass. "Did you think you four were the only gods-gifted in the family?"

Klaern hisses, his lips drawn back in a snarl, and turns to my mother. "Witch magic! Your Highness will not permit such base misuse of the *quinsatra's* gifts in my presence, will you?"

Mother, however, studies the altered reflection closely. Resentment roils inside her. She does not want to acknowledge any value in the daughter of her rival. But she knows better than to waste resources. "Can you do the rest?" she asks.

"Your Highness!" Klaern splutters.

Lyria's smile is smooth as butter. "Of course. Anything to serve."

"Do it then."

Ignoring the Miphato's protests, Lyria sets to work. She circles me, drawing little marks on my skin that burn briefly before sinking in, all the way to the bone. Unlike with Klaern's magic, which only influenced perception, this magic alters reality. It's strange, unsettling, but not exactly painful. I hold myself very still, trying not to flinch. Funny how I never considered the possibility that Lyria too might have received a gifting. Though she does not bear our father's name, she is nonetheless a king's daughter. How much do the gods care for things like legitimacy anyway?

"Now," Lyria says, standing in front of me. "The last part is always the most difficult. Close your eyes."

I obey. Lyria places one hand on the back of my head. The next moment I cry out in pain as she presses two fingers hard against my closed eyelids. The magic plunges deep, right to the center of my eyeballs, like two long pins. If not for her grip on my head, I would jerk away.

The pain is brief, but the weird sensation lingers even after Lyria draws back. "Have a look," she says.

Blinking against tears and rawness, I peer into the mirror. A pair of chocolate-brown eyes gaze back at me from a face so like Ilsevel's, it makes my heart stop and stutter. More tears brim, not from pain this time. They roll down my cheeks, mocking all efforts to dash them away.

"Not bad." Mother's voice is coldly approving as she bends to scrutinize Lyria's work. She pokes my cheek, my nose, and then uses two fingers to pull my eyelids open. "If I didn't know any better . . ." She doesn't finish the thought but looks up sharply. "Will it hold?"

"It should." Lyria shrugs. "She must not wash her face, however. Water will wash those runes on the eyes away at once, and the rest will hold for no more than an hour or two after. If you want something more permanent done, I can try. There's a good chance she'll end up stone blind, but—"

"No!" I say hastily.

To my relief, Mother echoes me: "Certainly not. We cannot send a blind girl to the Shadow King. Faraine must simply avoid water until after all is settled. It shouldn't be too difficult." With that, she steps back and draws her chin high. "Very good. You may send your mother in now."

Lyria offers a quick curtsy and slips from the room, casting Mage Klaern a last smug look as she goes. I blink in surprise and try to catch my mother's gaze. She won't look at me directly. Possibly because she does not want to see her dead daughter's face.

"Mother," I inquire softly, "why have you sent for Fyndra?"

Mother's throat tenses as though she's trying to swallow something nasty. When she speaks, however, her voice is calm. "It was your father's particular request. He wants that woman to instruct you in the art of seduction. For your wedding night."

My jaw drops. "What?"

Mother shoots me a bitter look. "Look at you, girl! Even with your sister's pretty face, you're so ill prepared for what awaits you. But make no mistake, you *must* secure this marriage. Kingdoms rise and fall in the bedchamber. If you fail to please your husband, do you think for a moment this alliance will survive?"

She's right. I drop my head, shoulders bowing. I am unprepared for what's coming, dreadfully so. I have practically no experience with men. The most sensual moment of my entire life thus far was the moment Vor took my hand and pressed his lips to my knuckles at our last parting. I'd experienced such a shock of sensation at that barest touch, it shot straight to the quick of my heart and left me trembling with desire.

Beyond that? I'm a complete novice. But somehow I must endure a wedding night without either betraying or disgracing myself.

"I understand, Mother," I say softly.

Mother nods once. Then, in a rustle of heavy skirts, she makes for the door. She's not quick enough; Fyndra appears in the doorway. She smiles prettily and sinks into a deep reverential curtsy before her queen. I don't need any gods-gifting to feel the white-hot animosity burning between the two. Mother sweeps past her without so much as a glance of acknowledgment.

Chuckling softly, Fyndra turns to me and utters a little squeak of surprise. "Bless my soul, I almost thought I saw a ghost!" She places a hand against her breast. "You do look so like your sister. Are you truly Princess Faraine?" Without waiting for an answer, she waves away Mage Klaern, who still lurks in the corner of the room. "No need for you to be here! Wouldn't want you sharing a lady's most intimate secrets among your fellows."

Klaern draws himself up haughtily and makes good his escape, casting me an unpleasant glare as he goes. Though I suspect that glare isn't for me so much as for Lyria's rune work.

Once the room is cleared, Fyndra draws a chair up beside me and takes a seat, settling her skirts grandly around her. "Now, my dear, your father has entrusted me with a sacred duty. I must make you ready for your first mounting."

My face heats as Fyndra's laugh rings out. I've scarcely exchanged more than two words with this woman over the course of my life. As soon as I was old enough to understand what role she played at court, I was also old enough to recognize just how much hurt she caused my mother. A daughter's natural loyalty made me resent the woman I perceived as coming between my parents. Later on, I easily picked up on Fyndra's feelings for me and my sisters. She puts on sweet smiles and fine displays of kindliness, but I don't need a gods-gift to see through to the rancor coloring her spirit. It's noxious.

"So, where to begin?" Fyndra says, tapping her full lip prettily. "To start with, you need to get it into that pretty little head of yours that it's not going to be pleasant. Not for you. So, any ideas of romance and delight you've been harboring—*ffffbt!*" She snaps her fingers. "Begone! Now tell me, are you aware of the basics? The mechanics of it all, I mean?"

I nod mutely.

"Well, that's something at least. But allow me to let you in on a few little secrets."

Fyndra goes on to describe certain aspects of the night to come that I had never before heard, sheltered as I've always been. My face grows warm and cold by turns, nausea swimming in my gut as her words batter my ears.

"Ultimately, it's all very simple. Your husband must be satisfied. That's all that matters. To him. And to you. But—now listen, child, this is important—your husband will be more satisfied if he believes he has satisfied you. Such is the fragility of manly ego. Which is why no matter what he does to you, no matter how badly it hurts, you must act as though you're enjoying yourself. Do you understand? Until the consummation is complete, it is your job to make him believe he is your everything; his happiness is your only desire. And you desire it *voraciously*."

She shows all her teeth in a great smile, then slowly licks her lips. When I turn away, pressing a hand to my stomach, Fyndra snorts. "Is it too much for you, delicate creature? Well, we none of us get to hold on to our delicacy for long. You've enjoyed yours far longer than I did mine. But I survived and eventually thrived. You can too if you listen closely."

From there, she vividly recounts techniques I might find useful. How to thrust my hips, how to arch my back, how to turn any whimpers of pain into moans of pleasure. She presents a little box, opens the lid, and shows me certain balms that may be used to help matters along.

"I shouldn't worry too much, of course," she finishes. "I've had a good look at your King Vor. No doubt such a magnificent specimen has taken plenty of lovers in his time. He'll bring his experience into the bedchamber. Which should relieve your maidenly mind no end!"

Perhaps it should. But it doesn't. If I'm honest, I would be happier knowing I wasn't the only novice in the room; would prefer to learn such intimacies *with* my partner rather than live wondering how I compared to those who came before me. It would be one thing if I too had known previous lovers. As it is, I hate feeling at such a disadvantage.

Gods on high, what am I going to do? Fyndra's instruction has filled me with more dread than confidence. How can I possibly fulfill everything expected of me? And all while deceiving the man I once thought I could . . . still wish I could . . .

"Now keep in mind," Fyndra's voice breaks through my thoughts, drawing me back into the present. "Men are like musical instruments. The music may be the same, but the method with which to make them sing is unique. It may be that your husband prefers a shy and shrinking bride. Even a frightened one. In which case, your night will be much simpler." She laughs then, tossing her bounteous hair. "Oh, the look on your face! Our woman's lot is hard. We must fight for everything we have. And the fight in the bedroom is the bitterest of all, for we cannot let them know how they wound us. But if we are clever, if we are skilled, if we learn and learn quickly, we may all be queens in our own right."

Her bitterness is sickening. I've never been close enough to Fyndra to get such a strong sense of her. She's always seemed so confident. Only now, in this moment, do I realize how thin that veneer of confidence is, and how vulnerable and sad is the woman underneath.

She goes on to give me a few more words of advice, enough to make me blush and clench my fists. I can do nothing but sit there and take it, try to accept it, try to let it sink in. Soon I'll be facing these moments she describes. Best to know what I'm in for.

At last, Fyndra rises and bobs a little curtsy. "I'll say a prayer for you to Nornala. After all, the fate of the kingdom rests on your . . ." Her gaze lowers to my lap, then slowly rises back to my face. ". . . shoulders."

The next moment, she's gone. I'm alone in the room, gazing at my sister's face before me in the mirror.

Ilsevel.

Would she forgive me for what I'm about to do? Would she thank me for doing it?

Oh, Ilsevel.

I cup my own cheek. In the mirror, my hand caresses my sister. But it's not Ilsevel's emotion that surges through my palm. There's only me. Alone. Lost. Drifting in a world suddenly devoid of hope.

Someone knocks. I drop my hand, surprised. They've been coming and going so much, men and women alike, without any care for my modesty or exhaustion. Why should anyone bother knocking now? "Enter," I say dully.

Lyria peeks in. "It's time," she says, looking me up and down before catching my gaze. "Larongar wants to perform the ceremony. Are you ready?"

I shake my head slowly. "I've never heard of this Law of Ap— Appela—"

"Appellative Benefaction?" Lyria supplies. "Oh, it's an old one—positively decrepit! It dates back to an age when kings required heirs to bear their names. Something to do with the oldest son carrying the life force of his father via his name or some such nonsense. Thus, if an oldest son was lost in battle or sickness before he took the throne, a younger male relative could, by law, be given his name and essentially *become* that son."

"But that doesn't apply here at all! I'm neither a son nor an heir."

She shrugs. "I believe the legal term for a situation like this is *close enough*. Come on then. Let's get it over with."

She leads me from the room, down the winding stairs, and out to the courtyard. There, Father stands with his council arrayed behind him and Mage Wistari at his elbow. He looks me over and, to my surprise, his face crumples with sudden pain. "As I live and breathe," he says thickly, "you're the very picture of my Ilsie."

I duck my head. For an instant I'd been foolish enough to think that jolt of emotion was for me. But no. My father mourns the loss of his favorite daughter. That is all.

The ceremony of Benefaction is performed. It's all a blur: a priest, a basin of water, a knife. Nine drops of blood, three from my hand, three from each of my parents. I'm made to repeat a vow, spoken for me in deep monotone. The blood is smeared across my brow, then wiped away with a pure white cloth.

When it's all over, Father stands back, looks me hard in the eye, and says, "Ilsevel Cyhorn, do you understand what is required of you? Will you perform your duty to crown and country?"

"I will, my king." I sink into a curtsy, my head inclined. As I rise, however, I cannot help trying one last time. "Father, please. I understand I must take Ilsevel's name. But I beg you, do not send me with this face. Let me explain to the Shadow King what has happened. Let me—"

"Silence." Father looks at me like I'm some sort of worm, then turns from me to Mage Klaern, standing by. "Be vigilant. Take care that she does nothing to compromise this alliance."

Klaern nods. It is he who takes my hand and leads me to the carriage. Lyria is already there, waiting for me. She helps to bundle my long skirts in behind me, then climbs in herself and takes a seat on the opposite bench. I lean to one side, peer out the window. Theodre is riding on horseback, gorgeous in golden raiment and tall black boots. Mage Klaern climbs up to ride beside the driver.

I lift my eyes to my parents standing still at the top of the stair. Mother meets my gaze solemnly. When I raise my hand to her, she offers a short nod.

"Remember," Father calls out, "it all depends on you, girl. Save your people. Make this alliance secure."

While his words yet ring against the courtyard stones, the driver whips his horses into motion. With a lurch and a rumble, the carriage rolls into motion, and we pass under the arch of the gate, leaving Beldroth behind.

20

Vor

Our bargeman steers the craft up to the landing, settling it neatly so that there's barely any gap. We step from the gently bobbing barge onto more solid footing, wobbling a little as we adjust our balance.

Before us lies the town of Dugorim, a trolde holding some five leagues downriver of Mythanar. It shines beneath the peak glow of lusterling, its winding streets busy with life and commerce. The people of Dugorim are primarily miners, hunters after that rare *virmaer* ore that is so prized among the fae lords and ladies of Eledria. Lady Xag, mistress of this town, has grown quite wealthy off fae greed.

The lady herself stands at the end of the dock. She is a sight to behold, with perfectly chiseled features; plump, full lips; and sumptuous curves almost carelessly clad in the richest *hugagug* silk. Towering over everyone in the vicinity, she's like some sensual warrior angel brought to life. Her pure white hair is styled in a coiled crown on top of her head, lending her still more height. Beside her, Hael looks positively petite.

Sul steps off the barge and staggers. "Gods smite me!" he hisses. "You didn't tell her we were coming, did you?"

I glance his way, my mouth tipped in a wry grin. "Are you more afraid she'll wallop you or kiss you, brother?"

"Oh, the latter. Infinitely." Sul pivots as though to climb back on the barge and finds himself face-to-face with my captain. "Ah! Hael, darling. Do us a favor and put me out of my misery before that woman gets her hands on me, will you?"

Hael shoulders past him onto the dock. Yok hastens after, a little awkward and still favoring his wounded arm. "What's wrong with Lady Xag?" he asks innocently.

"Nothing," I say. "Only that she's in love with Sul."

"But then, aren't they all?" Sul heaves a long-suffering sigh. "It's the price of such beauty, I fear. The ladies cannot help themselves."

"Enough, Sul."

I take care not to so much as glance Hael's way as I lead them swiftly down the dock to shore. Lady Xag extends her muscular arms and beams a smile upon me. The next moment I'm caught in her embrace. She's taller than me by a good head and squishes me against her enormous bosom, lifting me right off my feet.

"Your Majesty!" she cries, her voice booming all the way to the *lorst* crystals high above. "Welcome back to my humble home. I've been preparing for your arrival and will escort you to the gate myself."

"Oh, that's not at all necessary, Lady Xag." I manage to pry myself free of her grasp and step back to regain my balance. "I know the way, and I wouldn't want to take you from your daily duties."

"Nonsense! I'm always glad of an excuse to ride. It's not every day one's king goes world-walking and brings back a new queen, am I right?" With this she turns from me to Hael and Yok, approaching behind me. Her mouth twists, and she rises on her toes, looking over their heads. "Ah! Sul!" she cries, not in the least concerned who among the river workers might overhear her. "It's no use trying to escape now I've spotted you. Am I too soon to hope the drums played for your brother's wedding will put ideas into *your* head? Surely it's time you settled down!"

Sul makes a flying leap to Hael's side, avoiding Xag's grasping arm. "Hide me!" he yelps.

Hael sneers at him, but Lady Xag laughs. "I heard that!" she says, and punches Sul in the shoulder. "Mark my words, little Prince, one of these days I'm going to chase you down in the *marhg*. When I've got you in my arms at last, we'll see what you think of that!"

"Romance by blood sport." Sul shudders. "How delightful."

Still laughing, Xag calls for our morleth to be brought up from the barge. They've traveled in shadow form but take on solid substance the instant their hooves hit the shore. She's had her own morleth brought down to the river as well, and we are soon all four mounted. "Is this all your party?" she asks.

I look over my small band—Sul, Hael, and Yok. I'd wanted to bring only my brother and captain, but Yok was so eager to go, and Madame Ar cleared him for duty, stating his arm was as good as new. I hadn't the heart to tell him no. This journey to the Between Gate is neither long nor arduous, after all, and there's no reason to expect trouble along the way.

"It's enough," I respond.

Xag tuts and spurs her morleth into motion, leading the way up from the river and through the streets of town. "I would have thought you'd want to show off a little. Throw a parade or some such for the human princess."

"There will be plenty of time for celebrating once we reach Mythanar," I answer with an easy shrug. The truth is, I don't want to frighten poor Ilsevel more than necessary. I know the passage through the Between Gate will be difficult enough as it is. This beautiful world of ours will be a nightmare to her human senses. I hope to give her a chance to adjust without hundreds of watching eyes analyzing her every move and expression.

Before Xag can press me further, I ask, "Will you be joining us at the ceremony tomorrow?"

"That depends. Will there be dancing and feasting and riotous revelries?"

I smile. "Do you doubt it?"

She casts me a sidelong glance. "Hard to say. You've always been such a serious fellow. If it were that pretty brother of yours, now, that's a different story!" Xag turns in her saddle, shooting a blinding grin back at Sul. "Once he and I have performed our hunt and swum the *yunkathu* waters, you can bet the revelry will be riotous enough to bring the crystals crashing down on our heads!"

Sul hunches in his saddle and mutters loud enough for all to hear, "Gods spare me from the love of powerful women."

Hael maintains a stoic expression even as Xag laughs again, throwing her beautiful head back. She's so confident in her purpose, part of me won't be at all surprised if she manages to snare my brother in the end. For Hael's sake, I hope I'm wrong about that, but it might be better for my brave captain to give up her impossible infatuation. Sul would make her a terrible husband.

We leave the streets of Dugorim behind and make our way into the forest above the town. Xag takes the lead, guiding us between the tall smooth trunks, following a trail I can scarcely discern. The air is alive with the hum of *olk*, which dart shyly from our path, leaving trails of glittering dust in their wake.

"I always forget how beautiful it is here," I say, breathing deep of the sweetly perfumed air.

"Aye, it's the prettiest spot in all the Under Realm if you ask me."

There's pride in Xag's voice, but something else as well. Something that makes me turn and study her as she rides by my side. "What's troubling you?"

She lifts an eyebrow and casts me a sidelong glance. "Oh, I don't know if I should mention it just now. What with you on your way to fetch your bride and all. Don't want to put a damper on the joyous occasion."

"You can't very well drop a hint like that and expect me not to pursue it. Come, my lady. Out with it. You may as well tell me."

"Is it your sovereign command?"

"If you like."

"Very well." She draws a long breath, then leans in her saddle so she can lower her voice, though I rather suspect the three behind us hear her loud and clear. "Have the stirrings been bad in Mythanar recently?"

I nod grimly. "They've been increasing in intensity, yes. But not what I'd call *bad*. Not yet anyway. Why?"

"Did you feel the stirring last dimness?"

"Yes." My mouth goes dry. "We felt it."

I'd woken in my bed to feel the whole room shake. It had lasted only a few seconds, and the damage was minimal. The palace cook claimed a few bits of crockery were broken, and Master Vret, the building master, reported a few new hairline cracks in the foundations. Nothing more.

"Well," Xag says, "it was big enough here that a portion of the south wall caved in, burying five houses. I've got people even now hard at work digging folks free. There's a new crack running through the town center as well that wasn't there yesterday. Folk are saying they smell *raog* poison rising from it."

My heart goes cold. This is serious news indeed. "And have you seen any signs of *raog* poison yourself?"

"No. But I've been having strange dreams lately."

"How do you mean?"

She bites her full lower lip. "I don't like to say. They're . . . bad. And I wake to find I've done things while sleeping. Things I regret." She drops her gaze to the pommel of her saddle, her fingers playing with strands of coarse morleth hair. "I had a pretty little *olk* pet, you know. Sweet thing, would perch on my shoulder. Liked to hum from lusterling to dimness. Drove me batty, but it was such a nice little creature."

She goes silent for a long minute, leaving me wondering how any of this pertains. I'm just about to question her further when she speaks again all in a rush: "I woke this morning to find its wings were in shreds. Little bits and pieces, spread across the floor. I found it in the corner of the room, all curled up on itself. Dead."

I frown. "What could have done such a thing?"

"That's just it! There was no one in the room but me. Just me and the little *olk*. Bip, I called it. But it was all torn to bits, poor thing, poor thing . . ."

We ride on, her words echoing dully in the silence between us. My stomach is a stone in my gut. Xag is such a great soul, so full of life and vim and laughter. I've never even seen her in a bad mood. This heaviness now bowing her shoulders feels wrong.

We reach a crest in the road. I turn in my saddle, gazing down on the village below us. All that life, all that bustling energy. But ah! There, off to the south, I see the scar in the cavern wall where the avalanche took place. Much of that bustling energy isn't miners about their business, but rescuers attempting to dig out their friends and family. I ought to be helping them. I ought to ride down there right now, hauling boulders, scraping dirt.

But no. I face forward through the trees, setting my jaw grimly. No, I'm doing what I must for those people. Right here. Right now.

The Between Gate comes abruptly into view, standing in a clearing in the middle of the forest. It's a great round arch, tall enough for three Lady Xags to balance on each other's shoulders beneath the highest point. Flat-headed fungi cling to the ancient stones in profusion, faintly pulsing with living light.

"Ho there, Kol!" Xag calls out. "Wake up, you old boulder. Your king is nigh!"

One of the fungus-covered stones at the base of the gate moves, stretches, and stands up into the form of a stoop-shouldered trolde. He grins, flashing gemstone teeth at us, and offers me a double-fisted salute. I answer with a nod. "How do you fare, Kol?"

"Can't complain, Majesty," the old gate warden rumbles in response. He moves to the large stone dial affixed to the wall behind him. "Will you be traveling to the human world again today?" He asks it as though I go world-walking as a general rule. In truth, I've only ever ventured beyond the Under Realm a handful of times, and then usually to the other Eledrian Courts. The human world has never held much appeal to me, despite my heritage.

"Yes, Kol. Thank you," I say.

Kol begins to turn the dial. The air beneath the arc shimmers with magic awakened. It's a strange sensation, for though I can see the forest on the far side of the arc, I feel different air blowing through. The sudden largeness of expanding worlds opens before me, layer after layer of realities, like doors flinging wide.

Young Yok curses behind me. This is only his third time traveling between worlds. In many ways the second time is worse, for you know what to expect but haven't yet built up a tolerance. I cast him an encouraging smile. "Go on then, Yok! Lead the way."

The boy grimaces but sets his shoulders bravely and spurs his morleth forward. The beast tosses its head, irked at being made to travel back into the human world, but Yok gets it under control. They pass through the opening and vanish.

Hael goes next, her sword drawn. One never knows exactly what one will meet on the other side of the gate, after all. Sul follows her, tossing a last look back at me before he goes. "Coming, Vor? Or are you getting cold feet?"

"I'll be there," I say. Sul shrugs and passes through, disappearing into the rippling curtain of magic. I turn to the woman beside me. "I promise, I'll look into these events, Lady Xag. And I hope I will soon have means to offer real help."

"I pray to the Deeper Dark you're right," she answers softly.

I spur my beast into motion, approaching the gate arc. The heat of living magic warms my skin and makes my morleth flare his nostrils and show his vicious canines. "Steady, Knar," I say, patting his ugly neck. "Steady."

Then we pass under the arc and are ripped from our reality and sent hurtling across the worlds.

21

Faraine

They say the Between Gates simply appeared one day. That was five hundred years ago now. Our world has never been the same since. No one knows from whence they came or who built them. There are legends aplenty of course—all elaborate and complicated and contradictory, possibly each containing a small piece of the truth but never the whole.

Peering out the carriage window at the enormous arch dominating the landscape, I cannot help thinking it must be of fae make. The engineering involved in that construction is simply so far beyond anything I've ever before seen. Then again, aren't the fae notoriously incapable of *making* things of their own? So perhaps not fae then.

Perhaps it's trolde engineering.

The gate stands in a broad empty plain, incongruous and eerie. A white wall extends as far as the eye can see on either side. Is it truly that endless or merely glamoured to appear so? I wonder if it's possible to go around the wall and if anyone has ever tried. Going over it seems impossible—it's so tall and sheer. One would have to fly. I spy a flock of starlings passing overhead and watch to see if they vanish once they cross over the wall. But they don't. They fly on and away through red-streaked sky.

Our party rolls to a stop directly before the gate arch. The Shadow King and his people have not yet arrived, but that's no surprise. No doubt they will time their appearance for after sundown.

People set to work at once, making ready for the meeting. A pavilion is set up. When I am finally let out of the carriage, groaning and stretching my sore back, they bustle me inside. Lyria joins me and helps me peel out of my travel gown, down to my shift. Then she pinches my chin between her fingers and turns my face from side to side. "The spells seem to be holding. You've stayed away from water?"

"Yes." After three days of hard travel on lonely roads, I'm definitely feeling the worse for it. "How am I supposed to go through with a wedding night if I stink like an unwashed pig?"

Lyria clucks and pulls something from the depths of her voluminous sleeve. It looks like a bottle of scent, but when she undoes the stopper, my nostrils are assaulted by a strong whiff of magic. "This will help," she says, and douses me from head to toe. It leaves behind no scent but more of a sudden *absence*—as though all the topmost layers of aroma clinging to my body have been peeled away, leaving simple, unobtrusive cleanliness beneath.

"That's better," Lyria says, then sets to work scrubbing my bare limbs down with a dry cloth. It's rough work, and I feel ill-used. But by the time she's done with me, my skin is soft and glowing in the lantern light.

Lyria helps me dress in a gown of blush pink covered in delicate beadwork. The billowing sleeves are gathered by three silver bands:

one on my upper arm, one at my elbow, the other close to my wrist. The effect looks like wings, and the soft fabric flutters with the barest movement.

"Why the bother?" I ask, as Lyria fastens the last silver band around my left wrist. "Trolde tradition dictates I must be stripped of all my worldly belongings and enter my husband's world with only those gifts he has given me, right? If that's the case, what's the use of dressing me up like this?"

Lyria grunts. "You're a princess. Larongar can't very well turn you over to your new master in a dirty old travel gown, now can he?" She fastens a beaded veil to my hair, then steps back, looking me over. "That'll do. Now you wait here. When the trolde arrive, they'll send one of their women in to strip you down, inspect your body, and help you into whatever garment they've brought for you. I'll be on hand for the whole procedure to make certain nothing goes amiss. Don't worry—she won't sense the magic. Some of those runes I planted in your face were also disguises on those reeking Miphates spells."

Up until this moment, I'd never considered the possibility that this whole ruse could come undone here and now. My stomach knots despite Lyria's reassurances.

I'm given a chair to sit in. And I wait. Lyria leaves me at some point, and Klaern takes the opportunity to slip in, poking and prodding my face as though it belongs to a statue, not a person. He mutters viciously over Lyria's witch magic, only to cringe like a scolded dog when she catches him at it. She holds the door flap open and orders him out with all the dignity of a queen. He casts her a dirty look, which she answers with a simpering smile. Then, lifting her eyebrows at me, she steps out behind the mage, leaving me alone again.

Time crawls by, one moment listlessly pursuing the next. I wish Lyria would return. Or Theodre or even Mage Klaern. Anything would be better than being left with my own thoughts. At least from behind these curtains I detect only the vaguest impressions of the simmering mood without. All that roiling anxiety mingled with occasional spikes of true fear. The trip from Beldroth put us all on edge. Over the last three days, I've had an eyeful of just how bad this part of the country has been hit by Prince Ruvaen's forces. This territory is much too near his stronghold to be safe. But it's the only Between Gate in all of Gavaria. It's not as though we have any choice.

I try to settle my mind, to pray. But I keep thinking, *What if he doesn't come?*

Or worse still, *What if he does?*

My bridegroom.

Ilsevel's bridegroom.

Gods on high, how am I going to do this?

A sudden change in the atmosphere cuts through my awareness. At first I can't describe it, can't quite be certain it's even real. Then the ground beneath my feet begins to rumble. Voices outside are talking all in a muddle, and the anxiety I felt before triples in intensity. I jump from my chair, gripping the folds of my gown so hard, the delicate beadwork bites into my flesh. I want to run to the pavilion flap and peer out, but I've been given strict instruction to stay inside.

The rumbling ceases. Have the trolde arrived? I draw a long breath, hold it for a count of three. Then I creep to the door flap, tilting my head, listening to the muffled voices outside. Theodre's voice first, high and nervous. Then a deep, growling trolde voice answers. Could it be Vor? I cannot discern the words.

A footstep sounds close by. With a little gasp, I spring back to the middle of the pavilion and take my seat, assuming what I hope is a composed posture. At the last moment I remember to lower the beaded veil over my face.

The door flap opens. A trolde woman appears. I recognize her—it's the same woman who served as part of Vor's entourage when he visited Beldroth. I don't recall her name, but I certainly remember the stony skin creeping up her neck and the lower right side of her jaw. Despite this deformity, she is imposing and beautiful after the pale trolde fashion.

She steps inside and offers me a graceful bow. When she straightens, she pounds her chest, one fist after the other, a trolde salute. How am I supposed to respond? Ilsevel no doubt received preparation for this moment, but I'm totally lost. I merely incline my head, hoping the trolde woman cannot see how hard I'm shaking.

Lyria enters next, carrying a small box under one arm, and pulls the door flap shut behind her. When the trolde woman looks at her, she nods and indicates with a wave of her hand that she may approach me.

"My name is Hael," the woman says, drawing near. "Captain Hael of the king's guard. He has specially requested I serve as your lady."

My lady? I blink. I've only ever heard the term in reference to a lady-in-waiting. That doesn't seem likely, considering Hael's warlike aspect, her armor, her sword. Perhaps she means bodyguard?

Hael turns to Lyria, who offers her the box. The trolde woman opens the lid and withdraws folds of soft, shimmering lavender fabric. She holds it up. It's a gown . . . though hardly like any gown I've ever worn. It's a trolde gown: a single layer of clinging fabric that billows out in a long trailing skirt. No petticoats or undergarments required. The thought of wearing such a garment makes my cheeks heat.

"If you will permit me, Princess Ilsevel?" Hael says, dropping the gown back in the box. "I will assist you."

I bite my lip. Then, with a short nod, I stand and hold out my arms. Hael begins unfastening the silver bands which Lyria only just fastened. Next she unlaces the bodice, then guides the sleeves off my arms and lets the whole gown drop in a pile at my feet. I step out of the pink, beaded mound, shivering, and Hael begins her inspection. She lifts my arms, runs her hands down my flesh, poking, prodding. It's all very cold and clinical. Prickles rise on the back of my neck. At any moment she'll detect the magic. I'm sure of it.

But she doesn't.

At last the trolde woman reaches for my veil. My heart leaps. "Oh, wait—" I begin.

Before I can blurt out anything more, Lyria steps forward and touches Hael's arm. The trolde woman turns sharply, and her hand moves to the knife at her belt. But Lyria smiles placatingly. "It's our tradition," she says, "that the bride's face not be seen save by her husband until the consummation is complete. Then she is made new as his bride and may be revealed to him and to all."

Hael narrows her eyes. "This is a human tradition?"

"Yes."

"She is a trolde bride."

Lyria shrugs. "But she is still human. If your trolde king is to take a human for his wife, he must accept her humanness even as she must accept his troldeness. Yes?"

Hael considers, her gaze moving from Lyria to me and back

again. "She may wear the veil outside the pavilion. But first, I must ascertain that this is indeed my king's true bride."

The time has come. In the next moment, the lie may well be undone and the alliance right along with it. And I can't even decide if I'm hoping Hael will see through the spells or not.

The trolde woman lifts my veil, her gaze running over my face. I feel her strength of will. She is determined to serve her king, to protect him in any way possible. Vor is lucky to have such a woman in his service.

As for me? My heart seems to have stopped beating.

At last Hael grunts. She lets the veil drop and takes a step back. "There is no spot or mark on this bride."

I let out a breath I'd not realized I was holding. Before I can draw another, the trolde woman has gone, stepping from the pavilion to report to her king. The bridal exchange will proceed.

My knees give out. Lyria steps in quickly, gripping my arm, offering silent support. The touch of her hand against my bare flesh stabs through my senses. She's afraid. Far more afraid than I realized. But when I turn and catch her eye, something else reaches me as well: an unexpected protectiveness. It's there for just an instant. When she blinks it's gone, replaced by her usual resentment.

"Almost there," Lyria whispers. Though we both know it's far from the truth.

Hael returns to help me dress in the trolde gown. A simple process compared to the layers and lacings of my own gown, but I find it very strange. The bodice is rather like a corset but fitted right against my skin with no smock beneath. My shoulders are left bare, but sheer sleeves drape from my upper arms in swaths of shimmering fabric to gather at my wrists. The skirt is full and hangs in straight folds with no underskirts to give it body. It's so light, I fear I will soon freeze to death.

Hael seems to notice my trembling. "Don't worry, Princess," she says, her accent strong as she sounds out the words of my language. "It is much warmer in the Under Realm than here."

"Well, let's get on with things then, shall we?" Lyria snaps.

Hael nods and fastens a belt around my waist. It's set with violet gemstones that change to green when light glints across their faceted surfaces. I cannot resist running my fingers across them, admiring. Such an item would be worth a king's ransom in Gavaria. I wonder what my father would think if he knew his daughter was presented with such a gift.

A gift intended for Ilsevel. Never forget.

Last of all, Hael places the veil back over my face. It's not the right style with a gown like this, but I'm grateful for the little bit of covering it provides over my shoulders.

"Here, Princess," Lyria says, stepping forward suddenly. She holds out her hand, and I'm surprised to see my crystal pendant resting in her palm with its coil of silver chain. It must have fallen off when Hael was assisting me out of my gown. I reach for it gratefully.

Hael steps in the way. "You are not to take any items with you on the wedding journey. This must be sent for later."

My heart lurches to my throat. My pendant? Somehow it had not occurred to me I would have to leave it behind. How will I cope without it? I've depended on its inner vibrations for years now to help me manage the dark side of my gods-gift. My mouth opens, protests dying unspoken on my lips. I dare not fight, dare not draw unnecessary attention to myself. Not here. Not now. But if I don't . . .

"Your tradition states that a bride may bring nothing with her that does not belong to her husband, is that not so?" Lyria speaks up suddenly.

Hael casts her a wary glance and nods.

"Well, that settles it. This necklace is from Mythanar. So really, Princess Ilsevel is taking it home."

"From Mythanar? Truly?" Hael's brow puckers as Lyria holds the stone up for her inspection. After a moment she nods. "I had not realized. That is an *urzul* stone." She purses her lips, casting me a wary glance. "And how did you come by it, Princess?"

"I don't actually remem—"

"It was with the other wedding gifts, of course," Lyria answers smoothly. "Your King Vor did send such a lot of them, but this piece caught my cousin's eye out of the lot. So, you see? No reason she should not keep it now."

Hael grunts an acknowledgment. To my utmost relief, she makes no further protest. Lyria helps fasten the necklace in place. I press my palm against it, closing my eyes as the subtle vibration purrs. Then I glance quickly at Lyria, sending her my silent thanks. Does she realize what the stone means to me? Her expression is masked in a pleasant smile, but when she catches my eye, the corner of her mouth twitches ever so slightly. She's certainly not my friend, but she is my ally.

I stand tall as Hael makes her final inspection, circling me, adjusting the set of the gown, the laces, the way the belt hangs. She's surprisingly finicky for a warrior. At last, she steps back and nods.

"You are ready, Princess. Come. Your bridegroom awaits." With that she opens the door flap, holding it aside and motioning for me to step through.

I look to Lyria again, searching for some support, some comfort. But my half sister is busy studying her nails. Whatever happens next, I must face it alone.

Drawing a deep breath, I duck my head and step out of the pavilion into the night.

22

Vor

Larongar has sent thirty horsemen. All fitted out with armor and many of them carrying magic-laced weapons. Also, to one side stands a Miphato, grim and silent, with a spellbook tucked under his arm.

"And you still think it was a wise idea to bring just us three?" Sul mutters as we watch Hael pass between two rows of armed men on her way to the pavilion.

"We have no need for a show of force," I reply. "Larongar must protect his daughter. Theirs was a long journey across the country. These men are a testimony to his love for her."

"A testimony to his fear of Prince Ruvaen, more like." Sul catches my quick glance. "What? It's not a bad thing, is it? It means Larongar is desperate. Another man's desperation is a powerful tool. For the first time, I think there might be some wisdom in this madcap marriage plot of yours."

I grunt. Hael has reached the pavilion entrance, where a woman in a long cloak greets her. Hael holds a box containing the first of my wedding gifts for Ilsevel—a gown and a jeweled belt, fashioned by Mythanar dressmakers after trolde fashion but to fit her more petite human measurements. The woman opens the lid, inspects the contents, and nods. She waves a hand for Hael to enter, then follows after, still carrying the box.

The human men stand with their backs to the pavilion, facing out into the night. At first, I think it merely a defensive stance. Then a lantern flares inside the tent, illuminating the interior and casting silhouetted shadows against the curtained walls. I recognize Hael's tall figure and that of the woman with the box. A third figure sits in a chair in the center of the pavilion. Ilsevel.

My gaze locks upon that shadow. I find myself striving to make something of it, to discern some feeling from that featureless impression. As difficult as this situation is for me, I know it is ten times worse for her. It is she who must leave behind her friends and family, everyone and everything she knows, for a strange new world where she is surrounded by people who do not share her face, her history, even her language. And none of this by her own choice. Of that I am too painfully aware.

I'll make it right for her. Just as I promised her sister. I'll treat her well. I'll make her happy.

The seated shadow rises, holds out her arms. Hael steps forward, and for a moment I don't quite realize what's happening. Then the gown slips from the girl's body, and I'm presented with the silhouette of a naked female form.

Heat rushes through my body. Drawing a short breath, I turn my back, one hand resting on my morleth's shoulder. Feeling watchful eyes upon me, I catch Sul's gaze. He smirks and waggles his eyebrows. Beyond him, Yok still stares at the pavilion. I clear my throat. The boy visibly starts, then whirls on his heels so fast that his morleth growls and yanks its head, nearly pulling its reins free.

Sul barks a laugh. "Best be the last time you're caught ogling your queen, little pip."

"I wasn't!" Yok looks to me, his nostrils flaring. "I swear, Your Majesty, I wouldn't—"

"Peace, Yok. I don't doubt your honor. Just try to be a little more aware of where your eyes fall, yes?" I shoot a glare at my brother. "Leave the boy alone. And turn around yourself, why don't you?"

Sul snorts. But he puts his back to the pavilion, sighing languidly. "I've said it before, and I'll say it again: Vor, my brother, you're going to squash that little slip of a woman like a *jiru* berry. *Pop!*"

"Sul?"

"Yes?"

"If you speak one word more, I will personally put your nose through the back of your head."

He opens his mouth, thinks better of it, and shrugs. Instead, he devotes his attention to the cuticles of one hand, tunelessly humming a traditional wedding song all the while.

I release a long sigh and face the Between Gate. Above me, the sky slowly spins, its distant stars twinkling like tiny *lorst* crystals as they pursue their heavenly dance. My stomach pitches with awareness of that huge emptiness. I close my eyes and try to draw the image of Ilsevel's face to mind. We'd known each other for such a short time, I can't recall many details. She was beautiful, I do remember that. Her eyes were dark and suspicious, but they sparkled when she laughed. Her feet were light, her hands graceful. And her singing. Now, that I recall well enough. Her singing was like no other.

I could come to love a voice like that. Surely.

"Your Majesty."

I look back over my shoulder. Hael hastens through the line of armed men, approaches me, and offers a sharp salute. "I've inspected the offered bride, Your Majesty. She is certainly Ilsevel Cyhorn. She appears to be unharmed, unblemished, and sound of body and mind."

I nod. "Very good, Hael. Please, proceed."

Hael hesitates. "There's just one thing."

"Yes?"

"Human tradition dictates she must wear a veil over her face. Apparently, none should see her until the marriage is finalized."

My brow puckers slightly. This had not been communicated to me earlier. "And you are certain the girl beneath the veil is Ilsevel?"

"I am, sire. I saw her face clearly."

"Very well. Let her wear a veil then. We must embrace the traditions of her people even as we guide her into our own."

Hael nods and returns to the pavilion. I spare a single swift glance for the lantern-lit walls, glimpsing the slim form standing with her arms wrapped around herself. Either out of modesty or simple cold, I cannot guess. I face away once more. My morleth paws the ground and snorts, shooting out streams of billowing steam.

"Taking long enough," Sul growls, forgetting my earlier warning.

I cast him a wry look. "Nervous, brother?"

"No, just damn cold."

Yok flashes a devious grin. "Eager to return to Lady Xag's warm embrace, eh? Ow!" He yelps and leaps back, rubbing his ear where Sul clipped him.

"Let that be a lesson to you," Sul says smoothly. "Children are to be seen and not heard."

Yok mutters darkly but doesn't push his luck. We stand in silence for some moments before there's movement behind us. I turn in time to see Hael exiting the pavilion. She speaks to Prince Theodre. I watch the prince breathe an audible sigh of relief. Which is odd. What had he feared would go wrong?

Before I have a chance to consider this question more closely, my bride appears. She's clad in the gown I'd ordered for her—lavender *hugagug* silk, trimmed in living gems, belted at the waist. The bodice hugs her figure, pushing up her breasts and displaying her round, soft shoulders. The skirt clings to her hips, her thighs, and floats from the knees, trailing in gentle ripples behind her with each step. Even with that odd, beaded veil covering her face, the effect is very troldish.

She's beautiful. I'd forgotten just how beautiful.

And soon she will be mine.

Theodre offers her his arm. She seems to waver before lightly dropping her fingers along his wrist. They progress through the guard, who hold up their arms in crisp salute. Hael and the other woman trail behind them.

I hope my face reveals nothing as I watch their approach. My head is a storm of feelings which I cannot arrange in any coherent form. Now that she's here, I feel a hunger I've rarely allowed myself to acknowledge roaring inside me. With that hunger comes shame. For I must take her, am eager to take her. Eager to know her as my wife, to discover the delights of the flesh promised to married couples. But I do not love her.

Curse that veil of hers! I should have refused to allow it, for it hides her face, preventing me from discerning any trace of her own feelings. Is she glad to see me? Is she angry, resentful, hopeful, fearful? Merely resigned? I cannot know, cannot even guess. And we will not have a moment for private conversation until we meet in the bridal chamber. At which point we are not expected to talk.

I draw a deep breath and compose my face into stoic lines as Theodre leads his sister to me. He holds her hand out like an offering. "King Vor, allow me to present your bride—Ilsevel Cyhorn."

I can almost discern the shape of her eyes through the elaborate beadwork. She seems to be gazing up at me. The air is suddenly caught in a frozen moment of stillness. As though some decision is even now being made. A decision that will determine the rest of my life.

Slowly, she sinks into a curtsy.

"No, no," I say. She looks up sharply, frightened. I smile, trying to make my expression kindly as I extend a hand to her. "You need not make obeisance to me. You are my bride. It is I who must honor you."

She hesitates. Slowly, she lets go of Theodre and places her hand in mine, allowing me to help her rise. I bow deeply and kiss her knuckles. For just an instant, as my eyes close, I step back into the cold, winter-locked garden at Beldroth. And it's Faraine's hand I hold; Faraine's fingers pressed against my lips. Faraine's shocked gaze I meet as I lift my head.

But there's no Faraine now. Just that beaded veil and that impression of a face studying me closely from behind it.

I rise, still smiling determinedly. She tilts her head, her hand trembling in my grasp. "I greet you in the name of Nornala, King Vor," she says in a low voice somewhat muffled from behind the beadwork. "It is my honor and my joy to become your wife."

There's no joy in her voice. The words are rote, heavy. We stand there looking at one another, neither of us daring to make the next move.

Theodre clears his throat loudly. "Well, go ahead then. Take her, why don't you?"

I turn to the human prince, glad to have my attention diverted. "The wedding ceremony will take place immediately upon our arrival in Mythanar. You may expect the return of your eyewitness in two days' time." I glance at Ilsevel. "Have you said your goodbyes?"

"I've said everything I wish to say," she responds coolly without so much as a glance for Theodre.

With a last nod to the prince, I lead Ilsevel to my mount. She doesn't falter, much to my surprise. Most would flinch upon first encountering a beast as awful and savage as a morleth. But then, Ilsevel is a brave creature. Or so I've been told.

"Wait a moment. Wait a gods-blighted moment. How am I supposed to get up on that thing?"

The sharp voice draws my attention to Hael's morleth, standing close by. The other woman, the one who'd been in the pavilion with Hael and my bride, stands there with her arms crossed, her expression mulish and just a little frightened. I was so concentrated on Ilsevel that I'd spared no attention for her companion. Only now do I realize she's not timid little Princess Aurae but a stranger.

Frowning, I turn to Theodre. "I was given to understand that my bride's sister would be joining our party as witness for Gavaria. Is that not so?"

Ilsevel catches a short breath. When I glance her way, she drops her head. Have I offended her somehow?

"Oh, yes." Theodre twists the ring on his left middle finger. "Princess Aurae was . . . indisposed. Our, er, cousin was chosen to take her place. Allow me to present Lady Lyria."

I take a second look at the other woman. I find human faces a little difficult to differentiate sometimes, but there's certainly something about her that reminds me of the Cyhorn daughters. Something in the brow, perhaps, or the line of the jaw. I nod slowly. "Very well. Welcome to our party, Lady Lyria. You will be safe riding with Captain Hael, I assure you."

"And how do you expect me to get up there?" Lyria demands. "Am I to jump?"

"I'll help you up," Sul says smoothly, sidling over to leer at her over the back of the morleth. "I'm quite good with my hands, let me assure you."

"Back off, Sul," Hael growls. She addresses the lady, bowing her head respectfully. "I can assist you into the saddle, my lady. It is no trouble." She crouches and offers her hands for a leg up. Lady Lyria looks as though she'd like to protest, but when she catches my brother's lascivious smirk, she grabs a handful of mane, places her foot in Hael's palms, and pulls herself into the saddle. She very nearly goes over the other side, but Sul catches and steadies her. "There, see? Told you: good with my hands."

Lyria casts him a sweet smile. "And if you'd like to keep both of them attached to your arms, you'll remove them from my person at once."

"Step away, Sul," I snap. Not waiting to see if my command is carried out, I return my attention to Ilsevel. She stands still and silent, so impossible to read. My morleth swings its heavy head around, flashing its sharp teeth at her, and shakes its head so hard, every silver buckle of its bridle rattles. Ilsevel draws back a step. I put out a hand, touching the small of her back. She straightens at once, pulling away from me.

My gut tightens uncomfortably. This is so much harder than I anticipated. "Don't be afraid," I say softly. "Knar is a fright to look upon, but he's really gentle as a lamb, I swear. In time, I'll teach you to ride a morleth of your own. Would that please you?"

She turns her head, the beads of her veil winking in the lantern light. Slowly she nods. Just once. "Thank you, my king." So stiff, so formal.

"With your permission," I continue, "may I lift you into the saddle? You'll ride in front of me. It's very safe, I promise."

She nods and turns to me. Her hands rest on my shoulders as I take hold of her waist. It's not difficult to lift her—she weighs so little. She settles herself on the low pommel, grabbing a handful of dark mane for balance. She looks much more comfortable than I might have expected for a first time on morlethback. I swing up into the saddle behind her, wrapping one arm around her middle as I take hold of the reins. She leans back against me, and . . . Gods damn me, why must I again be reminded so acutely of her sister? If I didn't know any better, I should think it was Faraine in my arms again, not Ilsevel.

But this is wrong. I must purge such thoughts from my head. Now. Forever. Closing my eyes for a moment, I breathe out a prayer. Then I look down at the girl in front of me. My view is rather too good, straight down the front of that low-cut dress. Another rush of heat roils in my gut, and I avert my eyes quickly.

Prince Theodre sweeps the feathered hat from his head. "May the seven gods shine upon your union!" he says, offering a deep bow.

I nod once. Then I turn my morleth's head for the Between Gate. Time to get out of this world. Time to begin my new life together with this girl. This stranger.

23

Faraine

"You'll need to hold on tight, Princess." Vor's words breathe through the delicate fabric of my veil, tickling my ear. "The first time passing through the Between Gates can be unpleasant. Don't be frightened; I won't let go of you, I promise."

I nod and wrap my fingers through handfuls of morleth mane. I can do nothing else. I dare not even speak. Each time I open my mouth, I run the risk of revealing my true identity. I can pitch my voice low, hope the veil muffles my words. But I can't guard against the natural cadence and rhythm of phrases flowing off my tongue. It would take no more than a single ill-chosen word to ruin everything.

So I hold my tongue behind my gritted teeth as Vor spurs his morleth into motion. The beast's muscles bunch and surge underneath me as it lurches forward, and I cannot help leaning back into the strong, broad chest behind me. Vor's grip around my waist tightens. A rush of heat burns through me. Seven gods above, I'd not realized how badly I missed that embrace!

Get a hold of yourself, Faraine. His embraces are not meant for you.

I straighten as though an iron rod has been driven up my spine. Using all the muscles in my legs and core, I hold myself rigid, despite the rolling gait of the morleth, determined not to relax again. A prick of emotion stabs through my senses—disappointment or discouragement. Possibly both. Vor doesn't know how to interpret his bride's icy demeanor. It cannot be helped. We're both just going to have to endure this ride as best we can.

The air beneath the gate arc ripples strangely, like vapors on a hot day. There's a gleam of light, a color I cannot define, dancing in ribbons, almost invisible but not quite. Magic. Living magic, drawn from the *quinsatra* and ignited by the spells implanted in the gate stones. This is powerful work, ancient and ageless. I feel a blast of cold against my exposed skin. My stomach plunges with a sudden awareness of yawning depths. Panic thrills in my veins, some primal instinct screaming that we shouldn't approach such power—that we should turn back, duck for cover.

The morleth picks up its feet, flowing into a swift, fluid pace, its neck extended, its nostrils flaring with eagerness. Just at the last moment, just as the eerie colored light flares, I turn my head and bury my face in Vor's shoulder.

"Hold on," he says. As if I could do anything else.

The next moment, or perhaps the next hour—perhaps the next day, or year, or century—time has suddenly ceased to mean anything. All I know is pain. Or rather, not pain. More like the shrill ache in a tooth when you've bitten down on something too cold. Only this sensation shoots through my entire body, deep down to my bones. At first, it's all-encompassing. Then my bones seem to disintegrate, softly, gently, particles of matter and existence drifting away from one another, held together by delicate filaments of time and space. There's a sickening rush as if I'm falling and left my stomach behind. I cannot bear to open my eyes, can do nothing but cling desperately to my own reality, willing myself to remember that I still *am*, that I *have been*, that I *shall go on being*.

There's a sound like *blibt*.

Then I'm gasping. And what a wonder—I still have lungs with which to gasp! I still have a body that drinks in air, exhales it in a rush, then bends double with a spasm of sickness. Even that's a wonder, the fact that I can feel sick. The fact that I have a stomach to tighten and cramp, a head to spin with nausea, a mouth to cough and spit. I have a reality. I have existence.

"There, it's all right." Vor's voice is warm, comforting. He places a gentle hand on my back. I'm bowed over to one side, determined not to vomit on another intended bridegroom. The last time I did that, it did not end well. I hold the veil out of my way, heaving again and again. It would be a relief to bring something up, but nothing comes. I've barely eaten in days. All I can do is dry heave, convulsing. I would fall from the saddle entirely were it not for Vor's arm around me.

"There, there," he says as if I'm some pathetic creature in need of crooning. "Let it out if you need to."

I spit one last time and wipe my lips with the back of my hand. Shaking my head, I settle the veil over my face and lean back. I can't help it. I cannot maintain my rigid posture. Shuddering a sigh, I slump in the saddle. "I'm sorry," I whisper.

"Don't be," he answers at once. "You did well. Young Yok over there hacked like a mothcat for hours after the first time he passed through."

As though to emphasize his king's word, the boy rider appears through the gate behind us and utters a dismal groan. He bends over his morleth, grabbing its spiny neck and muttering in troldish. I may not understand the exact words, but the meaning is perfectly clear. Before he can recover himself, the king's brother emerges, his morleth running into the back of the boy's steed. The incoming morleth snarls and sinks pointed teeth into the haunches of the first, which bucks angrily, very nearly unseating its rider. Yok lets out a yelp and grabs on fast, then turns in his saddle and rattles off a stream of angry invective. The king's brother merely shrugs and spurs his mount out of the way just in time for Hael to pass through.

Lyria is there, perched on a pack behind the trolde captain. Her face looks positively green, and the moment they're through, she tips to one side, opens her mouth, and lets all the contents of her stomach spill forth. Hael barks something in troldish and catches Lyria by the back of her gown to keep her from tumbling to the ground.

"Is she all right?" I ask, momentarily forgetting to disguise my voice. Thank the gods, Vor doesn't seem to notice.

"Oh, yes," he answers easily. "Our physical forms were simply not intended to pass through so many realities so quickly. But once we're through, the sickness passes soon enough. It's only a problem for those who become stuck in the Hinter. That can cause lasting harm. If the individual is ever found again, that is."

I don't want to think about that. Closing my eyes, I inhale deeply. Calm surrounds me, welcome as a blanket on a winter morning. Funny—I'd not expected to feel this way again. Certainly not while wearing my sister's face. Somehow, I'd unconsciously believed my lie would prevent me from experiencing the same pleasant comfort I'd felt before in Vor's presence. But it's still there. And when I lean into the sensation, it swiftly expels the sickness from my gut, leaving me trembling and a little weak, but whole.

My stomach twists, this time not with sickness. It's sharp, painful, like a knife to the gut. I bolt up straight again, pulling away from his chest. The air is chilly against my back, but I don't care. What right have I to such comfort? What right have I to take pleasure in sitting in my dead sister's place, enjoying the warming presence of her betrothed?

Oh, Ilsevel. I'm so sorry.

A sudden stream of troldish draws my attention. Yok, recovered from his bout of sickness, is turning in his saddle, looking here and there. His brow wrinkles with puzzlement. He calls out to Vor, who also turns. He cups a hand around his mouth and calls in a deep rumble, "*Kol? Crorsvar tah, Kol?*"

"What's wrong?" I ask softly.

Vor grunts. "It's the gatekeeper, Kol. He's usually on hand to mind the gate. He left it open for us, but . . ." He seems thoughtful. After a moment, he speaks another string of troldish to the young rider, who dismounts and approaches a massive stone dial set in the wall. He grunts and groans but gets it turning. The magic rippling in the open air of the gate flares, then quiets.

"Sul?" Vor says, turning to his brother.

"*Ortolar?*" Sul answers.

"I need you to ride on ahead. Alert Lady Xag to our coming. She offered to provide refreshments for the princess upon our return."

"*Morar-juk!*" Sul pulls a face and rattles off a stream of angry-sounding troldish.

"Don't be a coward, brother," Vor answers calmly. "I've seen you throw yourself at cave devils with more enthusiasm!"

Sul growls something else I don't understand but pulls his mount's head around and urges it into motion, disappearing into the trees.

Only . . . I blink. Only they aren't trees at all.

"Are you quite recovered, Princess?" Vor asks.

I nod. I scarcely hear him. He calls out to Hael and Yok, speaking in a mixture of troldish and Gavarian, but I pay him no heed. My attention is completely taken up by the forest in which I find myself. A whole forest of absolutely enormous, tree-sized mushrooms. What I had taken at first for trunks were in truth mushroom stalks—smooth and leathery and ringed with delicate frills. The caps opening overhead spread wide as rooftops, and the gills pulse with a warm glow. The strangest, most otherworldly source of light, but undeniably beautiful.

I stare around me, jaw hanging open. I remember suddenly how Vor had answered when I'd asked if there was any light underground. *More light than you can imagine. More light, more color, more life. More everything.*

Maybe he wasn't exaggerating.

Suddenly aware of Vor's scrutiny, I glance up and catch his smile. "What do you think, Princess?" he asks. Eagerness radiates from him, a nice change from the anxiety. He does very much want to please me. To please Ilsevel, that is.

I lower my head, wishing I'd not reacted so obviously. "It's beautiful."

"This is Horba Gat, one of the oldest and largest forests in the Under Realm." He spurs his morleth into motion, and we proceed through the massive stems. The beast shivers and tosses its head, very solid and ugly under the pulsing glow. "Knar doesn't like it here," Vor says as though answering a question I'd not thought to ask. "Morleth don't care for the *horba* lights during lusterling, though you can often find wild morleth wandering among them at dimness."

I'm silent for a little while, taking in this information. "What is lusterling?" I ask at length. "And dimness?"

"Ah! I forget how much you have to learn." Vor's voice is kind, and that eagerness radiates a little brighter from his soul. "Lusterling is what we call our *day*. It is the period in which the *lorst* crystals come alive and glow, generating the light that shines overhead. Dimness is our *night*, for the crystals slowly fade, and the older ones go out entirely, casting our world into darkness. There, you see?" He points at an opening between two great mushroom caps. I peer up and glimpse a distant arch of cavern ceiling studded with crystals. Almost too bright to look upon directly, they gleam in a multitude of colors.

Now that I see the ceiling, however, it brings a sudden flood of awareness over me. Awareness of the huge, crushing weight of stone overhead. Tons upon tons of rock and earth. My lungs tighten. Panic burns in my veins, threatening to overwhelm me. Hastily I look down, staring at the strands of morleth hair twined in my fingers, trying to count them, trying to focus on anything other than that terrible, terrible heaviness.

"It will take some getting used to." Vor's voice is close to my ear, his chin nearly resting on my shoulder. I close my eyes, my body tensing. But at least he's a distraction. For a moment I'm too aware of *him* to care much about anything else. "I know this world is strange to you, but I hope you will come to love the Under Realm in time."

I nod. I should say something, I know. Offer some polite little nothing. But I can't.

We ride on in silence. Little flitting creatures dart among the mushroom stems, catching my eye. Their wings move so fast; they're a blur, generating a sweet humming. As we ride deeper into the trees, there are more of the creatures, and the humming increases.

The pendant on my necklace warms in reaction. At first I don't notice. Then, slowly, I become aware of heat against my breast and a vibration that wasn't there before. I place my hand over it, shocked by how much bare flesh I feel under my palm. I'd almost forgotten the revealing gown I wear, caught up in the wonder of this new world.

One of the little creatures flits close and lands on my hand. I catch my breath and slowly lift my fingers up before my face. Rather than flying away, the creature holds on with its six tiny, clawed feet. Those feet are attached to six furry, fat legs, which in turn correspond with six delicate wings, each like a single feather. Huge dark eyes stare at me from beneath what I first take to be long, rabbit-like ears, but which prove to be drooping antenna. It opens and closes a tiny beak, unfurling a delicate ribbon of black tongue. It's so beautiful, so strange.

"It's called an *olk*," Vor says suddenly. "There are many of them here in Horba Gat and hundreds of varieties throughout the Under Realm. They're not unlike your songbirds, I believe."

"They look a bit more like moths," I say, tilting my hand and watching the creature crawl around to nestle in my palm. Then abruptly, it spreads its six wings and flutters to my chest. I catch a breath.

"It likes your necklace." There's a smile in Vor's voice, warm and kind. "*Olk* resonate to the song of *urzul* crystals."

"*Urzul* crystals?"

"Yes. That is what you're wearing. Did you not know?"

I lift the pendant, to which the *olk* is still clinging. The crystal hums a deep, melodious harmony to the *olk*'s simple song. "I did not realize it came from Mythanar."

"Wait." Vor's voice holds a sharpness that wasn't there a moment before. His body goes rigid behind me. "Where did you get that, Princess?"

"What? My necklace?"

"I recognize it. That was Faraine's."

My stomach drops. Ice chills through my veins. What a fool I am! I never stopped to consider he might remember such a simple token. "Oh!" I force out the word, a thin little gasp of sound. Quickly I shake my head. Now is not the time to fall apart. "Oh, yes. This. She gave it to me. Faraine, I mean. As a wedding gift."

"When?"

"Um. Just before I left on my Maiden's Journey. It was a parting gift."

Vor is silent. The *olk*, as though sensing unpleasant discord, flies away into the mushrooms, trailing glittering dust in its wake. The morleth plods on several heavy steps.

Then: "I saw her wearing it. The day after you left."

My mouth goes dry. "Yes. How foolish of me, I forgot. It was after."

"You saw Faraine after your journey? I thought you traveled directly to the Between Gate from the last shrine."

"We stopped at Nornala Convent on our way over the Ettrian Mountains. I saw her there." The lie falls so easily from my lips. And as it falls, I feel something slip away from me. Something I can never reclaim. Some virtue, some goodness. Some worth.

He's going to find out.

Of course he is. Sooner or later.

Sooner. Not later.

And when he does, what then? He'll recount all these lies, one after another. And when he looks at me, what will he see? Certainly not the girl whose hand he'd kissed in the garden. Not her. Because she's gone now. She vanished the minute I allowed them to give me my dead sister's name.

This is too much. I can't bear it.

"Vor," I say suddenly, clearly. Dropping all pretense of mimicking Ilsevel's voice.

He starts behind me, his muscles tensing. "Yes?"

I open my mouth. Ready to say more, ready to tell him everything, *everything*. My confession is right there on the tip of my tongue.

Before I can get a word out, a voice rings through the forest: "*Ortolar! Hirak-lash!*"

"Sul?" Vor sits up straighter in the saddle, looking over my head. "Sul, is that you?"

"*Juk, ortolar, mazoga!*"

"What's wrong?" I ask, sensing the mounting unease in the man at my back. He doesn't answer but spurs his morleth faster. It leaps forward, weaving through the mushroom stalks, swift and fluid. I glimpse a break in the forest up ahead, and Sul, still mounted, poised on a rocky outcropping overlooking a sheer drop. He sees Vor coming and points. "*Hirark!*" he says.

Vor urges his mount up alongside Sul's. My stomach pitches. We've come to an overlook, and a strange landscape appears below me, a landscape totally unlike my world back home, all contained within a great cavern. A winding river sparkles under the light of distant *lorst* crystals, cutting through massive rocks and crags. The crystal light is not as bright as full daylight but bright enough for me to see the village lining the riverbank—a village of conical stalagmites, formed by the hand of nature. Only on a second and third glance do I begin to notice the doors and windows carved into those stalagmites and what seems to be a complex network of streets running among them.

It's all ghostly quiet.

Sul says something in troldish. Vor responds sharply. The roiling tension in his spirit mounts, morphing into real fear. "What's wrong?" I ask softly.

Vor looks down at me as though suddenly reminded of my existence. "I beg your pardon, Princess. There is . . . We are not . . . There may be trouble below."

"What kind of trouble?"

Sul speaks harshly, making an impatient gesture. He won't even look at me. Vor answers in troldish, his voice less harsh but urgent. A sound of hoofbeats draws my attention. I look around Vor's broad shoulder to see Hael and Yok arrive. Hael exclaims once, and Yok begins to babble, but she hushes him with a sharp gesture. They approach the overlook and go still.

Lyria peers around Hael's shoulder, gripping the cantle of the morleth saddle for balance. "What's that?" she asks, and points.

I look where she indicates. A great gash runs through part of the trolde town, appearing as though some spectacularly huge claw has torn right through the rock. At first glance I assumed it was a natural part of the landscape, but now I notice how the houses closest to it teeter perilously on the edge. Even as I watch, one of them crumbles and falls into darkness.

Vor and his people begin talking rapidly in troldish. I exchange glances with Lyria. Her eyes are very wide.

"Forgive me, Princess," Vor says, his sudden switch to my language jarring. "I don't mean to alarm you, but I must see to business below." Without another word of explanation, he swings down from the saddle, then reaches up and wraps his hands around my waist. I only just have time to grip his upper arms before he's pulling me to the ground. He's too abrupt, and I stagger. He catches me, rights me, then turns away. I feel the sudden chill of his absence like an icy slap.

"Ouch! Have a care, there!" Lyria growls. I turn in time to see Hael take hold of her arm and, much less gently, almost shove her off her own morleth. Lyria stumbles and lands on her backside, glaring furiously up at the trolde woman, who ignores her. Vor has already remounted and is speaking to Yok. The boy lets out a protesting bleat. Vor repeats himself, his tone final. Yok bows his head.

I move to Lyria's side as she picks herself up off the ground. We stand close to one another. Her anxiety spikes like daggers. Ordinarily I would withdraw to keep from being hurt. But she needs my support. And, in truth, I need her in that moment as well.

Vor turns at last to the two of us. "Princess," he says, his voice crisp, "I am placing you in the care of Yok here. He is charged with your safety. He is a brave warrior and will keep you from any harm."

Lyria snorts. "I'm not sure what that child is going to protect us from."

Yok shoots her a dirty glare. Apparently he understands human language.

Vor's morleth stomps and snorts, tossing its head. Vor holds it in check, the muscles in his upper arms bulging with effort. "I would trust Yok with my life. You will be safe. He will escort you to the house of Lady Xag. She is a friend. She will see to your comfort until I come for you."

"Where are you going?" I ask.

He doesn't quite look at me. "There's something I must do." He hesitates. His jaw works as though he wants to say something more. But he merely shakes his head and addresses himself to Yok again, speaking in troldish. Then, with a last swift glance my way, he spurs his morleth into the forest. Sul and Hael ride hard upon his heels, and I watch them vanish into the mushroom trees.

Suddenly, the massive weight of the cavern overhead seems worse than before.

"Well, this is a fine cauldron of gruel," Lyria mutters, crossing her arms. "Barely through the gate and already abandoned! Not exactly the wedding celebration I anticipated."

I take her hand. It's an impulsive gesture, one I almost immediately regret as pain spikes through my palm. I close my eyes and clutch my pendant with my other hand, feeling for its inner pulse. It's stronger than usual. Am I imagining it, or is there an answering pulse in the ground beneath my feet? A gentle rumble, a rhythm like an ancient song.

The trolde boy still stands at the outlook, staring down at the village. His face is grim. Finally, he draws a deep breath and turns to us. He considers a moment, then dismounts. "Please," he says, in stilted but understandable Gavarian, "if you would ride my mount, I would be honored to escort you to a place of rest."

Lyria snorts. "You'll never get me back up on one of those creatures. Not if my life depends on it. I'll walk, thank you."

The boy's forehead puckers. "It's three miles at least to Lady Xag's home."

"Good. I need to stretch my legs anyway." Lyria picks up her skirts and starts walking through the mushrooms, scattering a little flock of *olk* as she goes. "Come along, Ilsevel!" she tosses back over her shoulder.

Yok turns to me. "Princess?"

"It's all right," I say, smiling, though he cannot see it through the veil. "I've been riding in a cramped carriage for days. I would appreciate a chance to move."

He looks as though he wants to protest. To my relief, he simply nods. "This way then."

24

Vor

Our morleth's hooves ring out like stone-sharpened blades against the pavers of Dugorim's streets, echoing eerily off the walls of the vacant buildings. I lead the way, despite Hael's protests that I should allow her to venture ahead and make certain all is safe. I already know it isn't safe.

Holding the reins with one hand, I rest the other on the knife hilt at my belt. I didn't bring a sword, not for a journey like this, not for meeting and escorting my bride. Neither Sul nor I travel armed, though Hael has her sword and a big trolde club strapped across the cantle of her saddle. We make our way down the main village thoroughfare. Every door of every building stands wide open. I peer into dark passages and front rooms as I ride by, searching for some sign of life.

Nothing. Not even a whisper. Not even a flickering shadow of movement.

We reach the Upper Round, a place of gathering and ceremony in the heart of town. From here, my view sweeps from the council house to the humble village temple, and on down to the river docks. I see the miners' road as well, leading up from the primary digs. When I passed this way mere hours ago, that road was busy with workers traveling to and fro, hauling loads of stone and silt on their backs or in pushcarts. Those pushcarts are now abandoned. Some lying on their sides, contents spilled.

A wind blows across the back of my neck, prickling my flesh. I shiver. "Dismount," I say, swinging down from Knar. "Check the buildings. There must be someone here, someone we can ask where everyone has gone. Perhaps they've fled some foe and need our help."

"Your Majesty, allow me to urge we stick together," Hael says.

"Why?" I spread my arms. "There's no one here."

"You think that," she answers grimly. "You think that right up until the moment there *is* someone. Someone you aren't prepared to meet." She shakes her head. "We shouldn't separate."

"Gods save us, Hael, you've convinced me!" Sul declares. "I'm positively trembling in my boots. Will you hold my hand?" She gives him a look. "What?" He shrugs and blinks innocently. "I'm susceptible to the spooks!"

"Enough," I growl. "Sul, go check the docks. Make certain our barge is still there and have a look for our bargeman. Hael, you search the council house. It's the largest building around save for Lady Xag's; perhaps folk are hidden inside. I'm going to the temple."

Hael looks as though she wants to protest. Instead, she says, "Will you take my sword, Your Majesty?"

"No, keep it." I draw my knife. "I'll be fine. Quick now!"

The Dugorim temple is neither large nor impressive, being little more than a cave. I cannot stand up fully in it but am obliged to bend almost double, feeling my way with care. The light of the *lorst* crystals cannot penetrate beyond the opening, and there are no lanterns inside. But that's not unusual; the priestesses of the Deeper Dark prefer to dwell in dense shadow.

My fingers, trailing on the walls and ceiling, pick out the secret and sacred carvings hidden in the stones, marking the way. I meet no one. Ordinarily, there would be a dozen or more priestesses deep in their *va* sitting like statues just inside the mouth of the temple. I should have stubbed my toe on at least one of them by now. But the way is clear.

I venture all the way to the inner sanctum. My breath echoes hollowly in that empty space. I open my mouth, intending to call out, but cannot bring myself to do so. This cavern should be alive with the hum of holy women pursuing their *va-vulug*, the sacred songs of the Dark. This silence feels wrong. Sinful.

I back out again, trying to ignore the creeping shudders running up and down my spine. The *lorst* glow is too bright as I stagger out into the broader cavern. My chest is tight, and when I force myself to draw a deeper breath, I taste something bitter on the back of my tongue.

My vision is just clearing when the silhouettes of Hael and Sul appear, approaching down two different streets. Sul reaches me first, returning from the docks. "All the barges are there, including ours," he says. "No sign of the bargemen. No beasts either, not even a fluttering water *olk*."

"It's the same in the city center," Hael says. Her face is lined and tense. "I saw signs of a meal in the inner chamber. Food and drink, still fresh, but disturbed. Chairs overturned, dishes smashed on the ground. I think there was blood on one wall."

I try to swallow, but my throat is too dry. I know where we must go. But I don't want to. Drawing a long breath, I tighten my grip on my dagger. "Come on," I say, and turn on one heel, leading the way out of the Upper Round and on to the edge of town. My steps are swift and confident, even as my heart quails.

We pass the place where the avalanche had buried several homes, now half excavated. Digging equipment lies strewn all around. Four wrapped-up bundles of sackcloth lie in a neat row. I know what they are—the dead pulled from the rubble. One of them is small, achingly small. Were any others found alive? If so, where are they now?

I glance back at my two companions. They meet my gaze, silent and solemn. With a quick shake of my head, I continue, leading the way past the small disaster and on to the greater one. To that place where the ground is torn apart, a jagged crevice ripping right through homes and streets. It's a good fifteen feet across at the broadest point, and extends for half a mile, reshaping this whole portion of the Dugorim Cavern. But it's not the size of the break that makes me halt in my tracks, my heart suddenly plunging.

It's the clothes.

All those bits and pieces of clothing—miners' hoods, smocks, undergarments, vests. Tunics, cloaks, belts, jewels, rings. And shoes. So many shoes. Even a pair of small mushroom-leather booties that would hardly fit my big toe, lying close to my feet. All scattered along the length of the chasm in random piles. All leading to that edge.

My blood runs cold.

"*Morar-juk.*"

Sul's voice breathes close to my ear. I glance to one side. His face is drained of color, almost pure white. Hael stands on his other side, her expression a mask. She lifts her chin and sniffs suddenly. "What's that smell?"

I inhale and choke on a curse. "*Raog*," I say. "Quick, cover your faces. Try not to breathe deeply."

Hael reacts at once, tearing a bit of cloth from her sleeve and wrapping it across her nose. Sul, however, merely snorts and crosses his arms. "If there's poison in the air, a little bit of silk over our faces isn't going to make any difference."

I don't force the issue, though I do rip a strip of fabric from the hem of my own tunic and tie it around the lower half of my face. He's probably right; if the poison has dissipated enough, we'll be fine. If not, we're dead already, even if we don't know it yet. Still, it feels better to take some precaution, even a useless one.

My half mask in place, I step through the piles of discarded garments, trying not to bring my foot down on any of them. A skirt, a bodice, a tunic. A small, white nappy. I don't look at any of them too closely, but creep to the edge of the crevice and peer over.

My stomach convulses.

The drop is deep. Endless. Dark. But the walls are not smooth. Jagged rocks and outcroppings jut like savage teeth. And straight below me, a good fifty feet down, is a body. Pale and broken. Contorted in death. Naked.

I turn, searching along the crevice wall, both on this side and the other. There are more bodies. Not many, but a few. In one place, several have piled on top of each other, all grossly angled limbs and lifeless flesh. The *lorst* light only just reaches deep enough to illuminate them. Another yard down, and all is lost in shadow. Ravenous shadow.

I back away. With an effort, I swallow, tasting bitter *raog* poison on the back of my tongue. Gods on high! It's already permeated this far. How quickly will it spread? Is there still time to turn back this tide? Is there still—

"Vor! Help me, brother!"

I pivot just in time to see Sul off to my right scrambling over the edge of the crevice. "Wait!" I cry, and break into a run. His face is uncovered. Has he already breathed too much poison? Is he succumbing as well? "Sul, don't!"

His head disappears. I skid to a stop, drop to my knees, and peer over the edge of broken stone. There's a ledge. Some twenty feet down, sharp and uneven, protruding from the craggy wall. A figure lies there, her naked body weirdly contorted. Her head is thrown back, blue blood matting in her braided crown of hair. Her expression is twisted into something horrible, almost demonic.

Lady Xag.

Sul scrambles down the side of the cliff, quick as a skittering insect. Stone and earth crumble beneath one of his feet. My heart catches. But my brother adjusts his hold and continues. He reaches the ledge, finds his balance, and crouches over the lady. With unprecedented gentleness, he gathers her in his arms, puts his head close to her mouth.

"She's breathing!" he calls up to me. "She's alive!"

"I'm coming down," I answer at once, and start to swing my legs out over the edge.

A hand falls on my shoulder, gripping hard. I look up into Hael's face, her eyes stern above folds of protective cloth. "Don't," she says. "You are our king. We need you in one piece."

I shake my head. My brother is down there. "I'm going, Hael. I want you to find something we can use to pull Lady Xag up." Her eyes narrow. I fear she's going to protest. "At once, captain. That's an order."

She releases my shoulder. The muscles in her throat spasm. Then she nods, turns, and strides back into the ghostly village, making for the mining works.

"Hurry, Vor!" Sul calls from below.

I turn and lower myself over the edge, my hands and feet finding holds. I'm a trolde—rock climbing is in my blood. Even so, that yawning darkness is enough to reduce me to piteous trembling. So I shut my mind off, refuse to think of it. The stench of *raog* poison is stronger down here. How old is it? How potent? How much do I even now draw into my lungs? My arms shake, but I close my eyes. Breathe in. Breathe out. Then continue, down and down, one careful handhold after the other.

I reach the ledge a few feet away from Sul and Xag. His back is to me, and I cannot see the lady's face, but I hear her groan. Painfully aware of the drop on one side, I step toward them. She groans again. Am I wrong, or is that a garbling attempt at words?

I reach my brother, rest a hand on his back, and peer over his shoulder. The lady lies with her head thrown across his arm. Her eyelids flutter open. Her pale eyes look out, spinning and unfocused.

"Xag?" Sul says, bending over her. "Xag, it's me. I'm here. I'm here, you great hulking terror of a woman. You're going to be all right, do you hear me?"

Her head turns slightly, her eyes struggling to focus. She stares at Sul, blinking slowly. A thin inarticulate sound ekes through her colorless lips.

"There, don't trouble yourself," Sul says. Her hand reaches up, trembling, grasping at air. He takes hold of her fingers and presses them to his chest. "Vor's here too. Our noble savior king. He's going to get you out of this, and he might even convince me to help a little."

She grimaces, closes her eyes. "Sssssssuuuul."

"Yes! Yes, that's right. It's Sul. Come on, Xag! Pull yourself together. If you get up out of this trench, I'll let you kiss me. Did you hear that? You're never going to get a better offer."

I look up the side of the wall I've just descended. It's dizzyingly sheer. Grimacing, I address my brother. "Can she be moved safely? What about her spine?"

Sul shakes his head. "I don't—"

Her hand rips free from his grasp and latches hold of his throat. Sul chokes, eyes goggling. He grapples with her arm even as she sits bolt upright. Her eyes flare open. Only they aren't the silvery eyes of Lady Xag as I know her. They're green. Glowing.

With a cry, I lunge and grab her arm, fighting to pry her free. She elbows me in the throat, and I fall back against the wall, gasping for air. Stone breaks under my foot, crumbles away into darkness. I manage to catch the wall, find firm footing.

Sul gags, his face turning blue. Xag has him bent out over the drop.

I lunge again. This time, I bring my fist down sharp on the weakest part of her arm. Bones snap. Xag screams and lets go so abruptly, Sul nearly plunges. I'm just quick enough to catch him, to wrench him back onto the ledge beside me.

Then Xag's arms are around my neck, and she's ripped me off my feet. I twist, jab an elbow into her stomach, and manage to wrench around to face her. She grips my shoulders, whirls, and slams me against the rock wall. Sparks explode in my vision. I can see nothing but Lady Xag leering at me, green foam dripping from the corners of her mouth. She raises her arm, a black stone gripped in her fist. Survival instinct surges, and just before she can brain me, I get my own arm up to deflect the blow. Then I slam the heel of my other hand into her nose. I feel it crunch. She steps back. I slam her again. Blue blood flows over her upper lip, mingles with spittle and foam.

She steps back again, one hand still clutching the front of my shirt. She teeters. She's going over the edge. And she's going to drag me with her. I suck in a breath, my feet skidding on stone.

Then Sul hurtles into the two of us, knocking us off our feet. Xag's grip on me breaks as she falls, slips, slides. I'm too stunned to do more than try to catch myself on the ledge, but Sul surges, both arms reaching. He cries out. Shaking my head, I pull myself upright to see my brother, his body half-extended over the drop. He grips Xag by one arm.

"I've got you!" he cries. "Hold on! Hold on, Xag! I'll get you up!"

Her head is lolling, her body limp, lifeless. She's too heavy. Sul is nearly broken in half trying to hold her.

I scramble, catch my brother around the waist, struggling to haul him back. "Let her go, Sul!"

"No! I can get her! Help me!"

"You can't save her." I adjust my grip, clinging to his shoulders. The inevitable pull of gravity drags a cry from my throat. We won't last much longer. "*Sul!*" I roar.

A sob breaks from my brother's throat. I feel the terrible pitch as the fall prepares to claim us. I squeeze my eyes shut.

Then—relief.

The terrible weight is gone.

I open my eyes. Sul hangs out over the edge, staring into the void. His empty hands still extended.

"Gods save us!" I breathe, and pull my brother back toward me. He's trembling so hard, I swear I hear his bones rattle. "Sul! Sul, are you all right?"

He shakes his head slowly. "I could have saved her." Slumping, he rests his forehead in his palm. "I could have saved her, Vor."

"No, Sul. You couldn't. She was already gone."

"You don't know that. She may have been able to come back."

I exhale slowly. What can I say? Across my mind's eye flashes the image of a savage *woggha* spewing foam as it strives to tear my face off. Foam the same green as what I saw flying from Xag's lips just now. Is it possible for anyone to come back from such madness?

I bow my head heavily. Xag. Poor Xag. I've known her my entire life. There was a time my father even talked about a betrothal between us, and in my boyhood, I'd harbored a youthful infatuation for the older, beautiful woman. Those feelings long since faded, but I'd always held her in highest esteem.

I glance at Sul. My brother's face has gone slack. "We've got to get out of here," I say. "We don't know if the poison is lingering."

"Yes." Sul passes a hand across his forehead. "And you've lost your little kerchief in the scuffle, so you're probably as doomed as me now."

I grunt and pull him to his feet. Sul cranes his neck, peering again over the ledge. "Do you think it was all of them?" he says. "The whole village?"

I nod. I feel sick, helpless. This is far worse than any of the rumors that have reached Mythanar. Far worse than I'd dared imagine.

"I don't understand." Sul looks at me, his brow puckered. "Did they jump? Were they driven here? All the children and the animals too?"

I shake my head. "We're not going to get answers down here. We need to get back to Mythanar. It'll take magic to seal this crevice."

Trolde magic won't be sufficient. I know that already, all too well. Neither will fae magic be any use, even if I could get a fae mage to travel all the way to the Under Realm. Such magic will only shrivel up and disintegrate the minute it touches the foul *raog*-infused air.

We need the Miphates. We need written magic.

"Come, Sul." I gaze grimly up the sheer face of the wall. Grunting, I take hold of the stone and begin to pull myself up.

Before I've climbed more than a foot, Hael appears overhead, her face still half-covered in her cloth. "Your Majesty?" she calls down. Though I'm fairly certain her gaze has fastened on Sul.

"Don't worry, Hael, my sweet," Sul calls up to her. "I've managed to keep my pretty face mostly intact. Give us a hand now, will you?"

Hael vanishes, then reappears and lowers a harness of woven *hugagug* rope, no doubt taken from the mine works. "Send the king up first," she says.

Ignoring this, I put Sul in the harness. Both my captain and my brother try to protest, but after a stern reminder that I am, in fact, their sovereign, they shut their mouths. Hael's powerful arms strain as she hauls Sul up, using knots in the length of rope to aid her grip. Sul is uncharacteristically silent. I watch until he reaches the top and Hael hauls him onto stable ground. Then I turn and look down the chasm once more.

I can feel it down there. Deep, deep down, beneath that impenetrable darkness. Down to where darkness gives way to heat, and the pressure at the fiery heart of the world burns like living hell. Down to where something lies coiled upon itself. Vast. Endless. Enduring.

Waiting.

I close my eyes, still my mind, still my senses. Feel that heat, feel that pressure. Feel . . .

. . . *breathing* . . .

A scream rings out, echoing against the stones. Distant but clear.

My eyes flare open. The blood in my veins surges with sudden fear. I know to whom that scream belongs. "Ilsevel!" I gasp.

25

Faraine

This house is not at all like what I expected. It's carved directly into the cavern wall, with only the most subtle stonemasonry providing any semblance of a distinct outer façade. In fact, if it weren't for our young guide, I would have walked right past it without seeing a house at all.

The trolde boy stops, however, and stands facing what turns out to be a front door. Now that I look more closely, I can see the delicate scrollwork decorating the lintel. This leads me to scan higher up the cavern wall, and I can just pick out elegantly shaped windows among the rough crags. It's a unique combination of naturalism and craft. Rather beautiful, in its way.

The boy's face is a study. His white brows knit, and the simmering unease in his soul intensifies.

Lyria and I exchange glances. Lyria shrugs. "Well?" she says, folding her arms. "Is there a bellpull? Or are we to sing like carolers for admittance?"

The boy licks his dry lips. "The door."

"Yes? What about it?"

"It's . . . open."

"So I see." Lyria raises an eyebrow. "Hospitable folk in these parts, yes?" She takes three light steps as though to enter, but the boy catches hold of her elbow. "What?" she demands.

"You can't just walk into Lady Xag's house uninvited."

"Why not?"

"It's . . ." He struggles a moment, as though searching for the appropriate word. "In our tongue, we would say *ush.*"

"Rude?"

"Maybe?"

Lyria snorts. "Well, in *our* tongue, we would say it's much ruder to keep your future queen standing on the stoop twiddling her thumbs."

The boy's jaw works as he glances from Lyria to me and back to the door again. I don't know what's troubling him. It is eerily silent, but for all I know, that's just the way these trolde towns are.

"Really," I say, drawing his gaze back to me, "I don't mind waiting here. I wouldn't want to be an inconvenience to Lady Xag if she's not prepared to receive—"

"Nonsense!" Lyria snaps. "We've had a long ride, then a quick nip across worlds and realities, then another long ride, and a long walk. We've earned a respite and a bite. So what's it to be, Yok?" She addresses the boy again, her eyes narrowing. "Are you leading the way, or shall I go first and loudly announce our arrival to the household?"

He gives her a look as though he would very much like to bind her up by her thumbs and leave her dangling. But his tone is respectful if mildly resentful when he says, "Very well. But I'll go first and make certain all is safe. You wait here."

"Wait here?" Lyria tilts her head. "Alone and exposed and

defenseless? Do you think that's what King Vor had in mind when he left us in your tender care?"

"Fine," Yok growls. He draws his sword and turns to the door. "You can come with me. Stay close."

"Not too close!" Lyria takes my hand and tucks it under her arm as she falls into step behind the boy. "I don't want to get hit by that blade of yours if you start swinging."

She holds on tight to me, keeping me close to her side as we follow the boy through that half-hidden opening and into the entrance hall. I cannot help but perceive the tension emanating from behind her bold front. She grips my hand like a lifeline, sending sharp stabs of pain through my palm. A headache is forming fast, but I clutch my crystal, leaning into its calming pulse.

The inside of the cave dwelling is even more unexpected than the exterior. The floors are smoothly paved and polished, while the ceilings arching overhead are jagged with stalactite formations. The walls are curved and vary between smooth and rough natural stone. Little *lorst* crystals hang suspended in delicate chandelier arrangements, illuminating the darkness.

Yok leads us down the passage, scouting out the first several chambers we come to. They're all empty. He calls out only once, a tremulous, "*Grakol-dura?*" There's a questioning lilt in his voice.

Lyria sniffs. "What's the point in that mouse-ish whispering?" She cups her hands around her mouth and shouts, "*Is anyone there?*" Her voice echoes down the corridor, hollow and lost.

"*Juk!*" Yok growls, and I'm sure it's an expletive. He whirls on Lyria, his mouth working as though he's trying to say a number of things all at once and can't quite settle on which. Finally, he manages, "I wish you hadn't done that!"

"Maybe." Lyria smiles sweetly. "But I think you've got your answer. There's no one here. Your Lady Xag must be out paying calls or whatever your trolde ladies do for amusement. Be a love now, sweet Yok, and find the princess a place to sit. Her feet are quite throbbing, I tell you!"

Though her manner is abrasive, Lyria certainly knows how to get results. Yok mutters ominously but turns and leads us to one of the nearby chambers. It seems to be a sitting room, with several windows gazing out on a view of the village and the river close by. Light pours through those windows, so bright and golden, I could almost trick myself into believing it was the afternoon sun of my own world. It's warm too, much warmer than I'd thought it would be underground. Which is a mercy, considering how exposed I am in this trolde-style gown.

Yok prowls the room, checking behind furnishings and prodding at the tall curtains framing the windows. It's an elegantly appointed space after a trolde fashion. The chairs are all oversized for humans and shaped in deep curves as though to cradle the sitter. A big round boulder of red stone with a flat top serves as a table, in the middle of which stands a cluster of crystals the same pale blue hue as my necklace. *Urzul* crystals, Vor called them. They seem to have been gathered and displayed with the same care we might gather flowers back home. On another table close by is a large, clear crystal that flickers with movement inside. When I step closer, I find it's hollowed out and filled with water. Pale, eyeless fish swim idly around their tiny world, wafting fanlike tails in their wake.

I go to the nearest window. We're on the second story, overlooking the trolde village below, eerily silent in the *lorst* light. The river flows not far from here, and I see barges tethered to long docks. Still no people. No bustle. No sound.

"So, how fast can you sniff out a bite to eat, friend Yok?" Lyria says, sauntering to one of the big, curved chairs and sinking into the cushion. "I'm positively famished!"

"I don't know." The trolde boy stands in the doorway, looking uneasy. "I've never been here before."

"Well, why don't you go find something?"

"I can't go burrowing through Lady Xag's larder!"

"Why not? Do you think Lady Xag would be happier to know her future queen came calling and was summarily starved?"

Yok turns his apprehensive gaze upon me. I offer a smile from behind my veil. "Really, it's all right. I'm not hungry." The words have no sooner left my mouth when my stomach lets out a loud grumble. Gods, how long has it been since I last ate? I've scarcely been able to stomach a mouthful since Theodre's arrival at the convent.

Lyria laughs outright. "That, my friend Yok, was a most polite lie." She waves a hand. "Go on! Don't let King Vor return to find his bride fainted on the floor. If he does, I'll tell him exactly where to place the blame."

"Fine," Yok says shortly. "But please, both of you, stay in here. I don't want you to get lost."

"I assure you, I have no intention of budging." Lyria snuggles deeper into the cradling chair, pulling her feet up under her.

Yok sends me a last urgent glance, then disappears down the passage. I turn from the bowl of blind fish to face Lyria. "Really, you shouldn't bully the poor boy—"

"Shh!" She holds up a hand, her head tilted, listening to the sound of Yok's retreating footsteps. Then she pops up out of the chair, steps lightly to the doorway, and peers out. "All right, he's gone." She turns on me and raises her eyebrows. "How are you bearing up, Faraine?"

"Oh." I wouldn't have expected the sound of my own name to

strike so hard. But it does. I feel suddenly weak. That threatening headache gives a sudden throb at the base of my skull. I make my way to the nearest chair and perch on the edge. After a moment, I lift the veil from before my face and raise my gaze to meet Lyria's. "I'm all right."

She lifts an eyebrow. "I have to say, I think you're doing rather magnificently. I never would have expected it of you. Since returning to Beldroth, I thought you rather a mousy little thing. But you're far more deceptive than I expected! No one seems to suspect a thing."

My lips tilt wryly. "Is that a compliment?"

"If you like." She approaches me, takes my face in her hands, and turns my head from side to side. "Hmmm. My spells seem to be holding. You could almost go without a veil entirely." She studies my features contemplatively. Then her gaze shifts and meets mine. She frowns. "Don't look so forlorn. You always knew this would be your future, didn't you? None of us grew up expecting to marry for love."

I lower my lashes. A loveless marriage? If only that were the worst of my problems.

"I marry for the kingdom," I answer softly. "I marry for the crown. For I am but an extension of the kingdom and the crown."

"That's right." Lyria taps me smartly on the top of my head. Then she pats my cheek. "Cheer up. King Vor seems like a genuinely good person. There's a strong chance we're going to survive."

"Survive what exactly?"

"The wedding, of course." Lyria shrugs one shoulder and returns to her comfortable chair, dropping back into it with a sigh. "Were he any less *good* than he is, I would fear for our lives. Now, don't go all wide-eyed and shocked on me!" she adds a little harshly.

"You know perfectly well what a dangerous game we're playing. Believe it or not, I'm trying to be comforting. I tell you, I think we'll live. A man like that is unlikely to have us executed for this duplicity. He might even forgive you. Eventually."

I bow my head, letting my veil drop back into place. It disturbs me to hear Vor's virtues discussed with such a combination of frivolity and calculation. He doesn't deserve this. None of it.

"Why, Faraine!" Lyria sits up suddenly. "Does that long-suffering sigh of yours mean what I think it means?" She ducks her head, as though trying to peer beneath my veil. "No, I'm right. You have a soft spot for this Shadow King, don't you?" Her laugh rings in my ear as I turn and look out the window. "Ha! Well, that's perfect! You'll get your happily ever after. I must say, I feel much better about my part in all this now. I might even be able to chalk it up as one of my few truly *good* deeds in this life."

"There's nothing good about this." The words snap from my tongue like whip lashes. "There's nothing good about deceiving an honest man."

"Nonsense. If a little deception ultimately opens the door to your happiness, why should you complain?"

"Because my sister is dead."

Lyria's smile fades. "Right," she says, sinking back into her seat. "There is that, I suppose."

We lapse into silence. The only sound in the room is the faint bubble from the fish in their crystal bowl. Finally, Lyria huffs, "Where is that little troll boy anyway?" and gets up, crossing to the door.

Just as she reaches the open doorway, a sudden, bloodcurdling scream erupts, followed by a crash. A thud reverberates down the walls and floors.

I spring to my feet, heart pounding. "What was that?"

Lyria jumps a step back from the doorway, her face white. She draws a steadying breath, steps forward again, and looks out into the passage. A strangled cry bursting from her throat, she springs back into the room, grabs the door, and slams it. Just as it closes, something solid hits it from the other side, driving the door back open by several inches. With a shriek, Lyria hurls the full force of her body against it and manages to get it shut. But in that intervening moment, I glimpse something. Something I can scarcely describe. All leering jaw and dagger teeth, colorless flesh sagging from protruding bones. A savage snarling, like a last choke on gurgling blood, fills my ears.

The creature throws itself at the door again, and Lyria's feet skid back by inches. The door opens wider, and that awful, lipless, leering muzzle pushes through the opening. I'm in motion already, hurtling across the room. I fling my own shoulder against the door, and with our combined weight, we manage to get it closed again. "Where's the latch?" Lyria gasps, her hand moving along the smooth panels.

But there is no latch. No knob, no handle, no nothing. The door cannot be fastened in any way. The monster bashes against it again, jarring my bones. My feet scramble for purchase on the ground. I step on the hem of my dress, pulling myself to my knees. A talon claw curls around the edge of the door, mere inches from my nose. I scream and, summoning strength I did not know I possessed, throw all my weight into the door, crushing that awful hand.

The monster on the other side emits a sound for which I have no words. But it pulls back. For an instant.

"Hold the door, Fairie!" Lyria cries. She's got her back pressed against it, one leg braced on the nearest boulder-shaped table. She hikes up her skirts with one hand.

"What are you doing?"

She whips out a knife hidden in a sheath strapped to her thigh. Her smile is quick and dangerous.

The creature slams against the door again. This time, it pushes it a full half foot wide. I slide back along the polished floor, desperately trying to dig in my heels. But Lyria whirls, dodges around my thrashing legs, and stabs her knife straight down into the top of the creature's head.

The blade shatters.

"*Damn!*" Lyria shrieks just as the door bursts wide. The creature leaps through the opening, its head low, its awful elbows angled above its bizarrely curved spine. Green foam spatters between long, pointed fangs. It swings its sightless head back and forth, opens its mouth and lashes the air with a long, black tongue. Gathering its powerful hind legs, it springs straight at Lyria.

With a cry, she ducks to one side, hits the ground, and rolls. It slashes after her, talons tearing through her skirt even as she escapes beneath a long stone settee. She scoots as far back as she can, but the creature crouches, stretching its arm into the space. It hooks her skirt in its claw, starts to drag her out.

I can't just stand here.

I leap to my feet and catch hold of the nearest object within my grasp—the crystal bowl with its blind inhabitants. "Sorry!" I whisper, and leap forward, sloshing water down my front as I smash the crystal with everything I have into the monster's spine. Its feet shoot out to each side. It hits the ground, flat on its belly. Pale fish flop and gasp around it, dancing their death throes.

Legs scrabbling, the creature pulls itself upright. Its awful head twists around, its wagging tongue tasting the air. Green foam spills between its teeth in long streams. I feel it searching, searching.

Then it fixes on me. And a wave of emotion hits me like a blow to the head.

I stagger back against the wall. I'm flattened, smashed. For a moment, I'm convinced my brains will ooze right out of my shattered skull.

The beast crouches. My roiling vision manages to focus just enough to see it. To watch how its head lowers, how those awful elbows rise and bow. To see it open its mouth so wide, its tongue spills out onto the floor. It's going to spring. It's going to hit me in the chest, and those teeth will tear my throat out, and I will die. Suddenly. Horribly. Pointlessly.

No!

In a last, desperate bid for survival, I roll along the wall, reaching for the only thing my hand can grasp. This happens to be the display of pale blue crystals. I pluck up the centermost crystal and whirl in place, holding it out in front of me like a dagger.

A surge ripples through the atmosphere. A shockwave hum, like music, singing straight to the bones.

The surge strikes the creature just as it begins its spring. All force seems to go out from its body. It falls to the ground, its elbows up, its body low. Its neck cranes as though it's searching for me, twisting to grotesque extremes. But I scarcely see any of that.

Instead, I *feel.*

I feel the pulsing emotion emanating from the beast. *Despair.* Savage. Violent. Soul quaking. Wave after crashing wave, washing over the creature, washing over me, pummeling my defenses. But somehow that hum—that single note vibrating from the crystal—catches the wave. Holds it. Suspended like delicate thread in that space between me and the beast.

The monster tilts its head to one side. Its jaw opens and closes. A strange burbling rasps from its tortured throat.

My arms begin to shake. The beast's emotions work their way up that thread, pouring into me. The pain increases. I grit my teeth, a little scream clawing from my throat. The crystal in my grasp begins to shake.

Suddenly there's a burst of blinding white light in my head. I gasp, drop the crystal, and fall to my knees. Blinking, I struggle to make sense of the dark and spinning world around me. The creature lies in broken ruin on the ground. The end of a long crystal protrudes from the soft place at the base of its skull.

All that pain. All that rage. All that horror. Extinguished forever.

My dazzled brain can't quite make sense of what's happening. A pair of feet stepping over the carcass. A hand extended to me. Lyria's voice: "Faraine! Faraine, can you hear me?"

With an effort of will, I manage to get my hand up and place it in hers. She grasps me tight, pulls me to my feet. Her blue eyes swim before my vision, staring earnestly into mine. "What did you do?" she demands. "What was that?"

I shake my head. "I-I don't—"

A burst of savage snarling echoes in the passage outside.

"Gods spare us!" Lyria cries, leaping for the nearest window and dragging me after her. "Nothing for it, I'm afraid. Out the window!"

"What?"

Lyria pushes me to the sill. I stare down at the rocks far below. "Hurry!" she says, swinging out through the opening onto the craggy outer wall. Her skirts flare around her, but her feet are quick and sure. "Climb!"

I gather my skirts in both hands. The awful snarls down the passage are drawing nearer. At any moment, another hideous nightmare will burst through that door. I breathe a prayer, climb out the window, grip the sill, and lower myself down. One foot finds a hold. I lower myself further.

An explosion of garbled roaring bursts in the room above. I choke on a scream and nearly lose my grip. I must concentrate. Climb. Not fall and break both legs. One hand, then the other; one foot, then the next.

A monstrous head appears over the sill. Its slitted nose sniffs; its long tongue tastes the air. I freeze in place, staring up at the beast, not daring even to breathe. It angles its head. Its jaw sags open. Saliva falls in a long, green stream. I choke on a scream and raise an arm to cover my face. My movement is too sharp. I lose my footing. With a shout, I slip, dangling over the drop, hanging on by just a few fingers.

"Hold on!" I hear Lyria shout, but I've lost all track of where she is. My legs kick in empty air as I struggle to find a grip with my other hand.

The monster crawls out over the windowsill. It starts to climb straight down the wall, hissing, slavering. Its body contorts in strange undulations as its claws dig into the stone. A scream of pure terror rips from my lungs. Somewhere, distantly, I hear a voice shout, "*Let go! Let go, Ilsevel!*" But I cannot understand, cannot make the words make sense in my brain.

The monster draws near. It raises an arm, claws flashing in the *lorst* light. It lashes out.

With a last desperate cry, I let go . . . drop . . .

The fall is so quick, it feels instantaneous. One moment I'm struggling against gravity, rocks tearing into my fingers, my grip weakening. The next—

"Got you!"

I blink, look up. *Vor!* He holds me cradled in his arms, tight against his chest. For a moment—a blessed, beautiful, glorious moment—I'm overcome by the calm of his presence. It's as though there cannot be any monsters, not in this place, not in this world made up of just the two of us.

Then I realize—I'm not wearing my veil.

Hastily I drop my gaze, gripping the front of his tunic and staring at the hollow of his throat. His voice is a deep rumble in my ear. "Ilsevel, are you all right?"

"Yes!" I gasp. Before I can get another word out, I'm unceremoniously dumped into another pair of arms. I'm too disoriented at first to comprehend what's happening. Vor's voice seems a dull echo in my ear. "Take the barge. Get her to Mythanar. I'll follow as soon as I can."

"My king—"

"That's an order, captain!"

I twist in this new strong grasp. "Vor!" I cry. My whirling vision catches just a glimpse of him as he leaps up the wall, scaling it in quick bursts of strength. I see Lyria hanging from a window ledge, the horrible monster crawling along the wall straight toward her. "*No!*" I cry.

Then I'm slung over a shoulder and carted off like a sack of flour, all breath for further protests driven from my body.

26

Vor

Faraine.

Her name flashes through my head like a bolt of lightning as I stare down into a pair of bicolored eyes.

Then her lashes fall.

It's Ilsevel's face tucked into my shoulder, Ilsevel's hand clutching the front of my shirt.

Ilsevel. Only Ilsevel.

I shake my head. The screams of the *woggha* explode through my senses. Up on the front face of Lady Xag's house, Ilsevel's cousin balances precariously on a window ledge, too high to safely jump. A cave devil is scuttling toward her from the right and . . . seven gods save us, another one crawls out of a nearby window.

This is no time to fall apart.

I whirl in place just as Hael joins me, her sword drawn. "Here!" I drop my bride unceremoniously into her arms. "Take the barge. Get her to Mythanar. I'll follow as soon as I can."

Hael's eyes flare. "My king—"

"That's an order, captain!"

Before she can protest further, I pivot and launch myself at the wall. Catching hold of rocky outcroppings, I climb, hauling my body up as swiftly as a spider, making for Lady Lyria. She's not looking at me but faces the nearer of the two *woggha*. She's too far away, and the monster is much too fast. I'll never reach her in time, and even if I do—

"*Chathanglas!*" she shouts in a strange, hollow tone. In the same moment, she brings her fist down hard on the wall beside her. A burst of red light ripples out from the point of contact, traveling through the stone. It strikes the nearest *woggha*, which shrieks and springs away from the wall as though burned. It falls to the ground below, twitches once, and is still.

The ripple fades the farther it moves from its center. By the time it reaches me, I feel little more than a buzz of magic under my hand. Witchcraft. Human witchcraft. I'd not realized my bride's companion was a witch.

There's no time to dwell on this revelation, however. The lady, exhausted by her efforts, has collapsed against the windowsill, panting hard. Little sparks of red crackle from her hand and every bit of exposed skin. The spell has sapped her energy. She doesn't seem to be aware of the second cave devil climbing straight down the wall toward her.

"Watch out!" I cry.

She looks down at me first, startled by my voice. I let go of the wall with one hand to point, uselessly. She turns her head, sees the monster bearing down upon her. Its awful jaw opens in a triumphant grin, teeth flashing, saliva dripping. It raises one forelimb. The lady screams.

"*Morar tor Grakanak!*"

The battle cry rings in my ears. I look higher to see a figure sliding down the side of the wall. He aims straight for the *woggha* and thrusts his sword into that exposed place at the back of its head. The monster utters a final death rattle as it falls in a heap to the ground. Its killer, sword ripped from his grasp, just catches the ledge by Lyria's feet.

"Yok!" I cry. The boy dangles above me. There's a gash across his chest, and his face is fixed in a ferocious grimace. "Get down from there, both of you!"

Even as I speak, a third cave devil emerges from a lower window, not far from my position. I launch myself up the wall, pushing off with my feet. Catching the beast around the middle, I wrench it free of the wall. We hang for a crystalized moment, out in empty air.

Then we fall.

Wind rushes past my ears, and I just have time to think, *Well, that was a mistake.*

We hit the ground. Hard. Somehow, instinct made me roll in midair, and the cave devil lands first, taking the impact into its armored body. I hear an awful crunch. I don't even have time to take a breath before I'm rolling, pushing away from the monster as it lashes out, struggling to gather its limbs, to lunge after me, to tear into my flesh. I come up in a defensive crouch, my gaze wholly consumed by that eyeless, hideous face. It opens its mouth wide, offering me a clear view through a cage of fangs down its screaming throat.

A blade appears through the roof of its mouth.

The wagging black tongue vibrates as the cave devil shudders and falls to one side. Sul stands over it, a sword in his hand. Hael's sword, unless I miss my guess, though when and how he took it from her, I don't know. My brother smooths his hair back from his forehead and looks around, his expression mild. "Well, that was fun. Any more playmates to be had? No?"

Bracing with one hand, I pick myself up. My limbs are shaking, my breath tight, but nothing seems to be broken. My sturdy trolde bones stood me in good stead this time. I offer Sul a short nod, then look up to where the human lady and Yok are even now making their way down the wall.

"I thought you were dead!" the lady says. "I thought it must have killed you first before rushing in to ruin our little sit-down."

"And I thought *you* were dead," Yok replies, his voice shaking, though he's trying to hide it. He leaps the last several feet to the ground, staggers heavily, but rights himself. He holds up a hand to the lady. "How did you survive?"

"Dumb luck, mostly," she replies, accepting his aid. Her teeth are chattering, and her entire body quakes. She wraps her arms tightly around herself. "What was that thing, anyway? Some sort of troll housecat?"

"A *woggha*," I answer grimly, striding up to the two of them. "A cave devil. They're closer to your human wolves than any domesticated beast."

She shivers. "Subterranean demon wolves. How lovely."

I look to my young soldier, grab his shoulder, and inspect his chest wound. It's a shallow cut, though painful. "What happened?" I ask, speaking in troldish.

"I'm sorry, my king," Yok replies. "I left them in the front sitting room. It seemed safe enough, what with the house abandoned. And the princess was hungry. Her lady sent me to find food."

"Your job was to protect them, not feed them."

He hangs his head, ashamed. "I know. And when I reached the

kitchen, the *woggha* were there, eating whatever they could find. I tried to shut and bolt them in, but they overpowered me. I ended up pinned down in the pantry." His eyes widen, and he turns suddenly to the lady, switching to her tongue. "There was a fourth one! Another *woggha*!"

"I know," she replies, smiling mirthlessly. "The princess and I managed that one between us."

"The princess?" I snap. "She was involved?"

The lady tosses me a cool glance. "Not to worry. She mostly participated in the role of bait. But she served that role admirably, I'll give her that!"

I eye the woman. This cousin of my bride is more than she seems. That little display of witchcraft proved it. Perhaps she was chosen for this journey to act as bodyguard as well as witness.

"My king," Yok says in troldish, drawing my attention back to him. "There's something you should know. I don't know quite how to explain it, but . . . when I was trapped in the pantry, I thought they were going to burst through the door. There were three of them, and they were slavering and throwing themselves against it, and I knew I couldn't hold them off much longer. I was sure I was a dead man and had begun to pray to the Deeper Dark, when . . . I don't know. There was a sound. Like music. At first, I thought it was just a ringing in my ears. But the *woggha* reacted too. They went from slobbering at the door to absolute silence." He drops his head and draws two deep breaths. Then he looks up at me again. "When I finally dared open the door, they were gone. It was . . . it was like something had *called* to them somehow."

My brow furrows. I've never heard of cave devils acting in this way. And a sound, like music? What could it have been? Perhaps Yok had imagined it in his terror. He's still very young, after all.

I sigh. Either way, we've no time to dwell on mysteries just now. Clapping the boy on the shoulder, I scowl at him. "I'm disappointed in you, Yok. You shouldn't have left the princess's side, not even for a moment. But no matter! We live and we learn and we act better next time. Besides," I add with a half smile, "you redeemed yourself somewhat with that heroic jump out the window. Even your sister would be proud of you for a maneuver like that."

Yok flushes and drops his head again. I give him a last pat on the shoulder, then march over to Sul. My brother stands over the *woggha* he slayed, staring down at the carcass. His face is more pensive than I remember seeing it in a long while.

I stand behind him. For a few breaths, we are silent. Then I speak in a low voice. "Well, Sul? What do you think of my plan now?"

He shakes his head. "I don't like trusting humans to save us." For once in his life, his voice is blunt, hard. And honest. "They're so base. So crude. And they lie with every breath they take. I hate that we must make ourselves vulnerable to such creatures."

My brother's words send a dart of shame to my heart—shame at my own human heritage. But it doesn't matter if I am of a lesser race, that my blood is diluted or even tainted. For whatever reason, the gods have seen fit to make me King of Mythanar, Lord Protector of all the Under Realm. Thus I must do what I believe is right. And bear the weight of consequences.

I look down to the docks. Our barge is no longer tethered in place, and when I follow the river's flow, I do not see it. Which means Hael must have gotten away with my bride.

My bride . . .

I frown. Once again, that bizarre image passes through my memory—the image of bicolored eyes peering up at me in that unexpected moment of mayhem and terror. But no. No, it simply could not be. For the face I'd glimpsed was certainly Ilsevel's, not Faraine's.

"*Juk*," I mutter through my teeth so no one will hear. I've got to get her out of my head. Once and for all. For my sake. For Ilsevel's. For all of the Under Realm.

I let my gaze sweep across the silent, stricken village. The weight of those deaths threatens to crush my soul. Those deaths, and the deaths yet to come. Unless I can prevent it.

"Come, Sul," I say, squeezing my brother's shoulder. "I need to get married. Fast."

"Yes, of course." My brother chuckles dully. "And let's hope the power of true love is enough to save us all."

27

Faraine

The slosh of water echoes hollowly against the surrounding stone walls. We have long since left behind the enormous open cavern beneath the *lorst* crystals and entered a narrow waterway in a tunnel scarcely wide enough for the barge to pass through. Hael deftly guides the craft from her place at the prow, using some steering mechanism I don't understand. A glowing crystal suspended in a delicate silver frame illuminates the trolde woman's gleaming muscles as she fights the river current.

"Hold on, Princess," she tosses back over her shoulder. "It gets rough in here."

I sit numbly in the middle of the craft on a chair which seems to have been bolted to the boards. It's cushioned and richly draped in silks, a proper throne intended for a sovereign quite a lot larger than me. At Hael's command, I grip the arms. And just in time! The barge bucks suddenly as the current turns aggressive. Despite Hael's determined steering, we bounce off a boulder, rebound, hit the opposite wall. I choke on a scream. I can see next to nothing, which makes it all seem much wilder and more dangerous.

Then, with a stomach-churning dip, we are expelled from the tunnel and into another cavern. The river calms, turns gentle and languid, lapping the stone shore. More *lorst* crystals glow here. Not as numerous or bright as those above the village, but enough that I am no longer blind. I look around and catch my breath. The cavern roof is like a vaulted chapel ceiling: high, arched, and jagged. The walls on either side of us are strange, carved by the river into undulous sheets layered in variegated colors.

Still gripping the chair, I crane my torso to peer back at the tunnel exit rushing with churning white water. How in the worlds do barges travel back along that way to reach the village? Perhaps another waterway flows the opposite direction? I cannot imagine learning to navigate these treacherous grottos and fissures.

Though I'm not cold, my body shivers uncontrollably. I wish I could pull the silk drapes on the chair up and around my bare shoulders. Just now, however, I can't seem to pry my tensed fingers free of the chair arms. What has become of the others? I can't believe I left them behind to face those monsters alone. Not that I could have been much help. Not like Lyria. Good goddess above, who knew my half sister could fight like that? What exactly has she been up to in the years since her exile from Beldroth?

"Are you all right, Princess Ilsevel?" Hael asks from the prow. The trolde woman stands at ease, but her face is still severely lined with tension.

I nod, then manage to rasp, "I'm unharmed." Shuddering, I force my lungs to draw a full breath. "What were those things?"

"Cave devils." Her voice is grim.

I want to question her further. Something is wrong here, something more than the attack. There's an unsettling, sour sensation wafting out from Hael's soul. Stronger than mere fear. It's more like *desperation.*

Bile rises in my throat. I swallow it back. How many more such dreadful beings live in this strange, dark realm? Are attacks like this an everyday occurrence? Did those monsters have something to do with why the trolde village was so terribly silent and empty?

I close my eyes. And suddenly, I'm back in Vor's arms, wrapped in the safety of his embrace. I wish I could have stayed there, stayed with him. What will happen if my bridegroom doesn't survive to the wedding?

No. I won't think like that. I bow my head and pray for Vor, for Lyria, for the young trolde soldier. When those prayers run out, I try to pray for myself.

We travel by water for some miles through a bewildering series of caverns and tunnels. Sometimes, I glimpse villages bustling with activity beneath the *lorst* crystal glow. Pale troldefolk pause in their business to watch us pass. They stare at me with mingled fascination and apprehension. Do these people, living away from centers of political activity, have any idea who I am? I must seem very strange to them, traveling in the royal barge with only tall Hael as escort.

We pass through a final tunnel, this one illuminated by glowing green growth that looks like a combination of fungi and flower—I'm never quite close enough to see for sure which. Before I can decide, the tunnel opens into the most massive space yet.

"Princess," Hael says, turning to me once more. "We're nearly there. Look!"

I am looking. I couldn't stop looking if I wanted to.

The city of Mythanar rises before me, vast and white and shining beneath the radiance of a million *lorst* crystals. At first glance, it looks like a single, vast stalagmite, completely carved from natural elements. At second glance, I become aware of all the beautiful arches and buttresses, the carved handiwork of generations of brilliant minds and gifted hands. Light fills the tiered streets—luminous glows of a thousand colors that make the pale stone shine like a dream.

Apparently, this waterway is only one of many approaches to the city. Bridges arch like soaring highways overhead, stretching from the cavern walls to meet the city at various levels. And at the pinnacle of the city stands what must be the king's own palace—a lofty edifice with a central tower so tall, it nearly meets the hanging stalactites of the cavern ceiling above.

I've never seen anything like this. Not in my wildest dreams. The town surrounding Beldroth would be swallowed whole ten times over in a city like this. Indeed, this place could easily house all the people of Gavaria with room to spare. And this is only one of the cities under the Shadow King's rule. He truly is a power far beyond anything I'd imagined.

And am I to be queen of such a city?

I drop my gaze, unable to take in more. Instead, I focus on more immediate surroundings. We're approaching some sort of dam. Workers march along its upper walkway, and I see wheels and mechanisms I don't understand, which seem to be controlling the water flow. Hael guides the barge to a landing, and dockworkers hasten to grab lines and secure it. They're all so tall, so pale and otherworldly in their beauty. I shiver every time one of them casts a glance my way.

"Where is the king?" someone asks.

"Coming," Hael answers with such confidence, it's almost enough to raise my spirits. She holds out a hand to me. "Allow me, Princess," she says.

I exit the barge with more dignity than I boarded it, walking hand in hand with the trolde woman rather than slung across her shoulders. My legs shake as I struggle to reorient my balance, but Hael tightens her grip and does not let me fall. She guides me down the dock to solid ground, then says, "Wait while I summon the morleth."

To my great surprise, she puts her fingers in her mouth and blows a sharp, blasting whistle. The next moment, darkness gathers in a whorl behind her, and the ugly, toothy head of a morleth emerges. She takes it by the reins and draws it out, its hooves striking the ground in sharp percussion.

I leap back several paces. "Where did it come from?"

"From the shadow, of course," Hael says mildly, and beckons me to her. "Come, Princess. It's a long walk to the city. Better to ride."

I find myself far less eager to mount that beast without Vor to ride with me. But Hael is sturdy and strong, and after mounting, she easily hauls me up to sit on her pack behind the saddle. Once I am settled, she yanks the morleth's head around, heading for the nearest bridge.

An arched gate of white stone marks the beginning of the bridge. Troldefolk traveling along the highway gather in a tight knot, waiting for the gate guards to let them through. People part quickly to make way for Hael's morleth. When some protest and hurl what I suspect are curses at her, she points to the insignia on her arm and says, "*Aruk hrukta.*" This is apparently enough to make the grumblers bow their heads and step back an extra pace. The gate guards take one look at her and wave her on through, saluting smartly even as they ogle me.

We pass under the arch and out onto the bridge. All the breath leaves my body in a rush.

For some reason, I'd assumed the river poured into a lake surrounding the city. But it's not a lake. It's a chasm. A vast chasm surrounding the city, save for where it backs up against the far cavern wall. It's so dark, so yawning, so huge. I feel the hollow endlessness of it reaching up as though to claim me and drag me into its depths.

"It's best not to look down," Hael says even as she urges her morleth into a brisk trot.

I should listen to her. But of course, I don't. I cannot resist the urge to peer over her arm, over the edge of the bridge. Oh gods! It's worse than I thought. For it isn't darkness that waits at the bottom of that drop. Deep down flows another river—this one a fiery red.

I squeeze my eyes shut and duck my head to where my hands grip the cantle of the saddle, praying the morleth will pick up its pace. It seems like an age before Hael speaks again: "They're here to greet you, Princess. I would advise you to sit tall. Show them your courage."

Swallowing back a whimper, I pull my head up. We're near the far gate now, which juts out from the wall ringing the lower tier of the city. Folk are gathered just outside the gate—any number of pale troldefolk, most of them tall and white and stern. One figure, however, looms taller than the others. He is a great stony slab of a being, with white hair hanging in thin, straggled hanks to his enormous shoulders. Unlike the others, he is nearly naked, clad only in a thin loincloth, his muscled, rock-hard body on full display. He looks something like how I once imagined trolls would be, only somehow, he's still maintained some of the eerie trolde beauty.

Beside him stands a woman with gloriously long white hair streaked with black. She wears a headdress of shining silver like a tall starburst trimmed in dangling red jewels. Her gown is not unlike the one I wear—bare shouldered with detached sleeves draping from her upper arms, and a column skirt that clings to her curves. The black fabric shimmers with unexpected glints of gleaming red thread woven in, which calls to mind the fiery river in the darkness below.

Her face is what draws my eye the most, however. It's a very beautiful face, but hard. As hard as the stone man standing beside her. She looks as though she were carved from marble. I'm not sure there ever was or ever could be any warmth to her.

"Who are they?" I ask softly.

"The lady in front is Queen Roh," Hael responds in a low voice. "She is the wife of the late King Guar, and the current king's stepmother. Beside her is Targ." Her tone pitches a little darker. "He calls himself *Umog tor Grakanak*, Priest of the Deeper Dark. He is a great favorite of the queen. He has . . . influence in Mythanar."

Though she expresses no opinion, her unease is palpable. I look again at the huge rock-hide man. His glittering eyes are fastened on me. I cannot read their expression, but I suddenly want very much to lean against Hael, to wrap her cloak around me and hide.

Instead, I pull myself a little straighter, setting my chin. "And the rest of them?"

"Members of the king's council," Hael says, rattling off a series of harsh-sounding trolde names. "You needn't concern yourself with them. They've merely come to gawk and serve no useful function."

"Is there anything I'm meant to do?"

"No. Hold yourself as tall as you can, nod if addressed, and say nothing. No one expects you to speak troldish, but they will not speak human either."

My eyebrow quirks at this rudeness. But then, it's not as though my people had made any effort to speak the trolde language when Vor and his people visited Beldroth. It's my turn to be the stranger. Only, unlike Vor, I do not have the support of friends at my back.

Hael rides her morleth the last few lengths of the bridge and pulls it to a halt before the gathered figures. "*Grakol-dura*," she says, raising a hand in greeting.

Queen Roh's gaze crawls over me like a spider, her expression utterly unreadable. She takes her time with her inspection, ignoring Hael. I feel waves of displeasure rolling out from her, but it's oddly muted. These troldefolk emotions are more difficult for me to read than my own kind. I keep my head high and meet the queen's gaze, maintaining a firmly blank expression.

At last, she turns from me and speaks a stream of trolde words of which I recognize only one: *Vor*. Hael answers, and they go back and forth. Then Targ, the stone man, takes a heavy step forward and joins the conversation. His voice is like a great millstone grinding. I feel as though he could crush me with mere words.

But here's an oddness: I get no sense of feeling from him. None. Not even the barest whisper. It's as if the rock covering his hide somehow blocks out all emotion. I've never encountered anything of the kind. It would almost be a relief if it weren't so deeply unsettling. It's very . . . cold. Like death.

Hael responds to the priest, her voice sharper than before. I hear Vor's name. I suspect they're asking where he is. Hael sounds cool enough, but the gathered folk exchange uneasy glances and level anxious looks my way. I wish I dared ask Hael what was happening. Better to do as she said, however, and hold my tongue.

Finally, Targ takes a step back. When he does, the others follow his lead, parting to make way for us to pass through the gate. Hael spurs her morleth into motion. We pass between the council members, the queen, and the priest, and I enter Mythanar for the first time.

I have no chance to form even a first impression of the city. No sooner am I through the gate before strangers crowd close, all reaching up to me. Hael barks, drives them back, then swings down from the saddle and lifts me off it herself. "This way, Princess," she says, and bustles me over to what turns out to be a curtained litter. She draws back the curtains, urges me inside. The space is cushioned and much larger than I need, having been fashioned for a trolde woman.

"Don't worry," Hael says. "I'll be right beside you."

Then she pulls the curtain shut and is gone. I'm caught like a bird in a cage behind fabric so dense, I can discern nothing through it but glowing lights and flickering shadows. The whole structure lurches suddenly as it's lifted, presumably onto trolde shoulders. It's good that I'm seated, or I would have toppled right over, for there is nothing to hold on to. The litter bearers fall into a steady rhythm, however, and the initial lurching subsides.

I fight to gather my wits. Why does it feel as though I'm a sacrifice being carried to a foreign altar? I miss the morleth and Hael. Much more so, I miss Vor. I'd felt safe in his arms. I want to believe if he were with me, he would have kept me in the saddle with him, riding through the streets in full view of his people. That would have been preferable. At least, it would be if I were truly his bride.

As it is, I should be grateful. The less I see of Vor before the wedding, the better.

After what feels like forever swaying along inside that litter, I finally grab the curtain and pull it open a sliver, peering out. Just beneath me is the head of a litter bearer—a great, strong trolde man. True to her word, Hael is close by, riding her morleth alongside me. Beyond her is another litter, this one with curtains drawn back, its occupant on display. Queen Roh, reclining and resplendent.

As though aware of my scrutiny, she turns her head to look directly at me.

I gasp and pull the curtain shut again. "Gods blight!" I whisper. I shouldn't have done that. I should have met her gaze and held it. Now she knows just how frightened I am.

At last we reach our destination. My litter is carried right up the palace steps, through the doors, and finally set down. Hael appears again, sweeping back the curtain and holding out her hand. Grateful for assistance, I climb out as gracefully as I can and emerge into a huge hall. The scale is so staggering, I can scarcely take it in. Beldroth is positively minuscule by comparison. What must Vor have thought of us during his visit? All our posturing and pride, while he himself was master of such a magnificent domain!

Hael exchanges words with the widow queen and her priest. It's hard to say, but it sounds to me like an argument. Eventually, Hael turns to me and barks, "Come, Princess. It is time for you to prepare."

"But . . ." I glance around at the others, then back up at Hael. I feel her silently urging me to hold my tongue. So, I merely incline my head.

To my relief, Hael leads me out of that hall and into a side passage, which would have seemed large were it not for the enormity of the hall we just left behind. We proceed through a labyrinth of corridors, then up a flight of stairs. Finally, Hael opens a door and ushers me into a room full of steam. A bathing chamber—but such a bathing chamber! A pool in the center of the room is filled with steaming, scented water, illuminated by glowing purple crystals below.

My blood goes cold.

Hael snaps her fingers. Two trolde women appear through the steam, towels draped over their arms. Hael speaks to them in quick troldish, then turns to me. "May I suggest a bath, Princess? You'll want to be fresh for the ceremony."

Lyria's warning rings in my ear: *Water will wash those runes on the eyes away at once, and the rest will hold for no more than an hour or two after.*

"No!" My voice comes out in a burst. Hael casts me a strange look, so I hastily soften my tone. "I . . . I would prefer a simple cloth and a basin of water. And privacy."

Hael looks as though she will protest. To my relief, however, she turns to the attendants and rattles off another string of troldish. They cast me uneasy glances but swiftly fulfill my request, fetching basin, water, cloth, and a little stand on which to set them. Then, bowing and scraping, they walk backwards from the room.

"That is all, Princess?" Hael asks.

"Yes, thank you," I answer firmly. Then add, "Privacy too. If you please."

She bows and follows the attendants from the room. The door shuts firmly behind her.

I let out a long sigh, rolling my head back and staring at the crystals hanging from the ceiling. This is the first time in days that

I've been alone. Yet I'm very aware of the figures standing just on the other side of that door. I dare not relax my guard, not for a moment.

It's tricky business washing myself. I use the dry cloth to wipe dirt and debris from my face, arms, and shoulders, then dampen it slightly to cleanse parts of my body that won't be overtly obvious should the magic wear off. How much longer will these spells hold? Days? Weeks? Hours? And more to the point: how much longer do I want them to hold? Because the moment is fast approaching when I will have to decide. Do I go through with the wedding night as planned? Or do I reveal the truth to Vor and throw myself and my kingdom upon his mercy?

It's not Vor's mercy I doubt, however. I close my eyes, leaning heavily against the wash table. Once more, I see the cold gaze of Queen Roh. Once more I feel the inexplicable *nothing* of her priest and the many faces of the council members all blended into a jumble of antagonism and suspicion. The troldefolk are not my friends. They do not care what becomes of Gavaria. They do not care that Prince Ruvaen slaughters my people like animals. We are little more than animals to them. We are worthwhile only insofar as we are useful.

Which means I must be useful.

Suddenly a great booming reverberates through the stone walls and along the floor. Like a deep-bellied roar, it echoes and reechoes. I straighten, step away from the wash basin. That sounds like a signal horn of some kind. Could it be . . . Does it mean . . . ?

A tap at the door, followed by Hael's voice: "The king has returned, Princess. He and the others are back safe. You must hurry now. We need to get you dressed. The ceremony is about to commence."

28

Vor

Umog Zu and Lord Gol, one of my ministers, stand at the top of the palace stairs as we ride our morleth through the city and into the palace courtyard. I pull Knar to a halt, dismount, and toss the reins to a waiting groom, then mount the steps quickly, taking them three at a time.

"Is she here?" I demand. "Princess Ilsevel, is she safe?"

"Yes, yes, the girl arrived all in one piece," Lord Gol says with a dismissive wave of one hand. Though a chief member of my council, he voted staunchly against this marriage. He would have been just as happy if Ilsevel had been lost somewhere on the journey. "And what of you, my king?" he continues, his disapproving expression shifting to one of solemn concern. "Captain Hael told us what happened. How many cave devils were there?"

"Too many," I answer shortly. "But I won't discuss that now." I turn to the priestess standing silent and dignified, her eyes closed, her fingers forming the holy sign of the diamond before her sternum. "Umog, is all prepared?"

"The *yunkathu* waters have been sanctified," she replies, without opening her eyes. "The witnesses have gathered, and the Song of the Deeper Dark is ready to be sung. Go prepare yourself quickly, my son, for all wait upon you."

"Right." I turn and look down the steps to where Yok is just now helping Ilsevel's cousin off his morleth. "Lady Lyria!" I call.

She picks up the hem of her gown and climbs the stair to me, huffing and puffing, for the steps are built for beings far taller than she. When she reaches the top, I take her hand and offer it to Gol. "This is my bride's cousin, Lady Lyria. She is to bear witness to the ceremony so that she may carry word of its completion back to her people."

Gol offers the lady a studiously blank look. She raises her eyebrows, turning from him to me. "What's happening?" she asks in her own language.

"Lord Gol will escort you to the *yunkathu* hall," I say, "where the ceremony will take place anon."

"Not before I've seen my cousin." Her words are sharp, her eyes hard as flints.

"Ah." Of course. What a cad I am. Of course, she must be concerned about Ilsevel. "You will see her just before the ceremony," I promise. I turn to my minister. "See that the lady is brought to the inner chamber so that she may meet her kinswoman before she enters the waters."

Gol opens his mouth to begin what will no doubt be a prolonged protest. I don't wait around to hear it. Pivoting, I sidestep him and Umog Zu, dart through the door, and make my way swiftly to the bathhouses. The last thing I want is to enter the wedding waters while covered in the grime and gore I accumulated battling cave devils. A servant helps me remove my clothes and hastily scrubs down my limbs and torso before helping me into the apparel prepared for my *yunkathu*—a sleeveless silver garment with an open front and a pair of close-fitted trousers held in place by a four-braid belt. It's simple attire, but for this part of the wedding events, I need nothing more. I'll change into proper finery for the feast after . . . after . . .

Gods, I can't think about that. Not yet.

Sul finds me just as the servant finishes securing my belt. He stands in the doorway, hair dripping from his own bath, clad in a long robe with heavily embroidered sleeves. His bare chest, scrubbed clean of Lady Xag's blood and *woggha* saliva, shines pale and smooth as a polished stone. He looks me over.

"Well?" I demand. "I'm sure you have some clever quip to make. Best get it over with now. I'm not waiting around."

Sul shakes his head. Then he sighs. "Your wedding day, brother."

My wedding day. I set my teeth and nod.

"Tell me," Sul continues, "are you satisfied? Are you . . . ? I hardly know what I'm asking. Are you happy?"

It's not what I would have expected from him. Not in this particular moment. It's certainly not like Sul to express any tender feeling or sympathy. The events of the day must have struck him harder than I thought.

His question is still there, hanging in the air. Waiting to be answered. "I am king," I say, inclining my head slightly.

He holds my gaze a moment. In the depth of his eyes, haunting sorrow lurks. For a moment, I'm back in Dugorim with him—back on the ledge above that death drop, watching in horror as Lady Xag pitched, fell. What we witnessed today will linger with us both for the rest of our lives.

Somewhere not far off, the wedding drums begin to beat.

"Ready?" Sul says.

"Yes." I nod and pull back my shoulders. "For Xag."

A spasm passes over Sul's face. He hardens his jaw and echoes softly, "For Xag."

....

The Kathu Grotto is a sacred space, hallowed over ages of ceremony and tradition, wrapped up in legend. It's a cave hidden behind the Yun Falls, illuminated only by small blue *lorst* crystals growing naturally from the walls and ceiling, which cast a moody light upon the scene.

A pool runs straight through the middle of the space, cutting it cleanly in two. Sul and I stand on one side. On the other stands Lyria, accompanied by Yok. She paces along the water's edge, her face a mask of hard lines. When I appear, she shoots me a swift, wary glance. Odd—up until this moment, I'd believed Ilsevel's cousin supported this match. Perhaps she's not so keen to see her kinswoman married off to a trolde after all.

I stand and wait, tense with anticipation. Beyond the Yun Falls, I can just discern the murmuring of a hundred voices gathered in the outer hall. The wedding guests. My court, my people. Spectators at the performance of my life.

Resentment pricks my heart. If I were any other man, a man who made his own choices for his own reasons, I wouldn't be standing here now. I wouldn't be waiting for Ilsevel to appear on the other side of this pool. No, if I were free to choose as my heart willed, it would be another face I looked for now—

No.

Don't think of her.

Never again.

Ilsevel.

Ilsevel.

Ilsevel.

As though my thinking her name somehow conjured her, my bride appears. She steps through the opening on the far side of the grotto, guided by Hael into the *lorst* light. She doesn't seem to see me but instead lets out a little cry and runs immediately to Lyria, throwing her arms around her. Then she draws back, and they exchange words in hushed tones I cannot hear over the waterfall.

I drink in the sight of her. She's not wearing a veil anymore; it was ripped from her head in the fracas with the cave devil. I'm sorry for that, knowing it was part of her people's tradition. But I'm also glad. It gives me a chance to study her face, to remember those features which had faded from recollection over the last few weeks. Seeing her now, memories return to me—that thick chestnut hair, that determined jaw and wide mouth, quick to smile, quicker still to frown. Those dark eyes and the way they sparked with defiant laughter when we danced. Dark eyes. Not the bicolored gaze I'd thought I glimpsed in the midst of mayhem back in Dugorim. I had most certainly imagined that sight. Such a fool.

But I won't be a fool any longer.

Slowly, my gaze travels from her face down lower. She's wearing a traditional troldish *wokh* for the ceremony: a loose-fitting gown that reaches all the way to her ankles. It's rather shapeless, but the material is thin enough that the *lorst* light shines right through it, revealing much of her slender, graceful figure. A rush of heat floods my veins. Soon, very soon, I will be expected to explore that figure much more intimately. My throat thickens.

I turn away. Sul is watching me, but I won't meet his eye. I wait until Umog Zu's voice echoes suddenly from beyond the waterfall: "*Vultog drag kathu. Tog Morar tor Grakanak.*"

Let the two enter the one water. By the God of the Deeper Dark.

The assembly gathered echoes in a dull roar: "*Morar tor Grakanak.*"

"Gods go with you, brother," Sul whispers.

I draw a slow breath. Then I move to the pool's edge. It's too deep to step down into, so I sit and ease myself in. Gods, it's cold as ice! Couldn't they have found a hot spring for this purpose?

The sound of frantic whispering catches my ear. I look up to see Lyria and Ilsevel exchanging tense words. Hael approaches, speaks sharply to them, but they hold each other's hands and won't look at her. Ilsevel's expression, lit from below by the *lorst* crystals, is frightened. My heart sinks. Is she going to refuse at the last moment to make this plunge with me?

As though giving in to an argument, Ilsevel nods suddenly and steps away from Lyria. She draws herself up straight as her slow footsteps carry her to the edge of the pool. Her eyes meet mine for a fraction of a second before she looks down at her feet. I watch her draw another shaky breath, then sit and put her feet in the water. She hisses through her teeth, shocked by the cold. Slowly, she slides into the pool, grimacing, nostrils flaring. The water is up to her chest. Her eyes go very wide, and the *wokh* gown floats out around her body, making her look like some sort of watery ghost.

Umog Zu's voice echoes through the falls: "*Let the two join hands. By the God of the Deeper Dark.*"

"*Morar tor Grakanak*," the assembly choruses.

I hold out my hand. Ilsevel glances up at me again. Just for an instant, just long enough for me to see those dark eyes of hers shimmering with fear in the *lorst* light. Then she focuses her gaze on my fingers. Wading to me, shivering hard, she takes hold of my hand.

"It's all right, Ilsevel," I say. "I'm here. I won't let go of you."

She nods, still without looking at me. Slowly, we turn to face the waterfall. She has been briefed on the ceremony, hasn't she? To be safe, I lean a little closer and speak into her ear so she can hear me above the water. "I will do my best to pull you along after me. Kick your feet and keep your head under until you touch the far edge of the pool. It's a bit far, but I'll get you there. I promise."

She nods. Her breath comes in short, quick pants.

"*Let the two give themselves to the Dark*," Umog Zu intones. "*Let them sink into the waters of oblivion, losing Self in the name of Oneness. Blessed by the Deeper Dark.*"

"*Morar tor Grakanak.*"

"Ready?" I whisper.

She nods.

Then we plunge under the water. I hadn't realized how bright it would be, how vividly the submerged *lorst* crystals would glow, lighting the way. I push off with my feet, dragging Ilsevel along behind me. She's struggling already. She's probably never swum before in her life; most humans don't as a rule. I kick harder, compensating for her.

We reach the waterfall. I feel the pressure of pounding water coming down on top of us. A shock ripples through Ilsevel, but her grip on my hand only tightens. I haul on my arm, dragging her after me. How terrifying this must be for her. But she's not protested. Not even once. My bride is very brave.

Perhaps I can learn to love her. Truly love her. Any woman who would go through all of this without so much as a murmur of protest must be a worthy queen.

We're through the falls now, on the far side of the pool. In full view of the witnesses in gallery seats above. How many times have I sat in those same seats, watching this swim performed? How often had I imagined what it would be like to enter that pool myself, to swim beneath the Yun Falls, dying to my old self and reemerging new?

A vibrating hum fills the water around me—the song of *urzul* crystals, plucked from their gardens and planted here fresh for the ceremony. Their song creates a cocoon of light and sound that wraps around my bride and me. And I feel it—something inexplicable taking place. Something mystical. The hum enters my body, works down into my bones, runs through my hand into hers. Soon both our bodies vibrate to the same frequency, joined in this song. Who we were before this moment no longer matters. We have died to those selves. When we emerge, we will be reborn as one. *Yun*, as we say in troldish. *United.*

A strange realization comes over me as I feel that vibration passing from me into Ilsevel and back again. I know now what I had not believed possible before: I will never think of another woman again. From this time forward, there will be no one for me but her. This girl. This woman. My *yun*, who shares the song of my bones. Ilsevel.

"*Ilsevel.*" My lips form her name under the water, blowing out a stream of bubbles, the last of my air.

Then my fingertips hit the far wall of the pool. I hear Umog Zu's voice above the water, and though I cannot discern the words, I know them by heart: "*Uvulg tor ugdth. Hirark! Yuntog lorst.*"

Now have the Two died. Look! The One rises.

"*Morar tor Garkanak!*" the assembly rumbles as I pull Ilsevel up beside me. She finds the wall, grips its edge, and we both emerge in a surge of water and foam and gasping breaths. My heart soars with the newness of the song playing in my body. Does she feel it too? Has she experienced what I just have?

I try to catch her eye. Ilsevel wipes hair out of her face, water streaming. She turns farther away, shaking her head. I cannot tell if she is purposefully avoiding my gaze or not.

Umog Zu seems to manifest from the darkness, stepping into the glow of two great *lorst* crystals placed at the head of the pool. "The Dark has claimed," she declares. "The Dark has delivered. The Dark has made new." She raises her old hands, painted all over with sparkling *olk* dust so that they draw every eye. "New life from the water rises, in the name of the Deeper Dark."

"*Morar tor Grakanak!*"

I climb out of the pool, then turn to help Ilsevel. She's so short that I'm obliged to grip her under the arms and pull her out, setting her on her feet beside me. Small and shivering, she takes a step back. Her wet gown clings to her body, revealing the curve of her hips, the swell of her breasts. Hastily, she crosses her arms and turns fully away from me.

Lyria leaps forward, gasping as though she's just sprinted around the waterfall to meet us on the far side. She drapes what turns out to be the beaded lace veil over Ilsevel's head. So, it wasn't lost after all. A funny sort of modesty, considering the state of the princess's *wokh* gown.

Hael steps forward next, however, and wraps a thick blanket around my bride's shoulders. Sul is there only a half beat slower with a blanket for me. I avoid my brother's gaze and turn with Ilsevel to face the high priestess one last time.

Umog Zu holds a bowl of *olk* dust in her hand. Her pale eyes move solemnly from me to Ilsevel. "*Tog Morar tor Grakanak*," she intones one last time.

"*By the God of the Deeper Dark*," the assembly echoes.

The priestess sticks her thumb in the bowl, then smears its contents across my forehead and heart. She performs the same gesture over Ilsevel, then takes our hands and joins them. "*Yun*," she says, "greet your people."

I turn and look up at the assembly, gathered in the stone gallery seats. The *lorst* light does not reach their faces, but I can see their hundreds of shadowy forms and feel the weight of their gazes. I lift my bride's hand high, showing all that we are united.

The hall erupts in cheers. The sound echoes and reechoes across the stone, until it seems to me that it will fill all the Under Realm. Let every rock, every cave, every dark and crawling thing, let the fire at the very heart of this world know that Vor of Mythanar has taken a wife. And he will save his people.

Triumphant, exultant, I turn to smile at my bride. But her head is ducked low beneath her veil, and she will not meet my gaze.

29

Faraine

Hael leads me from the vaulting stone hall with its shadowed galleries and unseen onlookers. It's a relief to escape all those watching eyes. Like shrugging off an invisible burden.

My whole body trembles. If I'm honest, it's not so much to do with the cold. Although I am frozen straight through after that icy plunge, I scarcely note the numbness in my extremities. My mind is much too focused on what comes next.

The bridal chamber.

Lyria trails behind us, muttering under her breath as she struggles to keep up with Hael's quick pace. No one else seems to be joining us on this particular trek. A soaking wet, shivering bride is permitted some dignity, at least. I cling with one hand to the thick blanket Hael gave me, my other hand gripping my necklace. I'd not worn it in the pool, remembering how Vor had reacted when he saw it. Instead, I'd slipped it into Lyria's hand just before entering the water.

Which meant I was open to receive the full force of Vor's surging feelings. Feelings which started out as nothing more than anxiety and tension, but which, partway through the swim, as we passed beneath that bruising waterfall, transformed abruptly into something unexpected. An exultant delight, thrilling with promise and purpose, that sang from his soul. That song struck me so hard, I nearly gasped at the sheer joy of it. I've never experienced anything quite like it.

I wanted to respond.

I wanted to let my own heart echo his song back to him in joyful harmony. My body, my being filled up with light and warmth and eagerness and—

And then I remembered. His song wasn't for me.

Hael stops abruptly. I've lost track of the passages and stairs we've climbed, and blink blearily at the tall stone door before me. There's no visible latch, but Hael pushes it open, revealing a sumptuous chamber within. It takes me a moment to realize why the sight looks so odd. Then it strikes me: the furnishings are all human. Beautiful chairs and lounges, a tall painted screen before the hearth, little tables and ornaments, all of luxurious taste. Utterly unexpected in such a distinctly troldish chamber of stone, illuminated by hanging *lorst* crystals.

"This is the Queen's Apartment," Hael says, waving a hand for me to enter. "King Vor had it fitted out specially for you. He wanted you to feel at home."

I step inside, my jaw dropping as I look around. The curtains in the windows are trimmed in Valaayun lace, so intricate, so expensive, it must be worth a king's ransom. The rug under my feet is an Urivarian import, woven with intricate sacred symbols of all seven gods. It's big enough to cover more than half the floor space. Everywhere I look, I spy some other beautiful item, all works of human craftsmanship. I cannot say I feel at home, because it's all so much nicer than anything I've ever known. My father could only dream of such riches back in Beldroth!

"It's beautiful," I say, turning slowly in place.

Hael nods and indicates a door on my right hand. "There is the adjoining passage to the King's Apartment. All concourse between these two rooms is strictly private, of course. But tonight, he will come through the main door, escorted by his attendants and other witnesses."

I nod. Of course, there must be witnesses. And afterwards, both Lyria and a female trolde called the *uggrha* will inspect my body to make certain everything has transpired as it ought. An indignity I will suffer gladly rather than having onlookers for the consummation itself.

Hael steps across the chamber and opens the door at my left hand. "Come," she bids. I obey. This door leads to the bedchamber, of course. My stomach tightens. At least my nervous tension has warmed my cold blood, though I still cannot seem to stop my knees from trembling.

Lyria hastily steps to my side, facing Hael. "I will help the princess prepare for her husband."

Hael narrows her eyes. "The king has asked me to stand in as the princess's *murzol*. It is my duty to prepare her."

"Yes, and I'm her next of kin. It is my right and privilege."

The two of them stare each other down, as though each believes force of will alone can make the other spontaneously combust. I'm caught between them. I can't very well urge Hael to comply without seeming as though I'm fighting the practices of the troldefolk. But I don't dare tell Lyria to stand down. If the disguise spells were affected by my plunge in the wedding pool, I can't risk discovery. Not now, not when we're so close to . . . to . . .

"Very well." Hael's voice is abrupt as she steps back out of the bedchamber. "Your kinswoman may prepare you. But I must be permitted to inspect the room and your person before King Vor arrives."

"Right." Lyria flashes a too-large smile. "Be off with you then."

Hael tips her chin, her brow furrowed. "I said, I will need to inspect the bride and chamber before the king's visit."

"I heard you the first time." Lyria waves her hand. To my relief, Hael departs with only a single glance my way. She crosses the outer room and steps into the passage beyond, closing the door behind her.

Lyria hastily pulls me into the bedroom and shuts us in. It's fairly well lit by *lorst* crystals, though the light through the window is swiftly fading into trolde nightfall. Lyria pulls my veil back and makes a face. "It's all slipping badly now. It's a good thing you weren't depending on that idiot Klaern's spellwork!"

A mirror dominates the wall opposite the bed—a huge, perfectly clear glass set in a silver frame which, upon second glance, appears to be a great, coiling dragon. I peer at my reflection, momentarily shocked to see my own two eyes looking back at me. The rest still looks like Ilsevel, but it's all gone a bit blurry around the edges. "What can we do?" I ask, prodding at one cheek.

"Don't poke it!" Lyria pushes away my hand and scowls into the glass. "Well, you can request these lights be dimmed. There's no guarantee he'll comply, but your new husband strikes me as the accommodating sort."

New husband. A shiver travels up the back of my neck. But it's true. I've married him. I've bound my life to his—all in my sister's name. The name which is now, in every legal sense, mine.

I shake my head, stepping back from the mirror. A little table and chair stand close to the hearth, and I sink into the seat. "I can't do it. I can't lie to him like this." I look up at Lyria. "I have to tell him the truth before—"

"You finish that sentence, and I'll put a spell on your tongue so you can't speak for a month!" Lyria's face falls into stern lines. "I was given one assignment when I was sent here with you: to make certain you don't spoil everything before the alliance can be secured." Her expression softens slightly. She reaches out, pats my hand. "Don't you realize? You've gone too far now. If he discovers that Larongar has played him false before the consummation, he will certainly break off everything."

"But what about after? He's going to find out." I shudder, dropping my head. "What will he think of me?"

"It doesn't matter what he thinks of you." Lyria's fingers tighten around mine. "What matters is Gavaria will have the help it needs."

With that, she leaves me to begin looking over the room. I can't bear more than a glance around myself. A huge four-poster bed of human style but trolde dimensions dominates the space. Beyond it stands a wardrobe, which Lyria opens and rummages inside. "It looks as though they've had plenty of gowns made for you. I'm quite tempted to take one or two home with me; shock the court with these bawdy troll fashions! Ah. This is what we're looking for, I think."

She turns around, holding up a silky white gown. If you can call a garment so small and sparse a *gown*. Lyria chuckles at the look I give her. "Come. I'll help you get into it. It's got to be better than that soaking wet thing you're in."

That, at least, is true enough. I'm very thankful to let Lyria peel me out of the clinging wet ceremonial robe. She towels me off and helps me into the white gown. It doesn't take a lot of help, for there are no buttons, no hooks, no ties. It's styled in such a way to come off easily.

My throat feels dry and tight. "What am I to do, Lyria?" I whisper softly as my half sister runs a comb through my still-wet hair.

"You mean about . . . about what's going to happen?" She pulls a face. "I can't help you there, I'm afraid. Try to remember what my gods-blighted mother told you. And hope for the best. Vor seems like a kind man. Perhaps it won't be so bad."

Is that compassion I glimpse in her eyes? Probably not. Still, I wish suddenly the two of us had gotten to know one another a bit better before now. "What will happen to you?" I ask. "After it's done?"

She shrugs. "I suppose that depends on what goes on in here. If he doesn't find out right away, I'll carry back word of the completed ceremony and the secured alliance. If he does . . . who knows? He might kill me too. Send my head back in a box as a warning to Larongar." She smiles grimly. "That's politics for you."

She takes a step back and looks me over, her gaze critical. The gown hangs from my shoulders by little jeweled straps, the gauzy fabric draped low across my bosom. More jewels glint amid the folds like dewdrops in fine mist. It's light and lovely against the skin, and far more revealing than any garment I've worn before.

Lyria grimaces suddenly and touches my cheek, then my jaw, then my nose, murmuring. A frisson of magic tickles my skin as she tries to bolster her spell. I can tell it's not working. Lyria shakes her head and heaves a sigh. "It'll have to do. Just remember, keep your eyes closed as much as possible. If you can do that, the rest should hold for a few hours at least."

I nod mutely. My half sister looks as though she wants to say something more. In the end, however, she steps back. "I think it's time I let that hulking warrioress in to poke and prod about the place."

I agree, and Lyria fetches Hael. The trolde woman approaches me first, murmuring an apology as she makes me turn in place. She pats down my body, checking for weapons or poisons or I don't even know what.

She points at my clenched fist. "What's that?"

I open my fingers, revealing the crystal pendant, which has left deep indentations in my palm. Hael's brow puckers faintly. "Do you plan to wear it?"

"I . . . have not decided."

Hael grunts and moves on. To my great relief, she does not bother to lift my veil and study my face as she did back in the barter tent. With swift efficiency she inspects the rest of the room. When she opens the wardrobe and rifles through the dresses, Lyria snorts and says, "You won't find an assassin in there. I've stashed him away in my pocket for future use."

Hael shoots her a dangerous look. "Lyria, please!" I hiss. Lyria rolls her eyes and mutters a somewhat ungracious apology. But she keeps her mouth shut for the rest of Hael's careful scrutiny.

Satisfied at last, the trolde woman approaches me. To my surprise, she kneels, takes my hands in hers, and presses them to her forehead. "My queen," she says.

A shock rolls through me at both her touch and her voice. I've not been addressed as queen yet. I won't be crowned until the feast following the consummation. This is a signal of trust from Hael. Trust I do not deserve.

She rises, her head bent. "Your husband will attend upon you shortly," she says. "All of Mythanar will pray to the Goddess of Unity for you this dimness."

With that, she beckons to Lyria, guiding my half sister to the door. Lyria pauses, casts me one last look. I see the injunction in her eyes: *Don't mess this up. Our lives are in your hands.*

Then they're gone.

The door shuts behind them.

A little sob rises in my throat. I choke it back and sink down onto the edge of the bed. Realizing what I've done, I spring up again at once. Sitting causes the skirt of my gown to part, revealing the entirety of both legs. I clutch my crystal and step back to the middle of the room. How long will I have to wait?

Drawing a deep breath, I move to the window and gaze at the city below. Those strange white rooftops of fantastically shaped stone lead all the way to the massive wall edging that great chasm. I have a sudden weird sensation of floating. As though I and all the denizens of Mythanar are suspended over an endless, eternal drop. And one wrong move on my part will send us all plunging . . .

A sudden burst of voices sounds behind me. Trolde voices. Barks of raucous laughter and shouts, coming from outside my chamber. I turn in place, heart galloping. There's a sound of a door shutting. Followed by silence.

My hands are sweating as I smooth them awkwardly down the front of my pale gown. I'm still holding my crystal. Should I put it on? No, I shouldn't. I don't want Vor to see it, to start questioning me again about how I came by it. Should I try to stash it somewhere? No, there's no time. I squeeze it tight in my fist.

Footsteps in the outer chamber. Drawing nearer.

I drag a shuddering breath into my lungs, then pull up my chin. Peering through my veil, I face the door. It opens softly.

King Vor stands framed in the opening.

30

Vor

I'm given a quiet room in which to towel off following the ceremony. I never realized just how cold the marriage pool was! Not an experience I ever want to repeat. Gods willing, I never will.

I pause a moment, head bowed, listening to the murmur of people just outside the door. All the onlookers have come down from the galleries above the ceremonial pool. They're filing on their way to the feasting hall now, where they will make merry until Ilsevel and I appear. Tradition dictates the revelers remain until the bridal appearance, however long that may take . . . with the understanding that the longer it takes, the greater the cause for celebration.

I clench my hands in the towel as I pull it from my head into my lap. I stare down at my tight fists, then close my eyes. The image of my bride clambering out of the pool appears in my head. The way the fabric clung to her curves, leaving nothing to the imagination. The hard knots of her nipples protruding through the thin, wet fabric. Gods! I should hate myself for this surge of arousal. The poor thing was so cold, so small, so shivering. So exposed before all those watchful eyes. No, I'm a beast even to begin thinking of her as anything other than someone in need of my protection.

And just a few minutes from now? When I visit her chamber? She still deserves my protection.

"I won't hurt her." The words slide through my teeth, as solemn as any vow. "And I won't frighten her."

But I know too well how tentative this alliance is. I must send Lady Lyria back to her people tomorrow lusterling. And when I do, she must bear witness that the consummation has taken place.

I shake my head and bury my face momentarily in my towel. Why would anyone ever want to be king? Such a hopelessly impossible role for anyone who ever sought to be a *good* man.

A knock at the door. Before I can answer, it opens, and Sul sticks his head in. "Brother mine, are you hiding?" He smirks. "Has that puny little bride of yours got you trembling in your boots? Or perhaps you fear your mouse will turn into a wildcat the moment you're alone with her. Have no fear! Say the word, and I'll personally stand outside your door, ready to burst in and save you at the first cry for help! Though have a care, I'm liable to burst in at *any* cry, and that might be—"

His voice is muffled by the towel hitting him dead in the face. I rise and stand before my brother, looking him in the eye as he yanks the towel away, grinning at me. He sees my expression, and his grin freezes.

"Hear me, brother, and hear me well," I say. "Whatever else happens tonight, you will do nothing to bring either shame or embarrassment to *my wife*."

Sul's brow tightens at the emphasis. Then his slow smile returns. "What wife, brother? You have no wife yet. Not according to the contract drawn up with the girl's father. If you want to secure this alliance, you better get to it. Sitting around moping isn't going to save Mythanar. Or do you want to wait until another stirring sends a swarm of cave devils crawling into the city?"

I grab the fresh garment prepared for me: a silken shirt with gold collar and cuffs, belted at the waist. My skin feels tight and hot, and though I don't like to admit it, other parts of me are responding with anticipation of the hours to come.

Hoping Sul won't take one look at my face and read the truth of my physical state, I turn to him. "All right. Let's get on with it then."

Sul flings open the door and shouts to the waiting warriors standing outside. All of my people—Wrag, Toz, Grir, Lur, and even young Yok—clad in their feasting finery, drinks already in hand, egged into bawdy cheering by my reprobate brother. I step out among them, grinning as they clap me on the back and wish me well. At a signal from Sul, they heave me onto their shoulders, despite my roared protests, and carry me through the palace halls, their voices echoing against the stone. It's all in good fun, of course. I myself have participated in similar antics with members of this very circle following their own wedding swims.

The difference being that those were all love matches. Every one of them.

At last, they set me down before the door of the Queen's Apartment. Hael is there already, waiting for us. I stagger unceremoniously, nearly falling into her, but pull myself together. I cast them all a grin, determined to keep the moment as light as possible.

"Your bride is ready for you, my king," Hael says. Her voice, at least, is sober out of all those present. Lady Lyria stands at her elbow too, glaring daggers at me. I can't tell if she's protective of her cousin or . . . what? I avoid her gaze.

"Three cheers for our king!" Sul shouts, lifting a fist.

The others answer, their voices ringing: "*Rhozah! Rhozah! Rhozah!*"

"Go on, King Vor!" Wrag shouts. "See if you can make her shout half as loud!"

I turn to speak to him, but Sul claps me by the shoulder and pivots me forcibly toward the door. "We'll be waiting for you on the other side," he says close to my ear, "ready to greet our new queen."

With that, and a little push between my shoulder blades, I'm through the door. It shuts solidly at my back.

All is suddenly very still. Hushed.

I stand in place, staring into the room. The room I have taken such pains to prepare for my human wife. The human wife even now waiting for me. I glance at the bedchamber door. It's open just a crack, revealing nothing of the interior.

Drawing a long breath, I step to a table where stand a ewer and chalices. I pour two servings of pale, sparkling liquid. Traditionally a trolde couple would drink *krilge* together, but I know that brew would scald my bride's tongue. Definitely not how I wish to begin our first marital encounter. So I had an imported Lunulyrian brew prepared instead. It will be strong for a human, but not unmanageable.

I carry the chalices to the bedroom door. Then, squaring my shoulders, I nudge it open with one elbow and peer inside.

My gaze first goes to the bed. Empty.

Movement draws my eye to the window.

There she stands, silhouetted by the dimness glow. My heart swells in my throat. She's a vision. Ethereally beautiful, like some delicate angel descended from the high heavens into this dark world of earth and stone. She does not belong here, but oh! how the heart does long to take hold of her and make her stay! The fabric of her gown is flimsy and light, sheer enough that I can see the pinkness of her skin right through it, but folded in such a way as to provide a titillating sort of modesty.

Her stance is defensive. One of her hands is clenched in a fist and pressed against her swiftly rising and falling breast. And I'm ogling her. Standing in the doorway, staring at her like a hungry beast.

Hastily, I clear my throat and look where I think her eyes must be behind her veil. "Ilsevel. I hope you were given some refreshment upon your arrival? I know you must have been tired."

She draws a little breath before answering, "I . . . Yes. I have eaten. And drunk." A pause. "I have been well cared for."

"Good." I hesitate, then lift one of the chalices. "May I enter?"

She nods. I step into the room. That's one barrier down at least. Now what? I hold out the drink to her. "Here. I thought you might like this."

"What is it?" Her voice is pitched low.

"*Qeiese.* A Lunulyrian drink, generally considered palatable to humans. It's traditional in Mythanar for a husband and wife to . . . to toast the dimness hours ahead."

She silently approaches me. When she walks, her skirt parts, revealing the length of her leg all the way up to the thigh. I try not to look, try to concentrate on her face, what I can discern of it. She's trembling. Is she afraid I'm going to grab her? Hurt her? Is she preparing to spring back, to fling herself out that open window?

Finally, she's before me. She stretches out her arm, takes the cup. I lift mine and gently touch it against hers. "To the union of our houses, our people, our worlds," I say. "May Nornala smile upon us tonight and always."

"Blessed be the Goddess of Unity," my bride whispers. She holds the chalice under her veil to take a sip. Then she coughs and sputters hard, turning away.

I blink, surprised. "I'm so sorry! I saw you drink *qeiese* at Beldroth. I thought you had a taste for it. Perhaps this is stronger than you are used to."

She wipes her mouth with the back of her hand and offers the chalice back to me, still sputtering. Then she shakes her head, and to my surprise I hear a soft laugh emerge from under that veil. "Well! This is not an auspicious beginning, is it?"

The tension holding my shoulders taut eases at the sound of that laugh. Though, I must say, she sounds very little like the girl I danced with in Beldroth. If I didn't know any better, I would say she sounds like—

But no. I've made my vows. Never again will I think of another woman. Only her. This woman before me. My wife. My Ilsevel.

I take the two chalices and set them down on a table near the bed. *The bed.* It seems suddenly rather large and ominous. And even without looking at her directly, I am painfully aware of Ilsevel's lithe shape beneath that gown. I close my eyes, fighting against the fire in my gut. I am a man, after all. I cannot help the urges of my body.

But I can absolutely help what I do with those urges. I will not let them control me.

Inhaling slowly, I face my bride once more. She stands where I left her, one fist pressed against her heart again. Is she trying to cover her exposed skin?

I lick my dry lips. "I want you to know, Ilsevel, that I have no intention of hurting you. Not tonight. Not ever."

She regards me silently. Perhaps she doesn't understand.

"What I'm trying to say is, we need not do anything now that you are not prepared to do."

"It is our wedding night." Her voice is very soft.

"I know."

"The alliance . . ." She leaves the unfinished thought hanging between us.

"The alliance is important to me," I acknowledge. "But so are you. I want you to be happy here in Mythanar."

She seems to consider this. "My cousin must verify the consummation before her return." She pauses and then adds, "My father will be expecting her."

"A messenger can be sent in her stead, explaining the delay." She starts to protest, but I hold up one hand. "I don't think it fair that an arbitrary deadline should dictate our private actions."

A long, silent moment hovers between us. Only the distant hum of music rises from the feasting hall far below, underscored by the throbbing beat of drums.

"But," she says at last, "this deadline isn't arbitrary."

It isn't. I feel the terrible pressure of the alliance weighing on me. The needs of my people, my kingdom, my world. The chasm slicing through Dugorim village, the bodies broken on stones below. The stink of *raog* poison rising, filling our nostrils. It must be stopped. I must use whatever means possible to stop it.

And yet . . .

I look her in the eye. Though I cannot see her face clearly through the veil, I hold her gaze. "Ilsevel, you are to be queen of my people. But you are also *my* queen. You and you alone shall guide and dictate your desires to me. It will be my honor to act accordingly."

Another silence. So full of unspoken things. Fears. Longings. And everything in between. I stand there beside that bed, looking at this woman, this stranger, to whom I have just bound myself, heart and soul. And I wait.

She takes a step.

My heart hitches in my chest.

She takes another step. And another. I clench my fists, arms straight at my sides, like a soldier bracing for battle. My eyes long to devour her body, the way the skirt parts, revealing her shapely legs. Even as I refuse to look down, I cannot help the intense awareness of her flooding my senses.

She stands in front of me, peering up at me from beneath her veil. "May we . . . Would it be well with you if we lowered the lights?"

"Of course!" I answer a little too fast. I speak a word of command that makes the crystals dim, casting the room in deep shades of purple and blue. But I can still see her. The shape of her pale form, standing before me in the shadows. The *olk* dust from our ceremony shimmers across her forehead and breast.

Slowly, she slips the veil from her head, drops it at her feet. She lifts her chin. Her eyelids are lowered, as though she cannot bear to look at me directly. Instead, she fixes her gaze on my chest. Raising one hand, she rests her palm against my heart, covering the shimmering *olk* dust mark. After a breath, she removes her other hand from her breast, baring a view of that plunging neckline and the delights it reveals.

I know what she is waiting for me to do. I hesitate. Then, moving cautiously so as not to startle her, I rest my palm against her own shining sigil. Her heart is galloping, keeping pace with mine.

Her lips move in a gentle whisper: "Will you kiss me, my king?"

31

Faraine

My words hang in the air between us like silvery bells.

Every sense in my body is fixated on the largeness of his hand pressed against my heart. So great, so strong. And he himself, so huge and powerful. He ought to terrify me. Yet I cannot deny the heat coursing through my veins, longing for his hand to move, to draw its warmth across my prickling skin.

I count my breaths. Waiting.

Finally, his hand does move. Slowly, he lifts his palm from my chest and places a finger under my chin, tilting my head up. Quickly I lower my eyelids, knowing full well that whatever other enchantments I wear, my eyes will give me away in an instant. Thus, I cannot see him as I stand there, my body quivering with tension, with anxiety, with eagerness, wondering what he will do.

He draws nearer. The warmth of his breath tickles my face. He smells of the *qeiese*, a sharp, sweet, smoky scent, more intoxicating than the drink itself. I breathe him in deeply.

Suddenly, his lips are on mine. And something unexpected happens inside me. This is not like the last time I was kissed. Then, the point of contact between me and my would-be lover opened up a channel of overwhelming emotion that struck me like a kick to the gut, leaving me sick and nauseated for days.

This couldn't be more different. As our lips touch, I feel those doorways of spirit opening as everything inside his head and heart rushes to meet me. But there is no pain. Instead, a spark seems to burn straight to my core, where it blooms in a flower of fire. I'm shocked by the sheer brilliance awakening my body to sensations I've never before known.

He pulls back a bare half inch. I still feel the shape of those full lips of his, hovering just above mine. I let out a little breath, uncertain what will happen next. I'm frightened—I'd be lying if I said I wasn't. But I want to feel that spark again, to know how bright it can burn.

I rise on my toes, closing the space between our lips. He meets me, his mouth curving a little in a surprised smile as he kisses me back. The connection of our souls opens once more. He's eager, hungry, but also oddly restrained. He's concerned for me. I can feel it. He knows I'm afraid, and he doesn't want to frighten me further.

Who would have thought in a moment like this my needs, my comfort, would be uppermost in his mind? It would be pleasant to dwell in this space for a little while. To let him coddle me, keeping his passions carefully in check.

But I can't. Restraint won't get me what I need.

I part my lips. Just the barest of invitations, just to see what he will do. He responds at once. Lifting his finger from my chin, he cups my cheeks with both hands, tenderly framing my face. His lips are nimble and warm. Still restrained, though. I feel the hunger in him, burning bright in his spirit and communicating itself to me. But he's still holding back.

I let my tongue explore, flicking softly across his upper lip, running along the edge of his teeth. The effect is instantaneous. His hands slide from my cheeks to twine his fingers in my hair, drawing me to him with unexpected roughness. Then his tongue moves with mine. A shock of sensation bolts through me like lightning, branching into every part of my body. Suddenly, I'm receiving emotions from him so powerful, they should overwhelm me with his hunger, his desire.

Wary of a sudden onset of pain, I pull back. He yanks his hands out of my hair and holds them out to either side, away from me, as though to show he means no harm. He cannot disguise his ragged breathing, however, nor can he hide the desire roiling in the little sliver of air between us. He wants to continue. I've driven him to the point of physical urgency. And yet, at the least resistance from me, he holds himself in check.

Gods on high, he is bound and determined to make me lead! But how can I? I'm so inexperienced, my every move uncertain. The throb of the stone in my palm echoes the throb of heat rushing through my body, pooling in my center, where it mounts with increasing pressure. I can use that. Draw on those new and enticing vibrations, channel them.

I take a step toward him, careful to keep my eyelids lowered. His breath pants against my forehead as I study the hollow of his throat. "Will you touch me, my king?" I ask. It takes every ounce of courage I possess to get the words out.

Slowly he reaches for my face again, cupping my cheeks in his hands. "Is this what you want?"

"Yes."

He lowers his mouth, kisses me again. Another one of those achingly tender kisses. "And this? Is this what you want?"

"Yes," I breathe.

He lets his lips play with mine in a series of short, sweet kisses. None deep, but teasing, provocative. His fingertips trace my cheek, my neck; run lightly down my spine. Every bone he touches sings out in response, like he's playing an instrument. My back arches, my body naturally bending into his.

"Is this what you want, my queen?" he asks. The words tickle my ear.

"Yes!" I loop my arms around his neck. My right hand is still clenched around the stone, but my left hand wanders up, fingers twirling through locks of his hair. I can't say if I draw his mouth back to mine or not, but suddenly he's there. I sink into the depths of another, longer kiss. Though the room is dim and full of shadows, my head bursts with light, whirling with colors hitherto unimagined.

I become aware of his hands moving at my waist. One slides down over my hips, caressing my curves. The other slips up to my abdomen. His thumb traces below my breast, tentative, like a question. "Is this what you want?" he asks.

I whimper. He starts to pull away, uncertain how to interpret that sound. "Yes, yes!" I gasp hastily. I can't let this moment end. Not now.

And the truth is, something has changed inside me. As each step of this slow dance progresses, I cease to be the substitute bride and become more and more myself. Present here in this secret, private moment. My needs are mine alone, my desires selfishly overshadowing the cause of duty and kingdom. I did not know I could feel this way until now, in this darkened room, with this man who is nearly a stranger. My husband.

Vor's lips move from my mouth to my jaw to my ear, sparking small fires with each deft touch. His hand glides up my arm, raising gooseflesh. He toys with the strap of my gown. He seems to be fingering the jewels there, counting them one by one. He's so patient, so slow, so careful. It's maddening.

I roll my shoulder, maneuvering the strap until it falls. The gathered fabric of my bodice drops dangerously low. He chuckles softly. "Clever queen." His hand, deprived of the strap to play with, warms the curve of my shoulder, my throat. His thumb dances along my collarbone.

Suddenly, he takes hold of my hips, pivots me to the side. I bleat with surprise as he backs me up a step. My knees hit the bed, but he continues pressing so that I fall onto the soft mattress. I prop onto my elbows, draw up one leg. The split of my skirt opens, revealing the whole of my leg to view.

His hand finds my bent knee, slips softly up my outer thigh. So warm and strong. It travels further up, under the gown to my hipbone. His touch is caressing but eager. I close my eyes, my head falling back. He takes this as an invitation, lunging forward to kiss my exposed throat before catching hold of my chin and pulling my lips down to be claimed by his. I open my mouth to his kiss, letting the touch, the connection fill me.

My right hand unclenches. My crystal drops, rolls away. Falls with a light clatter to the floor.

I grasp the back of his head with both hands, draw him closer to me. Vor's kisses move in a line of fire down my neck to my collarbone. "Is this what you want?" he asks.

"Yes!"

With a sudden growl, he turns me around, pulling me up on my knees. His strong arm presses me against his muscled chest. He brushes my hair out of his way and begins to kiss the back of my neck and shoulder, eliciting new shocks of sensation throughout my body. I close my eyes. A shivering sigh escapes my lips. Who knew that skin could be made to sing like this? He slips the other strap from my shoulder and begins kissing that side as well. His hand reaches around me, caressing my throat, then down lower and lower, until his fingers trail across the bit of flimsy fabric only just clinging to the peaks of my breasts.

"You're very quiet," he murmurs even as he nips playfully at my earlobe. "Is there nothing you would say to me?" He kisses me again, just in that little patch of skin behind my ear. Another flower of fire blooms inside me. "We can talk, you know." Another kiss, another blossoming. "I'm happy to make conversation with you until lusterling." Another kiss. I moan softly and feel his smile against my shoulder. "You'll find I'm an excellent conversationalist."

I'm dizzy, drunk. Absolutely mad with desire. Turning sharply, I catch his lips in a kiss that's almost vicious. Then I wrap my arms around his neck and shoulders and pull him down on top of me, opening my thighs so that he can fit between them. If I was in any doubt of his passion before, that doubt is now fled. His need is all too evident, both frightening and exhilarating. I twine my legs with his, only to realize he's still wearing trousers, while my legs are bare. This strikes me as grossly unfair. I reach down, pulling at his belt.

Vor chuckles against my lips. "Patience, my bride. There's time enough for that."

"But I want you," I answer, breathless, greedy. "I want to feel you. All of you."

"Well, in that case . . ." He shrugs out of his loose shirt, tosses it carelessly to one side.

I stare. I cannot help it, cannot even remember to hide my telltale eyes. The dim *lorst* light gleams off his sculpted physique, catching the breadth of his shoulders, the chiseled contours of his torso. So strange and wondrous and beautiful. And mine. All mine.

I sit upright, my lips parted as though eager to take a sip. Almost of their own volition, my hands smooth across his chest, down his front, slowly exploring every muscled plain. Scars lace his body, some of which feel fresh, the healed wounds puckered and knotted. Somehow, they only add to his magnificence.

I can't seem to help myself from leaning in and kissing that warm skin, just in that shining place over his heart where the dust from our ceremony gleams in a sacred sigil. One kiss, soft, tentative, but hungry. He groans. I glance up to find his eyes closed, a look of pleasure on his face. So I kiss him again, and again, searching for places that might provoke more of that same sound. I'm shy, though. Uncertain and hesitant.

He doesn't seem to mind. His teeth flashing white in a smile, he catches one of my hands, kisses my palm. "Let me teach you," he says, his voice husky and low. "Let me learn you."

It's easy to surrender to him. He lays me down once more, nuzzling into my neck. His body is heavy on top of me, and his scent overwhelms me until I can no longer tell where the physical sensations end and the pulsing power of our souls begin. It's all one and glorious and new. I wrap my arms around his neck and shoulders, thirsty for his skin, drinking in the splendor of him through my palms.

His kisses venture lower, his lips and tongue featherlight and teasing. I moan, my longing for his touch intensifying with every passing moment. His fingers start to peel away what little of my bodice remains. I want to burst with yearning to be free of this flimsy garment. For my husband to take me, to taste me. To lay claim to every inch of me.

"Is this what you want?" he asks. "Ilsevel?"

Ilsevel.

A stabbing pain shoots through my heart. Sharp enough to make me gasp.

Ilsevel.

Not me.

This is not my wedding night.

These delights do not belong to me.

Every caress, every word, every blissful sensation . . .

Stolen.

False.

A sob wells up in my throat, threatening to choke me. The brilliance of light which had surrounded me dims, dies, falls into shadow. All that glory, all that beauty, gone in a flash.

But no! I cannot let this opportunity be lost. I'm here for a purpose. I have one job to do. I was wrong to lose sight of it, wrong to forget the real and terrible reason I'm here in this bed, right now. It's not too late. I can salvage this. I can push down everything I'm feeling, turn myself into something numb and small that knows neither this pain nor this pleasure.

One duty. For crown and country.

"Ilsevel?" Vor says again, his lips still hot against my skin.

My throat swells so tight, for a moment I fear I won't be able to answer. "Yes!" I manage, nearly choking on the word. "Yes!"

But I feel it. That jolt passing through his heart. His muscles stiffen, and the singing in his soul turns to a sudden clamor. Then stillness.

"You're not happy," he says. He drags in a breath, releases it in a gust. Once, twice, three times. His fingers tighten in the blankets on either side of me, his knuckles standing out white. His mouth still hovers just above my breast. For a moment, he lowers his head, kisses me softly. Tasting sweet temptation.

His lips pull back in a grimace. "I won't take a weeping bride." The words grind through his teeth like a growl. He wrenches upright, backs off the bed, and stands there, staring down at me. I lie exposed and small before him, my mouth open, unable to form words. His ragged breathing fills my ears as his fists clench and unclench. Then with an angry, "Gods!" he covers his face and starts toward the door.

I've ruined it. I've ruined everything.

"No! Wait!" I sit up hastily, pulling the straps of my gown back onto my shoulders as I scramble off the bed, nearly falling in my haste. I reach out, catch his arm, draw him back to me. "Please, Vor, I didn't mean—"

The moment I touch him, I realize my mistake. In that unguarded moment, I forgot to disguise my voice. I spoke as myself.

Vor whirls on me. I'm not fast enough. I don't look away in time. He meets my eyes, locks on to my gaze so hard I cannot retreat. I watch his expression in the dim crystal glow transform from shock to horror. To rage.

"*Who are you?*" he snarls.

32

Vor

Those eyes.

Every inch of my body is alive with fire, still urging me to take hold of my desire and burn us both into an oblivion of bliss. But I can't. Because those eyes . . . they don't belong to my bride. They don't belong to the woman with whom I swam beneath the Yun Falls. They don't belong to the woman whose soul sang with mine when we entered the waters and lost ourselves only to emerge reborn.

Those aren't Ilsevel's eyes.

I stand there, my question still ringing in my ears, staring down into that upturned face. Even as I watch, little bits of magic spark to life beneath her skin, melting away the outermost layers of perception, revealing the truth beneath.

A guttural cry wrenches from my throat. I shake her hand free and leap back a pace. My body quakes, all arousal abruptly doused in a flood of shock. Instinct drives me to reach for a weapon. There's nothing in the room—Hael made certain of that. So I lunge for the table, grab one of the chalices, sloshing *qeiese* as I brandish it over my head.

She screams, cowering away from me. Her foot catches on her skirt, and she falls, sprawling so that the split reveals all of her long, pale legs. Scrambling, she pushes herself across the floor into the corner of the room. There she huddles, staring up at me with those wide, fear-filled eyes.

Those eyes . . .

Those eyes which belong to . . .

"Faraine?"

My arm trembles, the chalice wobbling in my grasp. Violence rushes in my veins, commanding me to attack, insisting even now that it's an assassin who crouches on my floor, the last of powerful magic spells melting away from her features. I fight to master myself, force my arm to lower. "Faraine, is that you?"

With a last burst of sparking energy, the final spells fall away. The air stinks with broken enchantment, so foul and thick, I can't believe I hadn't realized it was there to begin with. Maybe this is a dream? Yes, that would make sense, wouldn't it? I've been fighting so hard not to think of this face before me, not to remember those eyes of hers, one blue, one gold, framed by those dark lashes. Perhaps my mind is simply offering up an image of what my heart has secretly longed for. If I can wake, I'll return to reality, to the bride even now waiting for me. To Ilsevel.

But though I blink and shake my head and blink again, the vision does not vanish. She's there. Faraine. Her knees drawn up to her chest, one strap of her white gown slipped down her arm, her hair tumbled and tousled where my fingers had played with it. Faraine. The other sister.

Not my bride.

"I don't understand." I press my palm to my forehead as though I can somehow push sense into my own brain. "I don't understand. Ilsevel . . ."

"I'm sorry, my king." Her voice is so soft. So sweet. That solemn, serious voice with the unexpected depths which had struck me with such force from the very first time I heard it. How could I have ever mistaken that voice for anyone else's?

My lips curl back from my teeth. "Where is Ilsevel?"

Faraine looks at me. She swallows hard. Her lashes rise and fall in a single blink.

"What is going on?" My voice is harsher than I intend it to be. She cringes, turning her face toward the wall as though I've struck her. Gods, how I hate myself for causing her such fear! But in that moment, I can offer no comfort. "Tell me!" I snarl.

She looks up at me, her eyes large and luminous in the crystal glow, swimming with unshed tears. Her lips move soundlessly, but when the words finally come, they're clear enough. "Ilsevel is dead."

I recoil. "Dead? But . . . but she was . . ."

She was just here in my arms. Her mouth responding to my kisses and drawing me in for more, her fear melting away to delighted trembling at my touch. I'd seen her, heard her, felt her, breathed her, tasted her. Ilsevel. My bride, my chosen bride.

But none of it was true. The realization comes over me with all the force of a thunderclap. Ilsevel was never here. The girl I held in my arms, riding before me on the morleth. The girl with whom I'd swum in the sacred waters. To whom I'd made my holy vows. She was never even here.

"*Hira!*" I speak in sharp command. The *lorst* lights obey, filling the chamber with their glow. Faraine winces and bows her head. For an instant, the spells she wore seem to wriggle and writhe around her, trying to reassert themselves. Now that I know they're present, it's all too easy to wave them aside, looking through the miasma of broken enchantment to the truth beneath.

"Tell me what happened," I demand.

Her shoulders rise to her ears. Is that another spasm of pain I see flashing across her face? I should not speak to her so sternly. But what can I do? Apologize? I'm not yet even certain whether or not she's my enemy.

So, I stand my ground, maintaining a cold silence. She reaches out, grabs the side of the bed, and pulls herself upright. Her skirts flare and open, revealing far more than they hide, and I cannot help the instinctive way my body reacts to that sight. I avert my gaze, staring at a crystal sconce across the room rather than at her. From the tail of my eye, I watch her step over to the bed and sit down heavily, her hands gripping the edge of the mattress.

"It was on her Maiden's Journey." Her voice is thin, tight. "The party stopped to make prayers at the Ashryn Shrine. No one thought Prince Ruvaen would venture so far north. He's never been seen in that part of the country before." She goes silent. I listen to her draw three long breaths. Then: "There were no survivors."

I find a chair by the little table, pull it out, take a seat. A chill passes over my skin. My bare skin. I glance idly at my shirt, lying in a puddle on the floor where I'd tossed it after Ilsevel—after Faraine—after this stranger begged me to remove it. Just before her eager hands began to explore my body.

Ilsevel.

Dead.

I don't know how to feel. I scarcely knew her. But I danced with her every night in Beldroth. I danced with her, spoke vows to her. And just now, I believed I made love to her. A dead woman.

"I don't understand." Each word falls dull and thick from my numb lips. "If Ilsevel is dead, then . . . then what is . . . what is she . . . ?" I stop. Looking up sharply, I catch Faraine's gaze. "You were sent in your sister's place."

Her lashes fall, brushing her cheeks. She wraps her arms around her middle, shivering so hard she's obliged to brace her feet to keep from slipping off the bed.

I bare my teeth, sucking in a thin stream of air. Then slowly, coldly: "Why wasn't I told?"

"It was feared the alliance would fall apart without Ilsevel." She addresses her words to the floor. "My father did not believe you would accept a . . . a substitute. Not willingly."

"So he lied to me. *You* lied to me."

A pause. Then, very softly: "Yes."

My chest burns with a roiling mixture of rage, sorrow, disgust, dismay, and more emotions I cannot name. Rising abruptly from my chair, I stride to the open window. All of Mythanar lies below me. My city. So beautiful. So beloved. So perilously poised on the brink of ruin. I would give almost anything to protect it. But this?

I whirl suddenly, facing the girl. She sits on the bed still, her torso turned so that she can watch me over her shoulder. That strap is still fallen down her arm, exposing the smooth skin in which I was delighting only moments ago. My stomach knots.

"How could Larongar do this? We had a contract. A written contract, with Ilsevel's name, not yours. There were no provisos in the case of death. Which means *you* cannot fulfill your sister's role."

"No. I cannot." She drops her chin. "But we have a law. Legal means by which one blood kin can be renamed to take the place of another."

I stare at her. The words make no sense at first, clamoring

against my ears like so much noise. Finally, I say, "So they changed your name?"

"By sovereign decree of King Larongar and the power bestowed upon him by the gods, I am Ilsevel Cyhorn." Her eyes flash in the *lorst* light. "Thus, I may indeed take my sister's place. With or without my intended husband's knowledge."

"You're telling me your human law allows for such deceit to be perpetrated against bridegrooms?"

"So long as the marriage is consummated, yes."

Her words are soft as drifting *olk* dust. They seem to shimmer in the air. Only they're the color of poison.

"Did you think I would not notice? Not care?" I wait, but she offers no answer. "Did you think I could make vows to one woman and make love to another without a second thought?"

Her body is still. Every muscle tensed.

"You should have told me."

She opens her mouth, hesitates. "I'm sorry," she breathes at last.

"Sorry? *Morar-juk!*" I cannot look at her. I cannot let my gaze linger even one second longer on that luminous skin, that tumbling hair, those full pink lips worried between her teeth. Turning away, I lean against the window frame, staring out at my city. My gaze is unfocused, my head a storm.

"The vows of the *yunkathu* are sacred. You have sullied the purity of the waters in which we swam together. You have made a mockery of my people's most ancient rites. I spoke those words from the depths of my soul. From the core of what makes me both trolde and king. And all the while, I spoke them to a dead girl."

I squeeze my eyes shut. Seven gods on high! I still feel her warmth beneath my hands, her writhing body responding to my touch, thrilling at my kiss. I would have gone through with it. All of it. I would have let myself be duped by this two-faced seductress and her monster of a father. Even now there's a part of me—a dangerous, twisted part of me—that urges me to turn around, lunge at that bed, take her in my arms. This is what I wanted, isn't it? This is the very dream I've been fighting these last many weeks. The dream of finding Faraine in her sister's place. Of opening my eyes and seeing her earnest, lovely face gazing up at me . . .

Gods, I feel sick.

I turn, march to the door, and stop there. "I knew your father would betray me if he saw an advantage." I glance over my shoulder, not quite looking at her. "I thought better of you. Now . . ." I swallow painfully, forcing bile down my throat. "Now I can only thank the gods I am not bound to so false a creature."

"Vor, wait—"

With a single stride I escape, slamming the door behind me. I stagger to the middle of the outer room, drawing breath between my clenched teeth. A roar builds up inside me, and every effort to swallow it back proves useless. It bursts from my throat, resounding against the stone. A little cluster of *urzul* stones shrieks in response, catching my voice and echoing it back to me in shrill chorus. I snatch them up and hurl them across the room. The crystals smash against the wall, shattering in a dissonance that shreds my senses like knives.

Voices erupt outside my door. My entourage. They're still waiting. No doubt they heard my little display. No doubt all of Mythanar did! If I don't make an appearance soon, Hael and Sul and all the rest will come bursting into the room. I'll lose whatever control of the situation I still have.

I don't know what I want to happen to Faraine. But I can't just turn her over to Sul.

Pulling myself upright, I run my hands through my hair. Damn, why didn't I pick up my shirt before storming out of the bedroom? Too late now. I must be king. I must take charge. I must get to the bottom of this and figure out where I stand, where the alliance stands. Then I must decide what will happen to the trembling woman hiding in our bridal chamber.

The door swings wide at my touch. A cluster of stares meet my gaze—Sul, Hael, Yok, and the rest. All ogling me and my state of undress, their jaws slack. "Vor?" Sul says, his irreverent attitude replaced with true concern for once in his life. "Are you all right? What's wrong?"

"Where's the queen?" Hael demands.

My gaze shoots to her. My friend. My friend who confirmed that it was Ilsevel Cyhorn sitting within that tent just outside the Between Gate.

"Did you know?" I snarl.

She shakes her head, looks truly baffled. "Know what?"

I push past her and Sul, elbow through the crowd. Behind me, Hael shouts, "My king? What has happened?" She sounds desperate.

I'll deal with her later.

Shoving past Wrag and Lur, I emerge into the empty space behind the gathering. There, standing beneath the light of a solitary crystal, is Lady Lyria. Her face is drawn, her eyes wide, her expression utterly blank.

I point a finger at her. "Arrest this woman. At once."

Silence. Then in a rush, Hael leaps forward, gripping the human by one arm. Lyria's mouth twists into an ugly sneer. "So," she says, "you figured it out."

"Figured what out?" Sul demands. He looms beside me, gripping my shoulder. "Vor, what's going on here? What has happened to Ilsevel?"

"Ilsevel is dead."

A collective gasp ripples through the gathering. "My king?" Hael says.

I turn and march away down the passage. My head spins, and the whole world seems to tilt on its axis. But while my people are looking on, I won't betray myself with fits and foolishness.

"Lock up my bride in her chambers," I call over my shoulder. "Don't let her out on pain of death. Post a watch under her window. Sul, with me! We have much to discuss."

33

Faraine

I sit on the edge of the bed, my eyes closed fast, my legs braced. Wave after wave hits me—the heat of fury, the ice of fear, the bitterness of betrayal. And sorrow. Deep, throbbing, dark as a pit. Vor's sorrow. It strikes my soul like a spiked mace, battering and stabbing simultaneously.

I cannot bear it. My body shudders, heaves, then curls in a tight ball, knees drawn to my chest. I press my hands to my temples, clutching at my hair as my mouth opens in a voiceless scream. The pressure inside my head mounts with each passing breath. It's going to burst, going to break my skull apart and spatter bits of brain matter across this lovely room. And there's nothing I can do to stop it, nothing I can—

A crash explodes in the outer chamber. My senses reel as a shattering of discordant sound rains down on me. It feels like a thousand and one tiny cuts across my brain. I cry out and curl even tighter. The shattering ends, but the pain does not. I can do nothing but lie there, shaking.

Another door opens. Shuts. A sense of solitude fills the atmosphere, dulling the pain like salve. Which can only mean one thing: Vor is gone.

But this is worse. Much worse. I'd rather wrestle with the pain of his rage and sorrow than be so suddenly emptied of him. I squeeze my eyes shut, trying to draw memory of our connection back to the forefront of my awareness. How my body had hummed in response to his touch, not unlike the song of my pendant stone. But this song was so much deeper, so much richer, with promises of more. What would it be like to plunge in headfirst? To see just how deep those promises might flow? To let ourselves be carried on powerful currents until we're caught in the swells of rapture and radiance?

But it's gone now. Every hope, every chance. I feel hollow. As though something has been carved out from inside my chest, leaving my insides scraped raw.

After what feels like hours, I find the strength to pull myself up, crawl off the bed, and hunt along the floor. The searing light from the *lorst* crystals has dimmed, leaving the room full of shadows. I feel around nearly blind and only chance to brush a finger against my pendant, rolled under the bed. With a little cry, I snatch it up. It's dull and silent, more lifeless than I've ever known it to be. Crooning wordlessly, I press it against my heart, indenting my skin with its edges. The pain is slight compared to the throbbing in my head, but it's something on which to focus. Slowly my awareness narrows to that small pinpoint of sharpness. I push deeper still, breathing in and out with careful precision.

There, in the heart of the stone—a vibration. Just a faint pulse of life. But it's something.

Slowly, slowly, I pull my mind up from the slough. Thoughts begin to form, muddy at first, but gradually clarifying.

Ilsevel.

Oh, Ilsevel.

He'd called me by her name. Even as he touched me with such intimate tenderness, he'd been thinking of my sister. My beautiful, my darling, my dead sister.

Why does everything feel so foolish suddenly? The pressures of Gavaria. The importance of the alliance. The power of Prince Ruvaen, laying waste to the land, cutting down my people. Why do all those needs suddenly seem so small?

Eventually, I pick myself up off the floor. My limbs are shaky, but the crystal has done its job, dulling the pain so that I can function. Part of me wishes the pain would come back. At least then I'm too overwhelmed to actually *think*. To consider what I've done, what I've brought on myself.

What will Vor do now?

I make my way to the window, gaze down at the city below. Some dull part of my mind idly contemplates the idea of escape, of climbing out the window and descending the outer wall like I had when eluding the cave devil. But that's foolish. Even if I somehow fled this room, managed to slip through the palace grounds undetected, found my way through those sprawling city streets and across one of those awful bridges . . . what then? I'm not fool enough to think I could navigate the dark tunnels of the Under Realm back to the Between Gate.

No, I'm trapped in this world. For better or for worse.

I sag against the window frame, leaning my back against it for support, and tilt my head, closing my eyes. For a moment, I simply hold my crystal, breathing in time with its pulse. Slowly, another sound breaks through. Small at first—a thin, high-pitched whining. Then another one, pitched even higher. And a third, a fourth, a fifth, all different pitches, so faint I could almost believe I imagined them. But I couldn't imagine the way my stone responds. How it seems to warm suddenly in my grasp, giving off a sense of . . . I don't know how to describe it. A *pull.*

Frowning, I look down at my stone. There's nothing to see. But that *pull* doesn't decrease. In fact, it intensifies. I take a step. The pressure lessens for a moment, only to redouble the next. I step again and again, and the pull leads me right to the door of the bedchamber.

I stop. The door is shut fast. I can still almost feel the shudder in the wall after Vor slammed it. Will it open for me? Or is this the moment I discover I've been locked in? My hand shaking, I touch the latch.

The door swings soundlessly out.

Immediately the pull is stronger. So strong, I stumble into the outer chamber and follow it, weaving between articles of furniture to the far wall. Gleaming shards of crystal lie scattered across the floor. They give off a faint, forlorn hum, so high and soft, I'm halfway convinced I imagine it. I kneel amidst the bits and pieces. My own crystal has stopped pulling now and lies still in my hand. I reach out tentatively, running my fingers along the little shards. There's something here, something caught and held in this space. I can't explain it. But the broken song surrounds me, and in its brokenness I feel . . . *pain.*

With a quick series of scoops, I gather up the broken pieces, drawing them together in a pile. Their bitter song intensifies, but I rest my hand over them, trying to still the sound which is not quite a sound. It's more like the heat of a candle flame beneath my palm.

It feels like Vor.

Not the Vor I've come to know, whose very presence I crave like air. No, this is the Vor I just encountered. Shattered, raging. Poisoned with internal turmoil.

I hiss sharply and pull back, pressing my blistered hand against my chest. The crystal shards shiver. My eyes must be playing tricks on me, for I could almost swear I see them moving. Then, one by one, they go still.

What did I just do? Slowly, I reach out, nudge the crystals again with one finger. There's something here, something I don't quite understand. Something my poor, dull brain *cannot* understand just now.

Sighing, I look down. I'm still wearing the skimpy gown, one sleeve drooped from my shoulder and sagging down my upper arm, nearly baring my breast. Without quite realizing what I'm doing, I brush my fingers along my shoulders, my neck, following the paths Vor's kisses had blazed. His hands on my body had seemed to make me new, the heat of his passion a refining fire. I would give . . . oh! I would give a great deal to have him here in my arms once more.

"Gods above spare me," I hiss.

Carrying the broken crystals with me, I return to the bedchamber. One of the empty chalices serves as a receptacle for my shards. I leave them and step to the wardrobe. While I await my unknown fate, I might as well clothe myself properly. The garments inside are all trolde style, most of them in colors far better suited to Ilsevel's complexion. I find a purple gown with long sleeves and silver embellishments that fits me and which I can put on with relatively little trouble. A little more digging produces hair combs and a net, and I soon have my hair up in a modest, simple fashion. Not a fashion Ilsevel would wear.

Once dressed, there's nothing more for me to do. I look at the bed. Though I am suddenly weary to my bones, I cannot bear the idea of lying down upon it. Not when those blankets are still mussed from our eager, hot-blooded dance. I might catch a telltale trace of the simmering song we'd begun to create, and that would be too excruciating.

So I sit at the table instead, a chalice of broken crystal shards my only companion. Outside, the world is as dark as midnight. If I let myself, I can pretend a black night sky arches over my head. I close my eyes, trying to imagine myself anywhere but here. Where would I go? My lonely room at Nornala Convent, the dreary endlessness of days stretching before me? My own chambers in Beldroth, where the very walls breathe whispers of how great a disappointment I am? Or perhaps in Ilsevel's room, both my sisters gathered close in my arms, still laughing, still weeping, still bickering and teasing. Still living.

The truth is, there is no place for me. Not anymore. I'm not convinced there ever was a place to begin with. The closest I ever came to belonging was in the arms of the man I just betrayed so cruelly, I have no hope of forgiveness.

My head sinks heavily, first resting in my hand, then all the way down to the tabletop. I'm bent, broken. Too exhausted to hold myself together any longer. Pressing my forehead against the cool marble, I let tears squeeze through the corners of my eyes . . . trail down my cheeks . . . fall . . .

. . . .

I stand before the yawning chasm.

I gasp and jump back a step. That fall opens beneath me, too great, too terrible to comprehend. Desperately, I tear my gaze away and look up. Up at the city. Up at the bridges that once arched from the cavern wall, now broken, fallen. The city itself is no longer the white, shining edifice I'd seen under the *lorst* light. The high towers and many peaked roofs are crumbled, sunken. One half of the city is nothing but rubble. I can no longer see the palace. It's obscured in dust and debris.

Slowly I become aware of a ringing in my ears. A discordant song, not unlike the broken crystals I'd . . . I'd . . . When had I seen those? And where? I can't remember. It seems so long ago and yet so recent. Time itself folds up around me, crushed by that song singing its symphony of chaos.

It draws me. A pull I cannot explain. One step. Two. I draw nearer to the chasm's edge.

I look down.

Clouds churn below. Dark, billowing. Laced with strange green luminescence. They rise fast, propelled by some intense blast. Heat scalds my face, burns away my clothes, until I am naked, blistered, but somehow still alive, still staring into that darkness. It belches from the chasm, overwhelms me, pouring into my nostrils, down my throat to burn in my gut, melting me from the inside out. I would scream, but there's too much heat, too much pain, too much, too much, too much.

My vision clears. Just for an instant. I stare down.

And I see it.

Beneath the cloud. Below the stone. Beyond the fiery river.

I see it.

....

I bolt upright with a gasp. I'm dizzy, disoriented. My bleary eyes struggle to focus, every blink pushing me in and out of a world of green-limned cloud and unbearable heat. My gown sticks to my body, soaked with patches of sweat, while strands of hair are plastered to my forehead.

What was that?

I shake my head, forcing my eyes wide. The shadowed room slowly comes back into focus. A dream. It was just a dream. A nightmare. Drawing long breaths, I will my heart rate to calm and try to call to mind the images I'd just seen. But no. They're gone. Melted into oblivion.

Just as well. My life has more than enough complexity without trying to worry about fantasies conjured by my unconscious. Groaning, I let my head sink into my hands, fingers rubbing at my temples. Gods on high, I'm so sleep-deprived, so exhausted! Perhaps it's time to give in and lie down properly on that bed. Who knows what the immediate future will hold? Whatever it is, it should be easier to face after a nap.

I rise and take a step toward the bed. Before I can take a second, a new sound plucks at my awareness. Not at all like the crystal song, which is heard more with the mind than the body. This is the rhythmic growl of drums. How long have they been beating? Has it been a while? Was this the sound that woke me suddenly from my uneasy sleep?

Bah-bah-boom.

Bah-bah-boom.

Bah-bah-boom.

The rhythm travels from a distance, rolling through the air, vibrating through the stones, to throb in the pit of my stomach. All thought of sleep forgotten, I step to the window, gazing out upon the city. I can't tell where the drums are coming from. But they're louder now than they were even a moment before. A ripple of unease seems to move like a fog through the streets below me. I can sense it even from this distance: not one set of emotions, but many. Hundreds, thousands even. All fixated on the growl of the drums, which sharpens and intensifies their awareness. Is this an alarm of some sort? Is the city in danger?

I take a few steps back. Something is wrong. Very, very wrong.

Suddenly, the door of the outer apartment bursts open. Footsteps pound the floor. I whirl. Part of me wants to jump forward and slam the bedchamber door, to barricade myself. Before I can bring my limbs to move, however, two strange trolde men fill the opening.

I draw myself as straight as I can. "Where is King Vor?" I demand.

"Nurghed ghot, uskta!" the foremost one snarls as the two of them enter the chamber and approach me. He grabs my arm. A spark of ice-cold unfeeling shoots through his fingers, sharp enough to make my breath catch.

I twist away, wrenching free of his grasp. "I'll come," I say, my voice as firm as I can make it. "But on my own. I won't be dragged about like a dog."

I hold the trolde man's gaze, refusing to blink. He starts to raise his fist, but the second man catches his arm. They speak together in a quick scattering of incomprehensible troldish. Finally, the first man nods and mutters consent. The second man turns to me, indicating the door with a wave of his hand. "*Drag*," he says. His tone brooks no argument.

I grip my skirts with both hands and draw in a tight breath. Then I step from the chamber between the two troldes.

Somewhere far off, the drums beat on.

34

Vor

Hael stands at the door of the council hall, her shoulders back, her eyes forward. Her face is set like granite, her mouth a grim, hard line. Members of the house guard under her command encircle the room, standing in the shadows just outside the low amber *lorst* light illuminating the central table.

I sit at the head of the table, my hands on the stone arms, fingers drumming. Someone—I don't remember who—found me a blue silk robe, which I've pulled across my shoulders, but my feet are still bare against the cold floor. Sul sits at my left hand, draped in his chair, one ankle propped on the opposite knee. While his pose may be languid, there's a glint of deadly intent in his eye.

The table is shaped in a wide U with members of my privy council seated on either side of me. The seat for the queen is empty on my right hand, but Queen Roh has taken a chair several places down. Her priest is notably absent. Instead, Umog Zu and another priestess of the Deeper Dark occupy the furthest seats at the two ends of the table. They have entered into a semi-*va* state and will offer neither advice nor opinions. It is their job to petition the Dark to guide us in the right way. Their gentle prayersong hums like a deep river running beneath the strained voices filling the room.

I look around at the other parties present. My minsters of finance, travel, agriculture, tradition, and, of course, war. The minister of trade's seat is empty; that one belonged to Lady Xag. The other members wear grim faces, a stark contrast to their elaborate wedding apparel. Their voices rise and fall, speaking over one another, their words lost in a dissonant chorus. Only Sul and his mother hold their peace. Roh's hands are folded neatly in front of her, while Sul rubs his curling upper lip with one finger.

Finally, Lady Parh, my minister of war, pounds the table so hard, the opposite end lifts several inches off the floor. "I do not see what the question is here!" she barks, drowning out the other members, who stare at her, momentarily subdued. "The humans have conspired against our king. They have defiled our holy waters, revealing themselves to be two-faced and vicious wurms. We must send them a clear message."

"I agree." My minister of finance nods enthusiastically. "We ought to send the girl's thumbs back to her father in a box. Let that be a lesson to them!"

"Her thumbs?" Parh sneers. "You're far too squeamish, Lord Gol. In King Guar's day, it would have been her head!"

All eyes in the room swivel to me.

I blink blandly. "I am not King Guar."

"No, indeed." My minister of tradition offers a kindly smile that is just a little too broad. "And, *under the circumstances*, one would not expect you to behave as your noble father did."

Sul sits up straight in his chair, his hand dropping away from his face. "Speak plainly, Lord Rath." The smile he shoots my minister is even broader, even more kindly, and far more sinister. "What circumstances do you mean? Pray, enlighten us all."

My minister squirms in his seat, his lips compressing into a line. He offers no answer.

Lady Sha, a deputy minister, clears her throat gently, drawing eyes her way. "Pardon my confusion," she says softly, "but what is the problem here exactly? The human bride *is* King Larongar's daughter, is she not? Thus, the contract is binding, regardless of which girl bears the name. Why all this fuss? The alliance may move forward, as approved by majority vote of this very council."

"Exactly!" the rumbling voice of Brug, my minister of agriculture, growls. He pounds one rock-shaped fist against the other to emphasize his point. "No fuss. No bother. Just get back in there and *grundle* the girl. Pardon my language," he adds with a nod to Umog Zu. She opens one eye to give him a look, then returns to her *va*. He shrugs and addresses me directly. "There's no call to be delicate about it, Your Majesty. You only have to do it the once. If you find her unappealing, shut her away somewhere safe and take yourself a pretty mistress or two. That's the way it's done."

Sul tilts his chair back on two legs, his foot now propped on the table edge. "This wise and noble council need hardly be reminded that if Larongar played us false once, he will undoubtedly do so again. He is human. He is not bound to the written words of the contract but may break them on mere whim. Whereas our king, should he, um, *complete his marital duties*, will be obliged to fulfill the oath to which he signed his mark. Which means soldiers sent to fight Larongar's enemies. How many of you want to send good troldefolk off to die for a human king's cause?"

"Exactly!" Lady Parh leans forward in her seat, her eyes suddenly bright. "Which is why we should have gone with my original plan in the first place—attack the humans, take their Miphates captive, and force them to give us the magic we need. Break a couple of fingers and toes, maybe kill off some of the lesser mages, and the rest will soon be compliant."

"We are not going to war with the humans," I answer coldly.

"Oh, no," the minister of tradition mutters. "No, *of course* the king wouldn't want that!"

Sul is out of his chair and on the table in a trice. Ignoring the shouts of the ministers staring up at him, he strides its length to plant himself squarely before Lord Rath. "Speak up, Rath. What have you to say? Loud enough for everyone to hear, if you please!"

Rath's lips twist. "I only meant that because the king is half-human himself, he may be loath to—"

Before he can get another word out, Sul plants his foot on the minster's head, driving his face into the table. "Do you want to keep spitting that poisonous bile of yours?" he hisses, bending to plant his elbow on his knee. "Because I'm really starting to enjoy it!"

"Sul," I bark. "Stand down—off my minister and my table."

Growling, Sul obeys. He backs up to his seat, never breaking Rath's gaze. The minister rubs his head, cursing and spluttering, but unwilling to voice further complaint. Not in my brother's presence anyway.

"You've been very quiet, Your Highness," Lord Gol says suddenly, turning to Roh. "You were King Guar's consort and have served Mythanar these many turns of the cycle. What do you believe should be done?"

My stepmother raises her pale lashes at last. "The answer is clear," she says. Her cool gaze travels around the table, taking in each council member by turn. She stops when she comes to me, her eyes round and unblinking. "The answer is clear," she says again.

"We must execute the girl and send her head home with her kinswoman as a message to the human king."

Ignoring Lady Parh's muttered, "Exactly!" I hold my stepmother's gaze. A mocking half smile twists my lips, disguising the sudden plunge in my gut. "And what good would such violence accomplish?"

"It would put an end to this foolish notion of an alliance once and for all."

At this, the table explodes into yet another storm of babble, underscored by the rumbling voice of Brug and punctuated by Lady Parh's pounding fist. Finally, Lady Sha's high voice manages to be heard above the rest: "But what about the Miphates? We'll never get their support by offending Larongar so."

"We should never have pinned our hopes for help on the Miphates in the first place," Queen Roh responds.

"Is that so?" Brug folds his great arms. "And how exactly do you expect to combat the stirrings? To stop the destruction of our world?"

"I don't."

Every pair of eyes fixes on the queen. Even the two priestesses give up all pretense of *va* to stare at her.

"From the Dark we have sprung," Queen Roh says calmly. "To the Dark we must return. Who are we to thwart the will of the Deeper Dark?"

"It is not the Dark which sends the *raog* poison rising through the cracks in the world." Umog Zu lifts her head. The little skulls adorning her headdress rattle and shake. "It is that which dwells in the Dark."

"And you are so sure they are not one and the same?"

"We don't have time for this *guthakug* holy-talk," Brug barks, rounding on Queen Roh. "Are you saying we all ought to just sit back and watch our world burn?"

"Certainly not."

"Then what *do* you propose?"

"I propose we prepare our souls for the inevitable."

All mutters, murmurs, and growls cease. Total silence descends upon the room, so absolute one can almost hear the hum of *urzul* stones deep in the walls. Though I know it must be my imagination, suddenly the shadows on the edges of the room seem darker, denser. Full of living menace.

Then Lady Parh snorts. "You've been listening to that stone-hide priest of yours too long."

Roh merely sits back in her seat and smiles demurely. But she's lost her hold of the room, and the conversation carries on without her. More advice is sent my way, some presented in gentle tones, some hurled with angry force. Around and around my councillors go until the room itself spins in the maelstrom of their words.

At last, when everything that can be said has been said, they all sit back. And look at me. In the end, after all, this is not their decision to make. I and I alone must decide my bride's fate.

I push back my chair and stand. Everyone else stands as well, respectfully bowing their heads as they await my spoken will. I look around at each of them in turn, feeling one last time the force of their earnest and mostly contradictory opinions.

"I thank you all for your wisdom and perspective on the matter," I say, choosing my words with care. "I will retire to think upon your words. I bid you await my decision here. I won't be long."

Putting my back to their bubbling protests, I turn and make for the door of the nearest antechamber. I don't have to say a word for both Sul and Hael to leave their places and fall into step behind me. I pass into the room, a fraction of the size of the great council hall, furnished with large chairs and long tables on which various charts and instruments lie at the ready. A pale moonfire burns on the hearth, casting a little half-circle glow.

Leaving Hael to shut the door behind me, I pace up to the hearth and lean heavily against the mantel, staring into the flames. My breath is tight in my throat. I feel as though invisible claws have taken hold of me, squeezing slowly. The white fire dances, but I cannot see it. My vision seems to be made up entirely of a black box lined with blue silk. Blue to soak up the blood so it won't be visible.

But humans bleed red. Faraine's blood would leave an ugly stain when her head fell into that box.

No! This is foolish. No need for such gruesome imaginings. I am king. They cannot execute anyone without my leave. And I'm not about to let Faraine suffer such a fate. I may hate her for what she's done to me, but I would not be the man I hope I am if I let such hatred drive me to act so cruelly.

Behind me, Sul rings a silver bell. I listen to the murmur of his voice as he orders refreshments. He does not speak to me until the servant returns with a pitcher of *krilge*. Sul pours, then steps to my side. "Here, Vor," he says, holding out a goblet. "Drink up."

I take the cup, but do not drink. I cannot. Drawing a long breath, I turn and face the small chamber. Hael stands by the door, watchful and silent. I'm too angry to acknowledge her just now. Not after her failure to detect the ruse. Gods above! She was my first and only line of defense against such deceit. She should have seen something, some hint, some clue that all was not as it seemed. I've always trusted Hael, would put my life in her hands. But now? I'm not sure how I can ever trust her again.

"What are you going to do, brother?" Sul's voice intrudes upon my dismal thoughts.

"I don't know."

"Do you want an opinion?"

I cast him a bitter look. "Another one?"

Sul shrugs. "I simply think you should trust your instincts."

"My instincts?"

Seven gods preserve me! My instincts are urging me to leave this room, storm back across the council hall, ignoring the cries of my ministers, and return to that dim bridal chamber. To finish what I'd started. To take Faraine in my arms, whispering her name over and over. To tear away that flimsy white gown. To pin her arms above her head with one hand, while my other hand explores her body—every curve, every valley, every warm and secret place. Stroking, caressing until she quakes and cries out in sheer ecstasy.

I pinch the bridge of my nose. "I'm not sure trusting my instincts is the right call just now, brother."

"Not your *human* instincts. It's high time you acted like a proper *trolde*."

"That's rich, coming from you. Aren't you the one always so quick to defend my troldeness?"

Sul places a hand against his heart. "You know I am loyal to you above all things. I will defend your right to rule with my last breath. But"—he shakes his head heavily—"it's time you woke up and realized how precarious your rule has become. Hear me out!" he adds, silencing my mounting protest. "You've been so fixated on this alliance, so distracted by rumors of cave devils and stirrings and poison, you've not paid attention to which way the river is flowing. Lord Rath's implications aren't the worst of it, not by a long shot. Whispers are crawling all over the city. Never concentrated enough for me to pin down, but my spies pick up enough. As the stirrings worsen, so do the whispers. People are losing confidence in your leadership." He drops his head, speaking his next words softly, as though afraid the very walls might be listening. "It won't be long before word of what happened in Dugorim spreads throughout Mythanar."

Weight seems to press upon my shoulders. The weight of rule. The weight of the kingdom. The weight of the disaster we all know is coming. Weight, which is always there, but which, most of the time, I can ignore. I can concentrate on immediate needs, immediate plans; tell myself if I throw my whole heart into my endeavors, I can outrun destiny and thwart the clutches of doom.

It doesn't matter. The weight is always there, slowly crushing me beneath it.

I meet my brother's eyes. Moonfire illuminates them with an uncharacteristically earnest glow. "Go on," I say. "I can see you have a plan for how I might strengthen my rule. What is it?"

"Send her head home in a box."

I'd just lifted the goblet, dampening my lips with its contents. At those words, I sputter, choke, spew out the mouthful to sizzle in the fire. I whirl on Sul. "You can't be serious."

"Oh, but I am. Deadly serious." He takes a drink from his own cup, then sets it down on the mantel. "That old battle-ax Lady Parh was right. It's what our father would have done. And his father before him and his father's father. Trolde kings are not gentle kings. They are not kindly or merciful. They are kings of stone, kings of darkness, kings of molten magma."

I don't want to hear this. I want to hurl the contents of my cup in my brother's face. I want to take hold of his head and dash it against the stone mantelpiece until his skull cracks. I want to . . . I want to . . .

"Your people need to see a leader," Sul persists. "A trolde leader for trolde people. You don't want them thinking the humans can make a fool out of you. Humans who flout our traditions and disrespect our king should suffer his swift and brutal vengeance."

"I can't believe I'm hearing this." I draw back a step. My vision narrows, darkness closing in on each side. "Stop it, Sul. Stop it now."

He shrugs, holding up a defensive hand, palm out. "The decision is yours. You must do what you will with your bride. But your choice will change everything. For better or for worse. If you want to save Mythanar, you *must* secure your throne. Otherwise, we might as well let the next stirring drag us all to hell."

Casting about, I catch sight of Hael, so silent and stern before the door. Her face is still the same careful blank it's been since she learned Faraine's identity. She must feel my gaze on her, however, for she shoots me a brief sidelong glance. Just a glance, nothing more.

"Vor?" Sul takes a step closer to me, his voice low, urgent. "What are you thinking?"

How can I possibly answer? I know I cannot do as he asks. I won't even consider it. Maybe he's right. Maybe this moment is the moment I lose everything. It doesn't matter. I won't harm Faraine. No matter what she's done. No matter what she might yet do. I won't let such a fate befall her. Not while I have life in my body.

"You're a piece of morleth *gutha*," I snarl, and toss back the contents of my drink. It tastes unexpectedly sour on my tongue and burns when I swallow. A sudden rush of heat ripples through my veins like spreading fire. Lightheaded, I lean against the mantel, set my goblet down hard. I don't quite manage to get it all the way onto the level surface. It slips from my grip, crashes to the floor, and rolls.

A droning whine pierces my ear like red-hot iron.

"Are you all right?" Sul's voice echoes strangely, as though it comes from a distance.

I shake my head. The droning stops. "I'm fine." I bare my teeth, my jaw clenched. "I'll be better when you stop pressuring me and offer real advice."

"I'm not offering advice. I offer nothing but my opinion. You are king. Make up your own damn mind."

"Yes. I am king." I draw a sharp, hissing breath. "I am king, gods damn it."

I gaze down into the firelight. Deeper. Deeper. The flames twist together, coalescing in a writhing figure. Pale skin, dressed in white, reclining on that bed. She looks up at me, her eyes hooded, full of moonfire. Her gown slips from her shoulders, falls from her breasts. Slowly she parts her legs, wraps them around my waist, draws me to her. I feel her hands on my chest, in my hair, down my neck. I feel her warm and willing breast pressed against mine, the fiery heat of her core burning against me. Burning. *Burning. Burning me.*

I yank my head back, look into her face. Her eyes are black, empty voids. Her sweet pink tongue lengthens, lashing and poisonous, covered in welts. She licks my chest, and my skin erupts in oozing pustules. Her delicate fingers tracing my shoulders turn long, black, sharp, with coarse hairs bristling from each knuckle. They pierce my flesh, needle-sharp points digging down through muscle, through bone, reaching for my heart.

With a cry, I leap back from the hearth and stare down at my own body. My aroused, enflamed, sweat-dripping body. Is that blood pouring down my chest from five finger-point wounds? I pass a hand over my face, look again. My skin is clear. But I can still feel those punctures. I can still feel the trickling blood. I drag ragged gasps into my lungs. My head, my heart, my groin are on fire.

"I am king," I rasp. Slowly I turn, face the room. Sul and Hael are both staring at me, their faces uncertain. I smile. "That demon bitch should die for what she's done."

"Really?" Sul blinks, tilting his head. "I've convinced you that easily? I was bracing for a speech on honor and mercy and—"

I push past him, striding to the door. Hael draws herself up and steps in front of me, blocking my way. She doesn't say anything. She just stands there, looking at me. I growl, wordless, and shove her to one side. For half an instant, I feel the strength in her, how easily she could resist me. But she doesn't. Because I am king. I am master here. My word, my will, is sovereign. Holy. Indisputable.

I burst through the door, stride back into the council chamber. My ministers scattered about the room, talking in little clusters. They all turn, and I feel the weight of their stares, the pressure of their needs and expectations. Gods, I would kill them all if I could! Maybe I will. Soon. But first . . .

I raise my arms. "I am Vor, King of Mythanar, Lord Protector of the Under Realm. I will not be mocked. Sound the drums and summon the *drur.* Bid him sharpen his ax. It's time we show Larongar what becomes of those who play false with the Shadow King."

35

Faraine

The drumbeats vibrate through the walls, the floor, reverberating under my feet and into my bones. It feels strong enough to knock me off my balance, to send me crashing to the ground. But that's only my imagination. I walk steadily, though my knees tremble and my gut roils with nervous tension.

I'm going to Vor. I'm sure of it. These great trolde guards have come to fetch me to him. And I will have to face him again, face his anger, his sorrow, his rage. His betrayal. All of those feelings, which will stab me like knives. Will there remain any trace of the peace I once knew in his presence? Have I ruined forever all chance of experiencing that peace again?

I grip my necklace hard, seeking comfort in its inner vibrations. It's alive in my grasp, but with a pulse far more aggressive than I'm used to feeling from it. The waves rolling out from it call to stones buried deep in the walls around me. I hear them singing back, a silent yet unmistakable song of fear. My own fear, reflected back at me. But at least it drowns out whatever I might otherwise receive from my two stern guards.

They take me to a long tunnel, lit only by a few red *lorst* crystals, hung from the ceiling at intervals of twenty feet or more. The effect is hellish and harsh. The shadows between the crystals are so deep, I am blind as the guards hustle me onward. At the end of the tunnel, I see bright light. Too bright after this darkness.

The guards push me out through the opening, and I throw up both hands to shield my face from the intense white glow. A sense of huge, open space surrounds me, but before my vision has a chance to adjust, the guards grip my arms, dragging me forward. They wrench me painfully off my feet, carrying me between them. I struggle, kicking, desperate to find my balance. All the while, many, many unseen eyes rake over me until I feel more exposed and vulnerable than when I climbed nearly naked from the wedding pool.

My scalded eyes begin to make sense of shadows and shapes in the glare. I see what looks like a set of stairs rising before me. Before I have time to register this, the guards are carrying me up, my feet bumping and stumbling over every tread. We reach the top of a broad, circular platform. I can just discern a cluster of figures standing off to my right, their heads hooded, their faces indiscernible. In the glare of sheer white *lorst* light, all I can say for certain is that their robes are blue. It is they who beat the drums, which roll like thunder in my ears.

Bah-bah-boom.

Bah-bah-boom.

Bah-bah-boom.

The guards set me down hard. I stumble, stagger, sink to my knees. The next moment, a hand grips my arm, smaller than those huge, rock-fingered fists that held me a moment before. "Faraine!"

I know that voice. "Lyria?" I blink again, turning my head and trying to force the blurry shadows into submission. My half sister's features come slowly into view. "Lyria, what's going on? Are you all right?"

"Don't worry, Faraine." She drops her head, speaking close to my ear. "I'm going to stop this. I swear it."

Her fear is so intense, it's like she's driving a heated iron rod straight into my temple. I yank away, the pain so great it momentarily blinds me. When I come back to myself, however, I'm able to see the world a little more clearly. The platform stands in the center of a great circular cavern. Rings of gallery seats rise many stories overhead, surrounding me. Hundreds of pale, beautiful trolde faces peer down at us with interest.

And directly in front of me, on a level with the platform itself, is an arched alcove carved into the cavern wall. It's hung with shining silk curtains, drawn back to reveal a great stone seat in the center. There sits Vor. My husband. Wearing a crown of black stone, his chest and shoulders bare.

My heart lurches at the sight. For an instant I feel hope. But no, that's wrong. There is no hope in that stern face of his, which is turned away, refusing to look directly at me. His expression is something I've never before seen, not even in those awful moments in the bridal chamber when he discovered my betrayal. Then he still looked like himself. Now, though they are the same handsome, strong features I've come to know, his face is that of a stranger. Hard. Cruel.

I try again to form his name, to call out to him across that empty space between us. In that moment, movement draws my eye. More figures appear at the top of a stair opposite the one I've just climbed. Two trolde men wearing blue robes with hoods pulled up over their heads carry something between them: a heavy block with a curved indentation across one edge. Behind them comes a slender female trolde, also in blue and hooded. She carries a black box in her arms. The open lid reveals blue silk lining within.

Behind them follows a great, stone-hide mountain of a trolde. He climbs the stair slowly, ponderously. Each step makes the whole platform shake, as though the support beams will give out under his weight. He carries a huge *virmaer* silver ax over his shoulder.

My mind is dull. Stupid. I cannot comprehend what I'm seeing. It's as though my spirit has stepped outside my body and retreated, observing all from a distance. Observing as that block with its indentation is placed in the center of the platform. Observing as the huge trolde with the ax takes up position beside it.

Bah-bah-boom.

Bah-bah-boom.

Bah-bah-boom.

The drums beat faster, faster, reaching a roaring crescendo. Then, abruptly, they cease. The drummers stand poised, hands in the air, the sleeves of their robes rolled back, baring their arms. Lyria squeezes my elbow so tight, her fingers threaten to pierce bone. I feel it, feel the pain, but cannot quite comprehend that it belongs to me.

One of the hooded figures separates from the rest. He steps to the front of the platform in the space between the block and the king's gallery. He puts back his hood, revealing a stern face lined with deep crevices of cruelty. His long white hair is streaked with black and swept back from his forehead. A wave ripples out from him, crawling along the floor of the platform, spreading like an ugly stain. When it reaches me, I struggle for a moment to recognize it. It's too strange, too unexpected, too horrible in a moment like this: *pleasure.*

My spine shudders. Lyria takes hold of me again and helps me to my feet. I fear I'm going to crumple and drag her down with me. With an effort, I brace my feet.

"*Tog Morar tor Grakanak,*" the trolde man intones.

"*Morar tor Grakanak,*" voices from the gallery echo in thundering chorus. It's eerily similar to the wedding ceremony of just a few hours ago.

The trolde man begins to speak in rumbling, rolling troldish. I don't recognize a single word. But that pleasure pulsing from his core continues unabated. I glance around, searching for the two different stairs. What are the odds that I could reach either of them if I made a dart for freedom? Nonexistent, I should think.

"Be brave, Fairie," Lyria hisses suddenly in my ear. I wince away from the assault of her terror just as she lets go of me and steps forward. In a clear, strong voice, she cries out, "Princess Ilsevel Cyhorn of Gavaria requires whatever is spoken in her presence to be stated in her own language or a translation provided."

The trolde man breaks off abruptly in the middle of his speech. He looks up to the gallery where his king sits. Vor does not look at him. His face is turned off to one side, his expression strangely blank. I can only see one of his eyes from this angle. It narrows slightly.

A figure steps from the shadows behind the throne and kneels beside him. It's Sul, his half brother. He inclines his head, whispers in the king's ear. Vor's lips move in answer. Sul offers some response. Vor nods, speaks a few short words, and motions sharply.

Sul rises, steps to stand beneath the open arch. He barks

something in troldish. The man in the robes sneers but offers a deep bow. Then he turns to Lyria, his eyes never once shifting to look at me. "Princess Faraine Cyhorn is charged with conspiring against Mythanar," he says in perfectly clear Gavarian. "She has perpetrated treachery against Mythanar's king in both falseness of intention and falseness of deed. She has broken the sacred alliance of brotherhood between Mythanar and her own nation of Gavaria, sowing rancor between our worlds. For this, she must face retribution."

Lyria tosses back her head and barks a laugh. It echoes strangely against the towering stone walls. "There must be some mistake! This is not *Faraine* Cyhorn who stands before you. By the will of Larongar, by the blood of Gavaria's king and consort queen, she is *Ilsevel* Cyhorn. There has been no treachery."

The trolde man sneers at Lyria. "Only humans would dare twist the truth with such audacity."

"Who cares so long as it *is* the truth?" Lyria takes a step toward the man. The two guards on either side of us shift ominously. She stops, glancing at them, then draws herself straighter. "You see before you Princess Ilsevel. The name is hers the same as though it were given to her upon the day of her christening. She had no say over the giving, any more than any of you chose the names you now bear. Thus, there is no betrayal. Ilsevel Cyhorn is innocent. Her only hope, her only desire, is to fulfill the will of her royal father and to please the Shadow King of Mythanar."

"She is a witch." The trolde man spits the word with vicious delight. "A human witch. She has entangled all of Mythanar in her spell. The king must protect his people from her wickedness."

Lyria growls, then steps swiftly to one side, looking around the man to the king's gallery. "Vor of Mythanar, you cannot mean to do this! You know perfectly well your bride is innocent. Your grievance is with Larongar, not his daughter. Do not punish her for her father's choices."

Vor leans to one side, whispering to his brother. Sul bends his head to listen, then straightens and calls out a string of short, sharp words in troldish. The man in the long blue robe inclines his head, then rounds on Lyria. "You will not address the king directly. You will keep your lying human tongue behind your teeth and observe with dignity what must take place."

"Like hells I will." Lyria plants one foot and leans back in a defensive stance. I realize suddenly that all the while she spoke, she was drawing sigils in the air with her fingers. Sudden magic sparks to life, summoned at her call. The two guards lunge at her, but she holds up both hands. Starbursts of red light erupt around her fists, forming two broad shields. She holds one out to each side, blocking the guards, and slowly backs up, taking position in front of me. "Stand down!" she cries. "Or I'll burn you to a crisp!"

I crouch behind her shoulders, sheltering in her spell. It's certainly strong, but it doesn't feel lasting. I know little about magic, but this spell gives the impression of a firecracker burning out: bright and furious, but too quickly over.

For the moment, however, the guards draw back. The man in blue grimaces, the light of her spell casting his face in harsh relief. "You cannot hope to stop all of Mythanar. Douse your magic at once or meet the same fate as the princess."

"Fine!" Lyria waves her right arm in an arc, her star shield flaring bright. "Execute me too if you like! But I'll take out a good dozen or more of you first, starting with you!"

Such brave words. Gods on high, I never realized what strength of spirit my half sister possesses! And to think she would put herself at risk for me. Sure, we were friends once. But that friendship died long ago. I've done nothing to deserve this loyalty now. Yet here she stands between me and my killers, her fear wafting out of her in powerful waves, her shoulders set, her jaw grim and determined.

I look around her, over her upraised arm and through the gleaming glare of her spell. All the way to where Vor sits. He does not look at Lyria. His face is still firmly turned away. From her. From me. From what he has ordered to take place here and now.

So this is it. This is the end.

I never truly believed Vor would kill me. I knew it was a possibility, but when I considered the man I knew—the man who had saved me from the unicorn riders, who had treated me with such courtesy, such gallantry; the man who had, so short a time ago, melted my heart with the warmth of his kisses, the heat of his touch—it simply did not seem possible this same man could order my death. I'd feared imprisonment or exile. Not this. Not public execution.

I turn my gaze back to Lyria. To that terrible snarl on her face as she whirls this way and that, trying to keep her eye on all our approaching attackers at once. Her fear is spiking, terrible stabs as violent as any blades. She's going to die. And she knows it. She won't submit to the block, so she'll be torn to pieces by these troldes. Still fighting. Still screaming. A terrible death.

I lick my dry lips.

Then, gripping my crystal hard, I take a single step forward and place a hand on Lyria's neck.

Everything rushes into me. All of her fear, bursting inside of me like an explosion, ready to rip me to pieces. But I close my eyes, centering on the vibration deep in my stone. I take hold of that explosion and simply . . . stand. Holding it. Cradling it in that space of connection between the two of us. I pull it out further, further, deeper into me. The pain of it rocks my soul, but I stand firm. Just a little more. Just a little deeper. Boring into me like a stake driven through my chest.

Then, when I feel I cannot bear a single instant more, I grasp hold of that connection and send back through the only thing I know how to send—*calm*.

Lyria goes limp. Her arms drop to her sides, the magic dissipating into the air in little sizzling pops. Knees buckling, she collapses. I have enough awareness left to catch her, to let her fall against me, dragging us both to the ground. I'm still shuddering from all that horror and fear I've pulled into me, but I manage to cry out, "Help her! For gods' sake, help her!"

Lyria turns in my grasp, looking up at me. Her face has gone slack, her brow blank. "Fairie?" she manages softly.

"I'm sorry," I whisper. "I've lost two sisters already. Please, please make it home. Make it home and live. For all of us."

A whimper burbles on her lips. I see her trying to form a weak "*No!*" but the troldes are upon us already. They rip her from my arms, drag her away from me. She hangs limp in their grasp, her head bent, her long fair hair hanging over her face and shoulders. "Gently!" I urge them, afraid they'll break her arms.

My crystal surges, emitting an audible hum. One of the blue-robed figures springs to my side, grabs my wrist, and pries my fingers open. I try to protest as my necklace is snatched away, but what's the use? I have no power here. Not anymore.

But I had enough to save Lyria. If that is to be my final act of will in this life, so be it.

Without my crystal to steady me, I have no barrier against the hatred and bloodlust raining down on me from those high galleries. It's like a thundershower, driving with relentless force. I cannot find my feet, and the trolde guards are obliged to drag me upright.

The drums beat their terrible rhythm: *Bah-bah-boom. Bah-bah-boom.* We move in time to that beat. They drop me before the block, and I sink heavily to my knees. The drums beat on: *Bah-bah-boom. Bah-bah-boom.* Faster now. Keeping time with my racing heart.

The hooded woman with the blue box glides gracefully to stand before me. She kneels, places the box in front of the block. I gaze down into that blue silk lining, cushioned and soft. Waiting.

Swallowing painfully, I lift my face to the gallery across from me. To the Shadow King on his chair.

He's staring. Right at me.

Vor.

His name is there. On my tongue. I try to speak it, but my throat is too tight, my terror choking all breath out of me. I can do nothing but gaze into his eyes. And suddenly there is no one else present. Not a single other soul in this great, echoing, cavernous hall. Just him and me.

I cannot speak. So I throw everything I have into my spirit and send it flying across that space between us.

I loved you.

I believe I love you still.

Even now.

Even now.

A breath shudders through my lips.

Across from me, the hooded woman rises, folds her hands. She speaks in heavily accented Gavarian: "Princess Faraine Cyhorn. It is time."

36

Vor

When they drag her into the open, my bewitched eyes see her as I once believed her to be—small, delicate. Lovely as a *mar* lily offering up a gentle glow in the deepest shadows. She is like that. A glimmer in the darkness, a promise of hope tasted on the tip of one's tongue. A dream I could let myself fall into even as the rest of my world succumbs to darkness.

Then I blink. The dream fades, revealing the nightmare beneath. The witch, the demon, with her void eyes and lashing tongue, her skin like rot, flaking away from her bones. An abomination, a horror beyond all imagining.

She must be stopped. She must be ended before she can infect all Mythanar with her evil.

I grip the arms of my chair, fighting the urge to launch myself from the gallery, to throw aside those two tall guards hauling her between them and . . . and what? Take her in my arms, sheltering her against my breast, whispering into her hair that she's safe now, that I'll let no harm come to her? Or wrap my fingers around her throat, throttling the life out of her, dashing her head against the stone floor until her skull cracks and her brains spill out over my hands? My heart screams, torn between these two equal urges. I fear I will be ripped in half right here, before the eyes of my watching court.

She must die. She must die.

I love her, and she must die.

The guards drag her onto the scaffold, half carrying her between them. I watch through a miasma of rippling green as they drop her to her knees. The other human—another witch—goes to her, speaks in her ear. She lifts her face, her void eyes searching, searching. My heart leaps and races, knowing they will soon land on me.

But when they do, they are those eyes I know so well. One blue. One gold. Full of fear and entreaty.

I firm my jaw, setting my resolve like iron. I will not let the demon bewitch me. Not again.

Someone begins to speak. Lord Rath, enumerating the wrongs of the accused, the sins against king and crown. The weight of his accusation burns the atmosphere until my whirling vision seems to see all through licking tongues of green flame, dancing higher, higher—

"Your Majesty?"

I turn sharply. Sul is beside me, crouched to bring his face level with mine. "Brother," he says, "the cousin of the accused demands the charges be spoken in human tongue. What is the king's wish?"

I gape. Then my eyelids lower for a flash. When I raise them, Sul is transformed. His pale skin is rotten, falling away from his skull. His teeth are long, pointed, stained blue with blood, and his eyes are dark pits from which shadows writhe and crawl.

Another blink. My brother's face is before me, his head tilted, his brow puckered with concern. My heart plunges painfully before relearning to beat.

"Yes," I rasp, realizing he's awaiting my answer. "Yes. Of course. Let it be done."

Sul looks for a moment as though he'll say more. To my relief, he changes his mind, stands, and faces the scaffold. I don't hear what he calls down to Lord Rath. I don't hear whatever response is offered. Voices clamor on the edge of my awareness, but I cannot make sense of them. I close my eyes, bow my head.

And I see Faraine.

Aglow in the light of a unicorn rider's sword, just turning to me. Her hair whipping across her face, her eyes wide, gazing up in fear, in hope.

Her fingers touching the exposed skin of my wrist as we ride out under a horrible open sky. The flood of calm pouring into my soul.

Her slim body in my arms as I whirled her in time to the strains of a lively dance.

Her hand in mine, trembling as I kissed her knuckles. As I bade her goodbye.

Bade her goodbye.

Goodbye.

Gods above me, I'd thought I'd never see her again. Then lo and behold, she was in my arms! I feel her now, her back pressed against my chest, the flutter in her throat beneath my fingertips, the beat of her heart, the heave of her breast. Her lips, so soft, so pliant, so full of everything she had to offer, filling me with the need to offer everything I had in return.

How was I so foolish to believe I could feel that way for someone else?

Faraine.

Faraine—

"Vor of Mythanar, you cannot mean to do this!"

The sound of my own name lances through my senses. I sit up straighter in my seat and look down at the scaffold again. Down at the two human figures standing among my own tall, powerful people. One of the humans gazes straight at me, her eyes bright with desperate fury. "You know perfectly well your bride is innocent. Your grievance is with Larongar, not his daughter. Do not punish her for her father's choices."

Even as I watch, the fire in my head burns away the falseness of their features, revealing the rotten monsters beneath. Two demons with lashing tongues and long fingers tipped with black claws. Savage rage mounts inside me. I grip the arms of my chair again, fighting to maintain control of my own murderous urges.

"Sul," I hiss. My brother inclines his ear to my lips. "Do not let the witches address me again."

Sul draws back, blinking down at me. Then he nods and turns, once more speaking to those below. Again, all words melt away, vanishing in roaring flames. I close my eyes, brace myself against the heat. Gods! It's like molten magma forced into my veins, pulsing through my body, burning me from the inside out. Nothing can help me. Nothing, save the death of that witch.

Why, oh why do they not get on with it? I should open my eyes, open my mouth, scream at them to have done with these delays! Throw that creature across the block and put an end to her life. Now. At once. No, better still, I should do it myself. I should fly over the gallery rail, take hold of both those witches, one with each hand. Break them to pieces, tear their limbs from their sockets. Only death can bring relief, death, death, death—

A hum of music.

A single note—sweet and clear as newborn *lorst* light. Radiant aura, rippling through the flames in my soul, dousing them one by one.

At first, it is only a single note. But as it grows, as it spreads, other notes join in. High, crystalline, joining in a harmony of light. The heat in my veins flows out, replaced with this song like the purest running water.

I come back to myself. I'm collapsed in my chair, shaking, drenched in sweat. Every bone and muscle in my body aches, like the ache of a deadly fever. But this fever is past. Though I'm weak and gasping, I'm no longer imprisoned by that heat.

Dragging in a ragged gasp of air, I push myself straighter in my seat. Where am I? No, wait, I remember. The gallery overlooking the *drur* yard. And that scaffold below . . . I ordered it raised, didn't I? And that block, planted in the center, and . . . and . . .

Faraine.

She's there. She's down there, kneeling before the block. The black box is already placed before her, ready to receive her head. But she's not looking at that. Her gaze is uplifted, fixed on mine. She stares up at me with a whole world of life shining in those eyes.

Faraine.

"No!" I shout, leaping to my feet.

The drums roar, their pounding beat drowning out my voice. I shout again, uselessly, knowing I can never hope to be heard.

I see her bow. Place her chin in the groove. Exposing the white curve of her neck. The *drur* assumes his stance beside her, bracing his great feet.

There's no time to think.

I spring forward, push past Sul. Ignoring the shouts of those around me, I jump onto the gallery rail and, with a single bound, propel myself across the open space.

The ax is upraised. *Lorst* light gleams on its edge.

I land on the platform, take three long strides.

The ax descends.

My hands reach out and catch the handle. The tremendous weight of it, the power of the *drur's* swing drives me to my knees. But I hold it. Stop its descent. It hangs poised in midair, scarcely a foot above the chopping block and its intended target. I gaze up into the face of the *drur.* Wide, shocked eyes blink back at me from beneath his blue hood.

A roar bursts from my throat. I surge upright, pushing the ax high. Adjusting my grip, I wrest the handle from the *drur's* huge hands, turn, and plunge the heavy blade into the boards at my feet. The whole scaffold rocks, threatens to shatter under that blow. I stand there, my hands still gripping the handle, panting hard.

Then I turn to Lord Rath. Releasing hold of the ax, I straighten and snarl, "There will be no execution."

A terrible silence holds the hall captive. All those watching eyes. All those frozen screams. All those beating hearts caught in shock-tightened throats.

"There will be no execution," I repeat, my voice ringing against the stone. Turning, I look down at the block. Faraine is still there. Lying with her head in place, her face turned just slightly so she can look up at me. And all that beautiful life shines in her eyes. I want to reach out. I want to take her in my arms. To cradle her against me, to weep and beg her forgiveness through my tears.

But then I blink. And for an instant, I see the flash of endless void in her gaze.

Wincing, I retreat a step. "Take her to a holding cell," I command, addressing the two guards who had brought her here. "See she is cared for. She is not to be harmed. Do you understand me? Touch one hair of her head, and your life is forfeit. The same goes for everyone."

The guards exchange quick looks. Then one of them steps quickly to the chopping block, bends, and scoops Faraine in his arms. I have to fight the urge to launch myself at him, to pound his face into the ground and take her back. But I stand firm, fists clenched, and simply watch as the guard carries Faraine down from the scaffold and away. The other follows quickly after, holding tight to Lady Lyria.

I turn slowly, looking to the gallery. Sul is there, his mother beside him. They gaze down at me with faces totally blank of all expression. Others watch me as well—my council, members of my court and household. Hael and her guards. Umog Zu and the priestesses. Everyone.

The fire in my soul is gone. Now I become aware of the searing pain it left behind. My head feels as though someone has opened it up and stuck a burning brand directly into my brain. I want to scream, to grasp my skull, to shake and writhe. But I don't. I pull myself even straighter, looking into each of those faces above me, one after the other.

Silence throbs in my ears.

I turn. Take a step toward the scaffold stair. Before I take another, something bright catches my eye. I take a second glance and see it: a crystal pendant strung from a silver chain. Discarded. Forgotten.

I would know that pendant anywhere. I'd recognized it in the forest above Dugorim. Even then, the first suspicions had entered my head, only to be brushed aside as more pressing needs took precedence. I should have paid more attention. I should have questioned further, should have pressed for answers.

I bend and pick up the necklace, hiding it in my palm.

37

Faraine

There are no windows in this cell. Not that it matters. Perhaps if there were some hope of sky to be glimpsed, I would wish for one.

As it is, I know my view would only consist of more stone. All those folds of endless rock, layer upon layer, built up over eons. All those carved and twisting passages through which blind rivers flow. All the heat and suffocation, all the cold and the damp, all the incalculable mass. Perhaps there is no sky. Perhaps this bulk of stone is all there is, forever and ever. Perhaps I am to be crushed to death, my bones pulverized to dust. Perhaps . . . perhaps . . .

The horror comes over me slowly, like a swelling wave. When it hits, it breaks me. I am a mere ball of huddling, burbling madness. But even in that madness there is no relief, for I am not mad enough to lose my mind entirely. I have enough understanding to recognize my own gibbering, to feel shame. But I have no ability to surface now that the wave has taken me. I can only be carried by it, tossed on its merciless currents until at last, tired of me, it deposits my bruised and battered soul on the shores of self-awareness.

I let out a long, shuddering breath. The horror has passed. I feel weak, tired. My body shakes from dry heaving, and my throat and chest burn with bile. I push sweaty hair out of my face and manage to pull myself upright. My hand searches for my crystal pendant. But no. It's gone. They took it from me.

I lean my back against the wall, drawing and exhaling long sighs. The room in which they've placed me is small, maybe ten feet across, furnished with nothing but a low cot. A dim *lorst* crystal hangs from the stalactites overhead, slowly brightening over time to illuminate the room. It's already much brighter than it was when they first placed me in here. Not that it makes much difference. The contrast between this cell and the Queen's Apartment couldn't be starker. How far I have fallen in just a few short hours!

Then again, I could be dead. In fact, I'm still not entirely convinced I'm *not* dead. Had I not placed my head on that block? Had I not felt the change in the air as the ax-head began to fall?

But Vor saved me.

He leaped across that wide, empty space and caught the ax as it descended.

I groan, burying my face in my hands. Gods on high, what does it mean? He'd ordered my death. Only to change his mind in so dramatic a fashion! I wouldn't believe it if not for the evidence of my own head still firmly attached to my body. Shivering, I press a little harder into the wall and wrap my arms around my stomach. What is my fate to be after all? I cannot imagine. Vor may have decided I should live for now, but for how long?

The sound of a heavy door swinging open catches my ear. I look up, heart leaping. Light flares in the passage beyond the bars of my cell. Are they coming to fetch me? Will I be dragged back to that scaffold, faced with the block and the blade yet again? If so, I'm not going like a shivering mouse, gods help me!

I push off the cot and stand at the bars, craning my neck to look down the passage. A trolde guard approaches, carrying a small blue *lorst* light in one fist. Behind him hastens another, smaller figure.

"Lyria!" I gasp.

She peers around the trolde's shoulder, meeting my gaze. Her eyes flash. With a quick step, she skirts around the trolde, who grunts and lets her by. In a few quick paces, she reaches my cell, gripping the bars and staring in at me. Her mouth works, and she draws several breaths before turning to bark, "I was promised a private audience with the princess."

The guard regards her through half-lidded eyes. Slowly he nods.

"Open this door then. Let me in."

The guard raises an eyebrow.

Lyria curses and makes more angry demands, all to no avail. I'm not convinced the trolde even knows what she's saying. At last, however, when she asks if we may at least speak in private, he shrugs and retreats up the corridor. We watch until he steps out the far door, shutting it behind him with a clang that rings along the stone wall.

Lyria whirls to face me again. "Here," she says, taking hold of my hand. She pries open my fingers and drops something in my palm. "Take this."

It's my crystal. "Where did you find it?" I ask, surprised.

"It was sent to my chamber." Lyria snorts, looking through the bars at my cell. "Gods, Faraine! What a nasty little hole! It's a good thing you're used to your sparse convent living. They're keeping me in nicer quarters. I guess no one said to have me tossed in a dungeon, so they just stashed me back in the room they'd prepared for me. Someone slipped this under the door. I didn't see who, and when I called out, no one answered."

I bite my lip. Then, hands trembling, I slip the chain around my neck and breathe a sigh of relief to feel the crystal resting against my heart. Already, the faint vibration in its core soothes my frayed nerves.

Lyria looks at me contemplatively, her eyes narrowed. "You did something to me," she says. "Didn't you? On the scaffold, I mean. One moment I was ready to go out in a blaze of glory, and the next . . ."

I meet her gaze. And offer nothing.

She pulls a face. "They all said the gods gave you a curse, not a gift, on the day of your christening. But I'm starting to think they were wrong. Maybe the gods knew what they were doing after all."

She reaches through the bars again and clasps my hand. I wince. I know she means it as a comforting gesture, but anxiety needles from her palm into mine, sending shocks of pain through my awareness. I want to shake her off, to retreat. But that's not what she needs right now. So instead, I squeeze her fingers back.

"I'm leaving soon," she says.

"What?"

She nods. "They're sending me back through the Between Gate. I'm to be escorted out of Mythanar within the hour. By Prince Sul, of all people. I'll be lucky if he doesn't try to murder me along the way! But the king has commanded I bear a message home to Larongar, so perhaps I'll survive."

"What message?" I ask, half-afraid to hear the answer.

"That you're alive. That you are, for the time being, safe in Mythanar." Lyria hesitates, then adds, "That you are *not* Vor's wife. Not yet. He has a month to decide what to do with you before the contract is rendered null. I'm to promise Larongar an answer before the month is out."

An answer. A decision. For my life.

"I don't believe he'll kill you," Lyria continues, reading my expression. "There's no benefit for anyone in your death. And you can be sure Vor will be watching for whatever benefit he can salvage from this mess. He may even marry you yet."

"So he may," I answer dully. And lucky me, I get to wait around hoping he decides to make me his bride after all. This man who nearly killed me.

Lyria reaches through the bars to take my hand again, squeezing with what I'm sure she believes is comfort. "You did everything you could, Faraine. You shouldn't blame yourself."

"Thank you, Lyria." Somehow, I manage a fleeting smile. "Thank you for defending me."

She shrugs and grins back. "It was my job." Then, to my great surprise, she reaches through the bars, catches my shoulders, and pulls me to her in an embrace. An upswelling of affection rolls out from her. It's like standing on a trash heap and inhaling an unexpected breath of perfume. It catches me off guard. In that moment, I cannot help how my own heart gives a sudden throb in response. After all, she is my sister. Perhaps not in the same way Ilsevel and Aurae were. But a sister, nonetheless.

We cling for some moments, each knowing this is likely the last time we will ever set eyes on one another. When I release her, Lyria will go. Off to face the perils of her return journey and whatever future my father has planned for her. I, meanwhile, will be left behind in this dark world of rock and shadow. Alone. Utterly isolated. Without a friend in the world.

I hold on a little tighter and whisper, "I don't know if I can do this."

"Of course you can!" Lyria's arms squeeze me almost painfully. "You can do anything. You're so much braver, so much stronger than any of the rest of us. You always were, you know. Now is your time to prove it." She steps back then, looking into my eyes. "You were born to be a queen, Faraine. Show these people the truth. Make them see what you really are."

I swallow hard. I wish I had a final word for her, some way to express what I feel. But all I can manage is a softly spoken, "Be safe, sister."

She nods. "And you."

In another few moments, she's gone. Vanished back down the corridor and out through the far door. Off on adventures I cannot join. I wonder how long I'll be able to hold on to the memory of her face. Or will she—along with Ilsevel and Aurae and all those I once loved—fade into the darkness of this world and be lost?

I return to my bed, perch on the edge. Opening my palm, I look down at the crystal. It glints in the *lorst* light. So familiar and yet so strange. I grip it tight, press it to my chest, and close my eyes. Deep down, I feel the vibration in its core. And beneath my bare feet, an answering vibration in this stone floor, running up along the walls and across the ceiling overhead. So faint, so very faint. Am I imagining it? No. It's real. I'm almost certain.

Finally, I breathe out a long sigh, lie down on my side, and draw my knees up to my chest. For what feels like hours I watch the *lorst* crystal suspended from the ceiling overhead. It flickers, shines, fades . . . fades . . . fades . . .

Goes out.

38

Vor

I stand on the brink of the chasm, gazing down to the fiery river below. It winds through the darkness like a living vein, carrying life and heat through the bowels of our world. For ages beyond count it has safeguarded Mythanar, encircling the city and warding off all who would seek to do her harm. Save those foolish enough to carry harm in on their own bowed backs.

Behind me, the Queen's Garden hums gently with life. Moth-cats leap and bound among the rock formations and clamber among mosses and draping *jiru* vines, chasing fluttering *olk*, only pausing long enough to groom their long, plumed tails. They do not approach me as they usually would.

A footstep crunches in the pebbles behind me. I tense but do not turn. Part of me expects to hear that footstep quicken suddenly, for hands to shove me hard in the spine and send me stumbling, arms wheeling, over the edge of the chasm. My stomach plunges with the sensation of a fall that does not come. Gods, will this paranoia ever fade?

"The company is nearly ready to depart." It's Sul, standing several yards back from the sound of it. Apparently, he's not about to make an attempt on my life. Not yet anyway. "Yok begged leave to join again. I figured you wouldn't mind. We leave within the hour. I wanted to speak to you before we go."

"Why?" The word slices from my lips like a dagger thrust. "Are you looking for another chance to poison me?"

Silence.

I turn, my shoulders hunched, my eyes narrowed. Sul catches and holds my gaze. His brow slowly creases. "What in the *morarjuk* are you talking about?" he demands.

I pivot my weight on my heels, whirling on him. In three long strides I cover the space between us, grasp him by the throat with both hands, and force him to his knees. Sul doesn't have a chance to cry out, to defend himself. I yank his face up close to mine, snarling through clenched teeth. "I've been thinking about our little heart-to-heart in the antechamber. You gave me *krilge* to drink. It tasted strange, and then . . . and then . . ."

How can I describe the fiery rage that came over me? The same rage which even now fights to take mastery of my body, my soul, driving me out of my mind, fueling me with pure savagery.

Sul stares up at me, eyes goggling. He grapples with my arms, a wriggling worm in my grasp. "My king!" he gasps, the words choked from his gullet. "I would never . . . never . . ."

I squeeze harder. "You would never put traces of *raog* into my drink? You would never drive me to madness to accomplish your own aims? You would never see done to me what was done to Xag and all the folk of Dugorim?"

His eyes are rolling, desperate. Green flames lick the edges of my vision and cast his face in a ghastly light. It would be all too easy to succumb to the urging of those flames. To let go all restraint. To forget myself and simply become that which the heat awakens inside of me.

"Brother!" Sul chokes.

With a roar, I fling him to the ground. He gasps, gags, drags in ragged breaths, his face pressed into the dirt. I plant my foot on his neck, pinning him in place. "Swear to me your loyalty," I snarl. "Swear you are still the brother you've always claimed to be. Swear it on the Deeper Dark. Swear it on the Dragon."

"I swear!" he sputters. His whole body goes limp and submissive beneath my weight. "I swear it, Vor! I would never betray you!"

A terrible choice looms before me. I may either believe my brother or not. There is no in-between. And if I cannot believe Sul anymore, what hope is there for me? How can I face a world in which my trust is broken so completely? Faraine lied to me. Hael failed me. And Sul? Would Sul stoop so low in his determination to do what he thought was right for Mythanar?

Perhaps. But I've always believed Sul's first loyalty lay with me. Above crown. Above kingdom. If I don't have my brother's loyalty, I may as well cast myself over the chasm edge here and now.

With a ragged exhale of breath, I remove my foot from Sul's neck and step back. His head still in the dirt, he twists to look up at me. His eyes are wide, frightened. "Rise," I growl, and pass a hand over my face. "Rise, brother."

He scrambles to his knees and sits on his heels, still gaping at me. Finally, after many long, steadying breaths, he says, "*Raog* poison?"

I nod. "In the drink."

"I would never do that to you. I would take the draught myself first."

I believe him. In that moment at least. "But someone did."

Sul curses bitterly. "I'll find out who. I'll hunt down the servant who brought the *krilge*. If he is not responsible, he may know who is. I'll get my spies on it right away, before I set out for the gate." He gets unsteadily to his feet, still breathing hard. "I promise, Vor. I'll find answers for you."

I turn from him, gaze out over the chasm once more. The threat of rising poison has been brewing for many cycles now. But this? This is something new. Someone has learned to harness the poison, to contain it in small, targeted doses, and used it to manipulate me. I never would have suspected anything so terrible. Next time, will anything stop me and my murderous impulses? Will anyone prevent me from destroying everything I love in this world?

"Make your journey swift," I say, casting the words over my shoulder. "I need you back in Mythanar as soon as possible. Until you are here, there is no one I can trust."

"You can trust Hael."

"Can I?"

"You know you can." Sul's voice is uncharacteristically earnest. "Don't punish her, Vor. The humans . . . they're clever and deceitful. And their Miphates magic is more potent than we initially thought. It's not her fault."

"Perhaps not." It's the most I can acknowledge. I won't forgive her. Not yet.

I drop my head, close my eyes. Feel the vastness of the drop below me and the rising heat of the river. "I was so certain," I say, more to myself than to Sul. "I was so sure I'd found a way to save us all. And now . . ."

Now I feel the mounting pressure of annihilation. A world-ending force beyond anything I have the capacity to face or to defend against. Did I really think my futile machinations could be effective against such elemental powers of destruction?

Maybe my stepmother is right. Maybe it's time we all prepared our souls for the inevitable.

My hands squeeze into fists. I'm not done. The alliance with Gavaria is not broken yet. And Sul is right—this deception has only proven the cleverness of those human mages. There may be a way to set things right, to gain access to the magic I need. If I can only find the right angle.

"Off with you," I say to my brother without looking back. "Escort the human woman to her people. See she is not harmed while in your keeping."

"And what of the princess, my king? What is to become of her?"

That is a question to which I have no answer. But I must find an answer. Soon. Because in that moment, standing on the brink of the chasm, I know only one thing for certain.

Faraine will be my life. Or my doom.

EPILOGUE

The sorrow is too great. Too heavy.

Better to curl in tight, tighter, tightest. Present nothing but the hardened outer shell that none can pierce, not even the sorrow itself. And then to sleep. Deep, deep sleep that may in time—in centuries, in ages, in eons—turn into longed-for death.

Ah! Death! Death would be sweet, the sweetest of all blessings. Death would mean escape at last. And possibly . . . reunion? Yes, yes, let sleep turn to death, one sinking into the other. No more stirring. No more breathing. Just stillness, stillness, perfect stillness.

But death will not come.

Only sleep.

And in that sleep, there are dreams. Always dreams. Dreams of glory. Dreams of joy. Dreams of great flights across wide blue expanses, endless and dazzling and free.

Dreams of *together.*

But this is good. This dream. Maybe it's better than death. Maybe it is best to stay in this place, to let the dream become reality. For what is reality save that which is dreamed? Yes, here is a place to stay, to be.

Together.

Forever.

Only . . .

What is that?

That weight. That heavy, crushing, terrible weight. The weight of stone. The weight of loss. The weight of worlds.

Curl tighter, tighter. Don't let it in. Become nothing, become death, become dreams.

But it will not go. It will not shift. Not until it is shrugged off. Only then can there be freedom and great, empty, endless sky.

Perhaps it is time. Time to stop dreaming.

Time to wake.

Stone shifts.

Foundations tremble.

An eyelid rises, revealing a boiling red disc.

ACKNOWLEDGMENTS

Thank you hardly seems enough. I'm not sure I have words big enough to encompass the gratitude I feel for all those individuals who contributed to making this project come to life.

To Amanda Jain, queen among agents. I was so nervous to step back into the world of traditional publishing after so many years, and the idea of querying gave me hives! But then my very first query letter just happened to land in Amanda's inbox. She wrote me back the next day . . . and the rest has been history! Chance, you say? I think not. This partnership is much too fortuitous to be anything less than ordained by the stars.

To Mary Baker, my editor, who missed her subway stop after being swept off her feet by King Vor. I knew from the moment she told me that story that she was the perfect champion for this series. Thank you for believing in me. I cannot wait to see what more we accomplish together!

To the whole team at Ace, who have worked so hard to bring the Bride of the Shadow King trilogy to a whole new world of readers.

To K. D. Ritchie, an absolute rock star among cover designers. I fangirled so hard when I heard she was going to be creating the new look for my series! I'm not sure I've recovered yet . . .

To my wonderful readers, who fell in love with Vor and Faraine's romance early on. Especially Anna, Stephanie, Andra, Marea, Chantelle, Nic, Renée, Rexy, and Rizzo. You—and so many others, unnamed but no less appreciated—gave me life and inspiration as I crafted this tale!

To Elise, Danielle, Alisha, Angela, Emma, Jenny, Meg, Melissa, Sarah, Barbara, and all the Noble Order of Female Fantasy Writers, for being the literary goddesses you are.

To Una, Rex, Leo, and Aurelia. You give my life meaning.

And most of all, to Handsome. You are my hero and always will be. Whenever anyone asks me how I write such swoonworthy men, I point to you . . . and suddenly it all makes sense.

BONUS MATERIAL

When considering what I might like to write as a delicious little extra for this edition of *Bride of the Shadow King*, the first character who leapt to mind was Captain Hael. I don't know what it is about this character, but she has always had a special place in my heart. Given time, I'm sure I could devote an entire novel to our stoic but deep-feeling trolde warrior. Her loyalty to Vor, her love for her younger brother, and that unspoken but undeniable *something* between her and Prince Sul leave plenty of room for intrigue. As the trilogy developed, so too did my interest in Hael, and you'll find her role in the story increasing with each passing book.

I was excited at the prospect of delving into her perspective for this crucial scene early on in *Bride of the Shadow King*—I see it fitting in just before Chapter 7 of the story. I hope you will enjoy getting a taste of her point of view, and I look forward to sharing more tidbits featuring this intriguing character in the next two books as well.

Captain Hael

"Do my eyes deceive me, or is our fearless leader paying homage to the wrong princess this fine evening?"

I do not startle when Sul's voice whispers suddenly in my ear, his lips hovering all too close to my skin. My instinct is to turn, grab him by the arm, give it a good wrench, and put my knee in the small of his back. All of which I could do in half a breath, and well he knows it. But I also know the absolute delight he would gain from causing me to make such a scene in the midst of the human king's welcome banquet. I won't give him that satisfaction.

I merely grunt. Only the fine hairs rising on the back of my neck reveal any reaction to the proximity of the man standing so close behind me. My attention remains focused on Vor, who stands across the room, hovering beside the chair of King Larongar's eldest daughter, the princess we rescued on the mountain road. I cannot for the moment recall her name. Human names are so long and flowery to my ear, it's difficult to keep track of them.

Sul steps from behind me and lounges at my side, leaning

against one of the carved wooden support pillars. I took up position here following the meal where I might be out of the way of the dancing and keep a close eye on all the goings-on in the hall. Though I am dressed in my finest and dined at Larongar's table along with my king and his brother, I am still on duty. I must guard and protect Vor. Though we are guests in this house, I do not trust the human king nor any of these strange, small folk. The stink of mortality stings my nostrils, and I cannot help wishing Vor had never conceived this idea of an alliance with humans.

As though reading my mind, Sul casts me a sly smirk. "Perhaps the younger sister will notice and take issue, and a *woggha* fight will break out. Swiftest way to undo this whole debacle of an alliance."

Taking care my expression reveals nothing, I cast him a sidelong glance. "Something tells me the young sister will not care if Vor's attentions are diverted elsewhere."

"True enough." Sul snorts, and we both of us turn our gazes to the dance floor, where the dark-haired favorite daughter of King Larongar dances with a human knight. "If looks could kill, my poor brother would have been gasping out his last before the soup was served. Her face is pretty enough, but that glower of hers could set a herd of morleth stampeding."

He's not wrong. The young princess has been shooting dagger glares Vor's way all night. She glances his way now as he converses with her sister, and I cannot tell if that deep line between her brows is due to jealousy or concern. Perhaps some of both. By contrast, the look on the elder princess's face is not at all unwelcoming. She gazes up at Vor with such rapt attention, if I didn't know any better, I'd think he'd quite captured her interest.

"So long as Vor favors one of the king's daughters," I muse, "does it matter all that much which one he chooses?"

Sul curses softly. “One, either, both . . . This alliance is a joke regardless.” He idly rubs his nails against his tunic sleeve. “I don’t see why Vor couldn’t just as easily have made a fool of himself over a trolde wench. Even an elfkin would have been preferable.”

I cast him another sidelong look. “Vor believes this alliance with Larongar is our only option.”

“Larongar is not to be trusted.” Sul’s voice drops an octave, and when his eyes meet mine, his expression is sharp, all traces of light-hearted mockery momentarily vanished. “Vor shouldn’t be dealing with him. You know it. I know it. I think Vor knows it too in his heart. Only the heart can be such a deceitful organ.”

My jaw tightens. I’m careful not to look Sul’s way again, but focus on Vor; watch the subtle changes in his face as he speaks to the human princess. I don’t think his heart is engaged just yet, but . . . it doesn’t take a great deal of insight to perceive the danger. I’ve known Vor all my life; he and Sul and I grew up together. And I have never seen him look at any woman in quite that way before.

I draw a slow breath through my nostrils. Sul is right—this alliance isn’t a good idea. Vor is desperate for a solution to Mythanar’s dire situation, and I cannot blame him. But will pursuing that solution lead the Under Realm into greater peril still?

“Deeper Dark devour me, what is he doing now?” Sul growls.

I blink, my eyebrows rising. For as a new song begins to play, Vor extends his hand to the human princess and guides her down to the dance floor. This is a definite show of preference considering he did not dance with the younger princess when Larongar suggested it. I send a glance the king’s way and watch his brow tighten into a severe knot as he watches Vor lead his older, less favored daughter forward. While I cannot read the king’s mind, his displeasure is evident.

But when Vor sweeps the human maid off her feet and whirls her around in time to the soaring tune, Larongar positively erupts from his chair. "How now, King Vor!" he bellows, storming to the dance floor and firmly placing himself between my king and his daughter. "Is this some troll practice wherein you maul a man's daughter right before his eyes?"

My hand goes for my sword, which isn't there. It would have been rude indeed for me to attend this banquet armed. Now I wish I'd risked it, to hells with offending humans. Not that it matters—I'll wade into any fray and defend Vor with my bare hands if I must. I take half a step, but Sul grips my wrist. I turn to him with a savage snarl. He merely nods and murmurs, "Wait a moment, my dear Hael. Let this drama play out."

The princess hastily steps forward, drawing her father's eye. She looks very pale. If I didn't know any better, I'd say she was in pain. But she speaks in a soft, sweet voice, too low for me to hear. Whatever she says, it has a swift effect; Larongar's brow softens from its grim lines, breaking into an abrupt grin.

"Come, my friend!" he declares with a booming laugh. "You must teach us all to perform such feats of manliness. I'm sure our women are as brave as any troll dame."

I grit my teeth at the casual use of that slur. Sul growls, "*Guthakug!*" and squeezes my wrist a little tighter, as though to ensure I don't leap forward and brain the king with one blow of my fist. I stand down, watching as Larongar summons his mistress—right there, before the watching eyes of his queen—and leads her to the dance floor. In the same breath, he commands his younger daughter to take the elder's place at Vor's side and continue the dance. The dark-haired girl looks none too pleased with this turn of events but doesn't argue with her father.

As for the elder, paler princess? She slips away as the music swells, lines of pain tight around her mouth and eyes. She casts a single glance back at Vor as he spins her sister round in time to the lively melody. Then she is gone.

"I suppose we must give the wench credit for averting that particular crisis," Sul says. His grip on my wrist relaxes finally. Rather than take his hand away, he slips his hand down, his fingers wrapping with mine. The intimacy of the touch shocks me far more than anything else he's said or done this night. My heart leaps to my throat, but I maintain a stonelike calm, ignoring the magma suddenly shooting through my veins.

"What do you say, my dear, sweet Hael?" Sul's voice is at my ear once more, his lips hovering just a breath away from my skin. "The human king is a most ungraceful clod. Perhaps we *trolls*"—he growls the slur with venom—"ought to show these creatures what true dancing looks like."

I couldn't speak if I wanted to. Is he asking me what I think he's asking? Not in all the years I've known him has Sul ever invited me to dance. I'm not the kind of woman he seeks out for such pleasures. Once upon a time he may have seen me differently . . . but when the *dorgarag* stone started creeping up my skin, I lost all chance of being an object of interest in the Prince of Mythanar's eyes. He is too beautiful to waste time on an imperfect specimen like me. I've known it since the day the gray, scaly hide crept up above my collar and spread across my neck and jaw. I'd thought I'd accepted the truth long ago.

And yet the mere suggestion of a dance is enough to transform me back into the blushing child I once was. I hate myself for this weakness . . . but I can't deny the faint flicker of hope which sparks in my heart. I turn to him, catch his eyes, so close to my own. Close enough, I could almost swear I feel the fan of his lashes when he blinks.

Then his face breaks into a devastating smile. "I think I'll go see if the king's bastard daughter is daring enough to give me a dance. After all, she's an unexpectedly toothsome morsel . . . for a human."

With those words he leaves me. Weaves his way across the crowded room, searching out a likely target for his charm. And I stand beside that pillar, my hand suddenly cold and empty. Like my heart. Gods damn me, why did I allow that momentary surge of hope, of excitement? Why do I keep doing this to myself, turn after turn of the cycle? Why can I not let that scoundrel go?

I draw my shoulders back, my hands forming fists. I'm not about to allow Sul's teasing to compromise my own sense of worth. I know who I am. Vor depends on me, and I have always made certain I am worthy of that dependence. I'm not some foolish maid to go sighing after a pretty prince. I could break Sul in half with one hand tied behind my back if I wished to!

So why do my traitorous eyes insist on seeking him out as he leads a golden-haired partner to the dance floor?

"Ahem."

The small cough interrupts my reverie. I look down . . . then down a little more into a pair of sapphire-blue eyes upturned to mine. The face those eyes are set in is striking. I would call it *pretty* were it not for a certain sharpness of both jaw and brow. It's the sort of face one doesn't forget, not even after a single glimpse. Though I've never been an admirer of human forms or features, even I cannot deny the effect of it; too bad it has the misfortune of belonging to possibly the most disagreeable person I've met in all my life.

"Would you like a drink?" Prince Theodre says, offering me a goblet along with a blinding smile. "I, erh . . . I noticed you didn't eat or drink much at dinner. I thought you might be thirsty. Though perhaps you don't care for, erm . . . human food?"

I drop my gaze to the wine in his hand, then slowly lift it back to his.

"Do you remember me?" he asks, tilting his head so that those golden curls of his fall fetchingly across his forehead. "We spent quite a little time together the other night."

How could I forget? The human prince was my riding companion last night after we rescued him and his sister from the clutches of marauding Licornyn Riders. The prince, finding himself suddenly surrounded by troldefolk rather than fae, had been less than comforted. Memory of his voice inciting the gods to blast our nethers with pustule sores still rings rather vividly in my ear.

"I remember," I say coldly.

"Oh, good!" He lights up. It's quite disconcerting, the blast of pleasure beaming from that altogether beautiful face. "I fear I didn't give the best impression of myself last night. The, erh, excitement of it all, you know? If I said anything truly offensive, I hope you'll pardon me." I narrow my eyes. He swallows audibly, his larynx bobbing. Then he raises the goblet again. "Do you drink? Wine, that is? I assume you drink something, though perhaps you don't? I confess, I know little about trolls and their ways. Based on the stories I heard, I rather imagined you ate . . . Well, actually, I suppose that doesn't bear repeating."

Give the man some credit for self-preservation. I turn away from him, facing the dance floor once more. "I'm on duty."

He's silent a moment. Then: "Ah, of course. That would explain the not eating or drinking. You're captain of the king's guard, aren't you? I got a glimpse of you with the Licornyn last night. Ye gods above, I never saw a more formidable display! You could have set the whole lot of them hightailing it back for Eledria on your own, I daresay."

I look down at him again, silent. His smile falters. He takes a gulp from the goblet he'd offered me and stares fixedly out at the dance floor again. After watching the whirling figures for a measure or two, he summons the dregs of his courage and blurts, "What I really meant by coming over here was to ask you for a dance. I suppose if you're on duty it's out of the question, but . . . well . . . What do you think?"

My brow puckers. "A dance?"

"You know." He moves the goblet in his hand through the air in something of a pattern, sloshing wine over the brim. "Like this?" He eyes the couples on the floor and adds, "Not that I could lift you up and twirl you like that, but . . . you know, if you wanted to fling me about, I wouldn't be against the notion. Only if you want to, of course."

I'm still struggling to fathom what sort of answer to give this proposition when the song comes mercifully to an end. I turn away from the prince's hopeful face and watch Vor bowing over the human princess's hand as the two of them exchange words. But my gaze doesn't linger there—it is drawn irresistibly to where Sul even now laughs with his own human companion. The woman he chose to dance with rather than me.

My stomach clenches.

"Ah well, too late," Theodre mutters, rubbing the back of his neck. "Looks like Father's got to put on an exhibition anyway."

"What?" I shift my gaze across the hall. Larongar has drawn Vor back to the long table, and the floor is cleared. I find myself standing directly opposite Sul, who leans against a pillar and smirks at me. I turn coldly away from him, pretending disinterest as the dark-haired princess moves to the center of the hall.

"Father's making Ilsevel sing," Theodre says, leaning toward me and whispering conspiratorially. "It's her gods-gift, you see. She's his favorite, in no small part because he finds her gift more useful than anything the gods doled out to the rest of us."

My brow puckers in surprise. "You are gods-gifted?"

A flush steals up his cheeks. "You, erh . . . couldn't tell?"

Before I can answer, music draws my attention back to the princess. She sits alone, an instrument in her hands, and plays a delicate, lilting melody. I've never developed an ear for human music but am nonetheless immediately struck by her dexterity and the clear tone she calls forth from the strings. When she begins to sing, however, I am truly transported. I've never heard anything like it—a song as unlike troldish music as anything I've heard, yet it calls to my heart. There's magic in this music, life-giving and life-ending all at the same time.

Suddenly I feel as though I'm back home in Mythanar, wandering the caverns just beyond the city limits. Sul is with me, laughing and wild. Vor is there too, more cautious than his younger brother but eager for adventure. I am with them every step of the way, venturing into dark caverns, searching for cave spider nests and hidden forests of towering mushrooms, hungry for whatever adventure we may find. We were so young and heedless of the peril all around us, as yet unburdened by the weight of responsibility we now carry. In this song, I shrug off that weight, for a little while at least. I am young again, and the world is full of beautiful possibility, and the bond we share can never be broken.

The song fades away. I find that I'm no longer looking at Princess Ilsevel but staring across the hall. At Sul. His expression has gone soft, as though a mask has slipped. In those few moments, as the last strains of that gods-gifted talent hold the room captive, I see his true face for the first time in years. But he does not look back at me, and the distance between us feels like an impossible gulf.

"Gods above."

The breathless words yank my awareness painfully back to the present. Frowning, I turn to find Prince Theodre gazing up at me like some wonder-struck mothkitten. My frown deepens. He blinks and ducks his head, his cheeks pinking in the warm glow of firelight. "Forgive me, Captain," he says, clearing his throat. "I don't mean to be rude, but just now, when you were listening to Ilsie's song . . . well, you rather took my breath away."

I cross my arms. Uncertain how to respond, I opt for silence. When another dance tune begins to play, and the humans gather once more to form lines with their partners, the prince bows deeply. "I don't suppose you'd care for a turn? This dance looks a little less physically strenuous, and I promise not to step on your feet. I'm really quite graceful, you know. It's part of my gift."

"I'm on duty," I state in a voice of stone.

"Oh, yes. Quite so, quite so." He clears his throat again and straightens the collar of his ornate jerkin. "But if you should change your mind?"

"I won't."

"Yes, well. In that case, I'll bid you good night, Captain."

To my great relief, the human prince bows and retreats. I make a point not to look for him the rest of the evening, though I cannot help noticing that he does not take to the dance floor with anyone else. Sul, by contrast, dances with many a human maiden throughout the revels. Not once does he look my way.

But I will not care about that. I will become *jor*—one with the stone. No heart to hurt, no dreams to disappoint, no feelings, no fears, no fantasies. For I am a servant of Mythanar. I will do whatever I must to protect my king and my kingdom. No matter the cost.

Photo by Chelsea Ann Photography

Sylvia Mercedes makes her home in the idyllic North Carolina countryside with her handsome husband, numerous small children, and a menagerie of rescue cats and dogs. When she's not writing, she's . . . okay, let's be honest. When she's not writing, she's running around after her littles, cleaning up glitter, trying to plan healthy-ish meals, and wondering where she left her phone. In between, she reads a steady diet of fantasy novels. But mostly she's writing.

VISIT THE AUTHOR ONLINE AND LEARN ABOUT
HER TWENTY-PLUS BESTSELLING ROMANTASY NOVELS

SylviaMercedesBooks.com
AuthorSylviaMercedes